SYRELL LEAHY ... ... parentage who ... ... Jersey with her husband and two children. Many of the characters in *Family Truths* appeared in her first novel, *Family Ties*.

SYRELL LEAHY

Family Truths

FONTANA/Collins

First published in Great Britain by
William Collins Sons & Co. Ltd 1985
First issued in Fontana Paperbacks 1986

The author gratefully acknowledges permission from
Warner Bros. Music to reprint lyrics from
'A Hard Rain's A-Gonna Fall', by Bob Dylan,
© 1963 Warner Bros. Inc. All rights reserved.

Made and printed in Great Britain by
William Collins Sons & Co. Ltd, Glasgow

*In memory of
my Uncle Morris
who was father to more
than his own children*

*And in memory of
my cousin Sara
who remembered more about
the history of New York
at the age of eighty-five
than I will ever know*

I met a young girl, she gave me a rainbow.

BOB DYLAN

Kann i gleich net allweil bei dir sein,
Han i doch mein Freud an dir;
Wenn i komm, wenn i komm, wenni wieder,
    wieder komm,
      wieder, wieder komm,
Kehr i ein, mein Schatz, bei dir.

If I cannot spend my life beside you,
My joy is still in you;
When I come, when I come, when I come,
    back again,
I'll return my love, to you.

FROM AN OLD GERMAN FOLK TUNE
TRANSLATED FREELY, AND LOVINGLY,
BY THE AUTHOR

PART ONE

June 1959

One

———◦———

Even the house seemed expectant as the dinner hour approached, all five storeys more than ordinarily well scrubbed as they awaited the first gathering since the spring holidays of the five members of the Wolfe family. It was June, and Judy had arrived home from Swarthmore College two days earlier to start her summer vacation, leaving behind her studies and her closest friend, Fern. It was a bright, warm Thursday late afternoon, colourful flowers already in bloom in the small garden behind the town house. Her bedroom window looked out on that garden, a peaceful view in any season but especially beautiful in the spring. When her mother entertained in warm weather, guests spilled from the ground floor dining room out to the patio, mixing outdoors and indoors so that it was hard to believe the setting was the East Seventies, half a block from Park Avenue in the most elegant part of Manhattan. Only tonight the peacefulness of the place and the time would not last through the evening. Her brother Davey was on his way home, carrying belated news of his marriage, news which up until today only Judy knew.

She looked at her watch. Nearly five-thirty. He would be on his way now. She felt sick to her stomach. Tonight she would be unable to eat and unable to explain why. She realized suddenly that Davey would not be home for dinner. Davey loved airline meals, plastic trays with packaged cutlery and assembly line food. He would be on a dinner flight and by the time he arrived, his mother would be a nervous wreck worrying about his safety and his father would be irritated at his delay. Careful planning. That was Davey.

Five forty-five. Her father would be coming home now, dropping the black briefcase in the hall near the table inlaid

11

with dragons, to be retrieved at some later time this evening. He would come upstairs and wash. Dinner was a prompt and formal affair in this house. Daddy adjourned court so that the family could eat together, so that everyone's family could eat together. She could hear him now in the room below hers, unsuspecting Daddy, thinking he had the arrival of his younger son to look forward to. She felt her stomach contract in pain. Davey, you ass, couldn't you forego a TV dinner to make it easier on your parents?

There was silence in the room below. She put a brush halfheartedly through her dark hair and walked out into the hall. The lift was elsewhere but she rarely used it going down. She skittered down the carpeted stairs, scarcely noticing the lighted shelves that contained part of her father's collection; small, pretty, touchable objects in jade and coral and ivory, a distant culture, another century. At the turn on the third floor, she stopped at the shelf with the Buddhas and removed her favourite for a quick rub. Luck and happiness, she thought, replacing it. We need it tonight. She had wanted to take that small piece of ivory to Swarthmore with her three years ago and her father had not allowed it. Down to the living room on the first floor and down the last flight to the dining room where the stairs ended in a grand sweep.

'Hi, Daddy.' They had not sat down yet and she kissed his cheek and felt him hug her.

'Hello, sweetheart. It's good to have you back.' It was the third successive night he had said it. 'Why is it I miss you so much when you're away?'

She took her place at the side of the table between her parents, who sat at opposite ends. 'No one challenges your authority when I'm away,' she said, spreading the heavy damask napkin over her lap. 'You're afraid you'll get rusty.'

'That must be it,' he said, smiling at her.

Across the table and to her right, the older of her two brothers sat beside the empty place setting reserved for Davey. Arnold French Wolfe, never called anything in his life but Frenchy, born twenty-four years earlier in the exact image of his father, was newly a graduate of Yale Law School and

12

would, in just over two weeks, marry the most wonderful girl either of her brothers had ever brought home for approval or for any other reason.

'No Davey,' he observed as the meal began.

'I don't think Davey'll be home in time for dinner,' Judy said, her stomach tightening.

'You don't?' Her mother, her pretty face lined with worry, turned to look at Judy.

'Davey likes to eat on planes.'

'Judy's right,' her father said. 'He'll be fine, Edith. Try not to worry.'

'Shall I take the plate away, Mrs Wolfe?' the maid asked.

'No. Thank you, Marjorie. We'll leave it. Just in case our predictions are wrong.' But Mother looked more relaxed, as if the feared accident had been averted, her son saved once again.

They retired to the living room upstairs after dinner, father and son reading newspapers. From time to time Daddy pulled his watch out of its little pocket, flicked it open, then shut, then pushed it back into the pocket again. The relief at dinner had been transient. Mother walked into the room at the front of the house, the family television and guest room, and looked out of the windows that overlooked the street. Eight o'clock came and went. It began to grow dark. Daddy switched on a lamp. What if Davey had changed his mind? What if he had decided he couldn't face it? Judy sat on the rosebud-covered sofa and looked across the room at the fireplace, at the dark painting above it, the carvings along the mantel.

There was a sound of chimes and Mother stood quickly. 'There he is.' In a moment, she was down the stairs and greeting her son effusively, the voices rising to the first floor. 'Oh, Davey, my goodness, look at you.' Sweet relief in her voice. 'Darling, you'll have to see a barber before the wedding. That beard is *much* too long. My goodness, I can hardly find anything to kiss.'

'Well, we've averted disaster,' Daddy said, waiting for Judy to stand and precede him down the stairs.

In the foyer, her mother stood flushed and happy, a smaller, sweeter version of Judy's face, her eyes glowing. Judy said, 'Hi,' and hugged her brother and he said, 'Thanks, kiddo,' and hugged her back. She moved away, watching her family like an outside observer.

'Good dinner?' Frenchy asked, giving his brother a friendly pat on the shoulder.

'Fantastic cherry tart,' Davey enthused. 'With the greatest fake whipped cream you ever tasted.'

'Oh, Davey, I'll have to have something brought up for you. We have the loveliest chocolate cake. Do you want it with milk or coffee, dear?'

Davey shrugged. 'I don't care. Milk maybe. Can't eat chocolate cake without milk.'

They started up the stairs, her mother, her brothers.

'Something wrong?' her father asked.

She shook her head and followed the crowd. Her mother would be so happy now, all her children under one roof for the last time before Frenchy's wedding. Everyone safe, no one in an airplane or a dormitory full of careless smokers or a car whose brakes had not been checked.

'A great year,' Davey was saying. He was on the sofa, loosening his tie. 'I'm really happy there.' The door opened and Marjorie came into the living room with a tray of chocolate cake and milk. 'Hey, terrific,' Davey said. 'You're learning how to cut them big, Marge.' He dug in, relishing the bite. Judy sat in a chair near the fireplace so that when he looked up, their eyes met. He took a gulp of milk and pressed the napkin to his mouth. 'Look,' he said, putting the fork down, 'I gotta tell you something.' He looked around the room, his eyes lingering on his sister's before moving on. 'I've got some news,' he said. 'It's really hot stuff.'

Come on, Davey. Just do it. Just get it over with.

They were all watching him.

'I got married.'

Three people said three different things at the same time. Judy surveyed the faces. Her mother looked startled. Frenchy looked amused. Daddy's face was unreadable but as her eyes passed over his, they met hers in a look that nearly frightened her.

14

'Davey,' Mother said, 'why would you do something like that without telling us?'

'Well, it's a long story. I started going with her the beginning of last year, when I was thinking about the rabbinate. We knew we wanted to get married but her parents said nothing doing till she graduated. So she transferred to Cincinnati last fall.'

'Did she graduate?' Daddy asked.

'Huh-uh. She's got another year to go but I don't think she'll make it.' He looked at his sister.

It's OK, Davey, she telepathed. You can say it now. Daddy understands. Just say it.

'She's – uh – we're gonna have a baby,' he finished sheepishly.

Mother said, 'Jerold,' shrilly and Daddy closed his eyes for a moment. Frenchy stood and said, – 'Judy, how would you like to take a walk?' and Judy said, 'I wouldn't, thank you. I want to stay right here.'

Daddy walked over to where Mother sat on the sofa beside her son and put a hand on her shoulder. 'It's all right, Edith,' he said, although it was obvious that it wasn't all right to Mother. 'When is the baby expected, David?'

'The doctor said October.'

'October.'

'She's in maybe her fifth month.'

Mother sat with one hand across her eyes and it struck Judy suddenly that she was crying, her calm, well-collected mother who had never before shed a public tear. And Daddy who had left his chair to put his hand on Mother's shoulder, had known at that shrill 'Jerold!' that Davey's marriage was more than an inconvenience in the family schedule.

'Hey,' Davey said, viewing the carnage, 'isn't anybody going to say how happy they are?'

'I'm happy,' Judy said. She walked across the room to her brother. 'I'm terrifically happy. Davey never wanted a big wedding anyway.' Her parents were looking at her, her mother wiping her eyes with the napkin from Davey's tray. She sat down next to her brother and hugged him. Her mother was

15

right. The beard was enormous. It had begun in a scraggly fashion two summers ago in Alaska and had grown, like a jungle, out of control.

'What the hell's the matter with them?' he murmured in her ear.

'I don't know.'

'David,' Daddy said, 'where is – what is your wife's name?'

'Rena.' It was a chorus of two voices. Judy had met Rena once during the previous year.

'Where is Rena, Davey?'

'She's on her way to Hartford with her folks. We had them meet us when we got off the plane so we could tell them. That's why I didn't tell you when I was coming home. I didn't know how long it would take.' He took a breath. 'We had a really neat scene at the airport.'

'Oh, David,' Mother said, sounding exhausted.

'What's the matter with you two? So I didn't tell you. So what? We've got a nice little place to live and we finished all our exams and we're happy.' There was a plaintive note on the last word.

'Dad,' Frenchy said, joining the group at the sofa, 'Davey's right. He's happy and we should be celebrating. This isn't a time for recriminations.' He stood with his parents and no one said anything.

'I think you're all crazy,' Judy said, looking at them in amazement.

'Judy,' her mother ordered briskly, 'go to your room.'

'I'm twenty years old. You can't tell me to go to my room.'

'Please, Judy.' Her mother's voice sounded weary and ready to break.

She got up and walked past the clustered members of her family, three intensely sane people who had become inexplicably irrational. 'I don't know how you can treat Davey this way.' She was afraid suddenly that she, too, might cry. Hurrying up the stairs, she passed the Buddha. 'Thanks,' she said grimly and went on to her room.

She closed the door so that she could scarcely hear even muffled voices. Something was wrong. Her parents had not berated Davey for the obvious and embarrassing sequence of events in his life. Instead they had acted frightened, as though this marriage had upset some delicate balance in their lives, all their lives. Her mother's incomprehensible reaction: '*Jerold!*' A cry for help, not a word of anger or irritation. Even Frenchy had acted stangely. It was like a mass hysteria that had swept three-fifths of the family, leaving her and Davey out in the cold.

It reminded her suddenly of something else, something that had happened a hundred years ago, or nine anyway, when she was ten and a half and her mother had acted inexplicably, packing the three of them up and taking them away to the Rosenbergs' apartment on Park Avenue, because the Rosenbergs were friends and they were away in Europe. It had been the most mystifying time in their lives, and frightening because they had not seen Daddy. They had not known for all those days or weeks or however long it had been whether they would ever see Daddy again. It had been the meanest thing Mummy had ever done and Mummy didn't do mean things. They had never really understood it. But Davey had had an idea. Davey had thought something terrible. About Mummy.

She put a record on, found a book she had been meaning to read for a long time, and lay down on her bed. It was officially summer now and she could read for pleasure, listen to music for pleasure, ride, swim and lie in the sun at their Pennsylvania home for pleasure. She wished Fern were here so that they could talk about what had happened tonight. Fern visited every Thanksgiving, had met the Wolfes, and would have an opinion on tonight's craziness. She had put her finger on it on Monday. *It's not a family of innocents. No family is.* She would miss Fern this summer . . .

Judy opened her eyes to bright light and a strange, repetitive whirr. She had fallen asleep before the end of the first side of the record and now it went around and around, the poor needle wearing itself out uselessly. She shook herself, got up, and turned off the gramophone. It was a little past midnight. Opening her door, she listened. The house was silent. She went up to Davey's room and tapped lightly on the door. 'Davey?' she called softly. There was no light from the room.

'I'm sleeping.'

'What happened?'

'I'll talk to you tomorrow.'

'Did they – is everything all right?'

'Everything's great. Go to sleep.'

She walked to the stairs, disappointed and once again apprehensive.

'Thanks, Jude,' her brother called.

She went down to her floor. At the foot of the next flight, there was light. Her father was working in his study. She followed the light and stood in the doorway till he looked up.

He put a pen down and took his glasses off. He was at his desk, tieless and in his shirtsleeves, the cuffs turned back several times to expose arms that seemed too strong for the kind of work he did. 'Come in,' he said. She sat near the desk, not saying anything. 'How long have you known?'

'Since April. He told me at the wedding.'

'I see.' He rubbed his eyes. There were reams of paper on the desk, covered with his handwriting. Open on the floor beside him was his black leather briefcase with J W printed in gold on the front. From where she sat she could see the inside flap where JEROLD WOLFE was stamped in plain gold letters on black leather. His briefcases never varied, one following the other at intervals her mother thought were far too long. When she was three, Judy had carried it around the house to her mother's amusement and her father's delight. Her mother had thought she had mistaken it for a woman's handbag but there had been no mistake. Even at three she had known she wanted to grow up to be just like Daddy. 'I take it you've met Rena.'

'She's very nice, Daddy. She's little and round and a lot of fun. I think she'll be very good for Davey.'

'I'm sure she will.'

'You were all just terrible tonight,' she said.

'Yes, it must have seemed that way.'

'It wasn't like you.'

'No, I'm afraid I didn't rise to the occasion. We'll talk about it some time, not tonight.' He glanced at the papers on his desk and she knew the events of the evening had disrupted his work. He would be awake far into the night.

'Good night, Daddy,' she said.

'Good night, dear.' They kissed and he rumpled her hair.

'Daddy – ' She was at the door and she hadn't meant to say it. He looked up. 'I thought about something tonight,' she said. 'About the time Mum took us to the Rosenbergs' apartment.'

'That was a long time ago.'

'But it came back to me tonight. Why did she do it, Daddy? Why did she pack us up that time and take us away?'

'It was a misunderstanding.'

'You mean she moved us out of the house over a little misunderstanding?'

'It was something rather complicated, Judy, something that required a good deal of thought. It was all settled many years ago. There haven't been any misunderstandings since then, large or small. You know that.'

She waited, but that seemed to be the end. She started out of the room, not quite satisfied.

'There was never any doubt,' her father said, 'that you were all coming back.'

She turned around and smiled at him and he returned the smile. For the moment at least, she had heard what she wanted to hear.

It was late when she finally tried to sleep again and late when she awoke the next morning. By the time she went down for breakfast, Davey, car and driver had been dispatched to Hartford to bring his wife back in the style to which the Wolfe family was accustomed. Things were hectic when he returned, what with his marriage and Frenchy's wedding so close, and although she tried, she never got to talk to him about what had happened during the hours she had been upstairs in her room and he in turn never offered the slightest clue.

Two

If you weren't packing, you were unpacking. Somehow the summer had vanished, hundreds of hours of riding and swimming behind her, the glorious wedding, the happy honeymooners home in their Manhattan apartment. At the very end she had seen Davey and Rena again, Rena as round as a tub and as bubbly as a little engine.

There was a knock on the door and a shouted, 'Judy!'

'Fern!' She looked up from her half-empty trunk. 'Oh Fern, you look *wonderful*. You look almost *tan*.' They were both laughing with excitement. It was their senior year. It was the beginning of the end.

'Jack kicked me out of the store the whole last week and said, "Rest." So I did. Lazed around. Pretended I was you.'

'I'll get you for that,' Judy said with a grin. 'God I missed you. God I'm glad you're back.'

They had met early in their first term, a chance meeting that had blossomed into a friendship. Fern Hall lived with her widowed father in Kansas – she had called him Jack all her life – where he ran the general store in the town she had been born in, hardware, groceries, almost anything you could imagine. Sometimes, she said, they pounded on the door and woke the Halls up because they needed something.

'He does it all himself?' Judy asked when they first talked about it.

'Jack's got sort of a lady friend. She helps out a lot.'

A lady friend. Judy had not inquired further. But when she found out that Fern could afford to go home only for Christmas, she invited her to spend Thanksgiving with the Wolfes, along with Margaret Townley, a girl from England who would not return home until June. They had had a good time together, the five of them, Frenchy and Davey taking the girls around New York on the weekend following the big event, the brothers a gallant twosome for the appreciative trio.

It was the year of Davey's religious conversion, of keeping it a secret until Davey had his own thinking straightened out. Early that December Davey hitchhiked from Brown to Swarthmore to confide to his sister his new religious feelings – not yet certain that they were beliefs. He was full of questions, full of a need to find truth.

It was the summer between their first and second years that it happened. Fern returned to Swarthmore so thin, there seemed to be almost a depression between her pelvic bones, like on the little Buddha that Judy loved that had been stroked for good luck.

'Worked hard,' Fern explained. 'Jack took his first vacation in years this summer. It was six days a week from dawn till darkness.'

'I thought you said he had a friend who helped out.'

'Vivien went with him.' Fern looked at her with a steady gaze, watching. It was almost a test.

'I – I didn't know she was that kind of a friend.'

'She is. She lives in the house with us.'

'I see.'

'Does it rattle your Park Avenue conscience?'

'Fern – you're picking a fight. I have no fight with you. We're friends. What your father does is his business. I was just – surprised.'

'I'm sorry,' Fern said. She looked sorry. 'I was picking a fight with myself, that's all. Anyway, I fell in love while Jack was gone and he's half the reason I'm so thin. Love makes me lose my appetite.'

It had been more than loss of appetite. On the first Friday of October someone knocked on Judy's door and asked her to go upstairs to Fern's room.

'Come in,' Fern called at her knock.

'What's wrong?' She closed the door and looked around the

21

room. Fern, in a nightgown, sat in bed, propped by the pillow and something stuffed behind it.

'Did she scare the hell out of you?'

'Yes.'

'Sorry. I think I scared hell out of her. I didn't mean to.'

'You have a temperature?'

'No. I'm all right, really. I just didn't want to be alone. Will you stay?'

'Sure.' She had the sense of walking in where she was not expected. Something was wrong and she could not put her finger on it. Fern was pale and her fair hair had begun to get straggly from leaning against the pillow.

'I got back about an hour ago.'

'From where?'

Fern looked at her, the look that measured, weighed, appraised. 'I had an abortion this afternoon.'

'Oh, *no!*' Cold, from her scalp to her feet, an involuntary shiver. 'Oh Fern, I would've – ' Would have what? What do you do when your friend has abortion? What is there to do? 'If I couldn't have talked you out of it, I would've gone with you.'

'Thanks.' Fern smiled as if pleased with her appraisal, but the smile was weak and hollow. 'You couldn't have talked me out of it and this is one of the things in life you do alone. Like birth and death and all the rest of that garbage.'

'The guy in Kansas?'

Fern nodded her head.

'You didn't tell him, did you?'

'And ruin his life?'

'Maybe it wouldn't have ruined his life. Maybe it would have made him happy.'

'He's married, Judy.' She seemed so worn out, as if she had come to the end of some long trip. 'Besides,' her voice began to shake, 'how could I do that to Jack?'

'Your father would understand.'

'Would he? Would yours? Would you tell your father you were pregnant?'

Judy looked down at her hands. 'No. You're right. I

22

couldn't tell him.' As if at last she had found the dividing line: I can tell him everything but I couldn't tell him that. 'And there was no chance at all of getting married?'

'Get married. Is that what Jack saved his money for for seventeen years, so I could go away to college for a year, get knocked up and come back home to be a mother?'

'Fern, it's not *dishonourable* to be a mother.'

'No.' She moved on the bed to a more comfortable position.

'Are you all right? Do you need a doctor?'

'I'm fine. I don't need a doctor unless I'm haemorrhaging and I'm not.'

'Something to eat?'

'Huh-uh. Tomorrow maybe. Tomorrow it'll all be behind me. Except I can't shower, or wash my hair, or play tennis, or run the hundred-yard dash.' She took a breath. 'Or have sex.' She smiled. 'It doesn't matter. It was the best summer of my life.'

'Then you have something to remember.'

'Yes. Something wonderful. He's a great man. Great men don't come along every day. I feel – I think I'm lucky to have had him for a summer. Could you turn off the big light, Judy?'

'Sure.' She went to the switch and flicked it off. Returning, she pulled the chair closer to the bed. It was getting late and the hallway outside the room was becoming quiet.

'Two hundred seventy-five dollars to get rid of a baby you don't want,' Fern said. 'Think of what I could have done with that money. He was my first experience. My first, my second, my third . . . I don't think I'll ever love anyone again.' She reached for a tissue from the box on her night table and nearly knocked over the lamp that was the only light in the room. She cried into the tissue for some time. 'Listen,' she said finally, 'I hate to ask – '

'You want me to go?'

'No. Please. I want you to stay. I just don't want to be alone tonight.'

'I'll stay.'

'Get my coat out of the closet. It'll keep you warm.'

Judy went to the closet and took out the brown coat that

Fern had worn the previous winter. Fern was tall and the coat was long. She sat in the chair and worked the coat around her like a blanket, feeling the lining warm to her skin.

'Strawbridge,' Fern said, blotting her eyes. 'Good coat. Jack wanted me to have a classy eastern coat for my first year.' She was crying again. 'Mind if I turn off the light?'

'Huh-uh.'

The room went dark and Judy listened, eyes open, to the sound of her friend crying.

'I wonder if it was a boy or a girl.'

'You can't think about that.'

'I can't think about anything else.'

'Fern, you made up your mind. You've done it. You're a strong, wonderful person. You've protected your father and the man you love. Now think of yourself.'

'I've been thinking of myself all day.' She sounded distant, as though in the dark she had moved to another room. 'I was a mistake.'

'Stop it, Fern.'

'It's true. I lied to you about my mother. Jack doesn't talk about it. He thinks because it happened when I was young that I don't remember but I do. I remember the whole thing. She didn't die. She left us, walked out, split. She never wanted me. She wanted Jack. That was all, Jack with no encumbrances. She went to someone when she was pregnant – she told me this when I was five years old – she wanted to get rid of me because I was a mistake but they said it was too late. She had waited too long. She had no choice any more. That's why I was born. That's why I'm here today. And here I am, not even nineteen years old, and I've done what my mother tried to do. Except I succeeded. I took care of it in time. I have no more encumbrance. Like mother like daughter.'

Judy pulled herself out of the chair and flung the coat around her shoulders. Feeling her way to the bed, she sat on the edge. 'You're not your mother,' she said firmly. 'There is nothing in you like what you've just described. You talked about love and she talked about encumbrances. You're your father's daughter, not your mother's. You're not walking out

24

on anyone who needs you. You're living your life the way you think it should be lived.'

Fern sniffed and there was the sound of a tissue being torn from the box. 'Is that what they say on Park Avenue?' she said, trying to make a joke.

'It's what I say. And you have to believe it.'

'I'll try.' Fern leaned back on the pillow. 'Anyway, that's why Jack and Vivien never got married. He can't. Somewhere in this world, he's still got my mother.'

Three

———•———

It was September and they were hard at work on their last year of classes. It didn't seem possible, but it was. It didn't seem possible that Davey's baby was imminent, but it was.

Judy made a station call to Davey's number and Rena answered.

'Hi, Judy,' her sister-in-law said in her girlish, bubbling voice.

'Everything OK?'

'Terrific. Except that I can't breathe, we're all doing fine.'

Judy noted the 'all'. It was as if the unborn child were already part of their family, as if it were someone you said 'Good morning' to when you got up, as if it really existed. She talked for a while to Rena and then asked for her brother.

'Hold on, I'll get him. Davey?' she called. 'Davey?'

'What is it?' Dimly in the background.

'Come and talk to Judy.'

Davey started to say something and Rena covered the mouthpiece so that the sound was reduced to an unintelligible murmur. When Rena returned her voice was subdued.

'He's lying down, Judy,' she said. 'I don't have the energy any more to drag him up. You should have warned me about how lazy he was.'

'It was a family secret.' She kept her voice light, trying to mask the hurt. Since June Davey had become strangely cool. The old intimacy had disappeared. They had scarcely spoken all summer. He did not call. Now he would not even come to the phone. 'I get disinherited if I tell,' she said, sounding coy. 'Give him my love, OK?'

'Sure. And you know you'll hear from us the minute.'

'I know. I can't wait.'

She called one more time, early in October, but Davey was out at a meeting and after that, she didn't try again. He had not written her a single letter although in past years he had written her so often that Mother complained that he misaddressed the letters he meant to send home. This year, apparently, there were no mistakes.

It was late at night when the phone rang. She answered without turning a light on, just stumbling out of bed to the desk before the ring woke the whole corridor.

'Hello?'

'It's me. Davey.'

'Davey!' She was so delighted to hear his voice, she nearly forgot why he would be calling at such an hour. 'Davey! It happened. Tell me.'

'It's – uh – something went wrong.'

Love and compassion and forgiveness flooding her all at once. Her brother had finally called. 'What do you mean?'

'I mean – uh – ' He sounded terrible, his voice failing.

'What happened, Davey?'

'It was born, uh, dead or maybe it died when it was born or I don't know. I didn't get it straight.'

'Oh, Davey.' The chill of night and darkness and Davey's news creeping along her arms. 'I'm so sorry.'

'Yeah, well, we're all sorry.' His voice seemed to break or disintegrate on the last word. 'You know, I felt it kick yesterday. I saw it move. They move. Did you know that?'

'Davey, is there something I can do? Anything you want?'

'I just wanted to talk to someone and I couldn't think of anyone except you.'

'I'll come out and stay with you for a few days.'

'No, please. I gotta clean this place up. All this shit around here, I'll never get it done.'

'Is Rena all right?'

'Fine, tip-top. She was sleeping when I left. Jesus,' he said. 'I have to call her mother, don't I?'

'You can wait till morning. You don't have to do it now.' The clock said three minutes after three.

27

'Yeah. I suppose it doesn't make much difference at this point. You better talk to Dad, Jude.'

'What do you mean? Why?'

'Nothing. I don't even know what I'm saying.'

'Davey, I'll be here if you need me.'

'Thanks, kiddo. Thanks for everything.'

You better talk to Dad.

She did not sleep until it was nearly time to wake up. *You better talk to Dad.* Something teasing at her brain. Something just below the surface that she should be able to figure out.

She went to breakfast and then hurried to her first class, realizing too late that she had carried the wrong notebook. When she returned, she tried Davey but there was no answer. *You better talk to Dad.* What did Daddy know that Davey couldn't tell her?

She got the operator and asked for her home number.

'Judy dear,' her mother said.

'Davey called me in the middle of the night.'

'What did he tell you?' her mother asked with a strange sharpness to her voice, a kind of fear sharpness rather than an anger sharpness.

'What do you mean?' She felt confused from lack of sleep, from sharing Davey's agony. 'He said the baby died. What do you think he told me?'

'I'm sorry you had to hear it that way,' her mother said evenly. 'I was going to call this evening to tell you.'

'What makes a baby die like that, Mummy?'

'These are accidents of nature, dear. No one ever knows when something like this will happen.'

'I want to talk to Daddy.'

'Daddy left for Cincinnati a little while ago.'

'I need to talk to him.'

'I'll speak to him tonight and tell him you called. We've all had a shock but we're all going to recover. Do you want to come home for the weekend?'

'No. I just want to talk to Daddy.'

28

'He'll call you, dear. I promise.'

After lunch she walked back to the dorm with Fern.

'Is that your father?' Fern said. 'Standing near the door?'

He recognized them at the same moment and came toward them with a smile.

'Hello, Judy.' A kiss. 'Hello, Fern.' He held out his hand and they shook.

'Hello, Judge Wolfe. Nice to see you.' She waved and left them.

'Mummy said you were in Cincinnati.'

'Later. Can we find a place to eat that's not too far? I seem to have missed lunch in my travels.'

'Come on.'

Her father looked awful. She could imagine he had been awake since four this morning. She had been awake nearly that long herself.

She walked him off campus to a little place they went to sometimes for pizza. 'You can't have a drink here, you know. Swarthmore's dry. The kids go up to Chester for liquor.'

'Coffee will do fine. It's a little early to think about alcohol, isn't it?'

'You don't look very good.'

He ordered quickly and she sipped a Coke.

'I have to talk to you about something,' he said.

'About Davey's baby?'

'About our family. What did Davey tell you?'

For the first time, she felt a chill. 'Why is everyone asking me that? He said the baby died. Isn't that what happened? Mummy said it was an accident. Wasn't it an accident?'

'In the sense that no one could have predicted with any accuracy that this would happen now, yes, it was an accident. In the sense that something like this is bound to happen in our family some time, no, it wasn't an accident. The baby died because it wasn't well formed, because it wasn't viable. If it had lived, it would not have had a normal life.'

Jerold! As though she were in that living room, she could hear the shrill sound of her mother's cry.

29

'You knew last June,' she said in a shaky voice. 'When Davey told you Rena was pregnant. You knew then.'

'I've known since I was your age. I've known since I was twenty.' He paused and took a breath that was almost a shudder. 'I intended to tell Davey in good time. I miscalculated. Not that it would have changed anything. Not that it should have.'

'How did you know?'

'It's come out here and there in the family.'

'Is that what you came here to tell me?'

He said, 'Yes,' then rather quickly corrected himself. 'No. I came down to tell you something else.'

An image flashed before her eyes, the apartment on Park Avenue Mummy had taken them to when they hadn't known if they would ever see Daddy again. Davey had thought something terrible about Mummy but Davey had been thirteen and slightly nutty. Now Daddy was going to tell her. He was going to fit the missing piece into the puzzle.

'We were not angry with Davey last June,' he said firmly. 'We've come to expect surprises from him over the years but I want you to know we were never unhappy with his decision to marry or with his choice of a wife. He married Rena because they were happy together. There's no better reason for marrying. You're twenty years old now. Sometime in the next months or years you'll find someone that you want to marry. The decision to marry and the choice of whom you marry are the most important decisions you will ever make, more important than whether you go to law school or which one you finally attend. I want you to know, now, before it becomes an issue, that your mother and I stand behind any decision and any choice you make. No one in this family will tell you or suggest to you or try to influence you to change your mind after you've made your decision.'

She looked at him, bewildered. 'What does this have to do with Davey's baby?'

'Everything. You know now that this can happen to any of us. You also know, having grown up in our family, that it probably won't. Judy,' he looked wearier than she had ever

30

seen him, 'I want you to make all your choices out of love, not out of necessity or expedience. I don't want you to weigh risks or to balance assets and liabilities or try to corner the market in some useless commodity. I want you to act from love, the way Davey and Frenchy have, the way I hope they have. The most important things we do in our lives have to do with love, and that's the way it should be.' He paused and ate a forkful of food, setting the fork down and chewing slowly.

She wondered if there were more but it seemed that nothing else was forthcoming. 'I don't really understand what you're talking about,' she said apologetically, fearing that she had missed an important message, perhaps the most important message he had ever tried to communicate.

'I know you don't, dear,' her father said gently. 'But you will. The time will come and you'll remember we talked. I'll write you a letter one of these days and you'll put it away until the time comes. But you don't need a letter. I know you'll do what's right for yourself.' He reached into the little pocket and took out his watch. 'I don't have much time now. I'm catching a plane for Cincinnati this afternoon.'

She sipped the last of her Coke and saw him close the watch and put it away. 'Daddy,' she said, 'why did Mummy pack us up and take us away that time? To the Rosenbergs' apartment?'

Oddly, the question did not seem to surprise him. He showed no sign that it was irrelevant to the strange monologue he had just concluded. 'We had some important things we had to think about,' he said quietly. 'Your mother thought it could best be done separately.'

'Both of you?' she asked. 'You said last June it was just Mother.'

'It was mostly your mother.'

'What kinds of things did she have to think about? Love things or asset and liability things?'

This time he did not answer immediately. It occurred to her that without meaning to she might have asked the question that brought this hypothetical advice down to reality and he did not want to face reality. Or worse. Perhaps he did not know the answer to her question.

31

'I think it was love things,' he said finally, his voice rather hoarse. He took his watch out of the pocket again. 'I'd better get started or I'll miss my flight.' He pressed the watch closed, took out his wallet, and laid a five-dollar note on top of the bill. He had scarcely eaten.

'I'm glad you came,' Judy said.

'Yes.' He smiled at her. 'So am I. Very glad.'

She left him at his rented car and went back to the dorm. Fern was writing a letter, her radio tuned to a station that played romantic melodies.

'Was anything wrong?' Fern asked, flicking the radio off as she saw Judy.

'I don't know.' Judy sat in the chair, still in her coat. 'He said a lot of things that he seemed to think were very important, but none of it made sense. I don't think I understood a single word.'

Four

———◦◦———

The invitation was waiting for her when she came home at Christmas, tea on Tuesday afternoon with Regina Rush. Baffled, she read it again, then telephoned to accept, leaving her message with the maid. She could not imagine why she had been invited.

They were cousins of her father, a couple who sent their children to family weddings but did not themselves attend. She could not even recall what they looked like. There was no reason that she could think of to be invited for tea. Dressing on Tuesday afternoon, she wondered how many others would be there, whether she would know any of them.

The building was two blocks north, on a corner of Park Avenue. Walking, she thought of Davey, whom she would not see this vacation. He had telephoned last week but sounded down in the dumps. He did not talk about the baby, only about how much work he had, and that Rena missed her parents.

The doorman held the door open and she entered the large, ornate lobby typical of the old Park Avenue buildings. She felt a chill as the old memory returned, the chill and the fear that she would never see Daddy again.

The lift rode up several floors and stopped with a small jolt, opening to a private hall with a man's umbrella in a stand and a bentwood chair beside the door. The door opened immediately and she recognized Regina although she was not sure from where, a small woman with a round face and a smile, a woman with a glow.

'Hello, Judy,' Regina said. 'I would recognize you anywhere. You look like your beautiful mother.'

'Thank you. It was nice of you to invite me.'

The maid took her coat in the bright, well-lighted hall, a

gleaming black and white tiled floor, a small, ornate mirror over a table and beside it a gold spade with a plaque to Mr and Mrs Mortimer Rush. She caught the words 'grateful' and 'generous' as they walked by. Funny, how similar the apartments were, the halls, the high ceilings, everything spread out on one floor instead of piled on five, and always the fear that she would never see Daddy again.

'Let's go into my study.'

She caught a glimpse of the living room as they passed, and the stairs that went to the second floor – it was a duplex after all. 'Am I the first?' she asked.

'You're my only guest today.'

'Oh. I didn't realize –'

'I thought it would be nice if we got to know each other. Frenchy and I had such a nice talk a few years ago.'

'I remember that.' They sat in the study with its antique desk, French loveseat and chairs; pretty china teacups near a tray of small cakes. The maid came in with the tea things on a silver tray and departed quickly and silently. 'You talked him into law school that time, didn't you?'

'Did he tell you that?'

'No, but after he came back, things calmed down between him and Daddy. I figured that was why, that somehow you had made him accept the fact that this was what he had to do.' She looked directly at Regina. 'I was kind of angry with you about it.'

'I don't blame you. I would have been angry at me too. In fact, I didn't talk Frenchy into anything. I talked him out of it.'

'Out of it?' She was mystified now, and curious. Who was this woman who sat pouring tea and calmly told Frenchy not to be the lawyer his father wanted him to be?

'I told Frenchy what I know your dad believes for his children, that they must choose freely. I think that when Frenchy understood that, he was able to do it, without feeling that he was pressured. I'm sure he made the right decision. Do you think he's happy?' she inquired.

'Very happy. He passed the bar.'

34

'I'm sure he did. And he has a beautiful wife. Our children are all doing well these days.'

Judy looked at her, wondering about the purpose, about why she had been invited to sip tea with this cousin of her father who had had such an influence on Frenchy's life.

'How is Davey now?' Regina asked as if in answer to the unspoken question.

'Sad,' Judy answered truthfully. 'Torn apart.'

'Yes.' Regina put her cup down and moved the cake tray closer to Judy. 'It lasts and lasts. Even after thirty years it's still hard to think about. We lost a little boy baby,' Regina said as if sensing her curiosity. 'In '28. It must sound like a long time ago to you.'

'It does.'

'Not so long really. Afterwards, we adopted Ernie.'

'Ernie? Your son Ernie?'

'Our son, yes.'

'I didn't know.'

'Is your dad – how is your dad these days?'

'It upset him an awful lot. Davey, I mean.'

'Yes, I should think it would.'

'He came down to school to talk to me but I really couldn't figure out what he was saying. He kept telling me to make decisions based on love, not to weigh the plusses and minuses.'

'That sounds very clear to me.'

'I just had the feeling – I don't know – that he was talking to himself, not to me.'

Regina sat for a moment, looking away. Then she smiled, as if she had just returned to the company at hand. 'You'll give him my love, won't you?'

'Of course.'

'And I'll give you something.' Regina went to the desk and opened a drawer. Taking out a small business card, she wrote on it. 'If you ever need me.' She handed the card to Judy. 'Anything at all. I'm always at one of those numbers.'

They left the study a while later and as they passed the stairs, someone came bounding down. They stopped and Regina said, 'Have you two met?'

35

The young man stopped on the third step from the bottom and Judy looked at him. He was wearing a plaid flannel shirt and tan trousers and he was intensely handsome, as though he had been born in the image of a beautiful woman, but distinctly, powerfully male.

'This is our friend from Paris,' Regina went on, 'Marcel Goldblatt. Marcel, my cousin, Judy Wolfe.'

Judy smiled and murmured, 'Hello,' and the young man said, 'Hi,' and then walked down the last three steps. Regina quite suddenly smiled in a strange way and left them.

'It's nice to meet you,' Judy said, her eyes on the beautiful face, on the collar of the blue plaid shirt.

The young man said, 'Yes,' and stood looking at her.

'I was just on my way out.'

'So long.'

When she reached the hall, Regina kissed her and asked her to be sure to visit again.

The lift went down without a stop the way it had that other time, the day Daddy had come finally to take them home, all the suitcases piled in the elevator and Daddy holding her hand. She had made Mummy call him early one morning, before breakfast even, and she had talked to him, reassured that he was still alive, still a phone call away, still her daddy. She had told him she loved him and then she had cried. A few days later, he had come to get them.

But for Davey it had not ended. Davey had misunderstood everything. He had thought Mother was going to run away with Mr Rosenberg, take the three of them and never go home again. Davey thought that she *loved* Mr Rosenberg, silly, foolish Mr Rosenberg who told bad jokes and couldn't hold a candle to Daddy. Davey had never believed that it was only because the apartment was empty that Mother had taken them there. He had dreamed up a whole crazy story about Mummy and Mr Rosenberg and that spring, after it was all over and they were back home, he had cut school to see if the thing he had dreamed up was still going on. And even though it wasn't, he had never forgiven her.

The lift opened and Judy walked through the lobby, out of the massive front door, and over to Park Avenue. Poor Davey. Even now, ten years later, life was harder for him than for anyone else she knew.

That evening, Marcel Goldblatt called and asked her to dinner on Saturday night. It was the best thing that could have happened, someone new, someone absolutely gorgeous, someone French.

She felt wonderful till Saturday morning, when the letter arrived: 'Dear Jude . . .' It was not a happy letter. 'Do you remember how Rena used to smile so much? Well she doesn't any more. I begin to see that other side of the job looming before me like a leering giant. After the studying and the nitpicking arguments and all the stuff that's fun, there are those other things written in indelible capitals: Leader, Guide, Comforter. I start to wonder.'

Suddenly, she lost all her enthusiasm for the evening. Instead, she wanted to take a train to Hartford and talk to Davey. She was his sister and it was clear that he needed her. Why were they up there anyway for two weeks when his family was down here?

But she had a date tonight and she was well brought up. Late in the afternoon she showered and dressed. She could not remember how tall he was so she wore heels that were not too high. Suddenly it seemed the epitome of absurdity that a man's height should figure so importantly in a relationship. When you fixed people up at school, it was the first, and often the last, question you asked. How tall is he? Didn't anyone ever care whether he had a brain or a soul or a heart that beat regularly? No, he just had to be over five foot eight for Judy and five foot ten for Fern.

Easy, kiddo, she said to herself as she put her stockinged feet into the shoes. Funny how she talked to herself as if she were Davey. The doorbell rang and she gathered her comb and lipstick into a small black bag her aunt had sent from Rome, fixed her hair one last time, and went carefully down the stairs in her heels. By the time she got there, her father and Marcel were deep in conversation. She said, 'Hi,' to Marcel and 'Good night, Daddy,' to her father, handing him Davey's letter as she kissed him.

'Princeton,' he said in answer to her question. They were sitting at a table in one of the Italian restaurants in the Village that the kids always went to on vacations, waiting for the antipasto. 'I finished in June.'

It was the same boring script she had gone through with every new date for three and a half years of college. 'What do you do now?' she asked, reading off the next line from memory.

'Nothing.'

She looked at him with some surprise. The script called for one of a group of answers at this point: law school, graduate school, working for a business degree, working at – fill in the blank with the job of your choice. 'Nothing?' she repeated.

'That's right.' He spoke nearly without an accent, just a hint of something that said France. 'Does that surprise you?'

'Yes. Why do you do nothing?'

'Because I'm different. Isn't it better to be different than to be the same as everyone else?'

'Not if there's no reason for it.'

'I hate this way of meeting people,' he said with feeling. 'Why is it always necessary to start with a life history?'

'Maybe it's a point of departure.'

'A point of departure,' he repeated with an echo of irony. 'Does that mean in your beautiful language that we are departing for somewhere?'

'It means – ' she began patiently.

'I know what it means,' he snapped, as though reluctant to have her believe there was something in this beautiful language that he did not understand. 'I come from here and I'm going there. Well, I come from nowhere and I'm going nowhere.'

She felt a momentary chill, had a fleeting thought of Davey. 'Why are you angry?' she asked.

'Am I angry?'

'Very angry, I think.'

'You're right. I am angry.' The admission seemed to calm him. 'I'm very angry.' He watched, without speaking, as the waiter removed the dishes, his eyes following the waiter's hands. He had a beautiful face. One could imagine it had been chiselled out of marble. His hair was dark and lush. 'I had an argument this morning, an old, old argument that I've been through so many times I can't keep my temper any more. I can't say anything new any more. And I can never win. Whatever happens, I always lose.'

She was struck by the sincerity in his voice, by the emotion. 'I'm sorry,' she said.

He shrugged his shoulders. 'It's nothing,' he offered, as though to lighten his last message.

'It wasn't with Regina, was it? She seems so nice.'

'It was with Morty.'

'I don't really know him.'

'He's a good person,' Marcel said, and she knew that something quite different was coming. 'But he has this company, a textile company. You know, cotton mills in the South. It's not something his father or his uncle gave him, you understand. He *created* it.' He spoke the word so that it conveyed awe. 'And it's become everything to him.'

'I can understand that.'

He regarded her for a moment. 'Yes,' he agreed, 'I can understand it too. But for him, not for me. For me it's a company that makes millions of yards of fabric with thousands of people working in dozens of buildings in North and South Carolina. It's not my great passion. It isn't even interesting to me. And I don't ever want to work there.'

'Then tell him you want to do something else.'

'Life must be very simple for you,' Marcel said.

In the moments that followed, the moments in which she gathered her feelings together, she was aware of a winey aroma. In front of her was a plate of veal and mushrooms that she had looked forward to and that she now wondered if she could even manage to sample. She felt angry herself now. The insult had been gratuitous. What did this handsome, spoiled boy know of the difficulties of life? How could he even imagine what Davey

39

had lived through in the last months? How dare he be snide. 'In our family,' she said very deliberately, 'we have absolute freedom to choose our own lives.' She knew now that it was true. Davey had chosen. She had chosen. Even Frenchy had chosen.

There was a trace of a smile. 'One can hardly quarrel with absolute freedom.'

'Maybe you have it too. Maybe you don't know you have it until you try to use it,' she said bravely, speaking of something of which she had only the faintest experience. 'I intend to study law.' She spoke defiantly, anticipating retaliation. Looking away from him, she began to eat.

'Because of your father? He's a judge, isn't he?'

'A federal judge,' she said. She always made certain that Daddy was not mistaken for one of those municipal judges who could be bought and sold by politicians. 'And I didn't do it because of my father. I did it for myself. I did it because it's the kind of life I want to live.'

'Judy –'

'I don't see why you make this fuss about Morty anyway. The Rushes aren't your family. Don't you talk to your family about these things?'

'My family?'

'In Paris,' she prompted. What was *wrong* with him?

'In Paris they want me to study law.'

'And you don't want to.'

'And I don't want to.'

'What do you want to do, Marcel?'

He looked at her for a moment, then shrugged and smiled slightly. 'Forget it,' he said. 'I'm just crazy.'

'You're not crazy. You're angry.' Completing the circle. 'There is something you want to do, isn't there?'

His eyes appraised her, judging her on the qualities she valued most – sincerity, honesty, compassion. 'Something,' he said grudgingly and she had the sense that she had failed the appraisal.

'Something secret.'

'I think it's what you call a pipe dream. Look, a friend of

mine has an apartment a couple of blocks from here. We could go there and talk.'

She knew he didn't want to go there to talk and she wasn't sure she wanted to spend much time talking to him either. Everything ended in argument or dissatisfaction. As for the alternative, she had been to young men's apartments but not many and not often. She would not go to his tonight.

'I don't think so,' she said.

'Judy – '

'Maybe we'll just take a walk.'

'It would be nicer at my friend's place.'

She shook her head.

'I'm moving out of the Rushes' apartment,' he said suddenly.

'You are? Why?'

'Because I'm – because it's stifling there. Because nothing will ever happen if I stay.'

'What will happen if you leave?'

'The arguments will stop. I won't have to fly down to North Carolina and see all the places I fit into the company the way I did this week. I'll be on my own. Isn't that what you want too?'

'I don't know. I haven't thought about it yet.'

'Come to the apartment with me,' he said.

She shook her head. 'Not tonight.'

'It's too cold for a walk.'

'Then we could – you could come back to my house.'

'And sit and look at you across the living room?'

'What would you like to do?' she asked with an edge to her voice.

'You know what I'd like to do.'

She felt her cheeks redden. 'I'm sorry.'

'So am I.'

She looked at him, trying to determine whether he was being nasty again or whether there was a note of sincerity in what he had said. She decided it was the former and felt, quite suddenly, both angry and nasty herself. 'Why did you ask me out?' she said.

'Because you were so beautiful.'

Of course. That was the other question. How tall and how good-looking. Of such profound values were relationships created. 'You must find me very disappointing,' she said in a low voice.

'Only a little.'

She put her fork down, her appetite finally and irreversibly departed. She could have taken the train to Hartford and seen Davey and Rena instead of wearing her favourite dress and being insulted.

'I think you asked me out for the wrong reason. I think I accepted for the wrong reason.'

'What was your reason?'

Now she was stuck. She could remember vividly the moment they met at Regina's apartment, the flash of something exciting that had passed between them. Surely she had not asked herself whether he had a brain or a soul or a heart that beat regularly. She had been attracted by his intense good looks and nothing else. What else, after all, is there to attract you in a momentary encounter? She knew her cheeks had reddened. 'I thought you were very good-looking,' she said.

She could see the smile at the corners of his lips. 'We aren't so very different. Are we?'

'I think we are.' She was embarrassed by her admission, angry that he had elicited this odious similarity. 'I'd really like to go home.'

'Really?'

'Yes.'

He turned and signalled the waiter, who came immediately. 'The bill, please.'

'Now, sir?'

'Right now, please.'

'Yes, sir.'

She sat uncomfortably, thinking that perhaps she should apologize, but not knowing what she would apologize for. The waiter brought the bill on a small plastic tray and Marcel counted notes from his wallet and left them on the table. They had said nothing to each other since he had called the waiter.

'Ready?'

'Yes.'

Her coat was beside her on the banquette and he helped her to put it on as she reached where he was standing. For reasons that she could not fathom he had made her feel guilty, as though she were the one who had ruined the evening.

Outside, on McDougal Street, he took her arm the way Daddy sometimes held Mother's, a kind of protective grip when they crossed the street or when a car appeared suddenly out of nowhere.

'There's a cab.'

They got in and rode silently uptown, the loudest noise the sound of the taxi's motor. Even the cabby refrained from wise-cracking or intruding his cabby philosophy, as though he sensed that the couple in the back seat would respond to him no more than they were responding to each other. He crossed Manhattan, went down Lexington, turned right and stopped in front of her house.

'Nice house,' the cabby said, with an awe that indicated he sensed the diminished value of his unspoken philosophy when compared to the Wolfe town house.

Marcel had the fare ready in his hand and they left the cab in the same silence. At the door he said, 'Tell your father it was a pleasure meeting him. He's a real gentleman.' It was like a slap in the face.

She rode the lift up to her room thinking, trying to determine what had gone wrong, where, and whose was the blame. She had met boys before that she did not like and certainly there had been those who had never called her back. Somehow tonight had been different.

On her desk was the letter from Davey and under it a note from her father.

Judy dear, After you left, Mother and I spoke to Davey and Rena on the phone. I took the liberty of not showing Mother the letter. Perhaps you'll call them yourself tomorrow. I'm sure they'd both like to hear from you. It's true that Davey is going through a difficult time but he has a good partner and they're going to see each other through these troubles. I think the best we can do now is remain available but intrude as little as possible.

I was pleased that you allowed me a few minutes in which to speak to Marcel Goldblatt. I met his father briefly during the summer of 1925 when he was a young lawyer, many years before he became Marcel's father. As you probably know, both of Marcel's parents were lost in the camps during the war but they were wise and unselfish enough to send their children to the country to be cared for by cooperating families and thus to survive. He seems to have become the fine young man his parents would be proud to have. I hope you enjoyed your evening together.

Dad

By the time she had finished the second paragraph, she had completely forgotten the first. The second paragraph was all the information missing from this evening's conversation, the things he had not said, perhaps because he thought she knew, perhaps because he could not speak of them.

But she had spoken of those things, crassly because she did not know, tauntingly because she had thought he was goading her.

Don't you talk to your family about these things?

My family?

There was no family, that was the answer, at least no immediate family, and what was left was tearing him apart. Someone in Paris wanted him to be a lawyer like his father and here in New York they were pushing him into a company he had no use for. She saw in a flash why he was living with the Rushes – because his parents were dead – a boy shunted from one place to another, a young man always beholden to someone, and she, Judy Wolfe of great compassion, had only made things worse.

She found her telephone book and looked him up, Goldblatt, M., at Regina's address. She dialled the number. It rang several times before he answered.

'This is Judy,' she said.

'Oh,' There was a brief silence. 'Sorry it took so long to answer. I'm packing.'

'Packing?'

'I'm moving out.'

'Marcel, I – My father left a note for me on my desk. He told me about – I didn't know about your parents and the war and what happened.'

There was another silence and she thought. Now he will open up and be warm and human and friendly.

Instead, he said, 'Is that what you called to tell me?'

She felt frustrated again by the tone of his voice. She said, 'Yes,' knowing it was inadequate, knowing the phone call had been a mistake.

'Thank you very much for calling,' Marcel said.

'Good night, Marcel.' She replaced the phone, forgetting to wait for his final word. She had spoken hers.

In the morning she telephoned Hartford and spoke to her brother and sister-in-law for equal lengths of time. Davey sounded fine, the old Davey, the kidder and joker. She wondered if someone else had written the letter and had him sign it. Or perhaps the week in Hartford had settled him down. Either way he seemed finally to be recovering.

A week later she returned to school.

It was a beautiful day for a graduation. The leaves were out and the weather was warm. Outside the dorm, girls met their families to make the walk to the last ceremony on campus. She found her parents and kissed them. Her mother took the cap and gown and folded the gown carefully over her arm.

'Who are you looking for, dear?'

'Fern's family. There they are.'

It was surely the second-worst day in Fern's life, the day she had been dreading for four years, the day she would introduce Jack and Vivien to the Wolfes.

There was no mistaking Fern's father. He was tall and lanky, a high forehead where the hair had receded, hair the same almost colourless quality as Fern's and that nose, the beautiful straight nose, the centrepiece, the character of the face.

Fern smiled as they approached and she spoke with pride. 'This is my father, Jack Hall.'

Holding out her hand, Judy said, 'Hello, Jack. I'm Judy Wolfe,' hearing her mother gasp a footstep behind her, such shocking behaviour, to speak to a stranger with such familiarity.

'Well hello, Judy,' Jack Hall said. 'It sure is good to meet you. I'd like you to meet Vivien.'

'Hello, Vivien.' Vivien was tall, too, and thin, with dark hair sprinkled with grey, pulled back in a ponytail. 'These are my parents.' She stepped aside and her father came forward and held out his hand.

'I'm Jerold Wolfe,' he said easily, 'and this is my wife, Edith.'

'You must be the judge, sir,' Jack Hall said.

'Not until I get back to New York. Well, I don't know how we're going to get through Thanksgiving this year without Fern.'

Judy turned to look at Fern, who was watching the exchanges of greetings with disbelieving eyes in a sombre face. She made a half turn and Judy saw her shoulders move, as if she had taken an enormous breath and let it out in relief. When they started walking again, the four parents were together in a congenial group and Fern and Judy were behind, Fern brushing tears from her cheeks as fast as they overflowed.

She put her bag down on her dresser and fell into the chair, hot and needing to cool off. She had had lunch with a friend and then gone into a few stores. She had bought a bathing suit for the summer and a matching robe. Elegance for her solitary walk to the lake. At the end of the summer she would choose her clothes for fall. The acceptance from Yale Law was pasted to one of the last pages of her Swarthmore Scrapbook. It was real now. She would not be a spectator all her life. She would be part of it as her father was part of it, and her brother.

There was a knock on the door and the maid came in. 'Mr Frenchy to see you, Miss Judy.'

46

'Oh.' She went quickly past the maid.

'In the judge's study.'

She flew down the stairs, leaving the elevator for the maid.

'Frenchy.'

'Oh, hi, Judy. Where's Mum?'

'Out somewhere.' She watched his face for a sign. His whole face was the sign.

'I'll come back later.'

'Frenchy?'

His eyes were hollow. 'Very bad,' he said. 'Very, very bad.'

'How is Diana?'

'OK.'

'Can I visit her?'

'Not today. Maybe tomorrow. I don't know. She may not want to see anybody. I'm not sure she wants to see me.'

'I'll tell Mum you were here.'

'Thanks.'

It was at that moment that she knew that Davey had been the lucky one.

The son of one of her mother's friends called her and two days later, on Wednesday, they went out to dinner in the Village. He was twenty-five and very handsome and she could tell that he liked her but she felt nothing. Frenchy's poor, misshapen baby was two days old and soon they would have to decide how to care for it. It was a decision she would never have to make herself. For Judy there would be no pregnancies, no births, no disappointments. She would practise law and have men as friends but not as husbands.

'Want to walk down Eighth Street?'

'Sure.'

It was a pretty street, interesting shops with jewellery and clothes and books. She would come back by herself one day and look more closely. Tonight it took all her energy to be decent company.

A message came the next morning asking her to meet her father after four-thirty at the courthouse. He would want to talk to her about Frenchy, reassure her, but she could not

47

accept reassurance. Since Christmas she had figured it out. It was in at least two lines of the family and both her brothers were affected. She would not take the chances they had taken. Today she knew, finally, that she would never marry.

He was waiting for her when she arrived, sitting at his desk with the black briefcase open on the rug beside him. Gold JW on black. That would be hers one day. When you knew that a piece of your life was forever denied to you, you compensated. She would compensate. She would love law with the kind of passion she saw sometimes in those courtrooms she had haunted all year.

'Hello, dear. Why don't you sit down.' He capped his pen and put it away in an inside pocket. 'I don't think we'll see Davey this summer.' He was not at ease. His forehead was clouded. 'Maybe in the fall, before you go up to New Haven.'

'I hope so.'

'I talked to Frenchy this morning. Diana will probably go home in a few days.' He folded his hands on the desk blotter, then unfolded them. 'They've decided not to take the baby with them.'

'What'll happen to him?'

'He'll be placed where he'll get very good institutional care.'

'Poor Frenchy.'

'Yes.'

'Will they visit him?'

'I don't know, Judy. Nobody knows. They'll make up their minds as time goes on.'

She looked around the room. It had panelled walls and bookcases built in nearly everywhere. An air-conditioner in one window whirred noisily but the room was blissfully cool.

'It was Regina who had a child like that once, wasn't it?' she asked.

'Regina?' He seemed surprised. 'No, nothing like that ever happened to Regina.'

'Really? She told me at Christmas they adopted Ernie because she had a baby that died.'

'That's exactly what happened.'

'I thought probably the family just – said that it died. To cover it up.'

'There was nothing to cover up. Nothing in Regina's life needs to be covered up.' He spoke with uncharacteristic agitation.

'You needn't sound so angry. I was only asking a question. You said it was here and there in the family and I thought it was Regina. That's all.'

'It wasn't Regina,' he said in a lower, more controlled voice. He looked down at his desk and then back at Judy. 'It happened to me.'

'To you?' She shuddered as though the air-conditioner had suddenly gone wild. 'What do you mean?'

'I was the father of a child like Frenchy's.'

'You mean Mother had a baby like that?'

'It wasn't your mother's.'

She looked at him, her father behind a massive desk. Judge Wolfe. JW, gold on black. 'What do you mean?'

'It was someone else's child.'

'*What?*'

He looked down at the desk and his eyes flickered closed, then open. 'It was ten years ago. Eleven. She was a young woman I met in my work.'

'Oh, no, Daddy. Not you.'

'The child died a few days after it was born and that was the end of it. The end really came long before that. It was simply an act of foolishness on my part.'

'Does Mother know?' She could hardly ask. She could hardly bear to listen.

'Your mother knows everything. Nobody else does.'

'How could she – ?' she began and then it all fell into place. 'That was when she took us to the Rosenbergs' apartment, wasn't it?'

'Yes.'

'Then she didn't – It was your fault she took us there, wasn't it?'

'It was my fault.'

'How could you – how could you *do* such a thing?' She could scarcely catch her breath. 'How could you *do* that to us?'

'Judy, if there were one thing in my life that – '

49

'Do you *know* what you did?' she cried. 'Do you know what you did to Davey?' She found she was standing, moving toward the desk. 'Do you know that he thought Mummy was going to run away with Mr Rosenberg and he's hated her ever since that time? Do you know that? How could you *do* that to Davey?'

She reached into her bag for a handkerchief. She could not remember ever crying so hard, ever being so angry, ever feeling such revulsion. Her father whom she loved. Her father who was her idol. Her father the judge.

'I know a great deal about Davey,' her father said in a quiet voice.

'Why did she go back to you? How could she go back to you after you did a thing like that? You're my father,' she said, trying to make him understand the impossibility of what he had told her. 'How could you?'

He stood up and walked around the desk. 'Judy, dear – '

She said, 'No,' and he stopped where he was. 'Don't. Leave me alone.' She slung the bag over her shoulder. 'Please leave me alone. I don't want – ' She went to the door. 'I'm not coming home tonight.'

'Judy,' her father said sternly.

'I'm never coming home. I'm never going to law school. I don't want anything to do with you. Ever.'

She walked quickly, out into the warmth of the June day. It was rush hour and there were crowds of moving people. A taxi dropped a passenger at the kerb and she ran for it, making it inside before anyone else saw it. Fern had a small apartment in the West Eighties. She would go there.

PART TWO

June 1959

One

———◦◦◦———

'Be OK without me?' Fern stood, dressed for work, looking down at Judy on the couch.

'I'll be fine.'

'I don't have to shut the gas off or anything?' Fern said very lightly.

'I'm not suicidal, Fern. I'm homicidal.'

'Much healthier. I feel just plain guilty. When I needed you, you stayed and held my hand.'

'You held my hand last night. Besides, if you held my hand today, I couldn't brush my teeth.'

'That's the spirit.' Fern took her bag off the kitchen table and slung it over her shoulder. 'There's a new toothbrush in the medicine chest, by the way. I bought it in case I was lucky enough to have a guy stay over. You're my first guy.'

Judy smiled. 'I wish I could make it up to you.'

Fern raised her eyebrows suggestively. 'Find me a guy.'

'See you later.'

She was grateful for the toothbrush but nervous and confused about the day that spread before her. She did not want to see her mother. She wanted somehow to tell her mother how she felt, to apologize for years of unspoken suspicions, but she wanted to do it without a face-to-face meeting. She could not look at her mother's eyes as they discussed her father.

Showering, she thought of Davey and began to cry, hot tears mingling with hot spray. He should know, but it was impossible to tell him. He would tell Rena and the story might spread. She could not let that happen to her mother. She did not want people looking at her mother with narrow, curious eyes and laughing when she turned away.

Dressing, she realized she would have to find a job. She

could not eat Fern's food without paying her way. In fact, she would have to rent an apartment somewhere until she decided what she was doing and where she was going. Somehow, she would have to get into the house to pack a suitcase, but she could not do it when her mother was there. She could not look at her mother.

She poured orange juice from a glass jug in the refrigerator, toasted bread under the grill, forgetting to turn it till it smoked and was black on the first side, and boiled water for instant coffee. Funny, the different ways there were to live. Fern used margarine instead of butter but Fern was happy and independent, working at the job she had wanted most at one of the broadcasting stations. She loved her father and however he lived, he would never disappoint her.

She was washing the few dishes when the phone rang. Drying her hands on the dish towel, she answered.

'Judy? Are you all right?'

'Mother.' As if struck by a thunderbolt, she began to sob. Her reserves depleted, she lost all control. It was why she had not wanted to face her mother. She could not be strong and she could not imagine her mother strong.

Words came into her ear but she did not hear them. There was a click and she hung up, crying into the dish towel. She could not face her mother but her mother would be here sooner than she could run away and where would she run? She went back into the bedroom and sat by the windows overlooking Eighty-seventh Street. She hated him now and it would hurt her mother to hear it. Was it possible that a year ago this had been a happy family?

The black limousine drew up before the house and her mother got out before the chauffeur had a chance to help her. Judy ran back, opening the downstairs door, and waited while her mother's footsteps came nimbly up the stairs, like a young girl at the start of life.

Edith Wolfe kissed her daughter and closed the door. There was nowhere to sit except the unmade couch that had served as a bed and her mother sat them there without a word. The tears

54

returned and her mother put a tissue in Judy's hand and took another to blot her face.

'Your father made two mistakes in his life,' Edith Wolfe said finally. 'The second one was yesterday.'

'How could he let us believe what we believed all these years?' she asked with anguish.

'You were eleven, Judy. You can't talk about things like that with an eleven-year-old.'

'Why did you go back to him?'

'Because he loved me.'

'What about you? Didn't you think about how you felt?'

'I knew how I felt,' her mother said. 'I loved him. I loved him the day I met him. I just had to be sure he loved me.'

'I hate him.'

'No. It's easy to say but it isn't true. You only hate what happened.'

'I can't ever look at him again.'

'Judy, it was a small infidelity. Ten years ago, when I found out about it, it was already over.'

'I didn't know infidelities came in sizes.'

'They do. The big ones destroy marriages.'

'And the little ones just destroy families.'

'I know how angry you are, dear, but you're being very hard on Daddy. Davey's coming along very nicely and you're going to come along the best of all.'

'Davey isn't coming along,' she said in a low voice. 'Davey's a lost soul.'

'He'll find himself the way the rest of us have. And if he is a little – ' her mother hesitated ' – a little lost, you can't blame all of it on what happened.'

'I wish he'd never told me.' Judy reached for another tissue from the pile her mother had placed on the coffee table. 'I think I hate him more for telling me than for what he did.'

'That's Daddy's blind spot,' her mother said. 'He's always felt so close to you, he thought he could tell you anything and you would understand.'

'He was wrong.'

'That's why it's his blind spot. What he sees so clearly in

other people, he doesn't see in himself or his family.' Her mother gathered the used tissues and found Fern's waste basket. 'Why don't we go home, Judy? Have a rest and you'll feel better.'

Judy shook her head.

'Would you like to stay with Fern for a few days?'

She nodded.

'Shall I send your clothes over?'

'I'll pack them myself. Is he home?' She could not bring herself to say 'Daddy.'

'Daddy's in court, dear.'

She folded the sheets and blanket, leaving them stacked at one end of the couch. Then, taking the extra key Fern had left, she followed her mother down to the car.

She would not allow her mother to help her pack. Alone in her room, she emptied drawers and went selectively through her closet. It was summer and she could not think more than a season ahead. It was hard enough today to think about tomorrow.

But she knew she was leaving. In her desk drawer she found her bank books and beneath them, her passport, which her mother always kept current. She shoved them into her bag and looked around for mementoes. She had no memory before this room. The crib had been in that corner because Mummy didn't believe in putting a crib near a window; it was too dangerous. The rug was Chinese. She had gone with her father to pick it out and they had agreed immediately as they always agreed on everything. She wiped the back of her hand roughly across her eyes. The lids were so irritated they stung at the touch of her hand.

There was nothing in the room she would take with her. What was there belonged to the room, not to her. She walked out, rang for the lift, and sent her luggage down on it, choosing the stairs for her own descent. She went slowly, regarding the figurines on the lighted shelves with a distant gaze, as though more than glass separated them from her. Finally, on the last curve to the living room, she stopped. The little ivory Buddha she had always loved sat laughing on the edge of its shelf. She had wanted it once but he had not given it to her. Now she would take it. She would make it hers. It was the only thing she wanted from her father's house. Opening her bag, she dropped it in and went down the stairs to say good-bye to her mother.

She bought a paper and looked at want ads and ads for apartments. She began to think, using the word 'Need'. She needed a place to live; she needed a job. She had never needed anything before, never had to fund her own life. Her father had taken care of everything but that was over now. It was over forever.

She looked in Fern's mirror and knew she could not apply for a job with red eyes. She bathed them in cold water but it did no good. The job would have to wait till Monday. And the apartment. Fern would allow her the privilege of a long weekend of hospitality.

In her bag was a pair of sunglasses. She put them on and went outside. It was well after noon but she had no hunger, only a mild inquisitiveness about the neighbourhood and a desire to make the day pass until Fern came back and they could talk again. Charitably speaking, the area was mixed. On Central Park West there was old, staid affluence, the buildings high, stone, sombre, and expensive. Toward the west, the neighbourhood deteriorated. Columbus Avenue was shabby, walk-up apartments over first-floor groceries and cleaning shops and hardware stores. She walked all the way to Broadway and turned south. When she saw the stairs to the subway, she crossed the street and went downstairs to the train. It stopped and started roughly, disturbing what might otherwise have been dreams. She saw finally that they were at Christopher Street and she got up hurriedly and left the train just as the doors began to close. This was the Village where Uncle Richard had lived in the twenties, where artists and writers, people going up and people who rejected the values of uptown, lived. Perhaps she would look here for a place to live.

She walked east and found herself at Washington Square Park. Children swung and played in sand in their own little playground while men played chess at stone tables and lovers walked with casual disregard for nonlovers. The pool was full and she stopped to observe her reflection in sunglasses.

She watched her image flutter slightly, wondering who she was. Her father had done more than shatter the foundations of the family; he had destroyed her dream. She could not go to law school. Thinking about it brought a taste of revulsion. She wanted to spit, but she had been brought up to swallow. Practising law meant being like him. She would have to find her own way, another way.

She turned from the pool. A young man in jeans and a T shirt was standing beside her like an eerie memory of the past.

'Hi,' he said genially.

'Hello.' She began to walk away.

'Hey. Wait.'

'Sorry,' she said. She walked away, marvelling at the innocence of the world. As if all the problems in one's life could be solved by a fling at love. If only it were all true.

Why had she wanted law in the first place? Because Daddy was a lawyer. Because it was cute for a little girl to say, I'm going to be a lawyer when I grow up. Because she wanted a briefcase with JW near the latch in gold. She thought of the courtrooms she had visited and the trials she had seen. Had it all been her father? Was she no one without him?

She was through the park now and near the buildings of NYU. It was a pretty area, prettier than Fern's. She wished she could remember where Uncle Richard had lived. After she checked the paper again, she would come back to see what was available near Washington Square.

She walked up University Place to Eighth Street and turned right. She would look at the pretty shops, clear her mind of everything else. Halfway down the block, she could see she had lost her way. The shops were different from the other night when she had walked here with a date whose name she could no longer remember. At the corner she found with relief that she was on Broadway, which was where she had started her journey hours ago. There was a subway and she went down and took the first train that stopped, hoping to orient herself as it travelled.

The train, she realized as it began to move, was on the BMT line, and she felt a slight panic at the possibility of landing in Brooklyn, a foreign country for someone brought up in the East Seventies. The train was crowded and it struck her that it was now late in the day and she was caught in the rush hour. When it stopped at Canal Street, she knew she was going in the wrong direction but it was too late to exit; the crowd was too thick and the doors began to close. Working her way to the door, she got off at the next stop and looked around to see where she was, hoping she was still in Manhattan. She was. She had landed at City Hall.

As she reached the street, she began to get her bearings. She was on Centre Street near Chambers and farther up would be Foley Square and the courts, the courts where she would never try a case because she would not become a lawyer. She walked in that direction, a slow pacer in a sea of rushing individuals, anxious to get away from here and home to there. She was in no hurry. She felt calmer than she had felt all day. It was still bright enough that she could wear the sunglasses without looking out of place.

She passed number 40, the federal court, and kept on going. Nothing there for her today, nothing there for her ever again. She came to 60, the beautiful Supreme Court Building with its mountain of steps outside, and passed it by. Across another street and just up the block was 100, the Criminal Court Building, with its timeless messages engraved in stone.

She recognized it as soon as she reached it, the building looming like an old friend. She was the only person going inside. The building was emptying for the weekend, the tide moving in one steady, strong direction. Maybe she would just go in and find and empty courtroom and look at it, see if it made a difference to her that she would not go to law school in the fall.

She walked slowly up the steps and slowly into the building and the crowd thinned. The few people now walking out were mostly men. The juries had all recessed at the start of rush hour. No one wanted to dispense justice after a certain hour on a hot Friday afternoon.

The interior was dark and hot. She found the stairs and walked slowly up, her hand on the brass bannister, the only person ascending. Two men came down, talking, arms moving, and she slipped out of their way. When they had passed, she stopped on the landing to take the sunglasses off, stuffing them in her bag and then continuing. A small man with white hair passed her on his way down and she wondered if he was a judge as her father was. More people. Everyone going home except Judy. She had nearly reached the second floor when a man in a great hurry went by. She raised her head to watch him and their eyes met fleetingly. Behind glasses, his eyes were quite blue. It took several seconds for her mind to make the connection and by the time it did, he was gone. The man was someone she knew.

She stopped and looked down the stairs and at the same moment, the man stopped, down at the landing, and looked up. Then, slowly, he came back up to where she stood watching him.

'I know you,' he said, but he looked puzzled.

She shook her head. 'We met once. A long time ago.'

'You're Jerold's daughter.'

'Yes.'

'Your name is – Judith,' he said at last.

She smiled. 'That's very good after so many years.'

'I'm Roy Kellems.' He offered his hand and she shook. 'Are you all right?'

'I'm fine.' She knew that even in the half-dark of this place, her eyes must look terrible.

He glanced at his watch. 'Where are you going at this hour?'

'I just wanted to look at a courtroom.'

'The building's practically empty. You shouldn't wander around by yourself.'

'I'll just be a minute.'

'I'll go along with you if you like.'

'Thank you.'

They went to the second floor, down a hall, and he opened a door for her. 'Let's try this one,' he said.

There were windows along one side so that it was bright even with the lights off. She walked down the centre aisle to the front, stopped, and looked around. It was very quiet, a silence without echoes or memories. She was only a visitor.

'There isn't much difference between them,' Roy Kellems said from somewhere behind her. 'One's about the same as the other. The magic is what you put into them yourself.'

She turned around to face him. 'There was a lot of magic the time I saw you.'

'Did I win or lose?'

'I'm not sure. They convicted him of manslaughter.'

'Not enough magic.' He smiled very slightly with thin lips. He was a tall man, somewhat angular.

'I was enchanted.'

She had been sixteen and Daddy had taken her out of school for a day to watch the turning point in a murder trial. Even now, almost five years later, she could remember that day, that trial, that unforgettable man.

They had sat near the front of the courtroom, behind a group of reporters whose conversation sounded more like gossip than journalism. Daddy pointed out the people at the prosecution table, told her what he knew of the judge. The defence came in together and she looked at them with detachment. Rather ordinary-looking people, she thought, to be handling such an important case, a case where a man's life was at stake. Suddenly someone nearby said, 'Jerold, well, this is an honour,' and she looked up to see a man shaking hands with her father.

'I've brought my daughter this morning, Roy. Judith, I want you to meet Mr Kellems.'

'Hello, Judith.'

She held out her right hand and shook his but although she opened her lips slightly to respond, she said nothing. She was transfixed by the pale blue eyes that changed from cool to warm as they held her dark ones. He looked like no one she had ever seen in her life, a nose so thin and straight that she was tempted to wriggle in her seat to see it in profile, sandy hair that was straight and loose, that he would need to brush away from his face now and then, a man from another place, a place she could not imagine, a place she had never visited.

'A pleasure to meet you, Judith.'

A pleasure to meet *you*, Mr Kellems. But she did not say it.

'I'll try to see you later, Jerold. Hope it'll be worth your time.'

'I'm sure it will.'

Her father turned and looked at her with some irritation. She had not responded politely as she had been brought up to do.

'How do you know him?' she asked, her eyes on the defence table, on the profile, on the straight nose and thin lips of Roy Kellems.

'He came to my seminar at Columbia,' he said curtly, and she was sorry she had disappointed him. 'He's not a man with a narrow mind,' he went on and now the hard edge to his voice was gone. 'You'll have to stand in a moment. The judge is on his way.'

They stood and were seated after the judge took his place and then there were some uninteresting details to be taken care of, lawyers approaching the bench, the jury eventually ushered out of the court while a point was argued, then the jury brought back with apparently nothing of consequence changed, and then it began and it was like magic.

She watched Roy Kellems as some earlier testimony was read aloud. He seemed deep in thought, alone in an isolated room. He was still as a statue except when he suddenly corrected a phrase in the reading. When the reading was finished, he began to question the man sitting in the witness box. Slowly, carefully, patiently, Roy Kellems poked holes in the prosecution's case. Gradually, as they listened, the case against the defendant weakened.

She did not take her eyes off the lawyer. When he moved, her eyes moved with him. When he smiled, ever so slightly, she smiled too, relaxed, glad he had made the point. He seemed intensely concerned with the testimony of the witness, as though they were having a private conversation of tremendous importance, as though this witness knew the truth and Roy Kellems had to know it too. His intensity carried through the courtroom, touching the spectators. Judy could feel it in the pounding silence, in the merged heartbeats. Even the gossipy reporters held their pencils away from their pads so as not to disturb the quiet.

He was the most magnetic man she had ever seen. There was nothing flashy about the way he comported himself. Daddy sometimes dismissed certain lawyers by calling them 'showmen'; Roy Kellems was not a showman. He was defending someone's life and it was costing him a piece of his own to do it.

Suddenly, the judge said something about lunch and the spell was broken. She could not believe it was past noon. She could not believe it was hours since that handshake.

'Hungry, dear?' Her father had stood.

She shook her head.

'You're speechless today.'

'Daddy – ' she stood and straightened her skirt, 'that's what I want to do.'

'That?'

'That kind of law. In a courtroom like this. I want to be able to do what he does.'

'Takes some practice to be that good. He's been at it over ten years.'

'I have time.' She looked up at ther father, who did not defend murderers or second-storey men or rapists but whom, until this morning, she had admired above all other men in the world. 'He's really special, isn't he?'

'Very special. Let's get some lunch.'

'I feel as if I suddenly know what I want to do with my life,' she said as they went down the stone stairs to the first floor.

'Well, my friend Roy certainly had an effect on you.'

'Roy?' She looked at him inquiringly.

'Mr Kellems,' her father said indulgently. 'The fellow we've been listening to all morning. I see he's made quite a mark on you.'

'Yes.' Yes. Funny that Daddy should see it more clearly than she. It was not just the artful practice of the law that had affected her this morning; it was the man. It was the way Roy Kellems practised the law; it was the way Roy Kellems walked from the table to the witness, the way Roy Kellems spoke, the way he shook hands, the way his blue eyes turned from cool to warm as he looked at her. The magnetism came from him, and the way he practised law was as much a part of him as the eyes and the thin, straight nose, and the handshake. The intensity in the courtroom that morning had come from his person and his spirit. Someone very special indeed.

'I was enchanted,' she said again, her eyes focusing on the present-day courtroom, her mind re-establishing the day and the time, sliding over the four and a half years, somewhat reluctantly.

'Doesn't take much to do that to a teenage girl. I've got one at home.'

She started back toward the door. 'I'm sorry I'm keeping you,' she apologized.

'Would you like me to run you home?' he offered. 'I'm heading uptown anyway.'

'I don't live at home any more.'

He watched her for a moment. 'You look as if you've been crying buckets.'

It surged back, the anger, the grief, wetting her eyes. 'I'm all right.'

'I don't think you are.'

It was not something she could argue. 'I'll be all right tomorrow,' she said, as though offering a compromise.

'You can't walk around this place by yourself. Not when it's empty. It's not safe.'

'I'm finished here now.' She started towards the door and stopped.

'Is there something I can do?'

She shook her head.

'Come with me,' Roy Kellems said. He took her arm and led her back to the stairs, down to the first floor and out the door. The light exploded in her eyes and she reached into her bag and put the sunglasses back on. They were at the top of the outside stairs and he had let go her arm.

'Thank you very much, Mr Kellems.'

'Where will you go now?'

'I'm staying with a friend. She lives on the West Side. I took

64

a wrong subway before. That's how I got here. I can find my way back.'

'Are you in trouble?'

'No. No trouble at all.'

He regarded her for a moment. 'You're not pregnant, are you?'

She looked at him in surprise and came close to laughing. 'No. Not even a little bit. Is that what usually gives girls my age red eyes?'

'Usually. I wouldn't want you to do anything stupid or dangerous. And you wouldn't have to worry about it getting back to Jerold.'

'My father knows what's bothering me. It's a family matter and I can't talk about it. What I need is to do some thinking. When I went into that courtroom, I decided something. Over the weekend, I'll try to decide the rest.'

'I'll run you up to your friend's place.'

'It really isn't – '

'My car's parked around the corner,' he said, taking no notice of her protest.

He paid for the car and told the attendant he would drive it out himself. 'West?' he asked, turning the car into the street.

'West Eighty-seventh Street. Just in from Central Park.'

He drove back to Chambers Street, crossed Manhattan, and got on the West Side Highway. It was thick with traffic and she felt guilty that she had allowed him to do this. It would cost him much time and she could have been back to Fern's faster by subway.

'Maybe we'll get a look at some ships,' he said as they reached the Thirties. 'I wonder what that one is up there. Ever sailed?'

'Yes. My father took us to Europe a few times.'

'Privileged childhood.'

'I used to think so.'

'But you don't think so any more.'

'I don't know any more.'

'It's the *America*.'

She turned to look, watching it go by. It was decorated for

tonight's sailing. Tomorrow, Saturday, the harbour would be empty. 'We sailed on it once,' she said.

He exited at Seventy-ninth and turned up the Drive to Eighty-sixth, then across to Central Park West. Two lefts and he was almost in front of Fern's building.

'It's that one,' she said, pointing.

He stopped the car, double parking, and looked at the building. Then he looked across the street, up and down the block, as though appraising the neighbourhood as she had done only this afternoon. Finally, he looked at his watch. 'Will your friend be home?' he asked.

'Probably. It doesn't matter. I have the key.'

He took the car key from the ignition and put it in his pocket. 'Let's go tell her I'm taking you to dinner. Then she won't worry, you won't cry, and we can talk about what's bothering you.'

She didn't stop to think about it. As he had said it, she had known she would accept. 'Thank you,' she said. 'That's the nicest thing that's happened to me all week.'

'West Virginia,' he said in answer to her question. 'My daddy was a country lawyer and I grew up wanting to be a city lawyer.'

'Maybe I'll be a country lawyer some day.'

'Now's the time to think about it.'

'I know.'

'You've finished college?'

'I just graduated. It's only a couple of weeks ago but I feel like it's been a year.'

'A bad year.'

'A very bad one.'

'A falling out with Jerold.'

'In a way.' She touched the lid of one eye and felt the sting. He had persuaded her to take off the glasses and had found a table where her back was to everyone but him.

'But you're not pregnant.'

She smiled. 'No. I promise you. In fact, when the time comes, I'll see to it that I never am.'

'That's a big decision for a young girl to make.'

'It's a necessary one. There's something in the family, my father's family. It's hit both my brothers. It's not going to get me.'

'Accepted. Where do you go from there?'

'I'm not sure. I need a job. I need a place to live. I can't stay with Fern forever. I – ' she took a breath that was almost a sob ' – I just left home this morning.'

'Then today's the worst day.'

'I hope so.'

'Say,' he seemed suddenly to be reminded of something, 'would you like a drink?'

'I'm not much of a drinker.'

'I don't drink at all and I sometimes forget to ask.'

'Is that your West Virginia upbringing?'

'Not exactly. It's something – shall we say – that's in the family.'

'I see.'

'But I don't mind buying for someone else.'

She shook her head.

'You were saying you left home this morning. Does that mean that until this morning you were a college graduate who thought she needed neither job nor apartment?'

'That's right.'

'Then maybe there was someone who was going to marry you and take care of all that.'

She smiled. 'No. I'm not a casualty of romance. Is that the usual line of reasoning? That everything can be explained by pregnancy or romance or a broken-up love affair?'

'It goes a long way,' Roy Kellems said.

'A guy in Washington Square Park tried to pick me up this afternoon and I thought, I bet a lot of people think that falling in love takes care of all life's problems.'

'You're very young, aren't you? When you're very young, you sneer at that particular thought. When you get a little older, you do an about face. You don't think, you *know* that falling for someone will solve everything forever. A little while after that, you realize that you were right the first time.'

'That's – that's a very pessimistic outlook.'

'Not at all. It just means you have to start looking for answers somewhere else. Maybe work a little harder.'

'I don't mind working harder.'

'Good. But you want to work at the right thing.'

'I don't know what the right thing is any more.'

The food was served and she ate with more appetite than she had thought she had. He did not press her on her troubles and after a while he let her ask the questions, answering with nostalgic remembrances.

'The regular army,' he said when she asked about the war. 'They let me finish law school and then they wouldn't let me use anything I'd learned in my whole life except how to survive in mud. I tasted the most expensive mud in France. Shame I don't drink the wine.'

'When did you finish law school?'

'In '41. They gave me a weekend pass to take the bar exam. I got married the next day, but I'd known her for some while. We went to college together.'

'You must have graduated about '38.'

'That's when I did. End of May, beginning of June. It was a nice day.'

Judy blushed. 'That's when I was born. May of '38.'

'Well, if I'm twice as old as you, maybe you'll let me help.'

'I think I feel better than if I'd stayed home with Fern.'

'Well I know I feel better than if you'd stayed home with Fern.'

'I'm afraid your wife must be angry.' He had called when they reached the restaurant.

'It comes with the work.' He sipped his coffee. 'Well, that's not quite true. It comes with me.'

It was late and dark when they left. He drove to Central Park West and turned into Eighty-seventh Street. Upstairs, she could see the lights on in Fern's bedroom.

'Well,' he said, switching off the motor, 'have we got you safely through the worst day of your life?'

'Quite safely. I feel – I'm much more relaxed than I was. All those things inside stopped shaking. You've been more than kind.'

'We all remember a time when we should have and didn't. And we've lived to regret it. I wouldn't want to have any regrets over a girl like you. You'll pull out of it. If I were Jerold, I'd feel pretty proud of you. You didn't let anything slip.'

'You didn't ask very searching questions.'

'Well, at my age maybe you start to lose the magic.' He looked as though he were enjoying his own joke. He reached into his pocket, took out his wallet, and slid out a business card. 'If you start plummeting again, you can reach me most days at the office.'

'Thank you.' She opened the car door and read the card by the overhead lamp. Roy C. Kellems. Attorney-at-law. 'What's the C for?'

'Calvin. My mother's affectation. We call my son Cal instead of Junior.' He looked at his watch and yawned. 'I think I'll stay in the city tonight,' he said.

'At a hotel? On my account?'

'I have a little place across the park. For late nights and when I need to work. Get a good night's sleep, Judith.'

'Thanks again.'

When she got upstairs, Fern was in a nightgown, reading a book.

'Surviving?' she asked.

'Mm.'

'Seemed like a nice sort. What does he do?'

'I think he works magic,' Judy said.

'You know you can stay here if you want,' Fern said the next morning.

'I can't. You need to be alone.'

'Then what about someone from school?' Fern nodded toward the telephone.

'Their parents think it's immoral. To live in an apartment while your folks are alive and a subway stop away.'

'So does Jack,' Fern said lightly. 'It's the thrill of his life that I'm doing it.'

The phone rang again and Fern, putting down a broom to answer, wailed, 'Will it never stop? I've got to get this place cleaned up.' A moment later she covered the mouthpiece and said, 'It's for you.'

For a moment, something clawed at Judy's heart. 'It's not my father, is it?' she asked in a low voice.

Fern shook her head. 'Doesn't sound like it.'

'Hello?' Judy said inquiringly.

'Judith, Roy Kellems.'

'Oh.' Judy sat on the couch. 'Oh. Good morning, Mr Kellems.'

'Life a little brighter?'

'Yes. Thank you.'

'What are you thinking about today, a place to live or your future as a country lawyer?'

'A little of both.'

'I'd like to talk to you about being a country lawyer.'

She did not know what to say. Fern had been watching since she said, 'Mr Kellems.' Now she moved away, on tiptoe, into the bedroom and shut the door. 'Is that a yes or a no?' he asked after a moment's silence.

'I think it's a yes.'

'How's two? We can walk through the park. Don't dress fancy. We'll grab something for dinner later on.'

For a second she felt like laughing. Then she said, 'I'll see you at two.'

After she hung up, the door opened and Fern appeared, leaning on the broom. 'Magic?' she said with a special look in her eye.

'Crazy,' Judy said. 'Just plain crazy.'

'What you're telling me is that you have in your hand an acceptance from a prestigious law school, a guarantee of support from your father for as long as it takes you to go through it, and you're giving it up.'

'I may not be giving it up forever,' she said with uncertainty. 'What I want to do now is – '

'You're giving it up for September 1959.'

'Yes.'

He was different from yesterday. Dressed in a sports shirt and cords, he looked like an older version of yesterday's boys in Washington Square Park, but today he badgered her pointedly. The future, the future; what was she doing about the future?

'Because you've had a tiff with your father and this is your way of saying "up yours".'

'No.' Finally he had made her angry. '*No*. I'm not saying "up yours". I'm not being nasty and vulgar to get back at him.'

'Aren't you?'

'I'm doing it because – ' She knew she could not say it without tears.

'Don't cry in public,' Roy Kellems said gently, touching her shoulder. 'It's not healthy.'

It made her laugh and she wiped at the eyes with the back of her hand. 'Mr Kellems – '

'Would you call me Roy so I know I'm not talking to a client?'

'Roy.'

'Yes.' He retrieved his hand. 'Yes. You were saying you're doing it because.'

She swallowed. 'Because I don't want to be like him.'

'Come on, Judith,' he said with real or feigned irritation. 'Don't be like him. Be like me. Be like Oliver Wendell Holmes. Be for God's sake like Judith Wolfe. Doesn't she have an independent existence?'

'I don't know.' She pulled her full skirt down over her legs. They were sitting under a tree in Central Park, she facing northeast. Behind her the sun was still high and hot. It was nearly four.

'Well, think.'

'What do you care?' she said in exasperation.

'I care because we made a little agreement yesterday when I met you on the stairs.'

'I didn't make any agreements.'

'When I said I'd go along with you to the courtroom if you wanted, you said "thank you." That was the agreement. I care

71

because we went into that courtroom together. I picked up a piece of the responsibility for you when we went in. I care because you're someone I know, or the daughter of someone I know, and when I saw you, you scared hell out of me.'

'I'm all right, Roy.'

'Then let me hear you think. Out loud. You're holding in your hand the absolute top, no question about it. There isn't any man in this world that I envy. I get up in the morning and go to work because I want to, not because I have to. I spent four years in the slime of Europe keeping myself alive so I could come back to this city and put on a clean shirt and stand in front of a jury and defend people. All right. You're giving it up. Well what are you giving it up *for*? What are you going to do Monday morning when you put on a pretty dress and look for a job? You want to be someone's secretary? Is that it? Answer his phone, make his lunch reservations, cross your legs when you take dictation, and call his wife to say he'll be late for dinner? Is that what Judith Wolfe wants to do with her life?'

'Not forever. But it might be a start.'

'It's an end, a dead end. A girl like you doesn't have to do that. It's what lesser women escape from.'

'Roy, I need a paycheque. You're talking glamour and I'm talking ninety dollars a week to pay my rent and buy my meals.'

'What were you looking for in that courtroom?'

'I was listening for something.'

He smiled in that faint, engaging way, his eyes brilliantly blue. 'You didn't hear it, did you?'

'No.'

'It wasn't there for you to hear. I hear it. Jerold hears it. It's what you put in that echoes.'

She leaned back against the tree. 'I'll think about it.'

'Will you?'

'Yes. I won't do anything about Yale for a few weeks. But I *will* get a job.'

'Get any damn job you want. Just don't make a foolish decision in haste. There're a lot of ways of slitting your throat. Don't pick one just because it's bloodless.'

She said, 'Thank you,' and to her immense surprise, he leaned over and kissed her on the lips.

'Surprised?' he said, leaning back.

'Yes.'

'Anything else?'

She smiled at him. 'Yes.'

'Let's walk.'

They stood and he put his arm around her. It was a comfortable way to walk.

'Was that a seduction speech?' she asked.

'You bet. I think law is very seductive.'

'I don't mean law.'

'I'm forty-two years old, Judith, and a member of the bar. I don't seduce little girls.'

'Thank you for caring about me.'

'It's my pleasure,' Roy Kellems said.

He bought them each an ice cream and they made their way east to Fifth Avenue. 'I like Jerold,' he said as they walked south along the park. 'He's a man of honour in a profession in which men should be but often aren't.'

'We know my father differently. I don't want to dispute his virtues or argue his faults.'

'You're right. We always know people differently. That's what makes a trial so interesting, listening to witnesses who see the defendant as pure evil and others who see him as a Christian gentleman. I'd vouch for Jerold any day as the latter, even if he isn't Christian with a capital C. He's a man who does things for people, good things, and the only time you hear about them is when the people he's done them for speak up. You might be surprised some day.'

'I've already been surprised. I don't want to be surprised any more.'

'But you can't let it change the design of your life. You're young. Your big responsibility is to yourself. Your only one, at this point. You have to ask yourself: "What do I want?" with the emphasis on "I".'

'It's too soon. I can ask myself but I don't have any answers yet.'

73

'I can't spend the summer walking you through the park and bullying you. I'm afraid that when I leave you, you'll take that job as a secretary and turn down law school. You wouldn't do that just because it's easy, would you?' He stopped in front of a bench where two elderly women and one small dog were conversing, the dog obviously the object of both women's affections.

'I hope I wouldn't.' His arm was around her shoulder now that they stood still. 'It's hard to know what kind of a person you are until you're tested. You grow up thinking you know and then one day I suppose you find out.'

'Then you're not young any more.' He kissed her as though they were kids at Washington Square instead of whatever they were on Fifth Avenue, and the chattering of the two ladies stopped abruptly.

'Come on,' he said softly and they continued their southward march.

'You said – last night at dinner you told me – ' she was flustered by the kiss – the kisses – and the arm that held her as they walked, 'that when you get over believing that falling for someone will solve all your problems, you find out that it was never true.'

'That's right. I did say that. What I didn't tell you was that I never reached stage three. Just a small case of arrested development.' They had nearly reached Fifty-ninth Street with its muddle of traffic. They would have to make a choice soon, a direction, a crossing. He slid his hand back and took her arm, preparing to guide her. 'Have you reached stage two yet?'

'I don't know.' Her voice seemed abnormally high and it floated away from her like smoke.

'Here's the light.'

They made their way across Fifty-ninth, the Plaza, and Fifty-eighth, slowing to look in shop windows: shoes at Bergdorf's, jewels at Van Cleef, summer dresses at Tailored Woman.

'You grew up to all this, didn't you?' Roy Kellems said as they passed the jewels.

'My mother was very strict about what I wore. Nothing

showy. My friend at school always wore clothes that looked very expensive and once her mother tried to get me to tell her what mine cost without seeming to ask. It was very embarrassing. I didn't know and didn't care. Everyone I ever liked was the scholarly type who would never make a living.'

'And you didn't care.'

'No, but it's something I don't think I'll ever have to face any more. She turned to look at him, hardly aware that the street was thronged. She felt quite alone with him now, now that they had passed the park, the shoes and the jewels, now that they had kissed and he had admitted he was in spirit no older than she was. 'If I can't have children, there doesn't seem much purpose in getting married, does there? I expect most men want to have families, just as most women do. If my mother had known, probably she wouldn't have married my father.'

He looked at her without asking and she realized something small had escaped.

'My brother's wife had a baby this week that they have to institutionalize. Diana's only twenty-three. I wonder how she'll live through this. My other brother's wife lost one last year. I think it was born dead. That's not a very good average, is it?'

He looked very sombre. 'No, it isn't.'

'Well,' she tried to smile, 'that's part of the problem. Frenchy knew before he was married but it can't have made it all that much easier.' She looked at him. 'Do you think?'

'No.' He seemed deeply saddened by her revelation. 'I'm sorry I've been at you this way.'

'You meant well. And you're right. I do have questions to ask myself.'

'Look,' he stopped on the corner, forcing passers-by to walk irritably around them, 'you must be tired. I've walked you miles and I've been very inconsiderate. Let's get a cab and find a place to eat.'

'OK.'

He manœuvred them to the kerb on the Fifth Avenue side and looked north. She could not imagine finding a taxi at this location and this hour but suddenly, one appeared and he commandeered it like a sergeant on the battlefield. Inside he gave an address in the East Thirties and then sat back.

'We'll stop up at my place for a minute and I'll change my shirt and pick up a jacket. Do you like Middle Eastern food?'

'I like everything.'

'That's your fine upbringing.' He patted her hand. 'No, on second thoughts, I think it's your good nature. There's a nice place just west of Fifth, one flight up, very plain, best food you've ever eaten. Outside of West Virginia anyway.'

'I'm not really dressed.'

'You're perfect,' he said. 'You're absolutely perfect.'

There were two locks on the door. He opened the top one first, then found the key for the bottom one and pushed the door open. It was an apartment like thousands in postwar New York buildings, a living room on the left, a kitchen directly opposite the front door, leading to a dinette, and a bedroom off to the right. It was a new building and the rooms were large and the floors parquet. He dropped his ring of keys on a small table in the hall.

'Make yourself comfortable,' he said, waving to the living room. 'There's a refrigerator, bathroom. I'll just be a minute.' He went into the bedroom and shut the door.

She walked into the living room and stopped. On the far wall was a small sofa and over it a large oil painting. She moved closer to look at it better. It was a man at a desk, a jacket over the corner of his chair, but everything about the figure was distorted, as though the artist had been angry or thought the man was. In the lower right-hand corner the name A. Jackson appeared in red. Judy moved back, trying to find a location where the painting would come into focus. She could guess who it was supposed to be and it angered her that anyone should protray him like that. It was ugly, nearly grotesque, the paint applied in slashes instead of with a fine brush. She turned away and looked at the rest of the room but she could feel the presence of the painting behind her back. Across the room from it, a desk with a lamp, papers and two open books faced the opposite wall. Next to it was a small television set, which could best be viewed from the small sofa.

The room seemed more an office than a living room. Books and magazines lay about, an empty coffee mug on the desk, an electric percolator beside it, a waste basket, nearly overflowing, on the floor. Across the windows that spanned the distance between the portrait wall and the desk wall, translucent curtains provided a hazy view of New York.

She turned back to give the painting a second look but her response did not change.

'Like it?'

She turned, slightly startled. He had put on a tan summer suit, shirt and tie. 'It's horrible,' she said. 'It's ghastly. Who is A. Jackson?'

'Annie Jackson. She's my wife.'

'Your wife!' She felt herself flush at the identification. 'How could your wife paint you to look like that?'

'She says that's me.' He shrugged carelessly. 'You don't agree?'

'No. I can't imagine that the person in that picture would have been as kind to me as you've been. That person is all slashes and angles. The feeling isn't there.'

'Maybe Annie's wrong.'

'I don't know how you can work with that in the room.'

'I face the wall,' he acknowledged. 'No mirrors, no likenesses, no graven images.'

'You look very nice.'

He touched her arm. 'So do you.'

He put his arms around her and kissed her, the third kiss of the day and it was still daylight, the sun near its solstice. It was a different kind of kiss. This time she could feel the power of his feelings behind it, sense her own drawn to the surface to match his. He was forty-two and did not seduce little girls but he wanted what all the twenty-one-year-olds wanted and in the same way. But the experience was different; it was new; she thought it might be unique, something she had waited for without knowing it would ever happen.

He held her tightly for a moment and then relaxed, letting

77

his arm slide across her back and down to take her hand. 'Your cheeks are very pink.' He kissed one pink cheek. 'We'd better get going.'

He took the keys from the hall table and locked the door, managing it with his left hand so that he never let go the hand he was holding.

'Can you walk? It's only a couple of blocks. Or have I tired you out?'

'I can walk.'

It was just below Thirty-fourth and by the time they got there, the streets were empty of people and traffic. They climbed the stairs to the second floor and Roy shook hands with the proprietor, a heavy, greying Lebanese man with a wide smile. They sat at a table for four not far from the windows and ordered a variety of dishes. The appetizer was a combination of stuffed grape leaves and concoctions of mashed chick peas and sesame seeds.

'We should have taken the car,' he said reproachfully, holding a piece of pita bread ready to wipe his plate. 'I forget how the city empties after five. You can park anywhere now.'

'It wasn't a long walk.'

'I've bungled everything today.'

'No –'

'I'm sorry about your brother. When I realized your problem wasn't what I erroneously surmised yesterday afternoon, I lost sight of the fact that it might be serious after all. I'm sorry for the sermons.'

'I enjoyed them.'

'I think now what you ought to do is chuck everything for the summer and have a good time.'

'It isn't very feasible.'

'No.'

'What do I want?' she said, mimicking him.

He smiled. 'Well, it wouldn't hurt to ask that a few hundred times while you're lazing around the swimming hole.'

'Or crossing my legs while I take dictation.'

'Don't take it from one of those grubby bastards in downtown New York.'

She wondered if he meant the members of his own profession. 'I think I'll like working,' she said.

'Because you like life. I bet you liked school,' she nodded, 'and you like Fern and Fern's apartment. You probably even like me.'

'I do.' There was lamb and eggplant in front of them now and her hunger was evaporating. 'When I got up yesterday morning, all I could think of was that there were things that I needed – an apartment, a paycheque, all the things you have to have to set up housekeeping. I remember thinking that I couldn't use the word "want" any more, not for a long time. Then you came along and turned it all around and said that was all that was important.'

'That's all that is important.'

'Now I have to get used to it again. I want, I want.'

'What do you want, Judith?'

She could feel her heart starting to pound as he asked the question and knew it meant she was going to answer it. She put her fork down. 'I think I want you.'

He looked at her very steadily and she wondered if when you were forty-two and a member of the bar your heart still pounded at certain moments. 'Was that a seduction speech?' he asked.

'I don't know.' But inside she knew. 'I've never made one before.'

'Because if it was, if that's what you meant it to be, I think you ought to know I'm going to accept. But you have to be sure. You have to know what you're doing.'

The pounding had begun to recede and she felt as calm as he had sounded. 'I accept your acceptance,' she said.

They took a taxi back and he didn't take change from his dollar although the change was more than the fare. Upstairs, she watched him fuss with the keys, the perils of New York delaying whatever it was that awaited them inside and whatever it was, she wanted it. Inside he turned the bolt and dropped his keys on the table. She put her bag down on top of them. This time she would stay for a while.

He kissed her cheek and she could feel the rim of his glasses against her face. 'Call Fern,' he said. 'Tell her you won't be back tonight.'

She went to the phone on the desk and dialled Fern's number. The difference between boys and men. The difference between Miss Somebody *in loco parentis* and living on your own. A telephone call instead of a crisis of conscience.

Fern answered on the first ring.

'I won't be home tonight,' Judy said.

Fern said, 'Oh,' as though privy to a revelation. Then she said, 'I'm so glad, Judy.'

'Thanks, Fern.'

'I knew she would say something nice,' Roy Kellems said as she hung up the phone.

She followed him into the bedroom. It was sparely furnished, a room where two people could spend the night and find a change of clothes. There was a large bed, two night tables, and two lamps and, opposite, a dresser. A telephone sat on the table closer to the window.

He was in no hurry the way the boys at school were. There were no curfews tonight, no inner clocks urging great haste. He was not anxious to get something over with, one way or the other, so that when it was done a tug here and a smoothing hand there and they were ready to leave; it was behind them, a memory to keep or discard as they kept or discarded each other.

Roy Kellems told her he wanted to make her happy and she didn't understand because she was happy, so happy since two o'clock when he had picked her up at Fern's. But he said it again when they were in bed and much later he told her a third time and after that she understood exactly what he meant.

He wore the trousers and she wore the shirt as they sat across the breakfast table. He had scrambled eggs ('You know how to cook?' 'Not awfully well.'), instructing her as he went along. Coffee was easy; she had done that at school in a four-dollar pot where you had to count the minutes yourself. Roy's took care of all that. And his eggs were good. ('You should see what I do with black beans.')

Her hair was a mess without a hairbrush and Roy didn't keep an extra toothbrush the way Fern did, in case a guy decided to stay over. But those were small inconveniences and when he leaned across the breakfast table to kiss her, the brushes didn't seem to make much of a difference.

He drank a glass of milk with his eggs and then began on the coffee. 'I survive on it sometimes,' he said. 'You a coffee drinker?'

'Only now and then.'

'Good with scrambled eggs.'

'Uh-huh.'

'And late at night when there's work to do. It doesn't help you stay awake. That's a myth. It only keeps you up when you're trying to sleep. Once I fell asleep at that desk after drinking a quart of coffee. Best rest I ever had but the worst shock when the light came through the window.'

'I slept well,' Judy said. 'I wasn't shocked when I got up. I felt very happy. Am I allowed to tell you that?'

'You're allowed to tell me anything.' He got up, kissed her and poured more coffee. 'I'd like to tell you something. I'd like to make a small suggestion.'

'OK.'

'Maybe you'd like to stay with me for a while.'

A small suggestion. 'Here?' she asked.

'It's fully furnished. Good location. Easy access to all means of transportation.' He sounded like a real estate agent. 'You wouldn't have to get a job you don't want anyway and that you'll probably give up in a couple of months. I could even get you a telephone with your own number.'

'It sounds very practical.'

'I'm inviting you, Judith. I want you.'

'Then I would take it even without the easy access.'

They drove to Fern's apartment to pick up her suitcase. The car was a Jaguar ('My extravagance,' he said), and she was surprised she had not noticed when he had driven her on Friday night. She had observed very little on Friday night and the contrast between then and now was pleasingly sharp.

They went up the stairs to Fern's third-floor apartment but there was no answer to their knock. Judy used her key and walked in, calling, 'Fern?'

The bedroom door opened as they entered and Fern came out, tucking a blouse into the waistband of her skirt. With a pair of girlish yelps, they met in the middle of the living room and embraced, leaving Roy to watch with an amused smile. After a moment he put an arm around each of them and kissed them both. Then he took the suitcase down to the double-parked Jaguar and drove Judy to her new home.

He left her three tens on Monday morning and told her where to go to buy a steak. She went to her doctor first and filled the prescription at a clean new pharmacy in Murray Hill. She took some money out of her bank account and opened a new account near Roy's apartment, receiving a small frying pan as a gift. Later, she would have to learn how to use it.

At midweek the new phone was installed and she called her mother and gave her the number. She told her the truth, leaving out Roy. She said the apartment was in someone else's name.

Then she called Frenchy.

'I guess you know all about it,' her brother said.

'Yes. I wanted to know if I could visit Diana.'

Her brother did not answer immediately. 'Give it a little time, OK? She's kind of run down. She doesn't really want visitors this week.'

'Is she all right?'

'She's fine, she's fine,' Frenchy said quickly. 'Do I get to ask now?'

'Sure.'

'Mum says you've moved out.'

'It's true.'

'Something between you and Dad.'

'Yes.'

'Is it about what's happened to us?'

'Not exactly.'

'You want to have dinner and talk about it?'

'No. I don't want to talk about it to anyone. Besides, Diana needs you.'

The only mirror in the apartment was in the bathroom. For Roy there was no lack of convenience. He shaved in the bathroom and adjusted his tie in front of the same mirror. His hair was straight and somewhat long on top and it seemed not to bother him when it fell across his forehead. Judy had never slept in a bedroom without a mirror. At home, at school, in hotels, a mirror always perched over the dresser. In her first days in Roy's apartment, she sometimes picked up her hair-brush and turned to the blank wall, expecting to see her reflection.

Roy saw her do it once and laughed. 'Maybe if I were as pretty as you, I'd want to look at myself too,' he said.

It was a small inconvenience and there were absolutely no others.

On Friday, when they were out to dinner, he said he would like to visit his family the following day. His son was not yet five, his daughters ten and thirteen, born in the years of scramble just after the war. 'I haven't seen the kids for a week. I'll be back by dinner-time and we'll go somewhere nice.'

'Will you sleep with your wife while you're there?' she asked mildly.

'No.' He looked at her steadily, openly. 'I won't sleep with Annie. Why do you ask?'

'Because I think sex has to be an exclusive relationship.' She had wanted to say 'love' but thought better of it.

'Did you think I didn't share your opinion?'

'I didn't know. I needed to know whether to wait for you tomorrow night.'

He looked startled and he put his hand on hers. 'Wait for me,' he said. 'I'm coming home to you.'

When he arrived, he brought enough clothes to fill a closet and most of the drawers.

In a way it was like that. She had known so little about him and he even less about her. Every day she learned something new, something endearing. That he loved chocolate. That he actually worked at the desk with his jacket slung over one corner of the chair the way the ugly portrait showed him. That he called her during the day to ask insignificant questions and tell her what time he would be home. He did not ask her what she wanted to do and he never spoke of an end to her lease on his apartment or his life. One day he brought her a pretty summer robe and when she put it on, she could feel something more than admiration in the way he looked at her.

A week after she had spoken to Frenchy, she went to his apartment without calling.

'Judy,' Diana said at the door. 'How nice of you to come.'

'I decided not to call,' Judy said, walking into the living room. 'Last week Frenchy said not to come. I really wanted to see you.'

'I'm glad you didn't call. I keep saying no to everyone and today I'm starting to feel a little lonesome.'

'Maybe that's good. Have you gone out yet?'

'Just a bit. Down to the corner and back. I have one of those old-fashioned doctors that thinks you should take it easy for a month after – ' she paused, 'after giving birth.'

'Why don't you go out to Pennsylvania for a while? It's much nicer than the city in the summer and you won't have any trouble resting.'

'Didn't Frenchy tell you?'

'Tell me what?' She felt the icy fear that came with the solution to old mysteries, the missing pieces to puzzles better left jumbled.

'Frenchy and I separated over the weekend.' Diana looked suddenly quite small, almost lost in the pillows of the pale sofa.

Judy shook her head. 'You couldn't have.'

'We couldn't stay together. I need time to think and I have to do it by myself. I have to think about what happened and what we've done about it. I'm in such turmoil that sometimes when I'm standing up, I think I'm about to topple over.'

'Frenchy wouldn't let that happen.'

'There's nothing Frenchy can do right now. I have to do it myself. He was very considerate. He let me have the apartment.' There was something final about what she said, as though it were not a decision but a legal agreement between them.

'Diana, you're a member of our family. You're not some girl Frenchy married. You're part of us.'

'Maybe that's what I have to find out.' Talking about it seemed to have drained her. She had become pale and her shoulders slumped. 'All the time Frenchy and I were going out together I used to think that when we were married, nothing would ever make me unhappy. I was very young and very naive.'

'You say that as if it were a fault.'

'Not a fault, perhaps, but a failing. There was so much I didn't see. Well.' Diana smiled. 'I shouldn't dwell on it. Frenchy told me you'd had a spat with your dad and you moved out.'

'It's true.'

'Are you sharing a place with a friend from school?'

'I'm living with a man.'

Diana's eyes widened and her face brightened. 'You?'

'Uh-huh.'

'How absolutely fantastic.'

'But you're the only one in the family who knows.'

'I'll guard it with my life. But how marvellous, Judy.'

'It is marvellous. But it sounds strange coming from you.'

'One changes after marriage. Things that seemed awfully important when you were single start to look rather inconsequential. I think marriage changes you more than anything else in the world – except maybe – '

'Except what?'

Diana's shoulders trembled slightly. 'Except having children.'

She answered one phone and he answered the other. She got up five minutes before he did and made breakfast. The apartment was air-conditioned and on hot afternoons she could stay in and read. Now that she was finished with school, she could read what she wanted, not what she had to, and doing it in Roy's apartment gave it an added pleasure.

85

She found he was the kindest man she had ever met, the most thoughtful, the easiest to talk to. There was so much he knew, so much he had lived. He seemed right about so many things and knowledgeable about so much more. Towards the end of their third week together, he asked her what she would like most to have.

'A cookbook,' she said without stopping to think. 'We can't live on steak and hamburgers forever. Or go out every night.'

'It'll tie you down,' he said cautiously.

'No. It'll free me.'

On Saturday night, when he returned from visiting his children, they went to the Village for dinner and then walked along Eighth Street where the bookstores were open late. She selected a thick classic, a traditional beginner's book. There would be time later to branch out, to learn foreign cuisines, after she knew what he liked. He paid for the book and carried it under his arm as they walked back across Eighth Street to Fifth Avenue and she saw where she had made her wrong turn three weeks earlier, the wrong turn that had taken her to Centre Street and Roy Kellems, the luckiest moment of her life.

'You're very quiet,' he said. 'Are you cooking something up in there?'

'I was thinking of the accident that took me down to Centre Street three weeks ago.'

'A lucky accident for me.'

'Even luckier for me. You had somewhere to go that night. I was feeling very lost.'

'But you're found now.'

'Yes. You found me.'

'No. You found yourself. I watched you. It was a star performance. You could have left me at any time and landed on your feet. I thought you were going to two weeks ago when you asked me if I was going to sleep with Annie. You were ready to, weren't you.'

'Yes.' She slid her arm around him. 'But I'm glad I didn't.'

'Me too.' He kissed her lightly and as the light turned green, they crossed Fifth.

'I like Eighth Street,' she said, looking back down the lighted stretch on the other side of the avenue.

'We used to come here when I was young and poor.'

'Now you're young and rich.' She grinned at him.

'No,' he said as a taxi turned up from the park and he lifted a hand to signal it, 'tonight I'm young and lucky.'

In the taxi, she asked to take a peek at the cookbook.

'Not yet. It's not yours till I give it to you.' He held it away from her, acting younger and luckier than she had yet seen him.

In the apartment, he sat at the desk and wrote something on the inside cover. 'You'll see it in the morning,' he teased. 'We have better things to do tonight.' He unbuttoned her blouse and kissed the base of her neck.

She could not imagine anyone being a better lover. Until he had made love to her, she had not been able to imagine the pleasures of sex. Now she could not imagine any pleasure without Roy. She wondered how girls could be satisfied with boys their own age. Didn't they feel somewhat cheated when they saw Judy Wolfe walk down the street with Roy Kellems? Didn't they feel short-changed to be made love to half-clothed between dinner and curfew? It was she who was lucky, really. It would be her pleasure to cook him good meals, to spend time perfecting them as he spent time making her happy, happy in every way she could imagine.

In the morning, she slipped out of bed while he brushed his teeth and opened the cookbook. Inside he had written the date, July 11, 1959, and the message: For Judith, Who chose freedom. Roy.

Two

He kissed her when he left on Monday morning and said he'd be home by six, no later. Still wearing the pretty, new robe, she sat at the table with the cookbook. They had eaten out the night before and today was cool enough that she could cook something to surprise him. She went through the cakes first, making a list of the ingredients she would need, then the salads, then the meats, and finally deciding on melon as an appetizer, making her choices as though she were going down the line at a cafeteria where they enticed you with dessert at the start so that you committed yourself to something sweet before you knew what the main courses were. Roy would like chocolate; Roy would like red meat with fresh vegetables; Roy would like green salad with more oil than vinegar. She would make everything that he liked.

She splattered chocolate on the cake page and red vinegar on the salad page. Now the book belonged to her as surely as a volume of poetry with passages underlined. The book was hers and the dinner his. They were reciprocal gifts. They did unto each other happy things and they were happy.

Late in the afternoon she bought a small bouquet of summer flowers and put them in a glass vase on the table. When the table was set, it looked festive and colourful. When she dressed at five, she matched herself to the mood and wore red. Tomorrow, she thought, she would buy candles.

He was not there at six and still not home at six-thirty. She turned the fire down in the oven, not sure of the procedure to avoid overcooked meat and not sure whom to call for help. When the phone rang at a quarter to seven, she was not sure whether she was relieved or angry.

'Judith,' he said, 'I'm going to be late.'

'Oh,' Angry, she decided and said nothing else. She did not know how to respond to the obvious.

'Ran into an old friend and we decided to have dinner together.'

'Dinner.'

'Yes. So don't wait up for me.'

'I won't.'

'Uhhh – '

'Enjoy your dinner.'

'Judith – '

'Yes.'

'I'll see you later.'

'Yes.'

She hung up. She had said yes. I'll see you later. And she had said yes. Why had she said yes? She would not see him later. She walked into the kitchen and turned off the oven and the lighted burner on the stove. She would not see him later. She had cooked for him, showered for him, and put on a red dress for him. But she would not see him later. He was having dinner with an old friend. She stopped to consider whether it was a man or a woman. It did not matter. The reciprocity of their affection was suddenly gone. If it was a woman, she could not lie in his bed again. If it was a man, why had she not been invited to join them? How could he treat her so cavalierly, she who would not think of doing likewise? She might not be ready to marry but she was not ready to be treated like a mistress.

And that meant she could not stay in Roy Kellems apartment any more.

She felt oddly detached, almost floating. She was calm, entirely without rancour. It was simply something that had happened, something she had learned. They had had three lovely weeks together and she had come out of it with a splattered cookbook and a pretty robe. She had learned to make love, learned to run a small household, learned how to live with a man. There were lessons in all that that would surely stay with her although the learning was by no means complete. She would miss Roy; it would be a while before a man would affect her as he had. But she knew she must go.

She went into the bedroom and opened her suitcase on the big bed. The robe went in first, then all the summer skirts and blouses and dresses. When she came to the underclothes, there seemed hardly enough room for them, as though her wardrobe had expanded in the three weeks as her heart had expanded to include Roy. Perhaps, she thought with a touch of sadness, it had not expanded enough. Or perhaps this was the truth about Roy Calvin Kellems. Three weeks away from Annie and a companion became a mistress. Then so be it. She had asked for nothing when she had met him and she had received far more than she had expected. It would be something to remember.

She pressed the suitcase hard and managed to close it. A shopping bag would carry the extra shoes and the laundry that would not fit. She carried bag and suitcase to the foyer and left them while she went to the kitchen and found her wallet. A ten, a five and two singles remained of what Roy had given her that morning. She left them next to his place at the table, the pretty table with summer flowers and melon warming at each setting while the hot foot cooled. The thickly iced cake was concealed in a cabinet as a surprise. When he put the dishes away, he would find it.

In the living room she phoned Fern.

'You sure you're doing what's right?' Fern asked.

'Very sure.'

'Great men don't come along that often.'

'It's over, Fern.'

'Well,' Fern took a breath. She sounded sadder than Judy felt. 'I'll make up the extra bed for you.'

'I'll make it up when I get there. Thanks, Fern.'

She hung up and turned to take a last look at the room. Over the sofa where Roy would not have to look at it was the painting. It seemed suddenly to have changed. Startled, she took a step toward it, then moved backward to find the perfect distance from which to view it. It was as if someone had drawn back one cloudy layer of film or one of several gauze curtains, revealing the subject's features with new clarity. There was truly something of Roy in the sharp face, something of Roy in the too-angular body. Even the angularity itself suddenly had meaning. Dressed in the unvarying costume of a lawyer, he appeared to have the stature of a fairly tall man of medium build, but without clothes, as she now knew, the structure of his frame was more prominent. The bones that formed his shoulders, elbows, hips and knees were visible and emphasized the sharpness of his jaw, which, when he was dressed, was scarcely noticeable. It was as if the artist had painted the man naked and then hung clothes on him, as if she had used her knowledge of his undressed body when she painted him dressed. It was as if the artist knew him intimately.

There was a sound of the key in the lock and she turned to face the door. Roy pushed it open, looked at the suitcase on the floor in front of him, then up at her, then closed the door behind him and stood with the keys in his hand.

'I told you I'd see you later,' he said in a low voice.

'It wasn't enough, Roy.'

'I know. That's why I came home.' He dropped his keys on the hall table, his briefcase on the floor, and glanced through the kitchen door and she knew he would see the dining table set for dinner neither would eat, the golden melon halves, the flowers, the pitcher of water in which the ice had long ago melted.

'I'm sorry,' he said.

'There's nothing to be sorry for.' She still felt the same calm she had felt after he telephoned. She had no desire to inflict hurt. He was a man she had learned to care for. It was simply time to go.

He looked back through the kitchen door again. The sight seemed to disturb him greatly. 'I behaved very thoughtlessly. It isn't what you think it was.'

She smiled. 'I didn't think about what it was. I just thought it was time for me to leave.'

'It isn't.' His voice caught in his throat. She wondered if she had become immune to the savoury smells of the meal she had cooked or if they had evaporated in the last hour. 'I thought you would shriek like a banshee when I walked in.'

She smiled again, this time at his innocence. 'There isn't anything to shriek about. I'm not angry at you, Roy. I just saw what my place was here and I didn't like it.'

91

'You saw wrong. I saw wrong,' he said, as though correcting himself. He came into the living room, walking toward her. For no reason she could think of, she began to tremble. 'I care for you, Judith. For you and about you. I care much more about you than about having dinner with Harry Pine. If you leave, I suffer a loss.' He was very close to her now and she had to raise her head to look at him. 'A great loss. One that can't be compensated by anyone else. You have a place here, Judith. I don't want us to live side by side any more. I want us to live together.'

She could not think what to say but she felt immensely – unexpectedly – happy. 'I told Fern to make up the bed,' she said lamely.

He put his arms around her and held her in a crushing embrace. 'God, I love you.' And from the sound of surprise in his voice, she knew he was talking to himself, saying out loud what he was just discovering, what she had hoped for weeks they would both discover until she had given up an hour earlier. 'We'll call her back,' he said, kissing her temple where the pulse throbbed. 'Tell her to unmake it because you're not leaving here without me.'

She reached up and kissed his lips, feeling them warm and dry and searching. His eyes would be an intense blue now but she knew his lids would be closed, as hers were. She had a sense of belonging to him as she had never belonged to a man before. They would not live side by side any more. They would live together.

'I didn't think you would come home,' she said, rubbing her cheek against his, feeling the beginning of a scratch, twelve hours since his last shave, since he had promised to be home at six, no later. 'Not until I was gone.'

'I bribed a cab driver.' He would not let her go. 'To run a few lights for me.'

'Roy.' She kissed him again, enjoying the new sense of possession. 'Make love to me. Would you?'

'With pleasure,' Roy Kellems said. 'With very great pleasure.'

* * *

He ate half the chocolate cake at one sitting, admitting to fondnesses that led to weaknesses. He told her he was taking time off in August and asked where she would like to go. She said she would like to swim and ride and he made arrangements to visit Maine for a few weeks.

'What about Annie?' she asked when they talked about Maine.

'Annie knows how to get along without me,' he told her and that was all he would say about Annie.

A few days later she wrote a letter withdrawing from law school and sent a carbon to her father.

They came back near the end of August and Roy gave her money to buy winter clothes. Over the Labour Day weekend he took his children to a friend's house in the Hamptons and when he came back, it was the start of a new season in New York, her first fall out of college, her first full season with Roy Kellems.

Her clothes were all different this year. The skirts, sweaters and loafers of college seemed now to belong to a different era. She bought suits and wool dresses, sheer, seamless stockings, pointy shoes with skinny heels and small handbags lined in a red leather to carry a woman's necessities. When Roy had a pre-trial hearing shortly after Labour Day, she put on the new black suit with a white silk blouse and black kid gloves and went to listen, watching him from the rear of the courtroom, remembering the day five years before that she had first seen him, the day he had so overwhelmed her that she had been unable to speak, the day she had first fallen in love with him. Now he was hers. Now she woke with him, brewed coffee for him, counted the shirts that she took to the laundry, baked seven different chocolate cakes for him, loved him with her heart always and with her body often. She was without regrets. She did not recall the day law school was supposed to begin. Perhaps it had already passed and she had taken no notice. She was doing what she wanted and she was happy.

Her mother had telephoned, distraught, when her father had received the carbon copy of her withdrawal.

'What are you doing, Judy? Why are you hurting yourself this way?'

93

'I'm happy, Mother. Nothing hurts.'

'Who is it, Judy?' Her mother sounded weary. 'Who is the person who's doing this to you?'

'I've fallen in love, Mummy. No one is doing anything to me. I feel very happy and very free.'

'You're living in his apartment, aren't you?'

'Yes.'

'Judy, dear, come back to us. Daddy and I both want you back. Think about the future and then come back to us. There's been enough sadness in the family this summer. First Frenchy and now you. Sometimes I wonder where it will all end.'

It was a question that Judy did not ask. She was happy to sit in the back of the courtroom and listen to the proceedings, marking up his gains, sitting with fingers crossed as the judge made decisions that would affect the trial. When, at the end of the day, he threw out a large chunk of prosecution evidence that Roy had challenged, she broke into an unladylike grin, which was nearly matched by the one Roy exchanged with his client.

When the judge adjourned the proceedings, she waited for Roy at the door, accepted his brief kiss and tried to match his stride as they went to the stairs. (Roy would not take a lift unless it was going up.) He was ebullient.

'That's their whole case,' he said. 'I wouldn't be surprised if they move to dismiss.'

'Why was it thrown out?'

'The cops broke into his house like storm troopers, beat him up, pulled up floorboards, threatened his wife and found something they thought was incriminating.'

'Was it?'

'It doesn't matter. They had no warrant. They inflicted injury and damage, none of which he was compensated for. If they had found a goddamn smoking gun, I'd want it thrown out – they didn't, by the way – as a matter of principle. What the police did was less tolerable than what they accused my client of doing. How are you?'

'Fine. Where are we going?'

'Stop up at the office for a minute. Mind?'

'Huh-uh.'

'Then I think I'm going to be very hungry. You look gorgeous, do you know that?' They were nearly at the kerb and he had stopped to look at her. 'You look shining.'

'Maybe I need a little powder.'

'Don't you dare. I like you shining. Hey. There's a cab.'

His office was busy with end-of-the-day activity, everyone waiting for his arrival before leaving. His secretary handed him a pile of telephone messages.

'Your wife called,' she said, not looking at Judy.

'Thanks.'

'I think you should call her right away.'

'Thanks.' He flipped through the slips, arranging them as he went.

'Well, good night then.'

'So long, Mary.' He opened the door to his office. 'Come,' he said, reaching for Judy's arm. 'Sit while I phone.'

She opened his briefcase and took the *Times* out while he sat at his desk and dialled.

'What's up, Annie?' She heard him say as she scanned the front page. 'Well how much is it? . . . All right, I'll send a cheque . . . Then I'll double it . . . No, . . . No, I don't think so . . . Look, Annie . . . I don't have the time now. Keep it till Saturday . . . I will. G'bye.' He hung up and Judy looked up from the paper. 'Orthodonture,' he said, meeting her eyes.

But she wondered if Annie wasn't starting to feel the loss of her husband, wasn't starting to sense that the loss might be permanent.

'Can you hang on half an hour longer?'

'Sure.'

'When I get done here, I've got a present for you.'

'A present. Why?' But she could feel herself tingling with anticipation.

'Because you deserve it.' He lifted the receiver and began to dial.

It took more than half an hour and she had nearly finished the paper when he hung up for the last time. 'Ready?' he asked.

'What is it?'

He reached into his briefcase and brought out a flat package wrapped in brown paper. 'For no one but you,' he said, handing it to her.

It was hard and barely half an inch thick, possibly a foot long and somewhat less wide. She tore the paper off carefully and removed the cardboard that protected the object. 'Oh,' she breathed, seeing herself. It was an old oval mirror, the frame of stained oak, the glass bevelled. 'It's beautiful,' she said. 'But it's against your principles.'

'I want you to be happy.'

Something of the tone of his voice in the conversation with his wife nearly an hour ago echoed in her head, contrasting with the sound of this last statement, with the depth of feeling. A whisper of anguish for Annie rustled through her. As the bond between Judy and Roy strengthened, that other must weaken. It was something she thought about now and then, something that picked at her with cats' claws when she looked at the portrait and thought she was beginning to understand it.

'I can hide it under my pillow,' she offered lightly.

'We'll hang it over the dresser, just high enough for you. There's only room for one face in it. Can't do too much harm to my principles.'

'Thank you.' She went over to the desk and kissed him.

'I love you,' he said.

'Roy.' Standing, she was able to hold his head against her breast. He took his glasses off and dropped them on the desk and she rubbed her cheek on his soft hair that never seemed quite in place. 'I never felt this way about anyone before.'

'I know.' He had his arms around her now, around her waist. He was still sitting, still resting his head against her. 'I'd like to keep it that way.'

She saw the mirror lying on his desk, reflecting light so that it seemed to blaze, a relaxation of principle by a man who did not often compromise. 'I would too,' she said, and while she wasn't entirely sure what she meant, she knew she meant what she said.

* * *

96

Two days later he called her while she was cooking dinner. 'They dropped the case,' he said triumphantly.

'The hearing I went to on Monday?' she asked excitedly.

'The same. They've got nothing without the junk they got illegally.'

'That's wonderful!' She was almost singing. 'You're marvellous.'

'I thought you'd want to know,' he said, sounding much calmer than she felt.

'Oh, yes. We should really open a bottle of champagne to celebrate.'

'No. Get one for yourself if you want. I feel pretty high right now without any outside help.' There was a sound of voices and he said, 'I'll see you later, Judith. I just wanted to let you know.'

She hung up and walked past the oval mirror over the dresser to look at herself happy. She was holding a dish towel, wearing a red shirt and jeans. A mixture of good smells had seeped into the bedroom where she had run to answer her phone. She walked past the kitchen and into the living room, standing opposite Annie Jackson's no-longer-ugly portrait of Roy. Although more of his right side was visible than his left, she had curved his left hand so that the thin gold band could be seen. The fingernails were quite perfect, short and rounded. She wondered how anyone could paint a fingernail. But it was the face, as always, that drew her attention, the face that had seemed so unnatural that first moment in June, so slashed with colours that were not really there, angles that Roy's face did not have. Looking at it, she knew suddenly that it was a face of conflict, of deep emotions struggling with one another. The real Roy looked almost placid, as her mother looked, trying to keep beneath the surface the shame and hurt her father had inflicted on her. Roy's emotions were different but just as vital and the artist had pulled them into the open, submerging the objective surface and exposing the man.

'I love you,' she said to the picture and when she turned to go back to the kitchen, she wondered which of the Roys she had spoken to.

The *Times* had a small piece on page seventeen about the charges being dropped and the reason behind it. She read it with a mixture of pride and irritation. The article was too small for the importance of what had happened. If the judge had been more intransigent, if the case had gone to trial, if the Civil Liberties Union had become actively involved (as they had said they might); if all this had happened and *then* the judge had made the same decision, the article would have hit page one and Roy would have been surrounded by reporters. Had Roy been less successful – or unsuccessful – the story might have been in the papers for days and weeks. Because he was good, because he had accomplished something immense in a quiet, efficient manner, his success could be dispensed with in three paragraphs.

But it was a success and she felt it in a physical way, as if it were her own, a thrill, an excitement, a pride. Colleagues called to congratulate him and she knew that the most important people had noted what he had done. She did not drink champagne. He was hers and that was enough.

'Hi, kid. How're you?'

'Is this Davey?' She sat up in bed, pushing sleep away. Roy had left very early for a breakfast meeting and she had slept later than usual.

'The same.'

'Where are you?'

'In New York. Can I come and see you or have lunch or something?'

She looked at the clock. 'Lunch. I can't wait. How's Rena?'

'I'll tell you all about it when I see you.'

'Well, it's like this.' Davey sipped his bourbon and water. 'Rena and I are no more.'

Judy could feel her face drain. She reached for the glass of sherry in front of her but changed her mind. 'What do you mean?' she asked in a low voice.

'It was a mistake. It didn't work. She spent the summer with her parents and I spent the summer in Cincinnati and when I saw her last week, we agreed the summer'd been better than

98

the winter when we were living together. So why make the effort?' He sounded deceptively offhanded.

'Was it the baby, Davey?'

'It didn't help.'

'Frenchy and Diana – '

'I know.'

'Mummy'll go to pieces.'

'I can't stay with my wife so mum can stay in one piece.'

'No.'

'Any more than you'll move out of your little arrangement to make her happy.'

'That's different. I love him.'

'OK.' Davey smiled through his beard. It was a nice beard, full and dark and nineteenth-century rabbinical. 'And I've left the seminary.'

'Oh, Davey.'

'It was all part of the same thing – Rena and religion and the search for truth. Look, I was a fucked-up kid. No one knows that better than you. There was a year in my life when I needed everything all at once. I needed answers. I needed a girl I could sleep with seven nights a week. You know what that's like, needing it every day? Shit, I shouldn't talk to you like this. You're my sister, not my mistress.'

'It's OK. I know what you mean.'

'Well, there she was and it worked like a charm. Till the baby, anyway. I think things're straightening out a little now. I think – maybe – I'm getting to where I have some answers. Not truth. There isn't any truth. There are just answers. I've got myself an assistantship at Brown and I'm going to do graduate work in philosophy. That's where I'm headed now. 'How's things with you? I hear you're screwing the old man.'

She felt herself flush. 'I'm not screwing anybody. My father and I had a parting of the ways. I've met someone wonderful. I live in his apartment.'

'Wonderful enough to give up law school?'

'That wonderful, yes.'

'You surprise me. I thought you were Miss Stability. A port in the storm. An oasis in the desert. A shoulder to cry on.'

'Not very original and not very imaginative?' She felt somewhere between irritated and nasty.

'I didn't say that. Tell you what. Maybe I'm jealous. Maybe I'd like it for myself. Maybe I'd like all those great feelings again, day after day.'

'It'll come back, Davey.'

'Is it forever?'

'I don't know.'

'Sorry. It's not my business.'

'I'm not offended. I don't even know what forever means. When you don't want children, you look at things differently.'

'Come on, Jude.'

She looked at him questioningly.

'You don't mean that,' her brother said.

'I don't want to live through what Rena lived through and what Diana isn't living through very well. What does forever mean for Frenchy? Have you seen him lately? Do you know what he looks like?'

'You've gotta believe, kid,' Davey said earnestly. 'Where's all that stuff inside you grew up with?'

'It's gone, Davey. I don't think you have to believe any more. I think that's childish. I've outgrown it. I think you have to learn. That's what I'm doing now. I'm learning.'

The picture grew on her. Sometimes she found herself talking to it. 'Look at how sloppy you are,' she would say playfully, drying a handful of silver. 'Why did she paint you sloppy?' And the eyes, behind the miraculously transparent glasses, would tease her. Sloppy because she knew him weekends as well as Mondays and Tuesdays. Eyes teasing because he must have loved her once, loved her greatly, and looked at her with teasing eyes when he loved her most. What had seemed to be unidentifiable trash poking out of the painted waste basket she finally recognized as the corner of a wrapper of his favourite Swiss chocolate. There were coffee stains on white paper. Ink dripped on a handkerchief. It was his damned leaky pen that he would never have fixed because he could not be without it.

'I saw Jerold today,' he said during a lull in the October trial.

'My father?'

'Yes.' He looked at her as if waiting for a sign.

'Do you think he knows?'

'I'm sure he does.'

'Was he rude?'

'Jerold is never rude. But I sense that whatever friendship there was between us is gone.'

'That's too bad.' She said it with a heartfelt sadness. Friendship was important. Friendship could save lives.

'Maybe, some day, there'll be an accommodation.'

Her eyes asked a question, but there was no answer.

The picture spoke to her. Hearing it, she looked at it and smiled. Roy dug deeply into his work. It was murder, a boy charged with the deaths of his father, mother and younger sister. The father was wonderful. The whole town loved the father. No one could understand what had happened unless it was someone else who had done it. Roy understood. There were witnesses who would testify to the father's real character. Roy would destroy the dead man. In the months preceding the trial, Roy had come to know him well.

The trial was in Westchester, not many miles from where the Kellems family lived. She drove up with him in the Jaguar, wondering if Annie would show up.

'Annie's busy,' he said. 'She wouldn't come to a trial if it were in her back yard. Besides, she's too proud.'

'Proud?'

'She wouldn't want me to see her there.'

The trial stretched into November. He worked late every night. She made coffee for him and then, emptying the pot, made more. Sometimes, exhausted, he slept until four and got up to work before breakfast. Sometimes he made love to her at ten or eleven and told her to sleep without him. When the alarm went off, he was there, warm and tired beside her. Sometimes he said, 'I'm glad you're here.' The picture said the same thing.

'Maybe we'll go away for Christmas,' he said, driving back to New York one evening.

'Somewhere warm?'

101

'Somewhere alone. I miss you.'

'I'm right here.'

'But I'm not. Not enough. I worry that you'll leave.'

'I won't.'

'Maybe if we were married . . .' He left it hanging inconclusively while her heart beat strongly. 'We'll talk about it when this is over. OK?'

'Yes.' Faintly.

'Did you say yes?'

'Yes.'

'Good.' He took her hand momentarily. 'Very good.'

The boy he was defending had two sets of grandparents. The paternal set would have nothing to do with him. The others were paying Roy's fee. It was a lot of money. He had hired detectives to find out more about the father and psychiatrists to find out more about the boy. The detectives brought forth witnesses whose testimony brought gasps from the audience. One of the psychiatrists brought tears. For Judy it was all love. She watched Roy with an intellectual admiration that metamorphosed into an almost physical passion. He was a father himself but in court he was this boy. He knew, he understood, he sympathized, he could make everyone feel as he felt.

He went up at the weekend to visit the boy in jail, intending to drive over to see his children afterwards, but the boy would not let him go and he returned to New York miserable and depressed and, suddenly, afraid of failure. She held him in her arms but he would not make love to her. He would only talk, alluding to the fear. She wondered how she could have doubted his feelings of involvement when she had first seen him years ago. When she had been with her father.

On Monday morning he said, 'Look, I'm afraid I'll be lousy today. Would you mind not coming?'

She said, 'OK,' poked around the apartment, shopped, read, talked to Fern on the phone. At noon he called.

'I'm sorry for what I said this morning,' he said.

'You didn't say anything.'

'You sure?'

'Positive.'

'I apologize anyway. You still love me a little?'

'A lot.'

'You might get a train up here – '

'I can leave in fifteen minutes.'

'I don't know.' He sounded a little discouraged. 'I suppose you'd only get here in time to drive back with me.'

'Wait for me.'

The case went to the jury the last week of November and he became suddenly calm. It was done and he was not dissatisfied. She was incredulous at his calm. She imagined herself in the same situation, unable to eat, pulse and blood pressure rising, conversation impossible. He was nothing like that. He was quiet, no less talkative than usual, no less hungry. He asked her to stay in New York while the jury was out. He would call as soon as he knew.

She heard first on the radio that she kept softly tuned to a station that would broadcast important bulletins. The trial had been in all the papers and the announcer was nearly breathless. They had not convicted the boy of murder. Probably he would spend his life in institutions.

Judy turned the radio up and looked at the portrait across the room. It looked triumphant. In Westchester they shoved a microphone in front of the defence lawyer and she heard Roy say that he was gratified.

When he came through the door two hours later, he put his arms around her and for a brief moment, Roy Kellems cried.

First there was peace, then there was passion. Then there was more peace. They talked about Christmas. They talked about 1960. For a few heady minutes, they talked about 1970. She knew now that she loved him, knew he loved her as well. It was a glorious week. More even than loving him, she felt that she knew him; they knew each other. He made her believe she was the person she had thought she was. There was much in her to know, to appreciate, and he knew and appreciated all of it.

On Saturday he left early to see his children. They would eat out tonight and then, after this weekend, maybe they would get theatre tickets, resume life again. The trial was over. The way he said it, he could have meant the trial in their lives. Something was past and something was beginning.

To her surprise, he repeated the trip on Sunday, returning in mid afternoon in high spirits. It wasn't until Monday morning that she understood. Brushing her hair in front of the oval mirror, she looked down at the little round porcelain dish on the dresser in which he dropped casually a tie clip he was not wearing or a pair of cufflinks: There, on top of the jewellery, was his wedding ring. She put the brush down and looked at the dish without touching. He had talked to Annie. He had done more than talk; he had told her something, and now the wedding ring lay in the porcelain dish with other unused jewellery.

Three

———◦◦———

She rested the bag of groceries precariously on her pelvic bone and manipulated the first key into the top lock and then the second into the lower one. Entering, she pushed the door closed with her right elbow and then leaned against it to make sure it closed securely. Hoisting the bag so that both arms held it, she caught a glimpse of someone in the living room. She screamed and backed away, the panic giving way to mere fear as she realized the person was a woman, a slender, long-haired woman sitting composedly on the sofa just to the left of the portrait.

'Who are you?' Her heart was still pounding with such force that it seemed to have made her body shake to its awful rhythm.

'I'm Annie Kellems.' The woman on the sofa stood. 'You're awfully pretty.'

'Mrs Kellems . . .' Judy put the heavy bag on Roy's desk and moved her shoulders to reaccustom them to weightlessness. 'How did you – ?'

'I've always had the key.' Annie Kellems met her eyes with a frank gaze. When she spoke, you heard West Virginia. 'I just thought the time had come to use it.' She had a narrow waist and a nice bust, long hair pulled back from her forehead that might once have been blonde but now looked more sunbleached than any definitive colour, a bit of light here and there among the background of shiny darker strands. She wore a cotton dress with an unusual design – perhaps someone had hand-blocked the print – giving her a village look, but with an expensive, sophisticated, mature chic. Her toenails and the soles of her feet were surely as clean and shiny as her long hair. The hair fell loosely down her back, showing off the cheekbones, which were echoed halfway down her body by her pelvic structure. She had stood with the grace of a cat or a ballerina. Whatever else had attracted Roy Kellems to Annie Jackson, he had surely married her as well for her face and body.

'What do you want?' It was a foolish question, asked with honest reticence.

'I want Roy.' She said it quietly, as though the question had been asked in earnest. It was an earnest answer.

'I see.' She was fascinated by the cheekbones, bust and hips of Annie Jackson, by the hand-blocked print of the cotton dress. The print caused her to wonder how a woman stood in front of a closet and chose the dress she would wear to meet the girl who was sharing her husband's apartment.

'Do you?'

'Yes, I do.'

'There have been others before you – I'm sure you know that – '

She didn't, but it didn't surprise her.

'They didn't last as long as you.' Annie Jackson opened the large brown leather shoulder bag on the cocktail table beside her, pulled out a tissue, touched her nose with it, and returned it to the bag. The bag had a design tooled in the leather. It was well made but it was not the kind of bag that wives of successful lawyers carried; it was the kind Annie Jackson carried. 'I don't think one of them was as pretty as you. I don't know whether he got tired of them in a few weeks or whether he got back a yen for me, but all the others were over in a month or so. This time I've watched the seasons change twice without him. It's too long. It's got to end.'

The voice made it a plea even though the words had the sound of an order. Annie Jackson wanted Roy back. Annie Jackson wanted Judith Wolfe to give him back. She felt a fierce sense of possessiveness. Since Sunday night the wedding ring had lain in the porcelain dish and now it was Tuesday. He was hers now, not Annie Jackson's. Annie Jackson had said herself that the seasons had changed twice since he had left. They would change twice again and he would still be hers. There was nothing casual or accidental about their relationship – not any more. They loved each other. They needed each other. Like people who were married, they had built a life together.

'Maybe you should talk to Roy,' Judy said, feeling herself gain control of her voice as she gained control of her emotions.

'I'm talking to you – frankly and honestly. I'm asking you to leave him, if you leave him, he'll come back to us. He has three children, you know.'

'I know that.'

'It's bad for them, not knowing where their pa is. And he loves those children.'

'I know.'

'He loves me too. You could think of it as sparing yourself a big hurt. He'd come back to me one day. You don't see it now, but I do. We're his family and sooner or later, he'll come back to us. It'll hurt more if it's later.'

'It would hurt now.'

'But not such a big hurt. Not the hurt I feel not having him. You're so young and pretty – you really are,' Annie Jackson said, seeing the cheeks redden slightly. 'Not surface pretty like the little girls on the TV who'll never grow old. You'll grow old wonderfully. Your face will improve. You'll see it when you're thirty. And look at those hands. Your hands are almost as good as mine are.' Annie Jackson smiled and looked down at the backs of her own hands, narrow with long fingers and short, rounded nails, bare except for a narrow, gold wedding band. 'Of course, I've had almost forty years to grow these.'

'Mrs Kellems – '

'Why don't you call me Annie?'

'Because we're not friends.'

'Maybe because I'm old enough to be your ma.' She looked at Judy significantly so that the implied connection could not be denied.

'My mother is older than you. She's older than Roy.'

'Not by much, I'll bet. Don't you want to find someone as young and pretty as you are? The way I did a long time ago?'

'I don't.' Her eyes filled at the thought of what she was being asked to do: give up Roy. Roy and Annie had talked over the weekend and on Monday morning Judy had found the gold band in the little dish on Roy's dresser. Today Annie Jackson was playing her last card. Half the pain Judy felt at the thought of giving up Roy was for Annie who had already lost him.

Still, her reaction astonished her. She could not understand why she was without rage, without even an honest anger at this woman who had entered her home without permission, who was asking that she voluntarily give up the one person she could not live without. She did not know why she had held her tongue, reticently, deferentially. She could have spoken sharply; she knew how to be intimidating. Yet at some point she had chosen not to.

'I'd like you to leave, Mrs Kellems,' she said quietly.

It was the first moment that Annie Jackson wavered. Her mouth was suddenly less firm; her eyes flickered slightly. She began to look as though she might even be forty. She picked up the handsome brown hand-tooled leather bag and put it on her shoulder.

'I don't even know your name,' she said faintly.

'No.'

'It puts me at a disadvantage.'

Judy looked at her without speaking. She was the daughter of a lawyer and the lover of a lawyer and whatever happened, she would say nothing that would damage her case.

She looked away from the troubled face of Annie Jackson, lifting her eyes to the portrait of Roy that she had come to love as she had grown to love Roy himself. It seemed almost impossible to believe that she had once disliked it so much. He was all there, the hard and the soft, the brilliance and the little boy, the passionate devotion to everything he loved, the playfulness, and most of all, she could see it now, the sex.

Annie Jackson tossed a glance over her left shoulder, like an offering of salt. 'You like my Roy?' she asked with something of her former spirit.

'Very much.'

'It takes a long time to get to love a man enough to paint a picture like that of him.'

The tears in Judy's eyes flowed over. 'Good-bye, Mrs Kellems,' she said.

Annie Jackson looked at her with an almost maternal compassion. 'Good-bye, little girl,' she said. 'I hope you're a nice little girl.' She let herself out and then, like a thoughtful mother, put her key in the lock and bolted the door.

She was crying and she was still wearing her coat. She took it off and dropped it over the chair that Roy sat in when he worked at the desk. It fell, oddly, almost the way his jacket did when he hung it over a corner, the way Annie Jackson had painted him in her portrait. Her portrait.

It was, after all, Annie Jackson's portrait. She looked at it through the distortion of tears but she could not see it as she had that first night almost six months ago. The barriers were all gone now, the mist all cleared away. She could see him as Annie Jackson saw him. Roy, she thought. I need you, Roy. The revelation was that she could not go back. She could no more stop loving him than she could be the person who had walked into this apartment last summer. Growth was a permanent change.

It was Annie Jackson's portrait and maybe it was Annie Jackson's Roy. She would make a cup of tea and let the day pass and when he came home, they would talk. He would tell her that Annie had had no right to come to this apartment, that he had talked it out with Annie on Sunday, that he and Annie were finished. He would say everything that Judy wanted to hear. He would make love to her and she would feel better and they would be happy.

She looked across the room. It was Annie Jackson's Roy. Judy Wolfe's happiness had been built on Annie Jackson's misery. I am a certain kind of person, she thought. Maybe I don't even know what kind of person I am. Maybe I have to find out. Maybe I have to find out now.

She went to the bedroom and found her suitcase where Roy had stashed it, high on a shelf in the closet where she could not reach it without a stool. If I stay until he comes home, I will never leave and the question of who I am will be forever answered. I wonder if I will like that answer. Maybe it is a question I should answer myself, without Roy.

The seasons had changed twice and the clothes would not fit in a single suitcase. She found shopping bags and filled one after the other, mementoes of love. He had liked this one. He had insisted she buy that one although it was frightfully expensive. She could not stop crying. She had caused Annie Jackson the greatest grief of her life and now she would try to make amends. She wondered if she could be half the person Annie Jackson was.

Fern was not in her office and she needed to leave, needed to drop the luggage somewhere. Taking a last look around the apartment she found the beginner's cookbook and placed it on top of one almost full shopping bag. She lifted the cover and read the inscription: To Judith, Who chose freedom. She would go to to Penn Station and check her things. From there it was only a short walk to someone who would surely help her. She would see Regina.

PART THREE

---◦◦◦---

December 1959

One

———•❖•———

It was a feeling Regina Rush understood well and painfully, the feeling of leaving someone. For Regina, it had been Jerold, time and again, the cousin she could not marry. The ties had been severed finally in 1926 when she married Mortimer Rush, the widowed husband of Aunt Maude who had died in childbirth, and the marriage had been a good one. There had been love and there had been children. Over the next two decades, she and Jerold saw each other from time to time at family weddings, the table at which the cousins gossiped and complained and laughed and renewed the unchanging relationships they enjoyed with each other.

All that had changed in 1949 with a phone call from Cousin Lillian, the news, delivered with triumph, that Jerold had fathered an illegitimate child, 'A monster, Regina.' The past had come back as the past always would.

Lillian, herself a wronged wife, was jubilant. Edith and the children had moved out. So much for the men in the Wolfe family.

It had taken Regina less than twenty-four hours to decide to go to him and once there, less time than that for both of them to know that she could not leave. She could still remember – on the rare occasions when she allowed herself to – nearly every minute of the time they had spent together. She could hear his voice, feel his body under the fine white cotton shirt, sense his presence. She could remember that last morning – not knowing it was the last morning – when the telephone had rung, scarcely a minute after the alarm, and he had heard his daughter crying into a distant telephone.

That was when he had given her the Buddha and she had held it in her hand until the moment before she left the house, not realizing until it was upon her that the last moment had come, that the choice was hers, that she had to make it. Her own youngest child was six then and she needed him. Perhaps she had needed him more than she needed Jerold. She had left the Buddha on Jerold's shelf and gone home with Morty. It had not been an easy year.

The rubble of her marriage was littered around her like thick shards of pottery. She had been tempted once or twice to step on them and reduce them to dust, but she had not. Instead, she had gathered them together and applied her life glue; she had resurrected instead of destroying. She had made the great effort of her life and eventually, she had had success.

It was 1953 when the event occurred that finally sealed her homecoming, the arrival early in the year of Marcel Goldblatt. Suzanne, Regina's friend from the twenties, now widowed by the war and caring for her own two children as well as those of her brother, had called to say she could not handle her nephew. He needed a strong paternal presence. If he were not soon taken in hand, she feared she would lose him.

For Regina it was more than the challenge of helping a boy who needed her, more than the debt of thirty years of friendship; it was a reason to remain a wife. It was something they could share once again. Ernie, her oldest, was married and Margot, her second, now at college. Adam was ten and independent. Before she even saw him, she wanted Marcel the way she had once wanted her first child.

He was sixteen and a half, sullen and difficult, but he had loved New York. He had roamed the city daily, riding subways as far as they would go, returning unpredictably, sometimes very late, worrying them. Suzanne had been right. He had needed a firm male hand. Morty had supplied it – with great success – and a year later Marcel had been accepted at Princeton.

They had not been easy years, but they were behind her. She had worked at her business and taken care of Marcel and her family. She had not seen Jerold again and in a small way was grateful for it. But she received news, not merely received it, asked for it, demanded it. Richard and his family came now and then from Rome or Korea or wherever they were and Richard was Jerold's brother and Richard brought news. So it did not come as a surprise when she had heard, that Sunday afternoon early in 1957, that her cousin was to be appointed a federal judge. What surprised her was that it was Morty who had told her.

'I just had an interesting phone call,' he had said, entering her study and seating himself in the only big, comfortable chair. 'Want to scoop your bitch cousin?'

'What do you know that Lillian doesn't know?' She had left her desk and come to sit on the small sofa beside the chair, picking a small piece of lint from his shoulder as she sat.

'It was one of Eisenhower's men,' he said.

'We don't have any government contracts.' She had frowned, perplexed.

'It wasn't about contracts. They're making an announcement tomorrow.' He stopped very briefly. 'Jerold's going to get a shot at a federal bench.'

She had felt the heat rush into her face and as quickly leave it. It was eight years this month since she had left her cousin's beautiful house and gone home with Morty.

'Why – ' her voice had failed her, 'Why did they call you?'

'I put some money in the right place during the campaign last year.'

'I see.'

'I thought he deserved it. He's a damn good lawyer. That was a good splash he made a couple of years ago when that building contractor sued.'

'It was very nice of you, Morty.'

He had looked at her steadily. 'I'm a nice guy.'

'I know.'

'He wrote to me,' Morty said in a quiet voice. 'After you came back, he put it all in a letter.'

'He *wrote* to you?'

'You wouldn't expect a lawyer to do that, would you, the way they're always covering their asses. It was handwritten. I thought he was pretty eloquent. Took responsibility for the whole thing. Said he'd called you and asked you to come and see him. That sort of thing.'

'He wrote that in a letter.'

'I sent it back. I didn't want him to think I'd ever use it against him although I'm sure that's one of the reasons he did it.' Morty had moved to make himself more comfortable in the chair. 'I appreciated the fact that he was honourable, even if he wasn't being very honest.'

'You knew he wasn't telling the truth.'

'I was pretty damn sure he was protecting you and I couldn't get very angry about that, except maybe at myself. I never cared much one way or another about Jerold up until that point although I can see what you saw in him. See in him,' he corrected himself, looking away from her momentarily as though afraid to read confirmation in her eyes. 'I suppose he's as decent a man as I've ever met.'

'I think it's all under control now.' It wasn't as she spoke, but it had been, just below the surface, uneasily still because she did not see him.

'Regrets?' Morty had asked finally, the sound of his voice almost startling her.

'No.' And then she had added what she had eventually come to accept as a truth of her life. 'I don't regret anything I've ever done.'

He considered it. 'Fair enough,' he said.

'Not fair, perhaps. Just true.'

He looked at his watch. The discussion was over.

It was nearly two years later, two months after Davey's baby was born, when Regina had walked into her office to find a telephone memo: Judge Wolfe will call back after four-thirty.

The little pink rectangle of paper destroyed her day. She cancelled an appointment and closed her door. It was almost ten years and they had spoken to each other only once, warmly and emotionally, when she had called him the day after Morty had brought her the news of his appointment to the bench.

She thought, We have handled this all wrong. If we had stayed friends – acquaintances – then a pink memo from you would not throw me into turmoil.

But even as she thought it, she knew it could not have worked. They could be lovers but they could never be acquaintances. In their lives, the sound of each other's voice must always be cataclysmic. So she sat at her desk, doing the kind of work that left her mind free, waiting, waiting, until at four thirty-six the phone rang and she heard his voice say, 'How are you, darling?'

He had called to talk about Judy. The family had been severely shaken after the birth of Davey's baby and he was worried about his daughter.

'I went down to Swarthmore to talk to her,' he had said. 'But I'm afraid I botched it.'

'Badly, very badly. I tried to tell her – I wanted her to know that what happened to Davey shouldn't affect her choices. I don't want her making the kinds of mistakes – ' He stopped momentarily.

'That we made,' she had filled in.

'We didn't make any mistakes, Regina,' he said firmly. 'We're simply different people and the times were different. What I meant to say is that I don't want Judy making the kinds of mistakes one makes after too much thought. I don't want this to inhibit her natural impulses.'

She could remember their conversation as though it had happened only yesterday and now, a year later, Jerold's daughter was an unexpected visitor at Regina's office.

'A Miss Wolfe to see you, Mrs Rush,' the voice announced on the intercom.

'Send her right in.' Regina pushed her rolling chair back and stood as the door opened. 'Judy,' she said brightly as her cousin entered. Then, with concern, 'Something's wrong.'

'No, everything's fine.' She didn't look fine. 'Well, yes, something is wrong, but it's a personal thing. It's not the family. I need a favour, Regina.'

'Go on.' They had both sat and Regina had had a chance to look at her cousin more carefully, at her eyes, at her drawn face.

'I need to make some phone calls, I have to call England.' Her shoulders fell as she said England. 'It's just too complicated from a pay phone.'

'You can use my office.' She hesitated, wanting to offer more

117

than a telephone but still singed from their repeated failures with Marcel. She did not want offers misinterpreted as the strong arm of the family, as a means to control. 'If there's anything else I can do . . .' she said hesitantly.

'Thank you. Just the telphone. I'm going to England. It's just become very important that I get away. I have a friend over there – she's visited us every Christmas – and maybe she can find me a place to stay in London that won't cost an arm and a leg. I've called some airlines already and something should come through soon, maybe tomorrow morning.'

'You're not in trouble, Judy.'

'No.' She sounded certain enough of that. 'I've been – living in someone's apartment since last June and the relationship has to end. I realized that this morning. And the only way it's going to end is for me to go away, far away. If I see him tonight, I won't be able to go through with it.'

'Maybe you don't want to go through with it,' Regina said, thinking of those other times, the good-byes neither had wanted to say. 'Maybe it shouldn't end.' Jerold had said only a year ago that he wanted Judy to act from impulse, that she should not weigh the plusses and minuses.

'I don't know.' Judy sagged suddenly, as though under a great weight. 'If I can just be alone somewhere for a while and think about it. If I can just go far away and – ' She straightened herself purposefully and leaned slightly forward. 'I do know, Regina. I think I've known from the beginning and I need to get away. I'm not awfully strong and right now I'm being carried along by the momentum of a very hard push I got this morning and if something stops me now, a lot of lives will be destroyed.'

'Then make your calls,' Regina stood and moved the telephone to the centre of the desk before she left it.

'I have one more favour to ask.'

'Whatever you want.'

'You said last year that when Frenchy came to see you, you told him to do what he wanted, even if it wasn't what my father had in mind. I'd like you to do the same for me. Don't tell them I've been here. If they haul me back like a wounded child and try to nourish me back to health, I'll lose the whole war.'

'It'll be our secret.' She watched as Judy made her way to the desk, as beautiful a girl as her mother had been that Sunday afternoon in 1932 when Regina had first seen her. How could she think that she wasn't strong? What might have happened that Saturday night last Christmas if Morty hadn't started the day by inadvertently enraging Marcel? Clever questions that had no answers. Judy was leaving the country and Marcel, after moving from one ill-paying part-time job to another, was now apparently relatively happy working as an orderly at a large Brooklyn hospital, although Regina could not imagine what pleasure he found there.

Regina asked her secretary to transfer her calls to another telephone and went off to talk to one of her designers. It would be a long time before all the pieces fell in place, before all the small tales wound together to make one story.

Two

———◦◦———

Margaret, Judy's English friend from Swarthmore, met her at the airport and drove her to the Townley home in Hawthorne Lane in a small, picturesque village an hour or so out of London. It had all turned out far more favourably than Judy had imagined it could as she picked up the phone that afternoon in Regina's office and asked for England. Professor Townley was spending the year teaching at Gottingen and had returned with his wife only for the Christmas celebration. When they left for Germany late in December, Margaret would accompany them. They were delighted to leave the house in Judy's care and more delighted to entertain her as the Wolfes had entertained their own daughter.

Before year's end, she was alone and alone was the way she wanted to be. She spent the days inside the house listening to the stillness and writing letters. She wrote to Fern, to Margaret in Germany, to her brothers and finally to her mother. The phone rang only three times and she told each caller where Margaret's family was and how to reach them. By the time of the third call, a week after Margaret had left, she had a sudden urge to invite herself to the caller's home for some human company. Her voice had nearly croaked when she said, 'Hello.' In New York she had talked to Roy morning and evening, and during the day she had talked to the portrait. Now not even the portrait was there to listen.

She had dug deep into her old shoulder bag on the first day she was alone and found the little Buddha. The label stuck to its bottom had faded to illegibility after half a year in her bag but the smile was the same and the shiny, rubbable stomach. She put it on Margaret's dresser in front of Margaret's mirror and touched it twice or more daily. She wanted to be happy, wanted it desperately, but she was an ocean away from the source of her happiness and she could not return.

Although she had the run of the house, she picked four rooms to use in a kind of sequence, plugging in the electric heater in one as she unplugged the electric heater in the other. She had not known that the English lived this way. It must have been a shock to Margaret to find that every building she walked into in the States was centrally heated, even small, not very expensive private homes.

In the morning she left the bedroom and went down to Professor Townley's study, managing to breakfast without anything more than the heat of the stove brewing her coffee. There was plenty to read in the study and a wonderful desk on which to write her letters. After her evening meal, she moved to the living room, sitting on one piece of furniture or another or on the floor with her back propped against the couch the way she had sat at college when she was young and innocent, before she met Roy.

When the telephone calls seemed to have come to an end, all three of them, she found her way to the grocery, the post office and the bakery. There, at least, she could use her voice. She posted her letters. She bought provisions. Then she went home to the silent house and made a decision.

She had always thought that people who spoke aloud to themselves were at least slightly crazy. She was sane, very sane, but she decided to speak the truth aloud. Davey had said there was no truth, only answers, and she had humoured him. But she knew there was truth and she would stay in this house in England until she had spoken aloud all the truths of her life. Sitting on the floor of the living room, she said, 'I am Judith Wolfe.' At the moment, it was the only thing she was certain of.

A few days later – she had lost track of time but it was January – a letter arrived from Fern, too soon to be a response to her own letter. She opened the envelope and saw that within the folds of Fern's letter was an envelope with the printed return address of Roy C Kellems, Esq. She did not open it immediately. Instead, she enjoyed the rush of feeling that it engendered. She savoured it sealed, running fingers along its edges, smelling it for some familiar scent. He had handwritten the envelope in his familiar black ink with the pen that leaked. The 'e' of Wolfe was a glob. Miss Judith Wolfe. The one fact that she was sure of, the one truth. She could feel her throat constricting with the emotion she had not been able to set aside and she held the letter while she forced herself to read Fern's first. That he had called. That she would not give Judy's address except to say she was in England. That work was wonderful and exciting; they had given her a raise and she had met a few people and she was happy. That the letter from Roy had come and she would forward it. Dear, wonderful Fern who would always understand.

She went to the kitchen and slit the top of the envelope with the sharpest knife she could find. Inside was a single sheet of letterhead stationery, that good, white textured stock with an almost translucent quality.

'Dearest Judith, I look in the mirror and see only your face. Please come back. All my love, Roy.'

It brought her to tears and it brought her also to the second truth. 'I love Roy,' she said. Deeply, she added in her head, completely, passionately.

She returned to Professor Townley's study and shut the door, retaining the heat. She had bought a spiral notebook in town, the cover printed with a design of spring flowers. On the first page she began to write questions: What do I want? What kind of person am I? Did I know I was hurting Annie when I moved into Roy's apartment? What does freedom mean for Judith Wolfe?

She wrote question after question, outlining the curriculum of her stay in England. When she was out of questions, she pulled out the plug of the electric heater, changed her clothes and took the train into London.

Near Paddington Station she found a bank and changed a twenty-dollar traveller's cheque into pounds, noting sadly that twenty of the former reduced to less than ten of the latter. Her entire savings were in the book of cheques in her hand. She exchanged pleasantries with the teller, enjoying the sound of two voices. She went outside and bought a street map of the city and then she found the Underground and bought a ticket to Leicester Square because it was a place she had heard of in a song. It was the right place to go. The street sign on the side of the nearest building told her she was on Charing Cross Road and as she walked she found the bookshops, old books, new books, prints. Her heart quickened, the signal of life continuing. The browsers were mature, pipe-smoking types in tweeds and younger, studenty types with hair longer than at home, glasses like Roy's, beards like Davey's. In one store a young man spoke to her, in another an older one. She did not think of them as potential lovers as once, in the spring, she had thought of the young man at Washington Square. She thought of them as voices.

'Fond of Eliot, are you?'

She turned to look at the speaker, one of the older, tweedy types, an unlit pipe jiggling slightly in the corner of his mouth as he spoke. She said, 'Yes,' and smiled, still somewhat awed at the sound of her voice, still wondering whether it would suddenly give way under the pressure of so much use after such a long period of lying fallow. In her hand was a slim volume of Eliot's *Old Possum's Book of Practical Cats* that she had thought about buying, considering that each book she acquired was one day's less food, one day earlier she would have to return.

'A very interesting man when you speak to him. Fine wit.'

'Do you know him?' She could scarcely imagine her good fortune.

'Yes, indeed. Met him several times.'

'How marvellous.'

'Why don't we have a cup of tea and I'll tell you about it?'

She left the book and walked up the street with the man with the pipe. They turned into a Lyons Tea Room and he ordered tea and cakes at a table. They stayed an hour and he did most of the talking. He had met Eliot on several occasions. He could remember what Eliot had said at this time and that time. Some years ago, in the early fifties, he had hoisted a few with Dylan Thomas after a reading. She listened enthralled. His memory went back to the thirties, poets she had studied and poets she had never heard of. She would have to write to Fern when she got home. Imagine meeting someone who had met Eliot.

'Do you write yourself?' she asked finally, glancing at her watch and realizing she would walk in the dark from the station to the Townley house.

'Just a bit now and then. Nothing awfully good. Are you staying in London?'

'No, in the country. With friends. They'll be expecting me for dinner.'

'May I call you?'

'I don't think they'd approve,' she said.

'Well,' he cleared his throat, 'it's been a pleasant afternoon.'

She sat on the train looking out at the darkening landscape, thinking about the man whose joy in life was meeting poets but not writing poetry. She knew it was important to think about, that it applied to her life in a way that was not quite clear, something she could almost sense if she closed her eyes, if she squeezed them and tried to reach with her mind. The train slowed to a stop and she realized with panic that it was her station. Grabbing her bag she ran to the door.

'No rush, Miss,' the ageing conductor said calmly. 'Still ninety seconds left. Mind the step.'

She said, 'Thank you,' and followed the small crowd to the exit. In the house, she closed the door of the study and plugged in the heater, keeping her coat on till the chill wore off. There would be time later to cook and eat, time to wash the dishes and listen to the BBC news, time to sleep. Now she had questions for her notebook.

She turned to a fresh page and began writing: Does loving mean giving up? Did I give something up to love Roy? Did I give up something essential in my life? What is essential? WHAT DO I WANT? Can I be happy loving someone and making that my life? I was happy that way, wasn't I? Wasn't I?

She unbuttoned her coat and read the page over. Then she went into the kitchen to cook dinner.

In the morning she went back into London. She had found the Central Criminal Court on her map and realized it was the

Old Bailey of old stories, located on Old Bailey Street. She took the Underground to St Paul's, the nearest station, and walked the few blocks to the court. It was cold and drizzly but she remembered the day in June that she had ended up at Centre Street, the stairs where she had met Roy, the courtroom he had taken her to where she had listened for echoes and heard nothing. This building was nothing like that other. The Old Bailey stood flat against the sidewalk, Justice on top with a sword in her right hand and scale in her left, and a message written in the stone: Defend the children of the poor and punish the wrongdoer. She went inside and sat with the visitors, trying to identify the players. That was the judge, that the prosecutor, that the counsel for the defence. She could not imagine any lawyer she had ever known wearing a white wig. Still, something ran through the proceedings, an undercurrent of familiarity, like sitting in a strange temple on a sabbath morning and hearing the Sh'ma. You might not understand a word but you knew they were speaking your language.

A few seats to her left sat a woman with short-clipped grey hair, watching intently. Like a spectator at a baseball game, the old woman commented vigorously under her breath. 'Roy,' she breathed hoarsely when the prosecutor made a good point. 'You tell 'im.' Judy watched her through the corner of her eye, the woman, for the moment, more fascinating than the trial. The woman growled like an animal, never moving her eyes, scarcely blinking. 'Make 'im pay,' although it sounded more like, 'Mike 'im pie.'

Judy turned back to observe the judge, who was delivering a little sermon, shaking his head so that his white locks jumped and bobbed. She wondered if the judge's wife was travelling to Harrod's in a black limousine, if the defence counsel's wife was home painting a portrait of him, if the prosecutor's wife was ironing the wash she had carried home from the laundry.

Spectators.

Wives.

People who lived through other people without doing it themselves.

I *loved* doing other things for Roy, she thought. I loved watching him in court. I loved seeing him glow after a success. When I cooked for him, it was all pleasure. When I made the bed in the morning, it was because he would enjoy getting into it at night. When I looked at myself in that mirror, I saw the mirror he had given me more than I saw myself.

The defence lawyer made a good point and as the spectators laughed politely, the woman to Judy's left snarled a nasty epithet. A woman who wanted blood. A woman whose idea of justice was the prosecutor's case. A spectator.

Judy moved away, finding a seat with a less adequate view but away from everyone else. The witness was faltering now, just a little uncertain, his memory not quite as sharp as it should be. The defence attorney – barristers, weren't they? – withdrawing at precisely the right moment, his point made neatly, indirectly, no need for overkill. The old woman would be growling again.

I love him, she thought. It had become painful to watch, painful to listen. Artfulness was Roy. Skill was Roy. Success was Roy. She blotted tears with a tissue, thinking for the first time in her life that the tissue had cost money, that the traveller's cheques were a dwindling supply, that there was no income, only outgo. She left the courtroom and wandered to where she could look at the nearby Thames. It was January cold, drizzly cold, too cold to stay for more than a few minutes. It was nearly lunchtime and she had begun to feel hungry but she didn't want to spend too much to eat because food was a trade-off against time. Her parents had not let her squander but she had never wanted for money. She had been taken care of for twenty-one and a half years, first by her parents, then by Roy, and when she had needed help, her friend Fern had come to her aid to fill the gaps between. Even now Margaret's family had given her a house so that she lived rent-free. Privileged child, silver spoon, Park Avenue rich. *What does Judith want?*

She found a coffee shop and had a sandwich and a cup of tea, sipping it slowly, remaining until she was warm. Then she began to walk. Even in the mist it seemed a nice city. Unlike Manhattan, the directions were elusive. There was no obvious uptown or downtown, no corresponding north and south. Cars and buses came at you from the wrong direction but already she had begun to make that adjustment. If one was young and flexible, one adjusted to life. One learned easily how to love. But even being young did not help one learn how to stop loving. What does Judith want? She could hear him asking the questions, lightly, almost playfully, after hammering at her that afternoon in Central Park. And that first kiss.

Surprised?

Yes.

Anything else?

Yes.

Anything else. She could not have put it in words at that moment, had not been able to for weeks. *Sometimes you make me feel as if my skin shimmered.*

I know, baby. In the husky whisper of bed, between his and her telephones. *I know.*

A good thing it rains in London in January. All the women in London were talking with tears on their cheeks.

He had cared from that first day – *What does Judith want?* – cared from the night before when he had met her on the stairs of the courthouse and taken her under his wing. That they had fallen in love was almost irrelevant now. He had cared when they weren't in love, would have continued to care because he was that kind of person. We fell in love with a good man, Mrs Kellems, you and I, and he's yours now because I gave him back. But will it ever be the same with anyone else again? Do I want it to be the same?

Spectators, wives, poets who don't write poetry. Looking for echoes in an empty courtroom. Knowing just when the point is made and withdrawing gracefully. You may not understand a word but you know they're speaking your language. My father and I don't speak the same language. I was so happy with Roy, but there'll never be anyone like him again. It's over and I'm on my own.

What if – the light was red so she rounded the corner just to keep moving, to keep the thoughts going – what if Roy had been a surgeon? Would she have dressed in the morning to sit in the operating theatre and watch him slice a sleeping body open, remove a diseased organ, and sew up the wound? She felt a touch of nausea as the images confronted her. The nausea was her answer, an answer finally after all those questions written and imagined. The answer was no, shouted in her head, screamed in her mind as her step hurried to keep pace with her thoughts. *No*! They couldn't drag me into a hospital to watch an operation. *No*! Even if it were Roy I wouldn't find pleasure in seeing a surgeon at work. It wasn't just that Roy did it that made it wonderful, it was what he did. I loved what he did. I still love it. I love *law*.

A collision.

'Oh!' Reeling from the impact of the revelation and the impact of colliding. 'I'm terribly sorry.'

'You all right, darlin'?' He was immensely tall, dark blue, and helmeted. She had run into a bobby who still held her arm tightly to keep her upright.

'Yes, I'm fine.' He let her arm go and she took a step back. 'It's all my fault. I'm so sorry.' Strange how the 'darlin' – ' from this huge, smiling man made her feel sweetly complimented while the New York salesgirl's 'dear' made her feel condemned.

'Didn't even take the shine off my shoes,' the policeman said genially. 'Can I help you find your way to wherever you're going?'

'I have to send a telegram,' Judy said, still breathless with the revelation that had propelled her into the collision. 'A cable to the United States. Is there a Western Union around?'

The policeman lifted his eyebrows briefly. 'You might try the post office, Miss. It's just halfway down the street.' He turned and pointed.

'Thank you. Thank you very much.' She started away. 'I'm really sorry I bumped into you.'

He touched his helmet, looking not at all sorry himself, and Judy looked back in the direction of her goal to avoid a second mishap. The post office was only steps away, warm and dry on the inside. She wrote the words in pencil, erasing and correcting as she went along. Yale Law Admissions, New Haven,

Conn. Please activate 1959 application. Would like to enter September 1960. Letter follows. Judith Wolfe.

She read it over, thinking of omissions that would save money. This was not the time to save. This cable was an investment. If it didn't arrive soon, it would be too late. She didn't want to be someone's secretary. Roy had been right. It wasn't for her. This was for her. It had always been for her.

'You can send this as a night letter, Miss. The cost is quite a bit less.' The clerk looked through the grillwork at her.

'It's very important,' she said. 'I'd like it to go as a regular telegram. Do you think they might get it this afternoon?'

The clerk glanced at the clock on the wall. 'I should think they would.'

'Then it's worth it.'

It cost more than any single day had cost so far but she left the post office nearly floating. The rain had let up and a dark cloud right overhead had a brilliant beam of light behind it. A good omen. Tomorrow she would write a letter that they would never forget. She had done it once when she applied to Swarthmore. Now she would do it again.

She took the train home and walked through the damp streets to Hawthorne Lane. The key turned, the door opened, she went inside and leaned against the door to close it. Then she shouted the third truth of her life. 'I want to be a lawyer!'

Three

———◆———

'Dear Roy,' she wrote finally, when she knew what it was she had to write, 'I can't. Love, Judith.' She posted it without a return address, dropping it in a letter box in London to assure the secrecy of her whereabouts. It was still touchy. She was still uncertain of her own determination should he materialize unannounced on her doorstep. She still dreamed about him, passionately, erotically, longingly. But she had no desire to find someone else, to seek a replacement. She wanted only to ask and answer her life questions.

After the letter to Yale, after the decision that prompted the cable and the letter that followed, after she began to see herself as a law student, as a future member of the bar, the time with Roy revealed itself in a way she had not imagined it could. Like the layers of gauze dissolving to uncover the essence of the portrait, the beautiful relationship showed its other side and she was struck with awe and surprise. That she had lived through him. That she had subverted her own life's desires to care for him. That she had done it willingly and with love. That she knew, finally, that it had been for one time only. Roy had been a time in her life and the time was past.

The dreams ended then. She became edgy about Yale. She went into London nearly every day so that she would be diverted from thinking about it. She visited the museums and attended the theatre. She marked off sights on her map and put an X in the circle when she had visited one so that soon the map was dotted with X'd-out circles. Returning to the house on Hawthorne Lane one evening, wondering if there was something there to eat because she was starving, she heard the telephone ring. There was something almost terrifying about the sound, it had been so long since she had heard it.

Unlocking the door and leaving it ajar, she ran for the phone and said a breathless, 'Hello?'

'Miss Judith Wolfe, please, United States calling.'

It was sheer terror now. Who – ? Who – ? 'Yes.' It was little more than a gasp. 'This is she.'

'Go ahead, New Haven.'

She began to cry. *Go ahead, New Haven.* She heard herself saying, Yes, thank you, how kind or you, of course I will, thank you, thank you. They just wanted to be certain. The address had changed and they didn't want to chance their acceptance going astray. Her letter had been so moving, her record at Swarthmore, the cable . . . She hung up in a flood of tears. For the rest of her life those four words would signify the renewal of life, a second chance, an upturn. *Go ahead, New Haven.*

She sent the deposit from the thinning wad of traveller's cheques, wondering what would be the first to go, the trips to London or the lunches. The Townleys would not be back until August but she feared her money would not hold out that long. She wrote to Yale and said she needed a scholarship.

A week later the phone rang in the morning and this time she answered with far less hesitation.

'Judy?' a familiar voice said. 'This is Diana.'

'Diana! Where are you?'

'At the Connaught in London. Can I buy you lunch?'

'Oh, my.' A friend, a member of the family. She could not believe her good fortune. 'I can be there by noon.'

'Wonderful. I can't wait.'

'But what are you doing here?'

'Well,' Diana sipped her gin and tonic and smiled. She looked marvellous, healthy, rested, shining. 'I've been repeating the grand trip of the past, the trip we all made the summer between our junior and senior years, you know, Paris, Amsterdam, Geneva, Rome. This is my last stop and I'm cutting the trip short.'

'But London is wonderful,' Judy protested.

'I remember. But I don't need London any more. Anyway, I can always come back. I'm going home to Frenchy tomorrow.'

'Oh, Diana.' The news was sweetly elating, emotionally overwhelming. She felt her throat constrict, as it had when the operator said, Go ahead, New Haven. 'I'm so happy for both of you. I'm happy for me. Do you believe that?'

'I do. It was something that you said last summer that really made me think. Do you remember what it was?'

Judy shook her head. 'I don't remember much about last summer at all, except what happened to me. What happened to me I'll never forget.'

'When you came to see me, a couple of weeks after I came home, and I told you Frenchy and I were separating, you said I wasn't just some girl Frenchy had married, that I was part of the family. Well, it took me ten months to find out you were right. I couldn't bear to think of either one of us married to someone else. And what would be the point of my marrying someone else? Why should I marry someone who's half the man Frenchy is just so that I could have children? I really want to be Frenchy's wife.'

'I'm so glad to hear you say it.'

'I had a few dates during the winter,' Diana said, apologetically, as though she had broken some rule. 'It was awful. It wasn't at all like dating when I was younger. When I was – single. There wasn't one man I went out with a second time.' She looked troubled, singed by the memories. 'Nothing was the way it had been with Frenchy.'

'I don't suppose anything's ever the same twice.'

'No, I suppose it can't be. Or we don't want it to be. Nothing was the same for me. I went back to work, at my old job that I used to love so much. They were wonderful to me but I couldn't recapture that feeling of independence and accomplishment that I had when I worked the year Frenchy and I were engaged. So I quit, took my earnings, and bought a plane ticket.'

'I know the feeling,' Judy said.

'I saw your parents just before I left New York.'

'How are they?'

'They've been marvellous, right through everything that's

132

happened. Your mother especially. She seems so mild on the surface but she's really very strong underneath. My mother's just the opposite. You think she can handle anything but at the first sight of blood, she turns into jelly. I'm afraid I do too.'

'Don't be hard on yourself, Diana.'

'I went to see – our child before I left.' She shuddered slightly and didn't speak until she had composed herself. 'I couldn't do it, Judy. I couldn't take him home and devote my life to caring for him.'

'I couldn't either.'

'But I *know* I couldn't.' She paused while the waiter served their appetizers. 'What I want is Frenchy. What I want is to be his wife. We'll just have to take everything bit by bit as it happens and go on from there.'

'That sounds sensible. And workable.'

'Yes. And it's going to work.' Diana smiled. 'You know, I looked at your father when we were having dinner that night, and I had the feeling I could see Frenchy thirty years from now. It was rather pleasing actually.'

'He's a handsome man.'

'Have you made your peace?'

'No.'

'You will, Judy. Whatever it is, I know he wants you back.'

'How's Davey?'

'The underground says he's having a very good time. Comes into New York frequently.'

'Does he see Rena at all?'

'I think there's a court date set for a divorce.'

'He didn't write about that.'

'Judy – ' Diana looked uncertain. 'What happened? I mean that made you come here? You seemed so happy last summer.'

What happened? She reflected that it was a question she had not asked herself, not written in the little notebook whose pages were filled with mostly unanswered questions. 'He was forty-two years old and a member of the bar,' she answered calmly, paraphrasing Roy Kellems, 'and if I live to be a hundred, I'll never have anything like it again. That's not the answer to your question. It's the answer to the one you didn't ask that preceded it. The answer to your question is that he was married and when I met his wife, I knew her claim was more valid than mine. I knew also that I couldn't be the kind of person who treated someone's wife the way I had treated her. She was a much better person than I and I regretted it.'

'Don't be hard on yourself, Judy. I think someone said that to me just a few minutes ago.'

'I'm trying to be honest. I am being honest. It was a wonderful half year, but it's over. When I got here I thought I might go back to him some time. I won't. I have other plans now, plans for myself, plans that don't include anybody else for the time being. You know,' it was her sister-in-law sitting opposite her but she had the sense of speaking to herself, speaking aloud in the house on Hawthorne Lane, 'there's something magical about a man who's twice as old as you, but it doesn't last long, maybe just part of a year. Another birthday comes and he's never twice as old again. He's just so many years older and it's not special any more. The magic is all in those few months. I think that's all it was ever meant to last.'

'It's been quite a year for both of us.'

'Yes.' Judy held up her glass of sherry. 'To the future. And bon voyage.'

She felt high sitting in the train out of London. Diana was going back to Frenchy. Davey's marriage was over for good but Frenchy's was back together and she knew they would be happy. For the first time since she had left him, she found herself hoping that Roy and Annie were together, that in the unusual off-again on-again relationship that characterized their marriage, they were happy. Her own mother would be very happy to have Diana back in the fold. It was the first move toward cohesion in nearly a year.

She leaned back and looked out the window. They had passed the grubby, coal-dusted near environs of London and were now out in the pretty countryside. The time had come to tackle the hardest questions of all.

Four

She could not think about him without becoming tearful and she recognized that the emotion had two opposing sources. What he had done to her mother was unforgivable and she would never forgive him for it. But there was all the rest. There were the years that he had been her god. There was the day he had come to Swarthmore to reassure her, and even if she hadn't understood what he was saying, she had appreciated the gesture and loved him for making it. There were all the things, big and little, that made him her father in deed. It was hard to set them aside but the anger she felt was still there, still very real.

It was funny how, when she thought about her father, her mind would flip over to Roy, as though there were some connection that she had never seen, something hidden that was waiting to be uncovered. Once again she would see herself in her father's chambers that afternoon last June, sense her revulsion upon hearing his confession and suddenly, there she was, sitting in Central Park with Roy. *I'm forty-two years old, Judith, and a member of the bar. I don't seduce little girls.*

It was she who had made the seduction speech. *I think I want you.* Knowing there was an Annie. Knowing there were children. He had *called* them the night before as she sat in the restaurant averting her red eyes from the curious.

She mounted a barrage of excuses against the onslaught of her own attack. *I was in trouble. I needed help. It was a crisis. I needed him.*

But you knew, the quiet, calm voice in her head asserted. He went home nearly every weekend to see his children. He talked to Annie about orthodonture and who knows what else. He had a family. You knew he had a family. And you weren't the first.

Did you know that at the beginning? Did you guess it? Would it have made a difference if you had known?

I wasn't the first, she said icily, but I was the most important.

The voice smiled.

I was. *I was.*

Sometimes she became so angry that she cried. Sometimes she flew out the front door, down the path that ran between the halves of the overgrown English garden that even now was starting to bloom. It was April and there were tulips. It was spring and there was life.

Why, she said to the voice in her head, are we arguing about Roy when I have to find out the truth about my father?

Why, indeed.

How could you have done such a thing? You? *He.* Some damned girl he met in a courthouse . . .

She drew in her breath and started back for the house.

I didn't mean to hurt anyone. I needed something and I didn't think. And her father's voice: *If there were one thing in my life that* . . . He would do it differently. He had as good as said it. If he had the chance, he would clean the slate, rub it out, eradicate the grief.

The memory of his words struck her with a kind of horror. Her father was full of remorse. And she – much as she wanted Annie to forgive her, much as she was sorry for the hurt she had caused, she knew, *knew* that if she could go back, if she had it to do all over again, if she had a second chance, she would do everything just – exactly – the same.

It was the final revelation. She had been looking at the wrong portrait. The truth she had discovered was about herself.

And she knew now she was ready to go home.

She wanted to put it off as long as possible. She had come to love this house. Judy Wolfe, who had never lifted a dust rag in her life, kept her four rooms spotless. Judy Wolfe, who had never washed more than a pair of nylons, now washed her clothes and set up an ironing board to press them. Judy Wolfe was going to law school on a very tight budget and looking forward to it.

The phone rang on the morning of May first and she got out of bed to answer it.

'Miss Judith Wolfe, United States calling.'

'This is she.' She pulled a chair over and sat down, a little breathless from her run down the flight of stairs to the only telephone in the house, a little chilly because mornings on Hawthorne Lane were always cold.

There were sounds and distant voices, then, 'Judy, this is Dad.'

She said, 'Oh,' and realized that her heart was beating wildly.

'How are you?'

'Fine. I'm fine.'

'I have some unhappy news.'

She waited, tense, not wanting to think what unhappy news might mean.

'My father died a few hours ago.'

'Oh. Oh, Daddy, I'm very sorry.' The first time in nearly a year that she had said it.

'I'd like you to come home for the funeral.'

'Oh course I'll come.'

'Good.' He sounded relieved. 'We'll hold it till Tuesday then. Can you get to the airport in London Monday morning?'

'Monday.' She looked around the tiny foyer of the Town-leys' house, the closed door that was the living room, the closed door that was the kitchen, her first private home away from home and she was leaving it tomorrow. 'That's tomorrow,' she said.

'Yes, I think it must already be tomorrow,' and she realized it was only four in the morning in New York.

'I can make it. I'll pack today.'

'Uncle Richard's on his way back now but Jeanne-Marie will be on your plane. They'll give you the ticket if you show them your passport. It's taken care of.'

The sudden flash of irony. Nearly three hundred dollars she had considered unspendable. 'Thank you,' she said.

'There's nothing to thank me for. I'm happy to pay for your flight home.'

'I'll see you tomorrow.'

'Yes. Tomorrow.'

Her aunt Jeanne-Marie never changed. She was tall with a long, slender neck and very dark hair that was always wound up in a way that suggested it had been set aside where it would do the least harm. She rarely stepped out without a camera or two slung over her shoulder or around her neck. Today the camera case was wedged under the seat in front of her and she sat unencumbered.

The stewardess collected the lunch trays and the man in front of Judy pushed the back of his seat irritatingly far so that she had the sense of being invaded. Her father had purchased a tourist ticket because Uncle Richard and Aunt Jeanne-Marie never travelled any other way. It was the way Judy had flown to England in December.

'Where do you stay in New York?' she asked, not recalling ever having visited them in their own residence.

'Near the Village,' her aunt said, the accent still strongly French although she was thoroughly fluent in English. 'Do you know Prince Street?'

'I've been there.'

'It's a nice little house.'

'I didn't know you owned a house in New York.'

Jeanne-Marie smiled and all the lines on her face joined the smile. 'We don't. It's Regina's. When they moved out about twenty years ago, they kept it and gave us the key.'

'Would you have room for me?'

'Of course, chérie.' Jeanne-Marie patted her hand. 'You aren't ready to go home yet?'

'No.'

'Then you'll stay with us.'

She slept for a while, but not for long. Flying west it never became dark. When they landed it would still be afternoon, still light. The time lost in December would be made up in May, life brought back in balance.

'How old was your grandpa?' Jeanne-Marie asked when Judy was again fully awake.

'Eighty-two this year.'

'A good life, eighty-two years.'

'He was sixty around the time I was born.'

'Yes, the same year as our George.'

'He's studying medicine now, isn't he?'

'In New York, yes. In New York.' Jeanne-Marie took a breath and let it out in a long 'Ahhh.' 'Always everyone wanted to be like Uncle Richard, to live in Rome and write for the papers and be invited to lecture. Frenchy came one summer and I thought he would stay forever. Davey came and we almost tied him up to get him on the plane.' She was smiling. 'Regina's son Ernie. All of them. Everybody wanted to be Richard. And for twenty-five years Richard says to me, "This is my last war." He said it in Spain in the thirties and then on D-Day I was sitting in Regina's apartment and shaking because I knew where he was and I thought I would never see him again. He came back after the liberation of Paris, after he saw what the *Boche* had done to the Goldblatts' house – '

'The Goldblatts?'

'Regina's friends. She lived there, you know, in the twenties, in better times. And Richard said, "This is my last war." So we went together to Korea and put George in school in Switzerland. No more wars after Korea, Richard said. Now I see he gets itchy again – '56 and he's itchy for Southeast Asia.'

'Mother says it's in his blood.'

'In his blood, yes, but that's the funny thing. Everybody wants to be like Richard except Richard's son. Today George studies medicine and talks about putting down roots.'

'Does that disappoint you?'

'Disappoint me? No. I'm not disappointed. I am just surprised that at fifty-seven I can still be surprised.'

She wore the black suit Roy had bought her last fall. It was too warm for wool, but she had no spring clothes with her. She sat between her father and Frenchy, amazed at the number of people her grandfather's funeral had attracted. They had all kissed when she arrived with her uncle and aunt in the car that had been sent to fetch them. She was still somewhat disoriented by the change in time and she had not slept well although the bed was comfortable.

The family gathered in the evening at her father's house and when Fern came to call, they arranged for Judy to move her things to Fern's the next afternoon. Before she left with her uncle and aunt, her father asked her to see him at four-thirty on Thursday.

She went down feeling tense and uncomfortable. They had said nothing personal to each other since her arrival and she knew everything they said this afternoon would be very personal. It was nearly a year, and the same day of the week as their last conversation.

She went into his office and he looked up from his desk and smiled. 'It's good to see you again.' he said.

'It's good to be back.' Two days and already it seemed as though England had never happened, as though it were a dream, all those months, those four rooms, London in the rain.

'Before we talk,' he glanced at his wristwatch, 'I'd like you to return the Buddha. The one I lent to you last year.'

She looked at him a moment, taking in the phrasing of his request, its implicit forgiveness. Then she dug in her bag and drew it out.

He took it and without looking at it put it in the centre drawer of his desk and pushed it closed. 'Thank you. I hope it served its purpose.'

'It did. I was very happy.'

'Then I'm glad you had it.'

She shook her head and it crossed her mind that what had happened a year ago had affected her more intensely than it had her father. He had never doubted her eventual return, never doubted the enduring strength of the bond.

'Do you have any plans?'

'Yale has accepted me for September.'

He was quite obviously surprised, more obviously pleased.

140

'That's wonderful news, Judy. You must have decided that you really wanted it.'

'I did. I learned a lot since the last time I was here.'

'One can't ask for much more out of life.'

'Well.' She smiled slightly. 'Maybe a little more.'

'Yes. Maybe a little more.'

'Yale's giving me a scholarship, tuition and enough to live on. I want to do this myself. I know how and I want to keep in practice.'

'Well.' He looked down at his desk and then up. 'Maybe you'll let me match Yale so that someone without your father's resources can have the same chance you're getting.'

'All right.'

'Grandpa Willy always said that those who could should pay. I won't get in your way. I'm sure you know that.'

Her eyes were full now. 'I know.'

'Are you at Fern's?'

'Yes.'

'Well, whenever you're ready, we'll be happy to have you back.'

'I'm not ready yet.'

Her father smiled. 'We've learned how to wait.'

She spent Friday shopping and being interviewed by a friend of Frenchy's who was looking for a secretary for the summer. When he gave her the job, she treated herself to some new clothes. It was time and she had money left from the unused airline ticket.

Late in the afternoon she met Fern at her West Side office and they went uptown together, Fern talking about her job, about a man whom she saw now and then, about how good it was to have Judy back.

They went in the front door and a head poked out of a first-floor apartment. 'Package, Miss Hall. For a Miss Wolfe. By special messenger, if you don't mind.'

'For me? But nobody knows I'm here.' She took it, rectangular, not too thick, medium heavy, and juggled it with her other packages as they walked up the stairs.

'Somebody must.'

In the living room, she tore off the brown wrapping, as curious and excited as a child. Her birthday was a week away but nobody had any idea . . . She saw the name of the store and said, 'Oh, Fern,' tears overflowing because she knew, knew exactly what it would be, knew that if she had thought about it, this would have been the thing, the only thing in the world she really wanted.

Inside the box, the tissue paper torn away, it was gleaming black and redolent of fine leather, JW in plain gold letters and inside the flap – she knew it without looking – Judith Wolfe. There was a card but it took minutes until she could see clearly enough to read it: Dear Judy, Welcome to the club. It just became a better place because you're part of it. Love, Dad.

Later that evening, she went home.

PART FOUR

April 1960

One

─────●●─────

It had not rained and that was a blessing since it was April and had been rather wet. Morty was south, Margot in her own apartment, and Adam away visiting Princeton, which was his first choice for fall. Regina had thus been left alone in the apartment with the maid and on nights like this, she preferred to eat in her study rather than in the large, formal dining room or the breakfast nook they had built into the kitchen. It was cozy and pleasant and the space conformed to her needs. When the phone rang, she was halfway through an article in the *Times* and nearly halfway through her main course.

'Hello?' she answered, expecting to hear Morty's voice at the other end.

'*Regine?*' It was Marcel, calling her by her name in French.

'*Oui?*' They had not spoken French for some time and she was surprised to hear it now.

'I'm afraid there's some trouble,' he continued in French.

'Trouble? What sort of trouble?'

'I'm in a police station.'

'*Attends!*' She completed her shift from table to desk. 'Yes, go on.'

'I've been arrested.'

'What?'

'I'm in a police station.' Articulating carefully. 'In Brooklyn. I don't know the address. I've been arrested.'

It was as though her capacity to think, to reason, to solve problems had suddenly deserted her. One of those times when she wanted to say, Morty, I need help. But she was alone with the maid. She was all the help Marcel could get.

'All right,' she said as calmly as she could manage. 'Find out please where you are. I'll be there with a lawyer as soon as I can.'

'*Merci.*' There was the sound of voices, then he returned and gave her the address.

'Are you all right?' she asked, her voice now echoing the fear. 'They haven't – they're treating you all right, aren't they?'

'I'm fine.'

The old childish affection for the men in blue mingled with the adult apprehension, the stories she had heard. 'It'll take an hour. Just wait. I'll be there.'

She sat at the desk for a moment after she hung up, wondering what she would do, whom she would call. Morty would take care of this better than she but Morty could do nothing over the phone. She didn't even know what the problem was, had been afraid to ask. What could Marcel have done? What could they *think* he had done? She picked up the phone and, because it was a personal affair, because she trusted her family with personal problems, she called Frenchy.

It was a part of life she had never experienced. After the police station, she and Frenchy drove to the court where they met Marcel, who was brought over in a police van, a drab, fearful-looking vehicle that kept its occupants locked in.

The magistrate who meted out instant justice was greying and appeared to be weary but why shouldn't he? Regina thought. What kind of a life could he have, seeing accused men and women – a fight with a policeman, a shoplifting, a mugging on a dark street – whom he would never see again and deciding on the spot: go home, spend the night in jail, let someone else make the interesting decisions on your life and alleged crime. Still, there was the title, the required respect, the eventual pension.

Frenchy was very calm, very professional. He looked like what he was, a well paid, well dressed young lawyer who commanded his share of respect – but did not demand it. Regina glanced around the courtroom once and then kept her eyes to herself. She was an object of curiosity, well and expensively dressed although she had not thought about it. She realized that she would always stand out in a crowd like this. Marcel, on the other hand, seemed pivotal. He was extremely clean, but he did not look rich. He was dressed as though he cared nothing for clothes, but he did not look poor. The contrast between him and Frenchy disturbed her. There were only two years between them but one was on his way and the other was appearing before a Brooklyn magistrate, having been caught in the street with stolen drugs.

They sat in the back of the Rush car, the only car Morty ever felt completely comfortable in, a long, black Cadillac limousine that made heads turn as it passed. It was late now and they were all on their way back to Manhattan. She had identified herself to the magistrate and seen his eyebrows lift slightly as she gave Park Avenue as her address. When he set bail at ten thousand dollars, Marcel had been visibly shaken but Frenchy had contacted a bail bondsman and the arrangement had been made quite easily. The Park Avenue address and the bail had been enough to let Marcel come home with her.

Frenchy sat facing them as the car worked its way through the streets of Brooklyn, the borough in which she had been born fifty-five years ago, but she could not get her bearings. Not that it mattered. It was the question at hand that she had to think about. It occurred to her that Frenchy was still very young, that this was not the kind of case one entrusted to the young, although he had handled everything as though he were often called upon to bail out clients.

'We have a date before the grand jury a week on Monday,' Frenchy said. 'That gives us a little time. We're going to get you a lawyer who's experienced in cases like this, Marcel. He may decide to waive the grand jury appearance, but that'll be his decision, not mine.'

'I think I ought to plead guilty,' Marcel said. It was the first thing he had said since they had left the court and he had said very little there, merely answering questions.

'You're not pleading guilty to anything.' Frenchy said it pleasantly but there was no question about his determination.

147

'I'm guilty, Frenchy.'

'I'm not asking whether you're guilty. I'm saying you're going to get a fair trial.' Speaking with a very ordinary calm, his father's son.

Marcel leaned back and closed his eyes.

'You don't have to worry about spending any time in jail. The bail has taken care of that.'

There was a silence and then Marcel said, 'Thank you,' as though he thought it necessary to acknowledge Frenchy's last remark.

'Regina – ' Frenchy said.

'What is it?'

'You don't intend to talk to my father about this, do you?'

'I don't intend to talk to anyone – except Morty.'

'That's fine.' Frenchy leaned back. 'Then I think we'll call Roy Kellems.'

He was moderately tall, slim, sandy-haired, and he wore glasses. It occurred to Regina as they shook hands that he was different. By choice or accident, most of the people she dealt with professionally were Jewish. While this man did not have the looks of a Wasp chairman of the board, he looked very much not a Jew. She wondered if it would matter. She wanted Marcel to be able to trust him but in fact, she did not know, after all these years of knowing Marcel, what kind of people he trusted, what kind of people he liked. She got along with him but beyond that, she knew very little about what he did, who his friends were, what on earth he wanted to do with his life.

Frenchy had reached the new lawyer from the Rush apartment and they had agreed to meet at Kellems' office at nine this morning. On the way down, they had picked Frenchy up at his apartment. Frenchy was living alone in the East Sixties. It was ten months now since the child had been born, nine since he and Diana had separated. Diana was abroad this month and there were no rumours about whether the separation might end. The child was still alive but no one knew for how long.

148

The perfunctory pleasantries over, the two lawyers moved away and spoke quietly for a moment. Then they shook hands.

Frenchy looked back to where Regina sat on the chair next to Marcel's. 'I'll give you a call this evening, Regina. And don't worry. You're in good hands, Marcel.'

Regina smiled and watched him go, her cousin who had not disappointed her when she needed him, like all her cousins, like Jerold.

The lawyer came back and took a chair facing them. 'Frenchy tells me you're his cousin, Mrs Rush.'

'His father and I are first cousins.'

'The judge.'

'Yes. My cousin Jerold.'

'A nice family,' the lawyer said.

'You know them.'

'I've known the judge for a number of years. I took his seminar at Columbia – that must have been '51 or '52. I admire him very much.'

She could sense herself relaxing.

'Mr Goldblatt.' The lawyer turned to his client. 'May I call you Marcel?'

Marcel looked at him for a moment as though making an assessment. 'Of course,' he said. 'Please.'

'I think we should set up an appointment when we can talk.' Kellems stood from his chair, leaned over his desk to reach a book, flipped a few pages, and ran a finger down one, stopping near the bottom.

'I don't have much to say,' Marcel said.

'Then it won't be a long appointment.' Kellems smiled cordially. 'I have a date in court this afternoon. Shouldn't take too long. How's four? I'll have a chance to look at the police report by then.'

'Four's fine.'

'Nothing formal,' Kellems said. 'No need to dress.' As though he sensed that the suit and tie had been worn for this occasion, to make the right impression. He reached into his jacket and took out a fountain pen and made a note on the

149

page. 'Just take the subway down and tell my secretary you're here.'

'OK.'

Kellems looked at his watch and closed the book. 'I'll be in touch, Mrs Rush,' he said and they all stood and went to the door.

'Do you want to tell me about it?' They had gone home for lunch and were sitting in Regina's study. Marcel had changed into slacks and a sport shirt. He looked pale and very sober. His birthday was coming in the next few days, his twenty-fourth.

'If you don't mind, I'd rather not.'

'If there's something we can do for you – besides the lawyer.'

'You think I'm on drugs.'

'I don't know what to think.'

'Regina, I want to plead guilty to this. I am guilty. I would be lying if I told you I didn't take those envelopes.' Four envelopes. Twenty-eight pills each in three envelopes. Thirteen in the fourth. A drug called Demerol.

'You can't plead guilty. It means jail now and your whole life later. You plead guilty and it's there forever. It follows you.'

'I don't think I care.'

'I care. You'll talk to the lawyer this afternoon.'

'Yes.' He put his fork down and moved the plate very slightly, indicating he was finished. He had changed physically in the last two years, becoming broader, more substantial. It made it easier somehow to talk to him. He was no longer the skinny child who ran away from his aunt's apartment as a protest against all the things he could not control in his life.

'Morty's coming home tomorrow night. We'll talk when he gets here.'

'There's nothing to talk about. I took the pills. It wasn't the first time. I suppose I knew they would catch me eventually. I'm just sorry it happened so soon. Let me pay my debts and try to forget it.'

'You weren't – selling them, were you?'

'I told you, Regina, there's nothing to talk about.'

'I can't understand why you called Frenchy,' Morty said. He had returned a day early and they sat in his library. It was late afternoon and Marcel had gone downtown to keep his appointment with Kellems.

'He's family. He was the first person I thought of.'

'He's a kid. He just got out of law school. We've got a staff of lawyers at Rush, any one of whom could have handled it for you and probably better.'

'I didn't think of them.' It was true though. One of their lawyers had got a salesman out of some serious and embarrassing trouble the previous year. 'When there's trouble, I think of my family. Besides, he's not just out of law school. He's been in practice nearly two years.' She knew what was bothering him. He thought that if Jerold were still in practice she would have called him. He was right.

'Who's this guy he recommended?'

'He's a trial lawyer. A defence lawyer. Frenchy said he's the best.'

'Did you make any other inquiries?'

'Morty, there's a grand jury hearing a week from Monday. We need to be represented. And I rather like him.'

'I'll make some phone calls,' he said. 'See what I can find out about him. It doesn't hurt to ask questions. You don't mind, do you?'

She looked at him and knew that in his own way, he was as nervous and upset at what had happened as she was. But for him there was something else too, the old ghosts. She had called Frenchy and gone along with his recommendation. Well, she thought, if he didn't like Kellems, they could always change lawyers. It wasn't worth internal strife to stick to their first choice. 'Of course I don't mind,' she said. Then she smiled. 'Thanks for coming home early.'

★ ★ ★

Marcel called that he would be late and when he arrived, he came with his suitcase. 'He thinks I should stay here,' he said to Regina.

'I'm glad. I'd like you nearby till this is over.'

'For the address,' Marcel said. 'Park Avenue sounds better than the Village. For the trial.'

'Yes, of course.'

'He says we should waive the grand jury hearing.'

'Hello, Marcel.' It was Morty, walking into the hall from the direction of his study.

'Hello, Morty.'

'Everything all right?'

'Fine.'

Regina watched tensely, hoping the friction between them would not surface at this already uncomfortable time. Morty would do anything for Marcel but she was not sure Marcel understood that. It still pained him that Morty wanted him to try working for Rush.

'Why are you waiving the grand jury?' Morty asked.

'Because Kellems says they'll indict. It's a waste of time. He wouldn't let me say anything anyway under oath.'

'That sounds kind of pessimistic.'

'Realistic,' Marcel said. 'I was carrying stolen drugs.'

'So I hear.'

There was a silence and Regina knew Morty was waiting for the inevitable explanation, the words that would clear Marcel, that would make everything that had happened understandable, acceptable. But no one spoke.

Finally, Morty said. 'Well, I'll be going upstairs,' and the conversation was over.

The next day was Friday. Regina and Morty ate their usual early breakfast but Marcel did not join them. About midday, the lawyer's secretary called Regina at the design studio.

'Mr Kellems would like to see you, Mrs Rush. Is there a time next week you might have an hour or two?'

'Any time. I'll work my schedule around his.'

'Then how would Tuesday be? About ten?'

'Ten will be fine.'

'Thank you, Mrs Rush. Mr Kellems would like to speak to you now, if you have a moment.'

'Yes, of course.'

There was a click and then the lawyer picked up the phone. 'Mrs Rush, Roy Kellems.'

'Yes, Mr Kellems.'

'You don't mind Marcel staying with you for a while, do you?'

'We're glad to have him.'

'Sometime in the next few days, he may want to talk to me.'

'The weekend is coming up,' Regina said, glancing at her calendar.

'Exactly. And I wouldn't want him to think that Saturdays and Sundays are off limits. I won't be in my office but he has my number at home. If he wants to talk to me, encourage him to use it.'

'Has something happened?' She heard the eagerness in her voice.

'No, nothing has happened. I think Marcel has a decision to make. A painful one but an important one. And quite soon. When he makes it, he'll have to tell someone.'

'Thank you. I'll keep my ears open.'

When she got home, the maid said Marcel had taken only a sandwich for lunch in his room and would not be down for dinner. Later, while Regina and Morty were relaxing in Morty's study with newspapers and television, there was a knock on the door.

'I'd like to go to Connecticut,' Marcel said, coming in. Connecticut was their summer home.

'Now?' Morty asked.

'Yes. Right now.'

'I'll call the caretaker,' Regina said before Morty delivered an opinion.

'Here's my car key.' Morty reached into a pocket for a keyring and detached one key. 'Regina has the registration.

153

You'd better be careful. It's Friday night. Everyone's leaving the city for the weekend.'

Marcel looked visibly relieved. 'Thank you,' he said, looking at both of them. 'Thank you very much.'

Regina met him in the hall with the car registration. He looked drawn, his eyes hollow. 'The phones up there work,' she said. 'If you have to call anyone – ' She left it hanging.

'I'm not calling anyone,' he said, taking a jacket out of the closet. 'I just have to think.'

She sweated through the weekend, wanting to call him in Connecticut and knowing she should not. Whatever it was, he would work it out alone or not at all. He did not return until Monday morning and by then Regina was already at work. The maid called to say he had arrived, had made a long telephone call, and would not speak to her.

The next morning she came punctually at ten to the lawyer's office and was shown in almost immediately.

'Did you get your phone call, Mr Kellems?' she asked.

'Phone call?' His forehead wrinkled. 'From Marcel. Yes, I got the phone call.'

'Does it affect Marcel's case?'

'It does.' He was obviously not a man to give anything away.

'Does it mean you can get an acquittal?' she asked, trying to pin him down.

'No, it doesn't mean that, Mrs Rush. This isn't a case where I can promise you an acquittal. The phone call means we have a strong case for forgiveness.'

'Forgiveness,' she echoed.

'That's right. Any other questions?'

Regina smiled. 'I don't think you're going to give me any more answers.'

'I'm sure you know why. If it's relevant, it'll come out in the trial. If it isn't, it really doesn't make much difference.' He smiled and his tone changed. 'I think we can use a strong character witness at the trial, Mrs Rush. I don't suppose you'd mind taking the stand for Marcel.'

'Not at all.'

154

He pressed a buzzer on his desk. 'My secretary will take some notes as we talk. Pretend she isn't even here.'

They were sitting in the chairs away from the desk and when the secretary came in, their backs were nearly to her so that she was almost invisible.

'You're not a relative of Marcel's, are you, Mrs Rush?'

'I'm afraid I'm only a friend.'

'Sometimes a friend can be worth a dozen relatives. Why don't you tell me how you came to know him. I'll stop you if I have any questions.'

Regina sat back in the chair and thought for a moment. 'Well,' she began, 'I suppose it goes back to 1923 when I was nineteen.'

'That sounds like a good place to begin,' Roy Kellems said.

That evening Morty came home with a report on Kellems. 'There were some surprises,' he said. 'Everyone I called had heard of him and everyone had an opinion.'

'Good or bad?'

'Depends what you're talking about. His personal life isn't exactly clean.'

'Morty, is he a good lawyer?'

'They say he's very good with a jury. He's had a few successes that everyone remembers. I'm just not sure he's the kind of guy you'd want to invite to your home if your daughter was going to be around.'

'What do you mean?' Unpleasant visions rippled in her mind, a mother's fears.

'He has a wife, but it's an on-again off-again thing. There are other women. That doesn't always sit well with judges. They're a moralistic bunch, even if they're out doing the same thing themselves.'

'You're probably right.' She felt struck, suddenly, by a mild wave of nausea. She had handled this all wrong. She had allowed her instincts to prevail instead of her intellectual acumen. She had called family when she should have called a professional and in doing so, she had hurt Morty. Marcel would disclose nothing about what had happened. He came and went, brooded in his room, ate alone. In six days he was visibly thinner. Right now he was having his second appointment with Kellems, a longer one than the first. It was nearly dinnertime and he had not returned.

'I have some names here.' Morty drew his small notebook from his jacket pocket and opened it. 'I met one of them once. Kind of a nice guy. Easy to talk to.'

'If you think we should make a change,' Regina said, 'of course we will. But we should ask Marcel first.'

The phone rang and Morty answered. 'Marcel – how's it going? . . . Sure . . . Sure . . . We'll see you later then.' He hung up and turned to Regina. 'He's having dinner with the lawyer.'

'Dinner?'

'That's what he said.'

'We'll talk to him when he comes home.' But she felt torn. She liked Kellems and she felt certain Marcel did. And beyond liking, she sensed a competence that was very satisfying.

'One of the people I called told me something kind of interesting.'

She looked at him, waiting. She had known there was more. At the beginning of the conversation he had said there were some surprises.

'Kellems had an affair last year. A girl moved into his apartment. The guy who told me about it said the girl was Judy Wolfe.'

'Judy . . .'

I've been living in someone's apartment since last June . . .

You don't intend to talk to Dad about this, do you?

Everything becoming clear except the reasons. Everything fitting into place except why.

'When Marcel comes home,' she said, feeling weary, feeling spent, 'we'll talk to him about changing.'

'I think that's a good idea.' He looked at his watch. 'Well, I guess we don't have to wait dinner.'

* * *

'Let's not talk about it,' Marcel said. It was nearly ten-thirty and he had just walked in.

'What's wrong?' Morty asked.

'Nothing's wrong. I've talked about it all night and I don't really want to go through it again.'

'Do you like this guy?'

'Kellems?' Marcel shrugged. 'He's fine.'

'You getting along with him?'

Marcel looked slightly dazed, as though the question had thrown him off balance. 'What do you mean?'

'I mean we got him in a hurry. There are other good attorneys around. Plenty of them. You're not stuck with this guy just because he took you to dinner tonight.'

Marcel looked quickly at Regina and then back at Morty. 'I don't want another lawyer,' he said. 'This one's OK. This one's fine. I want to get this over with. I don't want to fool around changing lawyers.'

'I just want you to know,' Morty said, and there was no doubting the sincerity in his voice, 'you're not married to this guy. If you change your mind, if you decide you want someone else, we'll get you another lawyer.'

Something that Regina had never seen before glimmered in Marcel's eyes, the look of being backed into a corner. 'I don't want another lawyer,' he said in a voice that seemed barely under control. 'I want Kellems. Do you have something against him?'

'Nothing,' Morty said evenly.

'I like him. I want him. He's the only person in this whole fucking business I can talk to.'

'That's what lawyers get paid for. You pay them enough, they take your case and they listen to you.'

'You want to believe that, you believe it. You're paying for this, you can do anything you want. But if you hire someone else to represent me, I'll ask Kellems to do it anyway and I'll pay him afterwards.'

For a moment, Regina was afraid Morty would ask, With what? and renew the old argument, but he ignored the challenge. 'I'm not hiring anyone else,' he said. 'I just want you to know that whatever you want, you can have.'

'I want it behind me. I want it over.' He looked briefly at Regina and then back at Morty. 'You have no idea what I've done. You don't have a scrap of an idea. I don't mean the drugs. That was the least of it. I've compromised someone. I've betrayed a trust. I don't mind fucking up my own life, it isn't worth much anyway, but someone else's . . .' He shuddered slightly.

'Does Kellems know this?' Morty asked.

'He knows. He knew before I told him.' His voice was very low.

'Then he must be good,' Morty said, giving in gracefully, as always a gentleman.

'Then lay off him, OK? Just let it happen. I don't want to talk about it and I don't want to hear about it. I only moved back because Kellems thought I should. When this is over, I'm leaving.'

'Marcel,' Regina protested.

'Good night.' Marcel walked out of the library.

'Well.' Morty ripped from his little notebook the page with the lawyers' names and crumpled it into a ball. 'I guess it's Kellems.'

She was a few minutes behind Morty going upstairs, having taken the tray of coffee things to the kitchen first. Marcel's door was open and as she passed it he called her name.

She stopped at the doorway, feeling the full impact of the growing misunderstanding. This was her son as much as Ernie whom she had picked out of a folder of photographs in 1932, as much as Adam whom she had borne the day before Morty's fiftieth birthday, the son for whom she had made the grand effort and remained a wife, and they had reached an impasse. She could not speak and he could not understand. Across this threshold was his room, once a room into which she could walk without thinking twice and now the room of a stranger.

'I'm sorry,' he said.

'There's nothing to be sorry for. We're all very edgy.'

'Come in.'

She stepped inside. It had been Ernie's room until his marriage. They had not changed the furniture, only the curtains and bedspread, a new rug, a new television set.

'I owe you so much,' he said.

'Owe? Love doesn't incur debts. It's given freely.'

'What does Morty have against Kellems?'

'Nothing. He doesn't know him and never heard of him before last week. He just wants to be sure you have the best.'

'He was in France,' Marcel said.

'He?' She could not think whom he meant.

'Kellems. The lawyer. During the war. He came over after the invasion.'

'I see.' A bond. Something that would appeal to Marcel. It had not occurred to her that they would discuss anything besides the case. 'I know that means something to you but it shouldn't deter you if you think he's not doing his job, if you think someone else could do it better.'

'No one can do it better. I took the pills. You know that, I know that, the police know that. I expect to pay for it.'

'We'll see,' Regina said.

The next Monday was the grand jury hearing. Marcel waived his right to appear and it was all over quite quickly. When they left the court, it was nearly noon.

'I'm going to take my client to lunch, Mrs Rush,' the lawyer said as they walked out of the building. 'I hope you won't mind being excluded.'

'Not at all. I have an office to go back to.'

'Of course. You're a textile designer, aren't you?'

'I keep my hand in it.'

'My wife paints. She's quite good. One of my daughters seems to have inherited some of her talent.'

'It's nice to pass it along. We don't seem to have that kind of luck.'

They stopped at the sidewalk. 'I'll be in touch, Mrs Rush: we're going to try for an early date for this trial.'

'Oh?'

'I think Marcel would like to have it behind him.'

Marcel did not acknowledge the remark. Standing beside Kellems, he looked anything but a prospective defendant in a drug case. He was wearing a dark suit, white shirt and conservative tie. His shoulders were broad but he was not as tall as the lawyer. He looked very respectable, very solid.

'The date makes no difference to us,' Regina said.

'Fine. Then we'll make the district attorney happy and settle on an early date.'

Sunday was the first of May. As on so many Sundays before, Morty began packing in the afternoon for an evening flight south. When the phone rang, Regina was in the bedroom, sitting with him, making notes of things he wanted done in his absence.

'Hello?' she said, setting the notebook aside.

'Regina, this is Edith.'

Edith. It was a shock, nearly as much of a shock, she thought later, as if Jerold had called. 'Yes, Edith. How are you?' Morty glanced at her and then went back to his packing.

'I'm afraid I have sad news,' Edith said. 'My father-in-law. Late last night. It seems to have been a heart attack.'

'Oh, no.' Uncle Willy, of all of them, her favourite. She saw Morty stop and focus his attention on her.

'The funeral will be Tuesday,' Edith went on. 'I hope you'll – '

'Yes, of course. We'll be there.'

'I know that will please Jerold. Richard is on his way from Rome.'

'Is there anyone I can call for you, Edith?'

'Well . . .' Edith hesitated and then went on uncertainly. 'If you have the time, I would appreciate your calling Lillian.'

Regina smiled. Lillian was no one's favourite. 'I'll call right now.'

'That's very kind of you, Regina.' Edith sounded sincerely grateful, unexpectedly so, as though she had not anticipated a kindness from her husband's cousin after so many years of neglect.

'We'll see you on Tuesday.' She hung up and looked at Morty, who had not moved. 'It's Uncle Willy,' she said, feeling the weight begin to descend. 'Last night. A heart attack. The funeral's Tuesday.'

Morty said something vile under his breath, his reaction to tragedy, and she knew he cared as much as she. Uncle Willy had set up their first partnership over thirty years ago, had known the answer to every question, had always been there.

After a moment, Morty began to unpack his suitcase.

There was an enormous crowd and it made her happy. Uncle Willy had been generous and kind and he had been loved. No one in the family had ever needed while Uncle Willy was alive.

Regina sat sombrely, her gloved hand through Morty's arm. Here and there in the crowd she picked out the cousins. Millie had come in from the farm in New Jersey and her sister, Adele, from Newark. For Adele, attending a funeral on a Tuesday meant missing a day of school, something she conscientiously avoided. Lillian and Aunt Martha sat beside Henry, who must have cancelled his office hours, and Sylvia, who looked permanently unhappy. Only Cousin Arthur was missing, the errant cousin who gambled away whatever he earned but retained the undying devotion of his sisters.

It was not until the brief service was over that she saw how completely the family was represented. They had entered when it was too late to speak to anyone and as the crowd broke up, she saw them: Diana walking with Frenchy, Davey with Judy beside him. Jerold had them back. He had lost his father but his children were home.

They walked outside to the street and she hugged her cousin Millie, who was in tears, heard Henry's wife say something foolish, caught a glimpse of Judy, too thin somehow but beautiful, slipping into a limousine at the kerb, and she had an absurd, irrational, overwhelming desire to go to a family wedding again, to sit at the table with all these people that she loved so much, she the only child in the family, all that love among the bickering.

'Come on, let's get out of here,' Morty said, pressing the gloved hand, and she knew he had seen and misinterpreted the tears.

'Yes.'

'We'll have lunch somewhere.'

'All right.'

They started down the street to their car, which was waiting just around the corner. It was May and Uncle Willy had died and after today the next important event in their lives would be Marcel's trial.

Two

Spring dissolved hotly into summer and there was nothing but dissension. Morty called Kellems and made an appointment to see him. He was courteous, Morty said afterwards, but he would not answer questions to Morty's satisfaction. Kellems' reason for doing what he was doing was generally that it was his judgement that this was the best way. Morty wanted chapter and verse. Kellems would not comment on how Marcel came in possession of the drugs or what he had intended using them for.

'You're not my client, Mr Rush,' Kellems had told him. 'You're paying the bill. Marcel Goldblatt is my client.'

'You know what we've done?' Morty said to Regina the evening of his appointment with the lawyer. 'We've abdicated our responsibility and handed it over to a twenty-four-year-old kid who's never demonstrated that he can make it in this world.'

'I don't think it's as bad as that,' Regina said, trying to soothe.

'You know, between us we have a lifetime of experience in business and we're acting as though we didn't know one damn thing. I don't like anything this guy has done. Maybe he could have beaten this before the grand jury but he didn't take the chance. He and Marcel are thick as thieves but he doesn't say anything to us except send us bills. Now he wants an early trial. Why? Because he has holiday plans? Why doesn't he take some time and prepare carefully? I don't know, I suppose I just don't like lawyers.'

As though it were all coming out after eleven years. It crossed her mind that perhaps he even resented her visiting

Kellems alone in his office, as if Kellems were a stand-in for Jerold, as if he did not trust her with a lawyer. For Morty lawyers were people who wrote contracts, who sued and defended against suits. What they practised was a skill developed from knowing where to find the answers to questions. If it was in black and white, if it was in a book they all agreed to consult, then it was law. What Kellems practised was something else – art, theatre, perhaps witchcraft.

'Except Uncle Willy,' she said in answer to his last comment.

'Willy was different.'

'Morty, I don't think Kellems was a mistake.'

'How do we know?' he asked with agitation. 'When do we find out – when they take Marcel off to jail? Listen to me. We got him on the recommendation of a twenty-six-year-old, we're keeping him on the advice of a twenty-four-year-old, he sleeps with little girls – what the hell is wrong with us?'

What was wrong was everything. What was wrong was Jerold. What was wrong was Marcel. What was wrong was that it was out of Morty's control and when he lost control, he lost confidence.

Nothing got better. By July it was sweltering. A date in August had been assigned for the start of the trial and Regina had had Marcel measured for three summer suits so that he could look fresh daily. She and Morty took brief trips out to their home in Connecticut but they did not relax. They talked about the trial and about Marcel and they worried. There was no indication that Marcel would be acquitted. Nothing had happened to show them why he had taken the pills. He was as silent as if he were uninvolved.

Suddenly, three-quarters of the way through July, Kellems called and said Friday had become available and he wanted to get started. Marcel said fine and that was it. On Friday morning she went to downtown Brooklyn with him to watch the jury selection.

The pool was a wilted and motley assortment. A man in his fifties who complained that his business was going to pot without him was excused by the prosecution. An imperious-looking schoolteacher who had never married was excused by Kellems. One by one they were questioned, examined, appraised, excused. Someone complained that Kellems was taking too much time. Kellems remained very calm. He did not shout or whine or plead. He looked at the judge and the judge allowed him to continue his questions.

It was late afternoon when the jury was finally assembled and Regina saw what Kellems had achieved: An elderly widower with arthritis, his cane beside his chair. A grand-motherly type with thick glasses and steelgray hair. A heavyset woman with a strong accent wearing a plaid cotton dress with long sleeves that she kept buttoned even through the worst heat of the afternoon when everyone else was fanning himself with a newspaper. Under one of those sleeves, Regina was willing to bet, a number was permanently marked on the skin, something the assistant district attorney, whose name was Murphy, was too young to know much about, but Kellems would know and he was betting along with Regina. When Regina gave her 'character sketch', these were the people who would weep.

Old rather than young, several Jewish names, not the healthiest group she had ever seen, one Negro woman with glasses and beautifully greying hair who had been widowed ten years earlier and had raised her only son herself.

It was too late when they had all been seated to begin and the judge recessed the proceedings until Monday morning. So be it. These twelve people would decide Marcel's fate.

When Monday morning came she was terrified. Morty was spending the week in New York but they had agreed he would not attend. She and Marcel went to Brooklyn in a taxi. It would not do to have a member of the jury see them leaving a limousine that cost as much as he earned in a year.

The fear had come over her during the weekend. Suddenly she appreciated the way Morty felt. They knew nothing. They had no guarantees. At the end of this week Marcel might be going off to prison and nothing they could do would stop it. She had put all her faith in a man she did not know and if the faith had been misplaced, Marcel would pay the price.

She sat where she could both watch the jury and glance over to the table where Marcel, Kellems, a young man and a young woman sat. Marcel had left her abruptly as they entered the courtroom and she had not been able to kiss him or wish him luck. She wondered if the lawyers, like actors in a play, walked into court the first morning with stage fright. He had seemed so composed on Friday, so in charge. Why could she not believe that he was?

The juror with the cane was the first to appear and the rest came in clumps so that no one was last. The judge arrived at the crack of nine-thirty as he had promised and as the trial got under way, she listened fearfully, but with interest, as the opening statements were delivered. We will prove, and she shuddered. Ninety-seven Demerol pills stolen from a nurses' station in a large hospital.

Why ninety-seven? she asked herself. Eight dozen plus one. But they were not packaged in dozens. They were divided into three envelopes of twenty-eight and one of thirteen.

Finally the man named Murphy called the first witness, a policeman who appeared in uniform, took the oath, sat in the chair, and answered the questions in a matter-of-fact, almost bored monotone. He stated his name and rank as though reading from a printed form and testified that on that Wednesday night in April (how long ago it seemed now, and how cool) he had arrested the defendant (he said *dant* as though it rhymed with can't) on the corner of this and that in Brooklyn at a certain time, having found on his person ninety-seven on and on; she looked at the jury, twenty-four eyes fixed on the policeman, hypnotized by the drone, concealed in two pockets – concealed. Did he expect a person to carry four envelopes in his hand? To wave them at passers-by? Later determined to contain . . . The whole case was in this man's brief testimony, which even Kellems did not contest in his short cross-examination. Kellems showed him a piece of official-looking paper and asked if he had filled it out after making the arrest and if that

166

was his signature. The policeman looked down at the paper, up at Kellems, and said, 'Yes, sir.' Then Kellems entered it as evidence and resumed his place at the table.

As quickly as that the first witness stepped down.

The second person called was Gail Fontana, a girl in her twenties with dark hair and somewhat uneven teeth. She was dressed in a sleeveless black blouse and matching straight skirt, tight around her hips, which showed knees and thighs as she sat. White high-heeled shoes with an obvious smudge, and a white handbag that she clutched rather nervously.

The assistant district attorney was very pleasant to her. What was the nature of her work?

'A nurse's aide,' she said. 'I work the floors. But I might go for my RN,' she told him with an air of confidentiality, 'if things go right.'

Could she identify the defendant? She looked for the first time toward the defence table and pointed, looking away quickly as though what she had seen had been very distasteful.

'And how did you come to know him?' Murphy asked.

'I was changing a bed one day and he came in to take a patient to therapy. We kind of – ' she shrugged, 'smiled at each other.' Her accent was deep Brooklyn. Othuh. Earlier, 'floors' had sounded like 'flaws'.

He asked a few more questions and finally got to the point.

'It was February,' she said, pronouncing it *Febuary*. 'In the afternoon, around the time the shift changed. He was at the nurses' station and no one else was around. I saw him empty a bottle of pills into an envelope.'

'What did he do with the envelope?'

'He put it in his pocket.'

'Did he seem to be aware that you had seen him do this?'

'No.'

'Did you know what the pills were?'

'I went back later, after he was gone. They were the Demerol.'

'Is it the usual procedure to put pills in a pocket?'

'No, sir.'

'And did you ever see him again at a nurses' station putting pills in an envelope and putting the envelope in his pocket?'

'Lots of times.'

'Every day?'

'Maybe once or twice a week?' She said it like a question, as though wondering whether the information would please Murphy. 'I guessed he was meeting someone after work to sell – '

'Objection,' Kellems said and everyone on the jury turned to look at him.

'Sustained.' The judge turned to the witness. 'Just answer the question, please.'

'I'm sorry,' the girl said, gripping her handbag more tightly.

'What did you do after you had observed this incident several times?'

'I stopped at the police station on my way home and told them.'

'And what did they advise you?'

'To call them the next time I saw him do it.'

'And did you call them on April thirteenth?'

'Yes.'

'Thank you.'

Murphy nodded at Kellems and Kellems stood and came forward.

'Miss Fontana,' he said pleasantly, 'when did you meet Mr Goldblatt?'

The girl shrugged. 'Last fall sometime. That day he came up when I was making the bed.'

'Back then, in the fall, did he seem to work conscientiously, to do his job well?'

'I think so.'

'Was he helpful to you?'

'Oh, sure. Like if something was heavy, he would help me lift it.'

'Was he kind to the patients – like the patients he took to therapy?'

'Oh, yeah.'

'Would you characterize Marcel Goldblatt as a friendly, helpful person?'

She looked at Murphy and then back at Kellems. Then she said, 'I guess so.'

'You testified a few minutes ago that when you saw him at the nurses' station on that first occasion, he emptied a bottle of pills into an envelope. How large was the bottle that he "emptied"?'

Quite suddenly she became flustered. He hadn't exactly *emptied*. He had poured some of the pills . . . Was it possible he had counted them? Possible, yes. She looked unhappy. He pursued. The size of the bottle and its capacity. A thousand? Five hundred? And the size of the envelope. She wiped sweat from her upper lip. Kellems, dressed in a tan summer suit, looked cool, almost cold, a man without sweat glands. The jury was sweating with the witness but they were rapt.

With almost no transition, he switched his questioning.

'Were you and Mr Goldblatt friendly last fall, Miss Fontana?'

'We were friendly.'

'He was helpful to you at work.'

'Yes.'

'And did he sometimes take you for a drink after work?'

'Beer,' she said as though 'drink' might have meant 'cocktail' and implied a generosity he had not shown.

'And did he sometimes take you to a movie?'

'Sometimes.'

'Or dinner.'

'Yes. A couple of times.' She looked distinctly uncomfortable now.

'And after the beer or the movie or the dinner, did you from time to time return to Mr Goldblatt's apartment with him?'

The girl's eyes widened and she looked pleadingly at the judge as Murphy shouted his objection.

'Overruled,' the judge said. 'Get to the point, Mr Kellems.'

'Yes, Your Honour.' He turned back to the witness.

'Answer the question, please,' the judge ordered.

169

She swallowed and said, 'Yes,' in a low voice.

'On those occasions when you were in Mr Goldblatt's apartment, did you have an intimate relationship with him?'

Murphy was shouting again, the girl was on the verge of tears, and Regina looked at the twelve faces. One man raised his eyebrows. Another smiled slightly. The heavyset woman with the buttoned sleeves, today wearing a dress of light green and white, looked at the witness stonily.

The gavel came down, halting the argument between the lawyers.

'Answer the question,' the judge said testily.

The girl had taken a tissue from her white bag and used it to blot her eyes. She looked angrily at Murphy as though perhaps he had reneged on a promise or failed to warn her adequately. She nodded her head and the judge told the jury she had answered affirmatively.

'How long did this intimate relationship last?' Kellems asked.

'Till January,' she answered softly.

There were a few more questions – when it had ended, how, how long afterwards she had first seen Marcel Goldblatt at the nurses' station pouring pills into an envelope. He did not prolong her agony. The point had been made and it had escaped no one. Regina found herself feeling sorry for the girl. To save his client, Kellems had to destroy. This was not a game in which anyone won a clear victory.

After she was excused, the prosecution put a pharmaceutical researcher on the stand. First he was qualified as an expert. Then he began to testify on the nature of Demerol. The testimony was dry and technical, words spat out of an encyclopaedia. Meperidine hydrochloride. A white crystalline substance, with a melting point expressed in Celsius. A bitter taste. The effect upon it of boiling.

Then Murphy pushed home. Could he describe the clinical pharmacology? I can, the expert said confidently, and went on to do so. It was a narcotic analgesic with effects on the central nervous system qualitatively similar to those of morphine.

The word brought a small, collective intake of breath and then a hush. It was the first time morphine had been mentioned. Until that moment, they had been talking about pills, little white tablets, medicine stolen from a nurses' station. Now they were talking about morphine.

And did there exist, Murphy asked, the possibility of addiction from repeated use of Demerol?

Quite frequently. Meperidine often produced the same kind of drug dependence associated with morphine and had the same potential for being abused. That was why it was available only by prescription and was subject to the provisions of the federal narcotics laws.

Murphy asked a few more questions and then sat down.

Kellems' questions had to do with pain. Was it likely that Demerol would be prescribed for a mild pain such as a headache? No. For what we might call moderate pain, a woman in labour? Yes, sir, but not orally. For severe pain, a patient suffering, let us say, from the effects of cancer? Yes, sir. It was often used in cancer treatment, especially in terminal patients when the problem of dependency was less acute.

When he was finished, it was after eleven-thirty and the judge recessed the trial for lunch. They would return at one-thirty and Regina knew who would take the stand first in the afternoon. The prosecution had concluded its case and Kellems wanted to start with a character witness. She went to find Marcel to take him to lunch, but she knew she would not be able to eat. She was next.

The heat was terrible. When they left the air-conditioned restaurant and stepped out into the street, it struck them like a wall. There was nothing but a fan in the courtroom and already before lunch, ties had been loosened, shirts unbuttoned. The judge used a handkerchief from time to time on his face but Kellems and Marcel did not show their discomfort, if they felt any.

Kellems had disappeared as soon as the lunch recess was called but he was at his table when Regina and Marcel returned.

171

'I suppose he'll call you first,' Marcel said with an echo of regret.

'I think so.'

'I'm sorry to do this to you.'

'There's nothing to be sorry for.' She knew he could sense her nervousness. Mostly, it was the idea of speaking in public that was causing it. Kellems had assured her it would not be hard. He would ask her questions and she would answer them. It would be as easy as that morning in his office a few months ago. But even then she had become tearful and she did not want to lose her composure in public.

The fan was whirring but the room was stifling. Kellems called her and she walked slowly to the front of the room. It occurred to her with some irony that she was wearing black also, as the last female witness had. But Regina's dress, a simple black shirtwaist of imported cotton, was a much more expensive and sophisticated version of the Fontana girl's tight skirt and sleeveless blouse.

She raised her hand and was sworn in and then Kellems came forward and smiled at her, relaxing and disarming her, Judy's lover, although Regina still could not believe it, this cool, calculating man who destroyed people to save his client.

He led her quickly through the distant past, slowing down in the thirties to allow her to tell how she and her husband had written pleading letters to their friends in France to leave while they could, how she and her husband had booked passage for the end of August 1939. She heard someone to her left, someone in the jury, draw a breath that was more like a gasp of recognition but it was so hot, it might only have been a difficult intake of air. She kept her eyes on Kellems' cool grey eyes, almost colourless eyes, and she spoke to him because he was now her friend. No one else was. She had glanced at Murphy a moment ago and seen the look in his eyes, stoic patience. He had proved his case this morning. The defendant had stolen ninety-seven pills of an addictive drug and had been caught with them on a street corner in Brooklyn. Nothing that she said

172

this afternoon could contradict that. All they could do now was create a sympathy that Murphy would demolish in his closing argument.

'Did you get to France, Mrs Rush?'

'The sailing was cancelled.'

'And then what happened?'

'War broke out two days later.'

'Did you try to contact your friends some other way?'

'My husband tried to telephone. The lines were down to Europe. They weren't restored until well after the end of the war. We didn't hear from them for a long time.'

'When was that?'

'After Paris was liberated.' She could hear her voice changing. 'A letter came.'

As though she had said something shattering, a sudden silence descended on the courtroom. Following the direction of the silence, she realized that the fan in the rear corner had stopped. Also, the little lamp over the stenographer's machine had gone out. There had been a power failure.

The stenographer, without missing a beat, reached for pen and paper. Kellems paused only long enough for everyone to turn once and verify the absence of the fan. Then he said, 'The letter from France. What did the letter say, Mrs Rush?'

'She wrote that she and the children were all alive.'

'The children. Was Marcel Goldblatt one of the children?'

'Yes. He was about nine.' She could remember that day when the letter came, the tissue-thin sheets with the story of the war in blue ink. Death had been in every line. She opened her bag and drew out an embroidered white handkerchief, catching a glance of the jury. They looked haggard, glistening. The men had their jackets off. One woman was pressing a handkerchief to the vee of her neckline. Only the woman in the green and white dress did not move, did not blot sweat, did not show pain.

There was a small commotion in the rear of the courtroom and everyone turned. Two men in work uniforms stood near the fan, talking, scarcely trying to keep their voices down.

173

The judge pounded his gavel and spoke in an angry voice for the first time. 'Quiet back there. I will not have this testimony interrupted.'

The men looked at him, then turned and walked slowly out of the room.

'Please continue,' the judge said in an apologetic voice. 'I'm very sorry for the interruption.'

'The children,' Kellems prompted, and this time he spoke very quietly because there was no fan, no sound, no breathing. 'The children all survived. What of their parents?'

Regina shook her head. 'Only my friend Suzanne lived through the war.'

'And Marcel's parents?'

'They never came back.'

'You say they never came back. Then they weren't killed by the bombs or guns of war.'

'Oh, no. They weren't that lucky. They finished their lives in a death camp.' She did not want to look at Marcel. In all the years he had lived with them or near them, she had never told him about the letter from Suzanne. She touched her eyes with the handkerchief and looked to her left. Every member of the jury was watching her and the woman in green and white had begun to unbutton her sleeves.

When Kellems had finished with her, about fifteen minutes later, Murphy waved her away. He would ask no questions. She went back to her seat and avoided eyes. As she sat, the fan started up with an uneven whirr and the breeze it stirred seemed almost cool. The stenographer adjusted his machine under the little lamp. She could scarcely believe how long she had been on the stand. It was close to three.

At the front of the room, Kellems and Murphy were speaking to the judge. After a moment, they withdrew to their separate tables.

'It's quite hot,' the judge said, looking at the jury, 'and Mr Kellems' next witness cannot appear until tomorrow morning.

174

We will recess until then at nine-thirty.' And with a bang of the gavel, the day was over.

In contrast to the streets, the courtroom was comparatively cool when they arrived the next morning. The fan was going and the windows were open. Marcel had said nothing on the way down and had left her as soon as they reached the courtroom. The evening before he had taken dinner in the kitchen with the maid. This morning he seemed distinctly unhappy.

There was a delay in starting and the judge seemed testy. Kellems had said this judge was strict about punctuality. The first witness was a woman in her fifties, Ann Mooney, Marcel's former supervisor at the hospital.

'What is your profession, Mrs Mooney?' Kellems asked.

'Registered nurse.' The voice of a commanding officer, the solid build of an armed guard.

'In what capacity did you know Marcel Goldblatt?'

'I hired him.' A statement of fact. 'He reported to me.'

'Would you describe the kind of employee you found him to be?'

'Agreeable. Hard-working. Effective.' The words came out like three pistols shots.

'Did you ever observe him removing anything from the hospital that did not belong to him?'

'No, sir.'

'Did you ever see him handling drugs of any kind?'

'No, sir.'

'Did anyone ever report him to you for stealing or misusing drugs?'

'No one.'

Regina the mother crossed her fingers. Regina the realist knew that a policeman had stopped Marcel on the street and found four envelopes of an addictive drug concealed on his person and none of this could eradicate that fact. A case for forgiveness. A lighter sentence. A suspended sentence. Guilty any way you looked at it. A record for life.

'Did Miss Fontana inform you that she had seen him pouring Demerol pills into an envelope and secreting them in his pocket?'

'She did not.' A hint of anger. She had been bypassed. An underling had abused the chain of command.

'Were you aware that drugs had been taken from a nurses' station?'

'I was aware.'

'Is it a common occurrence?'

Ann Mooney paused. 'These things happen,' she said in a softer voice, an apologetic voice.

'Then what Miss Fontana has testified to observing was not an isolated incident.'

'It was not isolated.'

'Were drugs stolen before Mr Goldblatt began to work at the hospital?'

'They were.'

'And since he has left?'

A sigh. 'Yes. Since has has left.'

'Can you tell us which people have access to the drugs stored at the nurses' stations?'

Ann Mooney took a breath. 'The rule is that the cabinet is kept locked and can only be opened by the nurse on duty. In practice, it doesn't work that way.'

'How does it work in practice, Mrs Mooney?'

'The cabinet is frequently left open because the nurse on duty may not be immediately available and a patient may require medication while she's gone. You can't go chasing after the nurse for the key.'

'And at such times drugs can be stolen?'

'Yes.'

'Did you have any reason to suspect that Marcel Goldblatt was one of the people responsible for the disappearance of any drugs?'

'I did not.'

'One last question. What kind of patients receive Demerol?'

'People in pain. Cancer patients very often.'

176

'Thank you, Mrs Mooney.'

Murphy was angry. Did Mrs Mooney mean to say that the hospital *tolerated* the stealing of drugs? That they *accommodated* it? That it was widespread and still the cabinets were left unlocked and unattended? And then there were her hiring practices. This young man had been little more than a drifter. Had she investigated him at all before taking him on? Was she aware of his work record or lack of it? Had she asked for no references? Or had she hired him in the same careless, hit-or-miss fashion with which she left drug cabinets open while knowing that the stealing of drugs – of addictive, morphine-type drugs – was rampant in the hospital? Or course Gail Fontana had not reported what she had seen to Ann Mooney. It was clear to Gail Fontana that Mrs Mooney would do no more about such a report than she did about keeping her drugs under lock and key.

Ann Mooney defended herself well but she was no match for Murphy's relentless attack. She stooped down, a tired-looking woman. She looked at no one as she left the courtroom. She had been put to shame as the Fontana girl had. Regina could only wonder who would be next.

'We call Mrs Grace Meade.' Kellems looked toward the back of the courtroom. The door opened and a uniformed man pushed a wheelchair inside. Seated in it was a small, white-haired woman sitting very erect and wearing a summer suit of a deep pink shade, a pale pink blouse, and a small straw hat. Accompanying her was a nurse in full white uniform.

Kellems went to the wheelchair and bent to the occupant. She shook her head and proceeded to stand, aided by Kellems and the guard, and watched intensely by the nurse.

'You may remain in your chair,' the judge offered.

'No thank you,' a crisp voice answered.

Marcel looked at her once and then down at the table as Regina took in the whole scene – the rapt jury, the unmoving members of the prosecution table, the tiny woman who was Kellems' secret weapon.

Quickly through the background. Age seventy-eight, eighteen

years a widow, a small house in Brooklyn where she had sometimes taken boarders, one son whom she had not seen since 1957, the disease that everyone feared and that would claim her soon enough. She did not smile, she did not cry, she looked only at Kellems. Once she faltered and the nurse stood quickly but the young woman at the defence table brought a glass of water and Mrs Meade said, 'Thank you,' drank from it, and continued.

'What kind of medication were you on, Mrs Meade?'

'A drug called Demerol.'

'And what effect did Demerol have on you?'

'At one time it eliminated my pain. After a while it only reduced it to where it was bearable.'

'How often did you take it?'

'Four times a day.'

'Four times a day,' Kellems repeated. 'Twenty-eight times a week.'

'That's right.'

And that was it, Regina thought with enormous relief. Three envelopes, each containing twenty-eight tablets, and one he had not yet filled completely.

'You had a prescription, Mrs Meade?'

'I did.'

'From a doctor.'

'Yes.'

'And how often did you fill it?'

'Every two weeks on a Friday.'

'Until when?'

'Until I became unable to reach his office. It was the end of January.'

'And what happened then?'

'I endured the pain until the young man came to see me.'

'What young man?'

She turned her head toward the defence table. 'That one,' she said without pointing. 'Marcel Goldblatt.'

'How did you come to know Marcel Goldblatt, Mrs Meade?'

'I was a patient at the hospital for a while. Later, when I

178

came for my appointments, he would help me to the hospital pharmacy to fill my prescription. He would find me a taxi. He paid for it too, sometimes, though I didn't like to take it. That's all. Just kindness. Just common decency.'

'Mrs Meade, did you telephone the hospital or a doctor who had treated you when you became unable to visit him?'

'The phone's been gone over a year. It was a saving.'

'Did the doctor try to get in touch with you some other way?'

'No, sir.'

'Or his nurse?'

'No, sir.'

'Or anyone connected with him?'

'No one.'

'Tell us what happened when Marcel Goldblatt came to see you.'

He had promised to get her the pills. He had bought groceries for her. Once the pain had receded, she was again able to keep the house in order although it would never be as it once had been.

'Then you would say he did you a service?'

'If you can call saving a life a service.' She looked toward the defence table where Marcel sat, still looking down. 'You don't have to be afraid to look at me, young man,' she said. 'You haven't done anything to be ashamed of.'

But the judge disagreed. The gavel came down heavily. 'The jury will ignore that comment. Please confine yourself to answering the questions, Mrs Meade.'

'Where are you living now?' Kellems asked.

'They've got me in a hospital,' she answered, her voice wavering for the first time. 'They won't let me stay in my house any more.'

'Thank you, Mrs Meade.' Kellems nodded deferentially and went back to his table.

Murphy rose slowly. The heat was beginning to accumulate and he had an unpleasant task ahead of him.

'Did Mr Goldblatt offer to take you to a doctor, Mrs Meade?'

'No, sir.'

'Did he ever bring a doctor to your house?'

'No.'

'Did you know that the medication he brought you was stolen?'

'I was in pain, sir.'

'I understand that and I am not unsympathetic. I am asking you if, when the medication alleviated that pain somewhat, you understood and accepted the fact that the pills had been stolen?'

'If I had thought about it, I would have known.'

'When Mr Goldblatt was arrested on April thirteenth, did the pills stop coming?'

'I had a terrible weekend. I thought – for the first time in my life, I considered taking my life.'

'I'm sorry.' Murphy sounded sorry. He sounded very human, very concerned. 'What happened after that weekend?'

'A social services woman came to my door.'

'How did the social services woman know you were in need of help?'

'I believe she was called by Mr Goldblatt's lawyer.'

'I see.' Murphy looked quietly triumphant. 'And that's how your testimony was paid for.'

'My testimony is not for sale.' Grace Meade said archly, setting her shoulders resolutely.

'Thank you, Mrs Meade.'

After lunch, Kellems called a doctor to the stand. He seemed as decent, concerned, and harried as any doctor Regina had ever met. She listened while his reputation was attacked, while his life work was diminished. Everyone was sweating again except Kellems. The doctor defended himself bravely but the jury looked at him harshly. He had abandoned his patient. He had made no inquiries. He had left a woman who might be suffering intractable pain. He had acted in a fashion that no one on the jury could condone.

They were older people, Regina saw now, who would

themselves be in need of medical care. They had all lived through the take-two-aspirins-and-call-me-in-the-morning experience. They all needed and loved doctors but at the core there was fear, there was hate.

Murphy resurrected him. They discussed the frequency with which patients changed doctors, the propriety of calling a patient to ask why he had stopped coming for his visits, the impracticality of this invasion of privacy and free choice. When he stepped down, the doctor looked wilted and angry but some of his self-respect had been restored. Regina wanted to apologize. It had become such a nasty business. Murphy had been right. Marcel could have called a doctor. He could have called a city agency. None of this would have escaped the jury. There was no case for acquittal and several lives had been damaged in the quest.

'The defence calls Detective Sergeant Michael Polovichak.'

There was a stir from the prosecution table, a rumble, a flurry of voices. From outside the courtroom a man in uniform entered. He walked down the aisle and looked at the people who had reacted so strongly to the sound of his name. He took the oath and sat in the witness chair. It was late and hot and there was no hope and Regina could not imagine what Kellems was doing. He had not proved innocence. He had only stirred emotions. Perhaps Morty had been right. Perhaps another lawyer – other lawyers – would have done the job better. She knew why Marcel had done what he had done and she loved him for his caring and thoughtfulness, but Murphy had proved his point. There was other ways. Marcel had destroyed himself.

'Would you identify yourself for the jury, please?' Kellems asked.

The policeman rattled off his name, rank, precinct.

Kellems was holding a piece of paper in his hand. 'On April thirteenth,' he said and then read off all the information on the arrest report that had been entered as evidence the previous morning – the time, the place, the circumstances, the name of the arresting officer – 'where were you, Sergeant Polovichak?'

'I was there, sir.'

'Did you in fact make the arrest, Sergeant?'

The policeman looked at Murphy and then back at Kellems. 'I did, sir.'

Murphy stood and Kellems, as though he had seen Murphy with the back of his head, stopped questioning. 'Your Honour,' Murphy said too loudly, 'the prosecution would like to approach the bench.'

Kellems had turned to watch Murphy deliver his brief request and Regina saw him standing there, the arrest report in one hand and a glint of something in his eyes that might have been recognition, might have been satisfaction, might have been something more.

The two lawyers walked forward and had a short conversation with the judge. When it was over, the judge looked at his watch, pounding the gavel, and said, 'We will recess for twenty minutes. You may step down, Sergeant.'

Regina watched with curiosity and a sudden surge of hope. Everyone seemed confused – the twelve members of the jury, the handful of spectators. The lawyers left with the judge, the jury went out their special door, and everyone else moved to the back of the room and out into the hall.

She caught up with Marcel in the back of the courtroom. 'What is it?' she asked.

'Something,' he said. 'Maybe nothing.' He looked as he had through the entire trial, neither happy nor unhappy, but accepting. 'Have you told Suzanne about this?' he asked.

'No.'

'Please don't. OK? Whichever way it goes.'

'All right.'

'I want to find the water fountain.'

She walked to where she could feel the movement of air from the fan. It was after three. The sun would be high. Perhaps next week they could go to Connecticut and swim in their cold, spring-fed lake with the waterfall that emptied into the creek below. Perhaps Ernie and the children would come. Perhaps Margot would come for a long weekend. Perhaps

Marcel would be free to join them. They would be a family again.

The jury began returning. The man with the cane was first as usual. The heavyset woman was next, today wearing a grey shirtdress with long sleeves rolled to just below the elbow. The mark on her forearm was plainly visible. She smiled at Regina, her first smile, and Regina smiled back, feeling that kinship that came upon one at moments like these, thinking, please be kind to my most difficult child.

They stood as the judge returned and then, to Regina's surprise, he asked that the jury be taken out of the courtroom. When they were gone, Murphy asked to speak.

'The prosecution moves to dismiss all charges against the defendant.'

As Regina inhaled surprise and joy, a murmur arose from the spectators who had sweltered through the trial for reasons Regina could not imagine. The judge banged the gavel and said, 'Let's have it quiet, please,' and Regina thought, My God, he's done it.

Kellems sat in his chair, looking somewhere between Murphy and the judge so that all Regina could see was his profile, a very straight nose, glasses, a classic shape. He was the only person in the room who seemed unsurprised, unmoved.

'I trust you have considered this move carefully, Mr Murphy,' the judge said, his testiness returning.

'I have, Your Honour.'

'The state has gone to considerable expense to assemble this jury and try this defendant.'

'I apologize to the state, Your Honour, and to the jury.'

'Please bring the jury back.'

They filed in, bewildered, fanning themselves, and took their seats.

'The charges against this defendant are hereby dismissed,' the judge declared. 'I appreciate the cooperation of the jury. These have not been comfortable days and you have shown yourselves equal to the heat and accompanying discomfort.

183

You are now free to leave. Mr Murphy, I would like to see you in my chambers in ten minutes.'

'Yes, Your Honour.'

It was over. Stunned, Regina did not move. At the defence table, Kellems patted Marcel's shoulder and spoke to him. The jury began to move out of the box and she heard the words 'unbelievable' and 'lucky' and 'travesty' as they passed her row.

She stood and made her way to the defence table. Everyone was standing and the two younger lawyers were smiling brilliantly. Of all of them, Marcel seemed the least elated, the least affected by the outcome.

'Go ahead,' Kellems was saying to him. 'There's still plenty of time.'

'OK.' He saw Regina. 'You OK?'

'Very OK.' It was not an expression she used.

'I probably won't be home for dinner. I'll see you in the morning. I'd just rather not talk about it tonight.' He loosened his tie.

'Shall I take your jacket home?'

'I think I'd better keep it with me.'

'Get moving,' Kellems said gently.

But Marcel stood very still. 'Thank you,' he said.

'My pleasure, Marcel.'

'Even so.'

'Marcel,' Kellems called after him. 'I see you tomorrow.'

'I'll be there.' He smiled, waved, and left the courtroom.

'Are you going to explain it to me, Mr Kellems?' Regina asked.

'Explain? Oh, you mean what just happened.'

'Yes.'

'We took a gamble and we won. That's all. Actually, there was nothing to lose. If they hadn't asked for dismissal, we still had the rest of our case.'

'I don't really understand.'

'Marcel will explain it to you. Tomorrow afternoon, after he sees me.' He had begun to look tired, worn, as though it had all

184

caught up with him at this moment. There was sweat on his face, fatigue in his eyes.

'May I buy you a drink?'

He smiled and she had the impression that his eyes might be blue after all instead of the hard grey she had thought they were. 'I'm afraid I don't drink, Mrs Rush, but I thank you for the invitation. I think I'll be heading home.' He had a hand on the back of a chair and he looked exhausted now.

For the first time in her life, she felt as if she had been turned down by a man. 'Thank you, Mr Kellems,' she said.

He nodded and picked up his briefcase. She watched him go, taking in the now empty courtroom as she turned, where the jury sat – what had become of the woman with long sleeves? – where the judge had presided. Kellems was nearly at the door. Between his shoulder blades, his jacket was soaked. The cool, calm machine had suddenly become human.

And then she understood. This was the man Judy had known, not the machine with cold grey eyes but this man disappearing down the hall, this tired, hot, successful creature who had needed her.

Something about lawyers. Something about being young. She found that she was crying. It was over. The jurors were gone from her life forever. But Marcel was free. He had been young and angry and stupid but now he had a second chance.

Three

'But what was it about the policeman?'

They sat in Regina's study over a cold lunch and a Chablis that Morty would not approve of because it still tasted faintly of the oak it had been aged in, a taste Regina rather liked.

'There were two of them that arrested me,' Marcel said, 'but only one name was on the arrest report. Kellems hired a detective and found out about Polovichak. He's been doing some work for the Brooklyn district attorney's office, a big drug ring they're trying to nail. Polovichak thought I was part of it. When he saw that I was really nobody, he pulled out of my arrest. They're afraid of the publicity. The whole thing is down the drain if the guys they're after get wind that the police are onto them. Murphy knew Kellems would expose everything. Kellems wanted to make a deal before the trial began, but they were still looking for Polovichak last weekend.'

'So when they saw him they gave up a conviction to save something much bigger.'

'Sure. It makes sense. I'm not the kind of person they waste time on. Polovichak wouldn't even have been there if he'd thought I was acting on my own.'

'He was a good choice, wasn't he? Kellems.'

'Regina, I'm very sorry. I acted very stupidly. I won't again. I want to make it up to you and Morty.'

'There's nothing to make up. Especially if you're sorry. Maybe it was just a lesson you had to learn.'

'Maybe. But I have some thinking to do now. I talked to Kellems this morning.'

'Why don't you take some time off, a trip maybe. You can think while you're away, or when you come back.'

186

'I can't go anywhere, Regina.' He looked down at the glass which she had just refilled for him. 'There's no one else who can visit her. Kellems wouldn't let me near her after I was arrested. You have no idea how sick she is.'

It was where he had gone yesterday afternoon. 'Of course.'

'I didn't want Kellems to put her on the stand. I was afraid of what the DA might do.'

'I think she enjoyed it, Marcel. No one's going to hurt her.'

'It's too late now anyway.' He looked at his watch. 'I'd better be going. I'll be back for dinner.' He kissed her on one cheek, then on the other.

She felt a great resurgence of hope, of satisfaction. He had come through. Everything was going to be all right. 'How did you like the wine?' she asked lightly as he headed for the door.

He grinned at her. 'It'll be great in a few years. Little too much tannin.'

She smiled, poured another glass, and sat back to enjoy it.

The cook had made a beautiful dinner. For the first time in months, they ate together, talked, enjoyed each other's company. Tomorrow, Thursday, they would leave for Connecticut for a long holiday. When he could, Marcel would join them for a weekend. There was a sense of high spirits at the table.

'I want to make you a proposition, Marcel,' Morty said as they began their salad.

'Thanks, but I think I'm not ready for any propositions.'

'It seems to me,' Morty said, 'that you need to build up some continuous work time, so your resumé looks good. If you come to work for us, even part time, you can do that.'

'Thank you, I don't think I'd like to do that.'

'You can't hang around doing nothing very long. Employers ask questions. You don't want a big gap in your record.'

'Morty,' Regina put in, 'I don't think Marcel's quite ready yet to – '

187

'Morty,' Marcel said, 'I don't want to work for a textile company.'

'This isn't "a textile company". This is Rush. This is your family.'

'I understand that. There are some things I have to think about. Maybe then I'll be able to – '

'You can think on the job. You can think nights. Marcel, you've been in one hell of a lot of trouble. Turn over a new leaf while you have the chance.'

'I've been talking to Mr Kellems – '

'Marcel, he's a lawyer. Your relationship with him ended yesterday when that trial ended. That's it. It's over. I'm making you the kind of offer that will put you back on your feet. Stay with it as long as you want. Stay forever. Leave next year. There are no hurt feelings if you get something better.'

'Morty, I don't want to work for Rush.' The voice controlling anger the way it used to in the old days, the bad days.

'Look, I've heard you say that before. I've also seen you mess up your life. I don't want to see it again. You've got a reprieve. Use it, for God's sake.'

'Excuse me,' Marcel said. He stood and turned toward Regina. 'Excuse me. Thank you both for everything. I've decided to move back to my apartment.' His voice was terrible, hard, everything suppressed. 'I'm leaving now.'

'Don't go tonight, Marcel,' Regina said, the old heartbreak returning.

'I think it's better for all of us if I do.'

She watched him leave the dining room.

'Coffee, Mrs Rush?' the maid asked.

'No thank you,' Regina said.

'I'll have mine in the library.'

'Yes, Mr Rush.'

'Don't tell me I'm too hard on him, Regina.'

She shook her head. 'It's a misunderstanding,' she said. 'It's nothing either of you can do anything about.'

'I cannot let him louse himself up again.'

'No.' She folded her napkin. 'I'll come along in a little while,' she said.

She went upstairs but the door to Marcel's room was closed and she did not knock. Downstairs in her study, she shut the door and sat at her desk. It wasn't Marcel, it was the company. Morty had fathered it and no one would keep it going. It was a constant hurt and now the hurt was spreading.

She heard the door close. He had left. *Some*body had to talk to him. Oh, Richard, why aren't you here this summer? You could talk to him. All the boys went to you and came back happy. My son needs to come back happy and to whom can I send him?

She looked at the telephone. It was almost a challenge. Funny that she remembered the number although it was more than a decade since she had called it.

'Judge Wolfe's residence,' the maid answered.

'Judge Wolfe, please.'

'One moment.'

'Hello?'

'Jody, it's Regina.'

'Regina. I thought I was the only one still in the city.'

'Jody, I need you to do something.'

'Of course.'

'It's Marcel Goldblatt. Maurice's son. There's been terrible trouble. Morty can't talk to him. He just doesn't know how. But someone must. Someone must very soon.'

'Give me his number.'

She recited it from memory. 'He'll be there in less than an hour. If he won't talk, you must go to see him. It's so important.'

'Of course it's important. I'll speak to him this evening.'

'If you could just *listen*.' She was overcome now, in tears. 'He needs someone to listen. I know you can do that for him.'

'I'll do whatever needs to be done.'

She let her breath out. 'Thank you.'

'Good night, Regina.'

She hung up, feeling better, feeling that something had been done. It was only a few minutes later, when she had rung the maid and said she would have coffee after all, that she realized she had said nothing personal to him, they had said nothing personal to each other. She had called as though he were Richard, had asked him a favour, and said good-bye. She was nearly fifty-six. Such a long time coming.

'I'll take it in the library,' she said as the maid came in with the coffee tray. She was sorry to make the extra work but she was not thinking very clearly. She was thinking of Marcel and Jerold and her own life and her own husband. She went to the library and tapped on the door.

The coffee tray was on the table, the larger pot, two cups. Morty would expect her.

She sat but did not pour. 'Morty, let's go away somewhere for a long time. Six months. Maybe a year.'

'I can't take off that much time.'

'Take it. I'm asking you to.'

'What about the company?'

'I don't *care* about the company.'

'You want me to sell?' The subtle difference in the question: You want *me* to sell? As though she had already relinquished her interest by not caring.

'Morty, you're going to be sixty-eight in three months. I want to spend time with you. I want to do things with *you*.'

He sat very quietly for a full minute. Then he said, 'I'll think about it.'

PART FIVE

April 1964

One

———◦●◦———

Davey was a little late – he had never been known for punctuality – and Judy ordered a glass of sherry while she waited. He was in town for some conference or other at which he had spoken this morning at a midtown hotel but he had declined this evening's banquet at which his philosophical colleagues would attempt to be entertaining but, he had said over the phone, would undoubtedly fail. He had elected instead to dine with his sister.

She looked up and saw him following the waiter and she beamed. He looked wonderful, the beard carefully barbered, the hair a little on the long side but well cared for. There was something to say for marriage.

'Hi, Kiddo.' He bent and hugged her, the beard brushing her cheek.

'You're good to look at.'

'And you're drinking already.' He turned to the waiter. 'Bourbon on the rocks. A little water on the side.'

'Yes, sir.'

'Show me pictures.'

Davey wrinkled his nose. 'I didn't think you would deteriorate into a maiden aunt so fast.'

'It's not deterioration. It's choice.'

'Aha.'

His drink came and he mixed carefully, then held the glass in a toast. 'To us,' he said.

'And to Mark.'

'Accepted.' He drank, put the glass down. 'How about a hot date with a cool philosopher?'

'I'll think about it. Let me see the pictures first.'

He put an envelope on the table, obviously prepared. Judy took the pack of snapshots out and went through them slowly. The first was Marilyn, Davey's wife of just over two years. She was small with a round face and dark hair – that much reminded one of Rena – but she was quite slender and only slightly busty. She was very pretty.

'Gorgeous,' Judy said, turning to the next picture as Davey made a comment of agreement. The little boy was a small Davey and something ached every time she looked at him. 'Is he walking yet?'

'Almost. Marilyn thinks I'll miss it being away this week.'

'Michael walked at one.'

'Jesus,' Davey said theatrically, 'you *are* a maiden aunt. Do you know when the teeth came in too?'

'Only the first one,' she teased. 'I know about Michael because Diana called to tell me. We're kind of buddies. From way back.'

'You're everybody's buddy. How about the cool philosopher?'

'You can give him my number.'

'He's a real comer,' Davey said. 'Marry him and you could find yourself the wife of the chairman of the department at the University of South Dakota.'

'Then I wouldn't see much of him, would I?'

'My sister, the lady lawyer.'

'Your sister, the lawyer,' she corrected him pleasantly. 'Your sister, the blissfully happy lawyer.'

'OK, OK. All you women with your jobs you love.'

'All? Are there many at Brown?'

'I was thinking of my wide range of acquaintances.'

She lingered over the last snapshot, then tapped the collection into a neat pile and put them back in the envelope. 'When he gets older, I'll take him away somewhere.'

'When he gets older, he'll take *you* away somewhere. He's a great kid.'

'Planning any more?'

'I think we should stop while we're ahead.'

Marilyn had miscarried once during their first year of marriage and the family had held their breath. The second pregnancy had been perfect. Mark Jordan Wolfe was perfect. It was now just a year since they had all stood together on a misty April day in 1963 as Frenchy's first son was buried. He had died of pneumonia before his fourth birthday and it was Diana, more than anyone else, who had seemed shattered.

'You're way ahead, Davey.' She patted the envelope of pictures and he took it and put it in a jacket pocket.

They paused to order and went on talking about his philosophy and her law. He had got his doctorate the year before, within a few days of her graduation from law school. Brown had made him an offer to stay on and she had had an offer from a law firm specializing in constitutional issues. It was a long way from the love of her youth, but a summer with a law firm that practised criminal law had convinced her it was not for her. Mostly nowadays she did research, but she was having a good time and they were even paying her for it.

'Three guesses who I saw walking through the lobby of the hotel this afternoon,' her brother said when they were eating their main course.

'Bobby Kennedy,' she began, knowing she would not be let off the guessing hook too easily.

'We're not at the Carlyle and you're way off base. Remember old Maxwell Rosenberg?'

'Oh, Davey.' She felt a momentary depression, a dip in spirits. 'Forget Mr Rosenberg. He was just a silly character in our lives when we were kids. There was nothing else to it.'

'That's what you think.'

'That's what I *know*. That's what you know too.'

'What is it, age? Or did you never really believe me when we were kids?'

'A little of both.' She saw the disappointment in his face. 'Age,' she said firmly. She had never disclosed her father's secret and she would not do it now. 'It's all much harder to believe now than it was then. I'll be twenty-six next month.'

195

'You're still a kid,' he said, lightening. 'Wisdom comes at twenty-eight. You'll see.'

'I hope so.' She sipped her wine. 'Staying with the folks?' she asked.

'Nah. Brown's paying for a hotel room. You know me, I never say no to a free airline meal or a free hotel room.'

'I know you,' his sister said gently.

Two

The philosopher was terrible. She wondered sometimes about Davey, about how he maintained the assorted friendships he claimed. Anyway, it was a one-dinner engagement as he taught in Boston and would not be down in New York again for a long time. For that she was grateful. Like so many of the men she had met since her return to the States nearly four years ago, he assumed she would accept his sexual advances gratefully. Like the rest, he was wrong. Age had made her more, not less, choosy. Well, perhaps it was experience rather than age.

It was now the Monday after her dinner with her brother. It was close to four-thirty and she had just concluded an interview with an elderly client whose offices were in the Empire State Building, a client too old, too respected, and of late too infirm to ask to go downtown. He had been somewhat put off that one of the partners had not shown up but Judy had managed to impress him suitably. Her boss had told her not to bother returning to the office after the interview and looking at the rush hour traffic on Thirty-fourth Street, she was glad of the reprieve. She started to walk east toward Fifth when she remembered suddenly that Regina's office at the design studio was not far from here and it was months since she had visited. Switching directions, she about-faced and walked west.

The lift in the building housing the studio opened and several young people walked out. At least some of them, Judy thought, must be Regina's designers. She hoped she wasn't too late. In the short walk from the Empire State Building, she had found herself looking forward to seeing Regina.

She got off the lift and went down the hall. Inside the design studio's door, the receptionist was putting away the paraphernalia of her job so that her desk would be neat tomorrow morning.

'Am I too late to see Mrs Rush?' Judy asked. 'It's a personal visit.'

The receptionist looked up. 'She's still here, wandering around, I think. Hold on and I'll try to find her.'

The receptionist disappeared through a door and a few minutes later reappeared with Regina.

'Judy!' Regina said, beaming. 'What a nice surprise. What brings you here?'

'Proximity and some time on my hands.' She leaned over to kiss her cousin. 'And I thought it would be nice to see you.'

'Come on in, or can I take you somewhere and buy you a drink?

'No, thanks. I'm having dinner with the folks tonight. I'd better save my appetite.'

They went into Regina's office and sat in two chairs away from the desk.

'You've done it over,' Judy said admiringly.

'A long time ago. You haven't visited me here for years. Morty's always after me to display my stuff. How do you like the rug? It's one of my designs.'

'Super.' Judy knelt and touched the rug with her palm. 'Feels good too.'

'It should,' Regina said with a knowing smile.

'Dad says the Museum of Modern Art has some of your designs in their collection.'

'It took thirty years, but I'm awfully pleased.'

They talked until nearly five-thirty. 'I ought to be on my way,' Judy said finally. 'Dad likes to eat promptly.'

'I don't blame him. Why don't we share a cab?'

They found one heading down Seventh Avenue and sat back for the drive north and east.

'You know,' Regina said when they were not too far from Judy's house, 'you might look up Marcel Goldblatt some time. He's in the phone book.'

198

Judy grinned. 'Our one and only date wasn't very auspicious, Regina.'

'He's changed.'

'Even so. I didn't have the feeling we were made for each other.'

'That was a long time ago. I think you'd enjoy meeting him again. I'm not sure he would call you if I suggested it but I think he'd be very pleased to hear from you.'

'I'll think about it.' The taxi was speeding up Park Avenue. 'Just stop at the corner,' she said to the driver.

The driver braked hard and stopped with a jolt.

'It was good to see you, Regina.' She leaned over and offered a kiss.

'For me too. Remember me at home.'

'I will.'

'And don't forget. He's in the phone book.'

'I won't forget.'

—

She didn't. When she returned to her apartment after dinner with her parents, she looked him up. Goldblatt, M. The address was on West Third Street, the Village. For most of the people she knew, the Village had been a time in their lives. It was something they passed through, something they gave up when they reached maturity or made an accommodation with life. If she was nearly twenty-six, Marcel should have made that accommodation long ago. As she had.

Still, she was curious. She was busy on Tuesday, too busy to think about it. Also, she had promised to have dinner with Fern after work so it wasn't till Wednesday that she thought about it again. He was in the phone book. He lived in the Village. He had changed.

She had a light dinner at her apartment, grilling a lamb chop for the main course, starting with grapefruit, and adding two vegetables to her plate. Simple, quick, moderately tasty. Her mother's meal on Monday had been rather heavy and she had eaten out with Fern last night. This would make up for two days of indulging. She had a good figure and like Fern, she had kept it lean.

She went through the paper quickly, feeling restless. The weather was nice and she began to think about what she would do with her summer. Her first annual vacation was in the offing and she had no plans.

The phone rang and when she answered she found, to her disappointment, that it was the awful philosopher calling from Boston. She put him off and hung up, feeling depressed. Why could men never read the signs? She had been everything but rude and here he was, calling to keep a nonexistent relationship alive.

Damn. As if that had been the last straw, she put a jacket on, took her bag, and left the apartment. She was wearing jeans for comfort, and a pair of sneakers. Her mother disapproved of such dress, but they had long ago made their peace and Judy dressed as she pleased.

She passed her car in the street, an old Volkswagen on the way to becoming ancient, and decided to leave it. Finding a space that would be 'good' tomorrow would be too much of a problem later on.

Continuing over to Lexington, she took the subway downtown. In the year since graduation she had learned the system by heart. Changing at Fifty-third, she ended up in the Village. It was a friendly place at night. There were people on the streets, shops still open. She went into one and looked at skirts and blouses, then left and kept walking. She knew the address and felt a certain excitement because she was heading there. After the dress shop, it was only another five minutes of ambling gait to West Third.

West Third was awful. There were girlie joints at the street level and she could see from the way the numbers ran that Marcel's entrace would be among them. She stopped where she was, having a surge of misgivings. A man walked by and made a comment that was not flattering. It made her angry. She had as much right to be here as he did, more, in fact, because she did not insult people on the street. Purposefully, she walked to the entrance with Marcel's number and went inside.

There were several mailboxes, each with a bell beneath it. She found Goldblatt and rang. A moment later, there was an answering buzz and she pushed the door, walked into the downstairs hall, and started up the long staircase.

His apartment number began with a four and she went slowly up the three flights, wondering at her own audacity. She had become nervous, as though she were about to be interviewed for an important job. She had a flood of second thoughts – she should have called first; she should not have come at all. He might not be alone. What had possessed her to do this?

The door to her immediate left on the fourth floor had a card with the name Goldblatt on it. She took a breath and knocked.

'OK,' a voice called.

A moment later, the door opened.

He looked at her for a fleeting moment without recognition and she smiled slightly, not certain whether to announce herself. Then he said, 'Judy,' in wonderment and then, 'Judy!' with absolute delight. He stood back and held the door open. 'Come in. Please come in. Sit. There should be room somewhere.'

He closed the door after her but she did not sit. She looked at him, wondering if he were the same person she had met once or some substitute with the same name. He had broadened and changed. He looked less as if he had been born in the image of a beautiful woman and more as though he were an attractive man.

'Please,' he said, gesturing with one hand. 'Anywhere.'

'Thank you.'

She sat in an old, comfortable wing chair and he took an overstuffed chair with a lower back in which he had obviously been sitting before her arrival. On a small end table beside it, a very thick book was open with a pair of glasses resting on the two visible pages.

'You look great,' he said.

'Thank you. You do too.'

He was wearing a pair of blue jeans and a blue plaid shirt, the sleeves rolled up a few turns. His hands seemed almost too clean, too well scrubbed, too well manicured.

'Can I get you something to drink? I have some beer.'

'No, thanks.'

'Grapefruit juice? I think I still have some bourbon somewhere.'

She shook her head. 'You aren't angry any more,' she said with some amazement. It was the most prominent feature of the new Marcel Goldblatt, the missing anger.

He smiled in a relaxed kind of way. 'I'm probably just too tired,' he said.

'I know the feeling.'

'You must be practising law now.'

'I am.'

'Judy Esquire.'

'Yes.' She would have to tell Davey that *someone* had not called her a lady lawyer.

'Are you going to tell me or do I have to guess how you got here tonight?'

'Regina said you were in the phone book.'

'Ah.' He nodded, knowingly.

'She said you probably wouldn't call me yourself but that you'd be happy to see me.'

'She was right – at least about the second half. What else did she tell you?'

'Nothing. She said you were in the phone book.'

'And that's all.'

'That's all.'

He looked away a moment, as though considering something. 'You must be out of law school a couple of years by now,' he said.

'I could have been, but I'm not. I finished last year. I took a year off before I started.'

'You? A year off?'

'Mm-hmm.'

. 'I thought you were so sure.'

'I thought so too. I wasn't.'

'"In our family,"' he quoted mercilessly, '"we have absolute freedom to choose our own lives."'

She closed her eyes in embarrassment. 'I apologize,' she said. 'I was only twenty.'

'I know. I shouldn't have brought it up. That wasn't one of the best days of my life.'

'Or mine.'

'But I would still ask you out. And for the same reason. With or without the esquire, you're beautiful. You're really extraordinary.'

She could feel her cheeks warming. She had a question to ask but she wasn't sure how to phrase it, how to say it without possibly hurting and she did not want to hurt. 'Are you – what do you do now?'

He looked at her appraisingly. 'Regina didn't tell you?'

'Regina said – '

'I know, I know. She said I was in the phone book.' He was teasing.

'She said one other thing. She said you'd changed.'

He considered it briefly. 'I guess it would seem that way to her.'

'Haven't you?'

'I suppose I'd like to think I haven't.' He rubbed his cheek. 'I took a couple more years off than you did. Did something stupid. Then I got lucky.' He took a breath. 'I'm in my third year of medical school.'

'Medical school. I thought you – ' She stopped, remembering bits of conversation from an evening she had forgotten without trying. 'They wanted things from you, didn't they?'

'Well, I wasn't the most cooperative kid in the world.'

'How did you manage it?'

'I told you. I was lucky. Someone took an interest in me. He was the first person in my life that asked me what I wanted. I told him. He said, screw them all. Do it. So I did. It took a little longer than that,' he admitted.

'You must be very happy now.'

'When I'm not tired,' he said, 'I feel pretty damn good.'

There was the sudden sound of a buzzer. Marcel said, 'Oh,' and looked at his watch, a shiny round face with several dials. 'Excuse me. I'll be right back.'

'I can go,' Judy offered, moving to rise. 'I don't want to stay if you have company. I just walked in off the street.'

He had stood. 'Stay,' he said. 'Please stay.'

'If you're sure.'

'I'm sure.'

He went out, leaving the door open. She heard him go down the stairs and open the ground-floor door. She could not hear him speak but a female voice – surprised, irritated – came up the stairs. It said, finally, 'You could have *called*,' and then the door closed. He was upstairs in a minute.

'Sorry,' he said, closing the door of the apartment.

'She's angry.'

'We were just going to study together. I forgot she was coming over.'

'OK.' She found she was rather pleased. 'I think I'll accept that drink now.'

'What makes you think I'm still offering?' he asked good-naturedly.

'Gut instinct.'

He stood. 'Come on. I'll show you the kitchen.'

The apartment stretched from back to front of the building, taking up half its width. The 'rooms' were only partly separated from one another but had no doors. Beyond the living room, which she had entered from the outside hall, was the bedroom, more of an alcove, really, with a double bed against the far wall and a night table. On the other side of the wall was the kitchen.

She had asked for coffee on the assurance that it would not keep him up and he made it, telling her nothing kept him awake any more. He was in his surgical apprenticeship now and he was working harder than he ever had before.

She sat opposite him at a square wooden table with old-fashioned legs that looked as though they had been turned by a wood-worker. She ran her palm over the smooth bleached surface.

'I sanded it,' he said, watching her. 'Stripped the paint off. It was aqua.' He smiled. 'That was a long time ago. Nowadays I'm glad to get the dishes done twice a week.'

'I like it,' Judy said. 'The apartment. It kind of looks like you.'

'I moved in the day after I took you to dinner.'

'Because of something I did?'

'Because of a lot of things I didn't.' He sipped his coffee. 'A guy I knew was living here and I slept on the couch till he moved out that June. I guess it's five years. I like the Village and I only have another year to go before I become respectable. You're respectable, aren't you?'

'Days,' she said. 'I'm glad you made it, Marcel. It's touch and go sometimes.'

'I wouldn't've expected to hear that from you.'

'Maybe I changed and you stayed the same.'

'What made you take the year off?'

She shrugged, wondering where it had all begun. 'A problem in the family, a disagreement with my – parents, a great love affair.' She looked across the small table at him. He was watching her with interest, his eyes warm. 'A love affair with someone my parents couldn't possibly approve of. Not that I cared. When I left him, I knew I had to find out whose person I was. I remember I had nowhere to go so I went to Regina's office.'

'For solace?'

'For a telephone.' She smiled. 'I had to call England to find a place to live. I spent almost five months there.'

'And whose person are you?'

'Mine, I think, but I'm afraid to say it. I'm afraid you'll come back at me in five years and say – '

'I won't come back at you. In five years I may not even be in the phone book.'

'You'll be in the phone book.' She said it softly. 'With an

MD after your name. I really feel – I'm very happy for you. They've all forgiven you, haven't they? For doing what you want?'

'They've forgiven me. I could have made it easier on them.'

'No you couldn't. If you could have, you would have. That's why lawyers always pick juries to decide their cases. Three-quarters of every jury remembers a time when they couldn't have done it any differently themselves.'

'Can I get you more coffee?'

She shook her head, then looked at her watch. 'I'd really better get going.'

'I'll take you home.'

'Thanks, it really isn't – '

'I'll take you home.'

'Thank you.'

They caught a taxi on Sixth Avenue and started uptown. Marcel said very little. He looked far away.

'I hope her feelings weren't hurt,' Judy said finally.

He looked puzzled. 'Oh, Joy. I don't think so. She's pretty tough.' He smiled at her. 'Are you tough?'

The question bothered her. 'I'm not sure I want to find out.'

'Maybe you won't have to.'

'I don't feel very tough.' In fact, she felt just the reverse. She felt like putty. She felt the way she had that day in December when she was twenty and he had come down the stairs and she had first seen him, that stark sexual attraction, mellowed now because he was somebody, not just a physical object, because they had taken parallel paths, because he had sent away someone who had obviously wanted to spend the evening with him.

'Look,' he said.

She turned, expectant. He would ask now. You free this weekend? I'm tied up this weekend but maybe early next week . . . I'd like to see you again. How can I get in touch with you if . . .

But he said nothing and she felt the taxi start to slow.

'I think we're here,' he said, reaching into his pocket for a wallet.

They got out and he stood for a moment before the entrance. 'Nice,' he said.

The doorman touched the brim of his hat and held the door for them.

'After living in a dark hole in New Haven for three years and plugging in electric heaters in England, I thought I was ready for the East Side. Besides, they gave me a concession.'

'Because of your charm.'

'Because they couldn't fill the building.'

They rode the lift up to eight and got out. Her apartment was down the hall and they walked side by side to her door. She stopped and took her keys out of her bag.

'Look, I'm glad you found me in the book,' he said. He didn't sound glad. He sounded dutiful, a polite statement required by the society he had learned to live in, the same one she had returned to.

'So am I.' She felt a raw sexual attraction of the kind one felt now and then towards the wrong man or in the wrong place, but this was right, for a change, and it wasn't working. She turned the key and pushed the door open. 'Would you like to come in?'

'No, thanks. I really have work to do tonight. Really.'

'Good night.'

'Good night, Judy.'

She closed the door, leaving the lights off, crossed the living room and looked out the windows. The apartment faced south and she could see all of midtown Manhattan before her in lights. She waited, thinking he would come back, because her instincts couldn't be that bad, couldn't be so perverse as to make her sense they were equally interested when in fact he was only being polite.

Finally, when nothing happened, she turned the lights on, got undressed, showered and went to bed.

He did not call. She had thought she would tell Regina she had been to see him but now she reconsidered. Something had gone wrong and she could not figure out what. He had asked her to stay when she had offered to go but when the evening ended, it had simply ended.

207

She concocted excuses for him, hating herself for acting like an adolescent. He had been busy that weekend and would wait till Monday to call. He was ending something with the girl who had come to study and he needed time to finish it properly. School took so much of his time . . .

Come on, Judy, the voice of reason said. Admit it. You misread the signs. You felt and he didn't. You've lived long enough to know it doesn't always work in both directions.

Monday came and he didn't call. She was so tense now, so angry, so disappointed in her own intuitions, that she felt ready to scream. Late in the evening, she called Fern and they made a date for dinner the following night.

They went to a Greek restaurant on the West Side. Fern had hesitantly embraced the varied cuisines of New York and as long as they didn't sting going down, she had actually learned to like most of them.

'I detect malice,' she said as an appetizer of stuffed grape leaves was placed on the table.

'Your powers of detection were never more accurate.'

'Someone at the firm has sliced you up.'

'You are very cold.'

'Someone at the firm has offered you a junior partnership if you share his bed on Mondays, Wednesdays and Fridays when once he shared the hour with his analyst.'

'You're way off. It has nothing to do with work. I am happy in my work.'

'That's even worse. You sound Orwellian – or do I have the wrong Englishman? Don't tell me you're falling in love?'

'I won't tell you.' Judy put her fork down. 'Fern, how could I have been so wrong about someone? It was there, I felt it, and when he took me home, he said good night and that was it.'

'Why does life never change?' Fern asked rhetorically.

'Because our anatomy doesn't. Because our nerve endings don't. Because, damn it, I can't help feeling that way about men.'

'I feel for you.'

'Why don't you get married, Fern? Don't tell me you haven't had the chance with a couple of nice guys.'

Fern looked down at her dish. 'Never the right time,' she said in a low voice. She looked up. 'I can't just get married and start knitting, Judy. I can't give this job up. It means too much to me. You know I have my own office now? I'm only twenty-six. You know how many women there who are forty will never have their own offices? Besides, the ones that want to marry me aren't great men.'

The statement gave Judy a chill. 'You aren't still – you don't think about the guy in Kansas any more, do you?' she asked.

'I think about him. Don't you think about the lawyer?'

'Not that way. Not any more.'

'Well, you gave him up. I made a compromise.'

'I don't like to hear about compromises.'

'Cheer up.' Fern smiled. 'You were born under a good star.'

She came home on Wednesday and got into the car to find a parking space for the following day. This was the dismal part of living in New York, moving the car from side to side of the street, finding the aerial broken now and then by a malicious vandal who had nothing better to do with his life than inflict damage. Her mother had never lived this way and she herself had been so proud of this life – until it got screwed up by a man.

She watched an inept driver try to ease a Cadillac into too small a space and she bided her time. When the Caddy gave up, she pulled in, pulled on the brake, locked the car. It was only a block and a half from the apartment.

Nearly there, she remembered her briefcase. She had left it in the car. Furious now she returned, unlocked the car, pulled it out, locked again and headed for home. She was breathing unevenly, transferring the anger onto New York, the parking restrictions – why? They never cleaned the streets when they promised anyway – the dirt that was now becoming mud in the gentle rain. She went through the front door, hardly acknowledging the doorman's nod, the anger building.

The apartment was stuffy but in this damned city if you

opened a window you had to shovel soot at the end of the day. She dropped everything and started dinner, a minute steak and two vegetables, frozen, which she could drop into boiling water, and when they were finished their tastes would be indiscernible from each other. Anger rose like an incurable infection of the upper respiratory system. Fern and her damned memories. What good were memories when you had to live today, Wednesday, April –

The phone rang. She slammed the grill door shut on her minute steak and dropped the pot holder on the counter. Calmly, she instructed herself, as though she were her own client – which, the old adage said, made her a fool either way you looked at it. It's Mum and you'll put her in a panic if she senses hysteria.

She stood beside the phone, letting it ring a third time while she filled her lungs once again. Then she answered. 'Hello.'

'This is Marcel.' The voice was nearly toneless.

She said, 'Oh,' but it came out like a sigh or an exclamation.

'I think I have to talk to you.'

'Yes.'

'Everything OK?'

'Fine.' She was afraid to say too much lest her voice betray the only slowly receding emotion.

'Can you say anything that isn't monosyllabic?'

She swallowed. 'I said hello.'

'I guess that'll have to do. Look . . .' There was a pause and she remembered suddenly that a week ago when he had taken her home, he had said, Look, and never gone any further. It was seven days and he had called to finish his sentence.

'Judy – last week – when you came down to my place – What I mean is, what did you come down for?'

She thought, This city is finally making me crazy. I have lost my ability to comprehend ordinary English. She said, 'I don't think I understand what you're asking.'

'I don't think I understand either.' A note of defeat sounded in his voice.

'If you mean,' she said, feeling the anger surge back, 'did I have some unstated motive, the answer is no. If you mean, were my intentions honourable, the answer is no. At best they were dishonourable. I'm not going to marry you, not now and not ever. You want to know what I came down for? Curiosity. Regina said you had changed. Boredom. I went out with a philosopher I couldn't stand and he called all the way from Boston that night so I wouldn't forget him. Diversion. There was nothing on the tube. Thirst. I wanted a cup of coffee and I didn't feel like making it myself. Sport. Because I thought I'd get a good fight out of you but you disappointed me. Is there anything else I can tell you?' She was fighting now to keep it down, to keep it from exploding.

'Just one thing,' Marcel's calm voice said in her ear. 'If I take you to dinner, will you talk to me without shouting?'

She said, 'Yes,' faintly, and then she smelled it. 'Oh, God, my dinner's burning.' She dropped the phone and ran to the kitchen. There was smoke and fire. She turned off the grill and opened the door, holding her breath. The flames petered out and she set the pan on top of the stove beside the fiercely boiling, already tasteless vegetables, which would now be the main course of her ruined dinner. What possesses a person to answer the phone with a minute steak under the grill? What's the matter with me? Am I crazy?

She didn't need the voice to tell her. It had been an implicit sacrifice. If her dinner burned, it would be Marcel. She brushed the dish towel over her eyes and went back to the phone.

'I'm sorry,' she said.

'I should have called at a better time.'

'I should have turned the stove off when the phone rang.'

'I would take you to dinner but I'm too tired to be very good company. I've been awake almost thirty-six hours.'

'I'll be better company another night myself.'

'Pick the night.'

She didn't vacillate or play the schoolgirl's game. 'Saturday's fine.'

'I'll pick you up at seven.'

The meat turned out to be only partially burned. She poured some brownish stuff on it from a bottle the supermarket had given her as a promotion and found it was the tastiest piece of meat she'd ever eaten. Halfway through dinner she felt a cramp.

Damn, she thought. It wasn't love, sex, New York, Fern or any other external thing. It was the female cycle. Tomorrow she would be normal again.

Three

The doorman called her at seven exactly. 'Mr Goldblatt is on his way up.'

She put a brush through her hair for one last time, as though it made a difference, and waited for the doorbell, feeling again as nervous as she had the night she went to West Third Street.

She opened the door and said, 'Hello,' taking him in with greedy eyes, a dark suit, a white shirt and a silk tie that he wore as easily as the jeans and plaid shirt. He came in and as she closed the door, he kissed her, not a kiss, but a *kiss*.

She stepped back when it was over, feeling a pounding in her chest, and looked at him.

'I've never started out that way before,' he said, almost apologetically, 'but since you said your intentions weren't honourable anyway.'

'I'm sorry about that phone conversation. I was a little – edgy.'

'Salvage dinner?'

'It turned out pretty good.'

He touched her arm. 'Let's go.'

'I have a car,' she offered when they reached the street.

He hesitated. 'I don't like driving other people's cars,' he said.

They took a taxi downtown to one of the restaurants on Fifth Avenue within sight of the arch at Washington Square and when they were seated, they ordered drinks.

'I really have to talk to you,' he said after the drinks came. 'Whenever you decide you've had enough, I'll take you home. No hard feelings. OK?'

'Maybe I'd rather not hear what you're going to tell me.'

213

'You're a lawyer, Judy. You have a nice, clean reputation. I don't want to put any tarnish on it.'

'I don't think reputations tarnish from drinks and dinner. And I don't think you – '

'Listen to me. I was going to tell you last week when you came down to the apartment but I changed my mind. I decided the easiest thing was to take you home and not call. Only it turned out it wasn't easy.'

Something inside fluttered softly. 'I'm glad you called,' she said. 'I wanted you to. Please don't worry about tarnish. We've all got little things, Marcel.'

'I'm not talking about girls and bastard babies. I'm talking about drugs. I'm talking about stealing them. I'm talking about being arrested and going to trial.'

She felt an unmistakable chill. 'But you're in medical school.'

'I had a good lawyer.'

'You must have had more than that.'

He sipped his drink and set it aside. 'I was working as an orderly in a hospital in Brooklyn. The patient was seventy-eight, had cancer, lots of pain. I used to help her over to the pharmacy after she saw the doctor. One week she didn't show for her appointment. I looked up her address and went to see her. She couldn't get out any more and she had no phone. So I took what I needed from a nurses' station between shifts. The day nurses leave early and the evening nurses come late. It wasn't hard. There was plenty of the same thing going on for other reasons. After I'd done it a few times, someone turned me in to the police.'

'A good citizen?'

'A nurses' aide I'd taken out a couple of times. Several times,' he admitted. 'I wasn't taking her out any more when she turned me in.'

'Did she take the stand?'

'She was their star witness.'

'Your lawyer must have made mincemeat out of her.'

'He did.'

214

'And the old woman?'

'She was terrific.'

'They arrested you with the drugs?'

'Mm-hmm.' He was watching her with interest.

'And he got you *acquitted*?'

'He did better than that. He got them to drop the charges.'

It was the old delight. 'Tell me,' she said, the child waiting for the happy ending.

'I was arrested by two cops but only one of them signed the arrest papers. The laywer looked into it and found out the other cop was involved in some big drug investigation for the Brooklyn DA's office. He brought him in as the last witness. When the prosecutor saw him take the stand, he nearly had apoplexy. They stopped the trial and dropped the charges. I guess they figured if this guy's work ever became public, the whole thing was down the drain. What I had done wasn't important enough to jeopardize something really big.'

'That's lovely,' Judy said with admiration.

'You really haven't heard anything I've said.'

'I heard.' Her voice was low. 'Marcel, they would have sent you to medical school, wouldn't they?'

'They would have done anything I wanted. I never told them what I wanted and in all the years I lived with the Rushes, Morty never asked. He kept offering me a job with Rush and my aunt in Paris kept writing and telling me to cut out this nonsense and come home and be a lawyer. All I ever did was turn them down and try to figure out how I could do it myself.'

'So you screwed yourself instead of screwing them.'

'Succinctly, yes. But that wasn't the end. The night after the trial was over, Morty started in again offering me a job with Rush and I blew up. I'd spent the afternoon with Mrs Meade – the one I'd gotten the drugs for. She was in bad shape. I think the day she took the stand was the last good day of her life. She died two weeks later and her goddamn son didn't show up till the funeral.' He stopped and touched the glass containing his drink, but he did not take any. 'Anyway, I moved out of the Rushes' apartment that night and went back to my own place.

It was probably the worst night of my life, worse than when I was arrested because I knew that was bound to happen eventually.

'Here I was, feeling I really had a chance to start over again, and nothing had changed. The war hadn't killed me, postwar France hadn't killed me, the fifties hadn't killed me. I was going to be destroyed by all the wellmeaning people who had set out to save me. I got up the next morning and got a job with the biggest textile company in America. I just wanted to be able to say, Look, I've done it and I never want to do it again.'

'Was it awful?'

'Would you believe it was the greatest job I've ever had in my life?'

'And you applied to medical school.'

'I took some bio at night and a couple of other things. I put some money away. I thought it would take longer, but I got accepted the next spring, '61.' He smiled, looking more relaxed. 'After that, I stopped relying on miracles.'

'Are you friends again? With the Rushes?'

'We're friends. Morty's OK. It's that damned company. He started it with a cotton mill back in the thirties and it's one of the biggest privately held textile companies in the country now. The problem is, his kids don't seem to want it. Ernie went into business for himself. He's got a trucking firm down in Washington. Margot's married and got a job with some magazine. If he didn't think of me as his own son, he wouldn't have been so hurt when I turned him down. Besides,' he grinned, 'I was a little shit. As you know.'

Judy shook her head. 'I don't know. And I don't want to be reminded. If you'd been brought up in a whole family, you would have known that what Morty did wasn't unusual. My father did that to Frenchy for a while. About law.'

'Your brother is terrific. I can believe he was born to it.'

'Frenchy?'

'He kept me out of jail the night I was arrested.'

'Regina called *Frenchy*?'

'They came down to the police station together.'

'Frenchy doesn't know the first thing about police stations.'

'You don't know your brother.'

'I guess I don't,' Judy said thoughtfully. 'His father's son. But he didn't defend you?'

'He got me a lawyer later that night. Guy named Kellems.'

She knew her face mirrored the internal shock wave. 'He's very good,' she said, holding her voice steady.

'He's better than that.'

'My father took me to see Roy Kellems in court when I was sixteen. He was a big part of the reason I decided to study law.'

'Anyway,' Marcel said, 'that's what Regina meant when she told you I wouldn't have called you and that's why you didn't hear from me last week and that's why you really ought to think about whether you want to spend time with me.' He met her eyes across the table. 'I want to spend time with you.'

'Shouldn't we look at the menu?' Judy said. 'I'm getting hungry.'

They ate a leisurely dinner, finishing with cognac instead of dessert. When they left, she felt high out of all proportion to what she had drunk. They went out to Fifth Avenue, walked toward the arch, and stopped on the first corner. He took her hand and kissed her and she moved closer to him, feeling his hand drop hers and slip around her back.

'My place isn't far,' he said, the understanding implicit, the message clear and not unwelcome.

'I don't think so,' she said, staying close. 'Not tonight.'

'OK.'

They did not move. 'The girl who came that night.'

'Joy? I told you. She's a third-year student. We study together.'

'Do you sleep with her?'

A second passed. 'Sometimes.'

'I don't sleep with people sometimes.'

'I don't want you sometimes.'

'I need time to think.'

217

He turned and they started walking slowly north. 'Let's walk uptown. When you get tired, we'll look for a cab.'

'It's not that I wouldn't like to.'

'You don't have to explain.'

'I'm glad you called.'

He tightened the arm that held her. 'Stay close, huh? I want to keep you for a while.'

It was a nice thought. She might just be ready for keeping.

At dinner she had told him about England. Walking, he told her about his family. His sister, Renée, was seven years older and had become a lawyer, partly assuaging his aunt's desire for the continuity of the family. Renée had not married. For nearly a decade, she had been in love with a left-wing journalist who was not Jewish and their aunt had absolutely forbidden a marriage on both counts.

'She's old enough to do what she wants,' Judy said, feeling a strong sympathy for his sister, who at thirty-five was still struggling for that elusive treasure.

'You say that because you're able to do what you want. Not everyone can.'

'You have to take freedom.'

'You were able to take freedom without hurting anyone. I couldn't do it for a long time. My sister can't do it. For my sister to do what she wants, she has to hurt someone who's been very good to her.'

'But it's wrong to deprive her of what's hers. I can't imagine my father ever limiting my choices that way.'

'Your father and my aunt have lived different lives. They don't hurt in the same places.'

'Even so. If your sister can't take what's rightfully hers, maybe someone has to give it to her. Maybe you do.'

He took a long breath and then he rubbed his lips along the side of her face. 'We'll talk about it,' he said. 'OK? Next week or the week after or the week after that.'

She said, 'OK,' and they kept on walking.

When they reached the Sixties, she knew there would be no taxi. She could not remember ever walking three miles on the streets of New York, nor could she have imagined enjoying it so much. The sight of her apartment house was at once a surprise and a disappointment.

They rode up to the eighth floor and walked down the carpeted hall.

'I sleep at the hospital alternate nights,' he said. 'Maybe we could make it next Sunday.'

'Sunday's fine.'

'I won't call you again at six-fifteen.'

'There's nothing wrong with six-fifteen. It was just me. You call me any time.'

'I may.'

'Would you like me to invite you in?'

He shook his head. 'I'd better be getting back.'

'The doorman'll find you a cab.'

'I'll probably walk. It clears the mind.' He took her key, opened the door, and turned on the light. He put the keys back in her hand and folded her hand over them. 'I feel like apologizing for that Christmas.'

'I feel like apologizing for the Second World War.'

'Well,' he said, 'I'm glad we got all the apologies out of the way.'

She lay awake thinking about his sister, his sister who was thirty-five and had not married, his sister who would not bear children. She had never thought before about a family coming to an end. Her own family had two little boys to continue the line. What she wanted was a man, a beautiful, young, soft-spoken, sexy man to be close to, a man who walked three miles and then, just as easily, walked three miles back, a man with scrubbed hands and too-clean fingernails, a man who understood dedication, a man like Marcel. She did not crave children. She and Fern. Perhaps that was one of the things that had kept them friends, not an antipathy, just a neutrality, a fortunate neutrality in her case. But a family coming to an end . . . She had known for years that she could not marry someone young and beautiful but she knew now she could not keep him for long either. Better that he spend his time with

Joy, who could share his dedication and make babies besides, or someone else who could at least be a wife to him, and the mother of his children.

The trouble was she wanted him, really, really wanted him.

The phone at her desk rang shortly before eleven on Monday morning.

'Miss Wolfe,' she answered.

'I tried you before.'

A nice voice, even and very calm, a voice that would bring order to disarray, quiet to the anxious. 'I was in the library. I spend a lot of time there.'

'Looking things up?'

'And drafting briefs.'

'Do they give you time off for lunch?'

'Generously. I don't even have to punch in and out.'

'I think I can manage a forty-five-minute lunch hour. Can you meet me up here?'

'Yes.'

'Maybe – ten to twelve?' She could see him checking the watch, doing quick arithmetic.

'Yes.'

'Are you dressed like a lawyer?'

The jacket of her pearl-grey suit hung from a hanger in a corner. She looked down at her white silk blouse, slim grey skirt, black patent shoes, the matching bag for which was locked in a drawer. She said, 'Yes.'

'I'll recognize you then. No one around here looks remotely like one.'

'Good.'

'You're going monosyllabic on me again. Will you let me kiss you in the street? Please don't say "maybe."'

'How's "yes"?'

'Yes is very nice.' There was a click as the phone gave a warning. 'I'll see you, Judy.'

She got there five minutes early and paid the cab. It was nice weather, a good spring and getting better. He came out of a door near the main entrance and waved. He was wearing the white coat she had seen medical students in. It seemed strange to be going out with a student, any kind of student. Most of the men she dated were well established. Now and then one was already divorced from the sweetheart of his youth and looking for the sweetheart of his middle age. She liked being with someone who was starting out. It made life look somehow longer and brighter.

'Hi.' He kissed her and put a white-sleeved arm around her grey-jacketed back. 'Can you eat chicken salad?'

'I can eat anything.'

They crossed the street. 'This place has great chicken salad but nothing else is worth eating.'

It was half a block away and they found an empty table for two. At other tables, young men and an occasional woman sat in similar white coats and ate chicken salad.

'If you look at the table over there with the three white coats, you'll see what future surgeons look like.'

She glanced across the coffee shop. 'They're younger than you.'

'Everyone's younger than I. I'm twenty-eight. I got a late start.'

'They look rather imperious.'

'I knew you could tell.'

'Is that what distinguishes them?'

'Partly.'

'Surgery doesn't interest you?'

'I'm strictly medicine.'

'People, not bodies.'

'Well, that's one way of looking at it.'

She glanced at the future surgeons again and then back to Marcel. 'When did you know?'

'I'm not sure. It may have been earlier this year and it may have been something I've known all my life. I don't have any clear memories before the end of the war.'

'I thought about your sister over the weekend.'

'I thought about you.'

She hesitated. 'My kind of law is more issues than people. Do I look imperious?'

'Magnificently.' He held her eyes. 'Did I take you away from a gourmet lunch with stimulating company?'

'You made it available.'

He stroked her hand with a finger. It was a small table and they were not far apart. 'I think the future surgeons are looking at you.'

'Maybe they're wondering what an imperious, issues-oriented lawyer is doing with a nice guy like you.'

'They don't have that much imagination.'

'I'm glad you do.'

He moved his finger along the back of her hand and then withdrew. 'You said you were thinking about my sister.'

'I wondered how she came through the war.'

'Very well. A lot better than I did. She was fifteen or sixteen when the Germans left. She remembers my parents, the place we used to live in. Most of it's a blank to me. I was still pretty young when the war ended.' He smiled. 'And I was very angry.' He looked at his watch.

'Time?'

'I'm afraid so.'

'I'd like to pay my share.' She put the black patent bag on her lap and opened it.

His face had a look she could not read, amusement perhaps or indulgence. 'My resources are quite generous,' he said.

'I don't see – '

'They are. And I invited you. I'd like to pick up the bill for any debts we incur together.'

'OK.' She closed the bag with a snap.

He left some change on the table and they made their way to the cashier near the door. As he paid the bill, she saw two of the future surgeons watching her with interest. When Marcel put his change in his pocket, she slipped her hand through his arm and held it as they left the restaurant.

He would sleep at the hospital the next night so she made a dinner appointment with Fern. They met at a small French

222

restaurant in the West Sixties and they both started with artichokes.

'I learned artichokes from you,' Fern said, dipping a leaf in the vinaigrette sauce. 'They scared me the first time I saw them. I thought they might attack.'

'Maybe that's a lesson, the Hall Theory of Artichokes. What looks threatening can be stripped to the core and rendered delicious.'

'Judy, you are *blue*.'

'No, but I will be in a few months. When I have to give him up.'

'You amaze me. An embryo affair and you talk about when you have to give him up.'

Judy said nothing. She dipped a leaf and pulled the tasty meat with her teeth.

'Let me guess,' Fern went on. 'Thirty-seven, very tall, married long enough to know when something better has come along, took one look at you and decided to leave his wife. Let's see, maybe an industrialist this time with a charming eighteen rooms at one of those places on Long Island where only the best people go.'

The description came as a shock. Each of the elements represented someone she had dated in the last few years, dated because he was attractive and safe, and in the end she had wanted none of them. There was something more than disappointing about the composite. There was something distinctly distasteful.

'He's twenty-eight,' she said in a low voice, her eyes on the tablecloth. 'He's never been married. He doesn't earn anything and he isn't going to for a long time. When I wear heels, he's just an inch or two taller than I. He's sexy as hell.' She lifted her eyes briefly to look at Fern, who was watching her. 'He and his sister survived the war in France but their parents didn't and he seems to have given up or lost his birthright.' She paused and neatly tucked the eaten leaf in the saucer with the others. She smiled, the thought of Marcel pleasing her. 'He speaks with a slight French accent, but so slight you can't really place it.'

'And he's crazy about you.'

'You know what it's like when you spend an hour with someone and you know?'

'Yes.'

'Well, then you know.' She looked up again. 'He's a third-year medical student,' she said.

'Take him,' Fern ordered.

'His sister's thirty-five. She'll never have children. He really needs to marry someone else.'

'Are you still on that?'

'I should look for that industrialist you described, with a house on the ocean.'

'Yes, exactly,' Fern said drily. 'Salt and pepper. You can be his darling. I can just hear him introducing you to all his retired friends at the clubhouse. "This is my Judy. She practises law during the day, don't you, dear? Of course we have a maid and cook so we don't need her at home and she does *so* enjoy it."'

'Sometimes you are unspeakable to.'

'Yes.' Fern smiled. 'Usually when I'm listening.'

He called her when he had a minute. Sometimes she was at her desk and sometimes not. She met him again for lunch on Thursday and the next time she saw him was Sunday. She had packed a lunch for the afternoon and they drove up to the Cloisters. She drove, feeling mildly irritated that he would not but the irritation dissipated. It was a beautiful day. They went through the rooms of the museum and then got the lunch and a blanket from the car and found a place to spread out where they could look down on the Hudson.

'This is what I like best about American picnics,' he said, helping himself to a foil-wrapped piece of chicken. 'Everything is wrapped in silver paper.'

'Don't they use it in France?'

'They didn't when I left. Even paper was scarce. I haven't been back for a while. And I never go in the kitchen.'

'Maybe you'll come to mine. I'll cook dinner for you next Saturday night.'

'That sounds very nice.'

'And you can take all the leftovers home in foil.'

'I accept without the added incentive.'

She stretched on the blanket. Her birthday was Friday. She would have dinner with her parents and celebrate the following evening with Marcel. As she thought about it, he covered her with his arm.

'It's nice here,' she said, meaning something quite different. It wasn't the here that was nice, it was the they.

'I'd like to take you home and make love to you.'

Yes, go somewhere comfortable and make love. Be happy. Feel wonderful. Make the kind of commitment that sex had meant for her since the first time. Just ignore the fact that this is not a man who had already fathered children.

'No more Joy?' she asked, avoiding the suggestion.

'I told you I didn't want you sometimes. No more Joy. No more anybody. All my affection is now divided between you and an old woman at the hospital who's post-op.'

'She going to be all right?'

'I don't know. I think so.'

'I'll share you with her.'

'I wrote to my sister about you.'

She moved closer. 'What did you tell her?'

'That you're a lawyer.'

'Is that all?'

'That's all I could tell her.'

'I told my best friend about you.' She got up on her forearm so that she could see his face. 'I told her you were sexy as hell.'

She felt his reaction, the voluntary and the other. 'I think I'll take you to Paris,' he said. He touched her chin, her neck. 'Not this summer, I have school. But another year. After I'm finished.'

'You plan so far ahead.' She felt dreamy thinking about it, thinking about making plans.

'That's still new to me. It wasn't till I sat down in my first class three years ago that I realized I'd made a decision for the rest of my life.'

225

'But you're happy with it.'

'Oh, yes.' There was almost an exuberance about him. 'Like nothing else I've ever done.' He stroked her arm below the short sleeve of her blouse. 'Well, almost nothing. I'm glad you think I'm sexy. It shows you're thinking in the right direction.'

They had lunch twice in the next week and on Friday she went to her parents' for her birthday. Frenchy and Diana came and Frenchy made an appointment to take her to lunch the following Monday.

Saturday she prepared dinner. The kitchen was minuscule but the stove was good and the refrigerator more than adequate. She made a soup because she liked soups. She made chicken in wine sauce because she reasoned that everyone liked chicken. She had bought a small box of wild rice because it was easy to prepare and added a touch of elegance. There were vegetables, a salad, a dessert. Two cookbooks lay open, one on top of the other, on the counter, the 'freedom' cookbook and a more sophisticated one that a man she had dated in the fall had given her after he had slammed the door and a cake had sunk in the oven.

She was nervous and quite excited. She had not cooked for anyone for a long time and she had not felt this way about anyone for even longer. She knew this would be the night she would sleep with him and the thought of it had clung to her all day, sweetening the work and making the heat of the tiny kitchen more bearable as that other internal one became less so. Now, with everything nearly done, she was dressed in a long black skirt of loosely woven cotton that she had picked up in Vermont the previous summer and a white blouse, long-sleeved, with a ruffled shawl collar and ruffles at the cuffs. At the waist was a black taffeta cummerbund. She had told him not to dress and she herself felt very comfortable, very casual, in what she wore.

The doorman called up at seven and she opened the door a few minutes later to his ring.

He said, 'Hi,' and kissed her, handing her a large, paper-wrapped bouquet of flowers, the tops peering out of the wrapping. 'Happy birthday.'

226

She smiled, pleased. 'How did you know?'

'Regina told me. I would have taken you out if I'd known sooner.'

'No. This is just what I wanted to do.'

'You said casual,' he said, eyeing the ruffles, the cummerbund, the long black skirt.

'I am.' She lifted the skirt to show bare legs and sandals. 'We picked the same colours.' He was wearing a short-sleeved white sports shirt and black trousers. It was mild out now and he had no coat. She opened the paper and said, 'Mm,' at the sight of the flowers, giant white mums, each of them inches across. 'Do you know, I don't own a vase.' She felt strangely deficient, as though she had failed him in some necessary way.

'We'll get one in Paris.'

'I have a jug,' she said. 'They'll be fine in the jug.'

It was glass and tall and she set it up on the serving table near the window where she had put out her liquor: bourbon, because Davey visited, Scotch because Frenchy did, and sherry because she lived there herself. 'Will you have a drink?' she asked, finishing with the flowers and pleased at how the table looked.

'Bourbon.'

'Why don't you – I'm not awfully good at it.'

He came to the table, helped himself to ice, and poured some bourbon over it. 'Somethings smells good,' he said.

'I forgot to ask you what you like.' She felt apologetic, inadequate. No vase and she had not asked his preference.

'I like everything. I was brought up without scruples and without prejudices.'

'But you have both now.'

'To some extent. Judy – '

'If you want water, you'll have to get it in the kitchen. The jug's doing extra duty as a vase.' She walked by him and he touched her as she passed. 'I think I need to stir something.'

She went into the kitchen and a moment later he came slowly after her. She lifted the cover on the soup, sensing his presence behind her. The kitchen was so narrow, they must nearly be touching. She stirred the soup carefully. It had been prepared earlier and was now reheating. Cautiously, she turned up the flame.

'Marry me,' he said.

The spoon clattered onto the stove top and she replaced the lid with unexpected difficulty. 'You don't know me,' she said waveringly, still facing the stove.

'You mean we haven't been to bed.'

'That too.'

From where he stood behind her, he put his arms around her, covering her breasts.

'I can't,' she said, the words hurting as they came out.

He let her go and she turned around. The glass of bourbon and ice was on the counter. 'I've never asked anyone before.'

'I've never turned anyone down before.'

'I would be very good to you.'

'I know you would,' sensing it as she said it, that he would be so good, that they would be so right.

'I love you, Judy.'

'I told you when you called that time that my intentions weren't honourable.' Her voice was very low. She had expected many things, but not a proposal.

'Then let me make a more salacious offer, without withdrawing the first.'

'I can't have children, Marcel.'

He looked momentarily perplexed, as though her statement had had several meanings and he was uncertain which of them she intended. 'I'm not asking for children,' he said. 'I'm asking for you.'

'But that's what marriage amounts to.'

'It doesn't to me. I can't even think of myself with a child. Maybe because I spent the first twenty-five years of my life being one.'

'But if you marry me, there's no changing your mind. There's no growing up one day and deciding you want a family. There's something that came down from my father's side, something that's probably in all of us. My brother's wives have all had – ' It welled up in her for the first time in years. She had protected herself so carefully for so long, circumventing situations that would call for explanations, avoiding men who were young and starting out, men who would want progeny.

'Can you leave the stove for a minute?' He put his arm around her and they went into the living room.

She had the shattered sense that the evening was ruined; worse, that the relationship was. She had made an agreement with herself that she would sleep with him on the condition that she would not let it last, that she would protect him, and she saw now that it had been a foolish agreement, that it had been doomed before its start. She was too old to be making empty promises, too experienced to be making them to herself. Yesterday she had turned twenty-six.

'Would you just accept it the way I said it? That I can't even think about children? That I don't want them? That it's just you?'

She leaned against him, feeling the shirt against her cheek. It had the soft, fluffy texture of unworn cotton, the pristine whiteness of something just unwrapped. It was the way she felt about him, that newness, that intensity.

'It's different for you,' she said. 'My brothers have sons now and the family will go on without me. But yours won't go on without you.'

'Is that what all this is about?'

'Yes.'

'Is that what your concern is about my sister?'

'Partly.'

'Come and sit down.'

They sat on the sofa. Her mother's sofa always had rosebuds but she had decided to be more modern, more forceful, and had chosen uneven blotches of colour, shades of brown and gold on beige, but now, as she sat, she thought how much smarter her mother had been, how much more restful and inviting the rosebuds were. Sitting beside Marcel, she felt a wave of love and sympathy for her mother.

'Can't we just let it go where it'll go?' he asked, beside her on the forceful, blotchy sofa.

'I don't know.'

'I don't care if we don't get married. I just want you there. I'll be coming home every night after exams.'

'I'd leave you one day.' She felt as sad as if she were already packing to go.

'No you wouldn't,' he said. 'No you won't,' he altered it.

'I shouldn't have gone down to see you in the first place. I should have known if I didn't hate you I'd love you.' She sounded melancholy. It was as if everything had caught up with her, as she had always known it would.

'I don't believe we're having this conversation.'

She slipped her sandals off and drew her bare feet up onto the sofa, covering them with the long skirt. She told him about Davey and Rena, about Frenchy and Diana, about Davey and Marilyn. She went back to Swarthmore, remembering phone calls and visits. Fern kept flitting through her mind as she talked, but she did not speak of Fern. She did not speak of her father. She did not speak of Roy. She spoke of what was important to Marcel, what was relevant to his life.

When she finished, she smelled something burning and she had the sense that it was all over. This was the way it had begun and this was the way it would end, with dinner burning.

She got up from the sofa quickly, feeling his hand reach for her, and went barefooted into the kitchen. Her beautiful cream soup that she had laboured over was boiling furiously. A spoon inserted cautiously lifted a burned scum from the bottom. She began to cry. Somehow it was easier to cry over a ruined soup than over a ruined love affair. Through her tears she saw Diana at the cemetery, crying for the child she had not been able to love enough to keep and not been able to give up when he died.

A hand reached in front of her and turned the burner under the soup to off.

'I don't know what you're crying about,' he said.

'The soup is ruined,' she said ridiculously, wailing through tears.

230

'Damn it, Judy, we're not talking about soup.'

'It was so perfect,' she mourned.

He took the spoon from her hand and threw it into the sink. 'Get out of the kitchen,' he ordered, taking her arm above the wrist and leading her – pulling her – into the living room.

'Don't touch me that way!'

'Then let me touch you the way I want to – the way you want me to.'

'Never!' She was surprised at the anger in her voice, at the absoluteness of what she said, more surprised at how right he was, how much she wanted him, how little she cared about all the things she had always thought were of prime importance.

'I'll take care of dinner.' He was angry, furious. His dark eyes flashed with his anger. He marched back into the kitchen and after a moment she heard the cookbooks slammed shut, dropped heavily on the counter. Another moment passed and he came back. 'Nothing will burn any more,' he said, still angry. 'Will you talk to me now?'

'No.'

'Why not?'

'Because there's nothing to talk about.'

He looked at her a moment. 'OK,' he said, more calmly now, the eyes warmer. 'Fine. That's just fine. There's nothing to talk about. Enjoy your dinner.' He walked to the door and stopped with his hand on the knob. 'I'm in the phone book,' he said. 'In case you decide we have something to talk about.'

The door closed behind him and she stood watching it, knowing he would come back, knowing he hadn't wanted to leave, knowing she wanted the chance to do it over, to make it all right.

He did not come back. She put her sandals back on and went into the kitchen. All the burners were off and the two cookbooks, both closed, were on the counter, perhaps a foot apart, as though they had been placed – or thrown – carelessly.

She had lost her appetite. She opened the pot in which the chicken had been stewing and removed a small piece. Steam lifted from the open pot and the smell filled her nostrils, like a beautiful memory. She bit the flesh off the bone, standing over the sink. It was delicious. It was perfect. It made her feel terrible. She had made a mess of it and in doing so, she had evoked anger. In the case of Marcel, that was not a minor infraction.

He did not return. She spooned, wrapped, and stored the food. When the kitchen was clean, she picked up the cookbooks to return them to the shelves in the living room. Carrying them, she opened the older one. To Judith, it said. Who chose freedom.

At the moment, she didn't even know what freedom meant any more.

Four

———◆———

She had lunch with Frenchy on Monday. They met at his club so neither of them had far to go.

'Something wrong?' he asked after they had ordered.

'No. Why?'

'You look as if you've been up all night.'

She knew he was right. Marcel had not called and she had spent two nights and one day wondering whether she should initiate a call which would revive the relationship. So far, she had not. 'I've screwed something up,' she said.

'Well unscrew it.'

'I don't know if I should.'

'Do you mean you want someone to tell you you should?'

'Don't get to the heart of things quite so quickly, Frenchy. It throws me off balance and my balance isn't very good to start with.'

'Do you know that this is a business lunch?'

She looked at him with interest. 'I didn't. What's it about?'

'I'd like you to do something for me.'

'Something constitutional?'

'Something related to the family.' He paused momentarily. 'After Aunt Bertha died this winter, the property she lived on in New Jersey was passed on to her daughter Millie.'

'Daddy's cousin.'

'Right. She's lived there all her life. When her husband was alive, they owned an additional fifty acres or so across the road but they sold those off a long time ago. Not enough hands to farm it. Millie's alone now. Her son's thirty-something and married and she wants to sell. She's moving to Newark to be near her sister, Adele, who I happen to know on very good authority is Uncle Richard's least favourite person in the whole world.'

'How can I possibly fit into this morass?'

'There are several houses on the property. Grandpa Willy owned one that hasn't been used I'd guess in a quarter century or more, and Regina's mother had one too that's falling apart now. Millie has emptied out whatever belongs to her and whatever the members of the family want but she says there's still some stuff in the original house that our great-grandfather built before the turn of the century. Millie says she can't decide how to distribute those last things and since there are so many lawyers in the family, she'd like one of them to come out and make the decision for her.'

'Oh, Frenchy.' She was dismayed. 'I'm not Solomon.'

'I talked to Dad about it – in his capacity as family member, you understand – and he indicated that someone with sensitivity ought to go out and do the job. I would guess that means you.'

She looked down at the heavy white tablecloth, feeling disappointed. When he had said 'business', she had thought, ah, something exciting, something to take her mind off Marcel. Now she saw herself handing out pots and pans that nobody really wanted.

'There's a fee in it,' her brother said after silence.

'I drive out to New Jersey?' she asked half-heartedly.

'We'll pay five cents a mile.'

'Oh, don't be silly,' she said irritably. 'Keep your fee and keep your five cents a mile. I'll do it because Daddy wants it done. I just thought it might be something juicy like that First Amendment case we were talking about last Friday.'

'Next time.' Her brother smiled and handed her an envelope from inside his jacket. 'Directions, names of the cousins, etcetera.'

'Thanks.'

'From what I gather, Millie's sort of – ' he hesitated, 'well, a little dizzy, let's say. Just humour her.'

'I'll humour her. I'll go out on Saturday.'

'Good. I'll tell her to expect you. You don't even have to dress.'

She smiled. 'You're a peach, Frenchy. In fact, you're really terrific.' She paused. 'I went out with Marcel Goldblatt a few times.'

Frenchy said, 'Oh?' but his face did not change.

'He told me. Everything. You before the magistrate. Were you shaking?'

'Not so anyone noticed. I couldn't figure out why Regina called me, except that she has this thing about family and that was a family problem. She couldn't call Dad, of course.'

'I'm glad you got Roy for him.' Her voice was low. She was talking about Marcel because it pained and comforted her at the same time.

'Well.' Frenchy continued to look inscrutable. 'You know more than he does now, more than anyone else, I daresay.'

'You kept it to yourself all these years.' She felt magnificently proud of him. 'You are really terrific.'

'Did I do anything that you wouldn't have done in exactly the same way?'

'I hope. I hope I would have.'

'No question,' Frenchy said. 'You've never been short on honour. By the way, I liked Marcel. Liked him very much. I think he's doing great things now. Hang on to him.'

She didn't answer but she knew her brother had put the obvious two and two together.

Five

He did not call. There were no messages when she got back to the office after lunch, nothing in the evening, nothing on Tuesday. She was not sure when he was on this week and when he was off. She thought about calling him – she thought about little else – but she knew it was right that they should not see each other again. If she could not have freedom herself, she could at least grant it to those she loved. He deserved – needed – a woman who would bear him children, even if he couldn't see it himself.

There was nothing Wednesday either and by then the pain was terrible. She had thought it would recede, thought, after talking to Frenchy about him, that she had gotten him out of her system. But her system was a mess. She sat in a conference with three other lawyers who were preparing a delicate case on the right of free assembly, a case she had researched with zeal, a case she had been thrilled to be part of, and she could scarcely concentrate. She wondered if men felt the way she did, if a surgeon's hand was less than steady because the woman he loved had . . . Mostly, she wondered about Marcel.

The phone rang and she tensed with hope each time she answered but it was always a business call or Fern or her mother. Once it was Frenchy confirming Saturday. Millie would be at the house on the farm until she arrived, not to worry about the time, she had plenty to do and her son would pick her up and drive her back to Newark where she already had a small apartment near Adele's house. Yes, Frenchy. Thank you, Frenchy. She had looked at the list of eight first cousins, among whom there were people she had met only once or twice in her life, and she could not think what principles she would apply to distributing the objects she would find in the old house. Well, she would do it and that was that. It would occupy her Saturday.

She got in early on Thursday and the phone rang shortly after nine. That would be her boss scheduling a conference or asking to see her before she got involved in anything else.

She picked up the phone and said, 'Judy Wolfe,' and waited for Sheldon's voice.

'Can I see you for lunch?' It was not Sheldon. It was low and almost toneless.

She said, 'Yes,' feeling an internal crash, the welcome end of her good intentions, the rise of hope, the confirmation that he cared. Her voice had sounded faint. Since Saturday she had lost even the energy to be monosyllabic.

'I'll try to make it at a quarter to.'

'OK.'

There was a short pause, as thought he were deciding whether to say something important or let it wait. He let it wait. 'I'll see you then.'

She was a wreck. She chided herself for being adolescent, for compromising her principles. If she saw him today, she would see him forever. She would not stop. Something cataclysmic would have to happen to separate them. She would see to it that it would not happen. Her spirits soared as her nervousness grew. She would apologize. She would tell him outright that she loved him. She would invite him to join her for the trip to New Jersey on Saturday. She would be good to him, so good, as good as she had wanted to be when she failed.

She gave a brief message to the switchboard operator at eleven-twenty-five and went downstairs to find a taxi. It was still early when she arrived and she took her position along the sidewalk, out of the way of pedestrians, within sight of his door. At noon she began to worry. White-coated young men had come out in great numbers since her arrival but not Marcel. At twelve-thirty she felt something like panic. It crossed her mind briefly that she had been stood up in the cruellest way imaginable and just as quickly she dismissed the possibility. He would not do that. He did not have it in him to hurt. How many people could she say that about? She wondered. About her parents and her brothers she believed it implicitly. But of whom else? Roy could hurt. Not her, but he could hurt. Marcel could not. Marcel healed. Marcel was the kind of man you looked for, hoped you would find, because he was worth waiting for, because he was someone you could trust. He did not hurt and he did not humiliate.

Two in white coats passed her on their way back to the hospital. One looked at her with recognition. She turned away before she was sure whether he was one of the future surgeons she had seen on that first lunch date, when she had been so happy. Marcel did not walk with that confident swagger that said, Clear a path. I am coming.

At a quarter to one she hailed a taxi and returned to the office. There were no messages. She went back to her cubicle – it was scarcely an office – and began to look over the draft she had been working on for the right-to-assembly case. Something had happened and he had not been able to call. She could feel doubts pushing to insinuate themselves and she repelled their attack forcefully. Someone came by and asked if she wanted coffee and she said yes, a big one, and handed him change. She would call him tonight. But she didn't know if he was *on* tonight. She had severed their relationship and she didn't know his schedule any more. Something awful had happened and he had not had time to telephone or dash out to the street to tell her. The kids in the case she was working on had assembled on a street near a consulate and two had overflowed into a parking spot reserved for a diplomatic vehicle. Come on back, Judy, and think about it. The police had dragged them away after they had stood, sat or slept there for fourteen hours. It was three o'clock and he had not called her. Six hours since they had spoken this morning. Think, she told herself. This day will pass but the law will be here forever. Three-thirty. Four. Four-oh-seven.

The phone rang and the sound startled her. 'Hello?'

'Judy, I'm sorry.'

Like an echo. *Go ahead, New Haven.*

He sounded exhausted, beat.

'It's OK.' It was more than OK. It was a new beginning.

'I couldn't get to a phone.'

'Is she all right?'

'She?' He sounded thoroughly mystified.

'Your patient. The one – the one I'm sharing you with.'

There was a short pause. Then he said, 'Oh,' and 'Oh,' again. 'Mrs J.' He laughed and she knew they both felt better. 'She's not all right but she's the same. It was something else. An accident came in about ten-thirty and we've been in surgery since then.'

'I'll call you tonight.'

'Oh, honey, I can't talk tonight.' She could feel his fatigue. 'I only slept two hours last night and when I get finished here – '

'I'm driving to New Jersey Saturday, Marcel. Something for Frenchy. Will you come?'

'Saturday.' He sounded as though he were trying to figure out whether that was a day or a month or a word he had never heard before. 'Sure. I get done here at noon.'

'I'll pick you up.'

'Make it one at home. I'll have to clean up.'

'I'll be there.'

The coin dropped. 'We OK now?' he asked with a measure of uncertainty.

'We're fine.'

'I'll see you Saturday.'

She hung up, leaned back in her chair, and stretched, her shoes nearly touching the wall against which the desk stood, her calves and thighs pulling hard. Maybe Saturday morning she would ride, make her body work a little. She felt wonderful – happy, satisfied, contented. She pulled her stack of papers in front of her and started from page one, feeling the excitement of the case take hold once again. Sloppy, she thought, using her pencil extravagantly. Where was your mind, Jude, old girl? You can do better than that.

She took fresh paper and started again, working without a break until a little after seven. She left then but only because she was finished, because it was now right. She was filled with energy, ready to go on for hours more.

It was beautiful out, still light, still mild. She got on to the uptown subway and looked out the window as she passed the station that was nearest to Marcel. He was asleep now and she sensed his peace. They were OK now. They were fine.

She turned into West Third just as he emerged from his doorway. She slid past the first girlie joint and stopped in front of him. He came around to her window and said, 'Hi.'

'Hi. Want to drive?'

'No thanks.' He circled the car and got in beside her.

'Tired?'

He nodded. 'I'll pick up in a while.'

She got back to the West Side Highway and drove north. By the time she paid the fifty-cent toll on the George Washington Bridge, he was asleep.

The trip took the better part of an hour and was not very scenic although the day was beautiful. She had hoped he would at least help her with Frenchy's directions but as it turned out, she had to fend for herself until the last few minutes, juggling the envelope, reading at high speed. As she made the last turn, he opened his eyes and straightened up in the seat.

'Sorry,' he said.

'We're almost there.'

'I must have fallen asleep. It's nice country.'

It was, at that point. 'I think that's it.' She slowed. There was a mailbox at the side of the road, and she saw it said Wolfe and another name underneath. There were no other cars around and she turned left with ease and bumped along what looked like an unpaved drive. She had been here as a child and it came back to her, the house near the road that had been Uncle Nate's, the one behind that was Millie's, the one far behind that that was Grandpa Willy's. The oldest house was directly back and a little to the right, rather grand-looking she thought, rather aristocratic.

She stopped the car near the house that was probably Millie's and opened her door. Marcel had his hand on the door handle but he had not moved.

'Something wrong?'

'It looks like – it just reminded me of the place I stayed during the war.' He opened the door and got out and stood looking around.

'Judy!' a woman's voice, high-pitched and excited, called from nearby.

'Hello, Millie.'

'Oh, isn't it good to see you? You're just as beautiful as your mother.' She was small and thin, wearing a print dress, her hair in greying ringlets, her face lighted with a big smile. As she came toward them, a car turned into the drive and stopped behind the Volkswagen. 'There's my Harold,' Millie said, beaming. 'Didn't we time it well?'

A man in his thirties got out of the second car and joined Millie. He looked nothing like her except for the curly hair, which had begun to recede from his widening forehead.

They shook hands and kissed and Judy said, 'I'd like you to meet Marcel Goldblatt. My cousins, Millie and Harold.'

'Oh, I know who you are,' Millie said, grasping Marcel's hand. 'Goldblatt. You're from that wonderful French family, aren't you?'

'I'm from Paris, yes.' He spoke with a certain reserve, a measured caution.

'That was a wonderful family,' Millie said, her voice almost singing, her eyes shining. 'Regina always wrote about them when she was there. I'm the one that used to take care of our grandparents, you know,' she said proudly, as though she had been singled out for the honour, 'and I was there when the letters came. She used to write about Suzanne – she was very beautiful, wasn't she? – and her big brother Maurice – he became a lawyer, didn't he? – and the little brother.' She stopped and looked thoughtfully at Marcel. 'I've forgotten his name,' she said with regret.

'Marc.' He said it in French, the vowel and the R sounding foreign.

'Marc, yes.' Millie smiled again. 'He was just a little fellow.' The smile faded. 'He died too, didn't he?'

'Yes.'

Judy looked from one to the other. Something strange had happened. Marcel had not taken his eyes off Millie since they had been introduced. Judy and Harold were on the outside of the conversation, looking in.

'Regina used to send me perfume in those days,' Millie went on with her disjointed recollections. 'Real French perfume. My cousin Lillian was jealous but Lillian was always jealous if you had something she didn't have. Regina wasn't. Regina was generous. I used to wear that perfume when I went to the bakery to see my Izzy. I couldn't have married Izzy if it wasn't for Regina. She talked to Grandmama for me. She told Poppi how important it was. Of course, she really knew. She went to Paris because she wanted to marry Jerold so much and she couldn't. Because they're cousins, you know.'

It struck like the cold blade of a knife. Judy shuddered and looked at the little woman with the bright eyes, tight curls and high voice who had dropped this terrible insinuation and now was hurrying on to amplify it.

'It was a secret in those days, or it was supposed to be, but any fool could tell just by looking at them.'

'Mum,' her son interrupted, looking with uneasy eyes from Judy's face to his mother's, but Millie was somewhere else; she would not be stopped or put off course. Her eyes had a dreamy quality and her voice fairly sang.

'I used to watch them that summer, how one would leave the pond and then the other. I never knew where they went, but there were lots of woods then. More than now. Poppa cut them down to make more farmland. You should walk through the woods, Marcel. Do they have forests in France?'

'Yes, they do.'

'These are virgin forests, you know.' She waved her hand, encompassing the whole farm. 'Those trees were here before we were. My grandfather cut down the first trees to build that house and start the farm. Someone bought half the land after the war, a builder, they told us, but he never built. We never even knew where his part began and ours ended. Now they'll build, now that I'm leaving.'

'You must be very proud to be the last in your family to have the land,' Marcel said quietly.

'Oh, I am,' Millie said. 'If my Izzy were alive, we would still keep the farm. Izzy loved farming. He died down the road, you know.' Her energy suddenly petered out. 'Walking home from shul on Saturday.' She bit her lips together as though the wound were still fresh. 'It's more than twenty-five years,' she finished.

'Mum, I think Judy'd like to get her work done,' Harold said.

Millie heaved a sigh and brightened. 'Come. We'll walk over to the house. I'm so glad Frenchy sent you. You look so much like Edith. It all turned out right in the end, didn't it?'

'Where are the things you want me to see?' Judy asked, keeping her voice even.

'Upstairs in Grandmama's room. The rest of the house is empty. You just make your decisions and Frenchy will take care of everything.'

'Won't you come up with me to help?'

'Oh, no,' Millie said with great seriousness. 'You're the lawyer. I wouldn't want to influence you. You just look those things over and decide who should get what. And if there's something you specially like, you take it for yourself.'

'Thank you.'

'And we'll see each other again, Judy.'

'I'll walk you back to the car,' Marcel said, and turning to Judy, 'I want to look around.'

She said, 'OK,' and watched them go, hearing Millie take up the narrative again. 'Those Goldblatts. What a wonderful family they were. And that big house on the avenue . . .'

243

Turning to the house, she went inside. It was eerily empty. Nothing lay about. She went up the stairs and looked in one room after another until, at the back of the house, she found the right one. The sight of it stunned her. It had been preserved like a museum. There was no dust. The large bed looked freshly made. The rocker was waiting for a mother with her baby. The dressing table with its large cheval mirror tilted to accommodate one seated woman offered itself to her. There were a dresser and a chest. Five pieces of furniture, eight cousins.

She pulled the envelope from her bag and took out the list. Frenchy had arranged brothers and sisters in an orderly fashion. Jerold Wolfe and Richard Wolfe below. A space, Lillian Schindler, Dr Henry Wolfe. A space. Mildred Benetovich, Adele Bergman, Arthur Wolfe. A space. Regina Rush.

It was not possible. Regina had gone to Paris because she wanted to study there. Daddy had told the story enough times when Judy was growing up. The woman was simply crazy. Frenchy had said as much.

There was a coverlet made of dozens of crocheted circles covering the bed. That would be for Regina. Beneath it was a handmade quilt. Uncle Richard. The bed, the dresser and the chest of drawers belonged together. They would go to Millie, Adele, and Arthur. That left the rocker, which was beautifully carved, and the dressing table with the large mirror, which she would have liked for herself but would give to her parents. But there were three recipients for the two remaining articles. What did this crazy cousin of hers want of her?

She stood staring at the contents of the room, the list in her hand, trying to think how to divide seven things eight ways, when she heard a sound behind her. She turned and saw Marcel in the doorway.

'She's crazy,' she said unsteadily.

'She's not crazy. She's a lovely old woman who remembers when things were better.'

'It isn't true what she said about my father.' She sounded as thought she were trying to convince him. In fact, she was trying to convince herself.

'It doesn't matter. It's not important.'

'Of course it's important.' She felt torn up, raging against shadows. 'Look at this room,' she said in despair. 'My great-grandfather died seventeen years ago. She's kept it like a museum. Nobody's used it since then. And there aren't enough things to go around.'

He put his arm around her. 'How many people do you have to satisfy?' he asked quietly.

Two, Marcel. You and me, and I think now that I never will. I think something happened last week that we haven't remedied because we can't. 'Eight,' she said.

He looked around the room, turning her slightly as he turned himself. 'There's more than enough, Judy. The night tables and lamps alone – '

'The night tables,' she said faintly, seeing them for the first time. 'I never saw the night tables.' There was a polished brass oil lamp, electrified, on top of each one. 'I'll give them to Lillian, the rocker to her brother, and then I can give my mother the dressing table.'

'That wasn't hard, was it?'

She shook her head and he let her go and started to unbutton his shirt. She watched him with the curiosity of the uninitiated, button after button, the shirt coming off to expose his bare chest. He dropped the shirt on the dressing table and looked at her.

'You're angry about something,' she said, thinking of her own anger when he had fallen asleep in the car, when she had heard her cousin speak foolishly of her father and Regina, when he had walked her cousins back to the car instead of coming here with her. 'Don't do it in anger.'

'Angry.' He said it as though he had failed to understand the word. 'I love you, Judy.'

She walked over to him and leaned against his bare chest, black with hair, kissed the smooth shoulder that still smelled of the soap with which he had washed before she called for him, felt his arms tight around her. He was a beautiful man. It was a long time since she had loved anyone.

245

She turned away from him to undress, crossing her arms in front of her to grasp the lightweight sweater she had worn over her shirt because it was a cool afternoon. She pulled the sweater over her head, shook her hair back, and saw herself, nearly full length, in the dressing table mirror, the reflection startling her. She had never seen herself in the moment before she made love. She looked at the face with the recognition reserved for one's own image. The surprise faded and she saw a slight smile replace it as she took the shirt off and unhooked the bra, the acceptance of her own good looks, the anticipation of great pleasure. It was a magnificent mirror, tall with bevelled edges in a warm mahogony frame, the mirror of a woman who enjoyed looking at herself, a woman satisfied with her reflection, a woman who kept herself beautiful for her husband, a happy woman.

She dropped her eyes, pushed off her sneakers with the tips of her fingers, opened the fly front of her jeans, and, bending, removed the remainder of her clothes in one smooth movement, leaving them in a careless heap because she felt careless herself now, careless and tense and somewhat anxious, hotly expectant and warmly loving. When she turned back, she saw he had not moved. He had watched her undress, standing barefoot in his jeans. God, he was a beautiful man.

It was a worn brown belt. He unbuckled it and finished undressing as she had, quickly and carelessly. She went over to him and invited his kiss, standing so that her breasts just touched his chest, moving her body very slightly as he kissed her. She could feel the restraint in his kiss and in his hands, as though he were waiting, putting it off one last minute, saving it. She touched his shoulders and ran her hands down the front of his body, passing over his nipples and the bones of his pelvis.

'You're so hard,' she whispered, feeling it move as she spoke.

'Been hard since you walked in my door last month.'

'I'm glad.'

He walked her to the bed and took Regina's coverlet off,

tossing it on Henry's rocker. He pulled Uncle Richard's quilt down, revealing white muslin sheets on somebody's bed, she had forgotten whose, their bed, and they lay down on it, finally down, lovingly down, deeply down, and when he touched her, the restraint was gone, all gone, such a beautiful man and he was hers to love.

Judy.

So good to her and she had made him angry over nothing. As though he had known her forever. As though he knew just how to make her happy.

Judy.

She would love him so much she would destroy him but he was so good, he would probably forgive her.

Oh, Judy.

She smiled at him and kissed him and he stirred as though she had aroused some lusty feeling not yet satisfied.

'I knew,' he adjusted himself next to her, fitting their bodies comfortably, 'that you would be the best thing that ever happened to me.'

It pleased her to hear it. 'When did you know?'

'That Christmas.'

'You hated me that Christmas.'

'I never hated you.'

'I didn't hate you either.'

He pulled the muslin top sheet up to cover her, an act of modesty more than a concern for comfort. 'What happened last Saturday night?'

'I was trying to protect you.' He had large dark eyes. 'I haven't loved anyone for so long.'

'And now? Is my protection gone?'

'Mm-hmm. You're on your own. I don't want to give you up any more.'

He got out of bed and walked to the rocker, touched the arm and stood watching it as it rocked. His back was to her.

'Was it Kellems?' he asked.

It gave her a start and she swallowed before speaking. 'How did you know?'

247

'The way people acted when I was arrested and his name came up. The way you looked when I told you.'

'It was a long time ago and when it happened, it was right.'

He turned around to face her. 'He was one of the people who helped save my life.'

'He does that for people. In the end, you saved your own life. In the end, I saved mine. I did it partly by leaving him. I'm sure he knew that.'

He came back and sat on his side of the bed. The rocker was still. 'At the beginning, he talked to me as if I were his son. He was in France when I was just a kid. With the invasion. Later on, when the trial was over, it was different. We talked differently. We used to go to dinner . . . Kellems doesn't drink.'

'I know.'

'I guess you would. I guess we don't have to talk about it any more.'

'Come closer,' Judy said, sensing that it was over now, that it had been said. 'Don't be so far away.'

He came back and lay beside her and she felt lightened. There were no secrets, just good feelings and some nice memories.

'I'm glad you came today,' she said. 'I couldn't have done it without you. Millie got me so shook up I couldn't even count.'

'Why don't you talk to your father about it?'

'I can't.'

'He's easy to talk to. I don't think he'd be angry.'

'You don't know my father. You met him once for ten minutes.'

'I know Jerold very well.' He rested on an elbow so that he could look at her. There was something in his eyes, something at the corners of his lips.

'I – I don't know what you mean.'

'Didn't you ever wonder who was paying my bills?'

'You said you'd – Well, I supposed the Rushes.'

'Regina called your father the night I walked out. He came down to West Third and stayed half the night. You grew up lucky.'

'I know that.'

'He sat down in one of my crummy chairs and said, "What do you want to do with your life?" and I didn't know what to answer. No one had ever asked me before. I said, "Well, my aunt Suzanne wants me to go to law school and Morty wants – " and he said, "I didn't ask you what anyone else wants. I asked you what you want." So I said, "I'd like to go to medical school," and he said, "in that case, we'd better find out what the requirements are and get hold of some applications." Then he had a drink, I had a drink, and we talked. Before he left, we made an agreement.'

She had listened with her eyes glistening. 'That's the real reason you wouldn't have called me, isn't it?'

He kissed her and put an arm across her. 'I'll have to tell him now.'

'I'll tell him.'

'No.'

She kissed the hand that held her shoulder. 'He won't approve,' she said, 'but he won't interfere.'

'I know.' He considered something for a moment. 'When we get back to the city, will I pack a bag and go to your place or will you pack a bag and come to mine?'

'I'll pack a bag and go to yours.'

'You sure?'

'Yes.'

'Maybe just till the end of the month. I don't think I want you living on West Third.'

'My place is more expensive,' she said cautiously.

'Not if we share.'

'OK.' She was glad she had made the first concession. They would get along beautifully. Already in the first minutes of being together they had worked out an agreement.

'Let's go home.'

They dressed and he helped her remake the bed. She sat at the dressing table and brushed her hair, watching her reflection. Marcel walked to the windows, buckling his belt.

'Some tree,' he said. 'I wonder . . .' He pulled the sheer

curtains aside and looked out. 'It might mean something to them if I went back.'

She looked at him questioningly, not following the train of his thought.

'The people I stayed with during the war. I never saw them again.'

'I think it would mean everything in the world to them. Just to see you.'

'Maybe next summer . . .'

'I'll go with you.'

He came over to where she was sitting. 'Then I'll definitely go.'

She got up, took her bag, and they left the room. At the foot of the stairs, he put his arm around her. She felt wonderful, light and happy, relaxed and contented. They chattered about nothing as they walked across the weedy expanse between the house and where she had left her car in the drive near Millie's house. She sensed the comfort in him. He was as happy as she. Something scarcely predictable had turned out unexpectedly perfect.

As they neared the little Volkswagen, she dropped her arm from around him and started toward the driver's side. He caught her arm and stopped walking.

'Where do you think you're going? I want you right here.'

'To the car,' she said. 'I'm driving, remember?'

He stood looking at her a minute as though something unanticipated had happened. 'Give me the damn keys,' he said finally. Then he drove them home.

When the phone rang, it roused her from a deep sleep. Unaccustomed to the new configuration, she turned to answer and banged her hand painfully on the wall. At the same moment, she heard Marcel's voice on the other side of the bed.

He said, 'Hello,' in a voice heavy with sleep, the accent more pronounced. It was so quiet she could hear the caller, a man's voice but the words were unintelligible. Marcel said, 'Yeah,' a few times and then, 'OK,' and then the man asked him something and it was a moment before he said, 'All right.' Then he hung up and lay back on the pillow.

She felt very tired. They had eaten at her apartment and made love at his. She has not thought about anything except them since they had left New Jersey and now resented the intrusion of the outside world. 'What is it?' she asked.

'A guy in my class,' he said. 'He's at the hospital. It's my patient. She wanted to know where the nice young man was.'

She reached out her arm and touched his chest. 'Is she dying?'

'Yes.'

'I'll go with you.'

'Don't be silly.' He sounded irritated.

But she was sitting up and her head had cleared.

'Judy – '

'I'll be dressed in a minute.'

He sat up and looked at her and she turned away and pulled clothes out of her open suitcase. He got out of bed heavily and moved slowly. She wanted to say something, something right, something comforting. but she could not think of what so she said nothing. She was ready before him and she stood at the door, waiting.

He opened the door for her and locked it behind them. She started for the stairs but stopped when she saw he had not moved. Finally, he took the car keys out of his pocket, handed them to her, took her hand and they went down the stairs together.

He showed her where to park and they rode up in a lift. It was quiet and dim. Doors were closed. She was twenty-six but she could not remember having been in a hospital more than two or three times in her life, always as a visitor and always reluctantly. When the lift stopped, he took off ahead of her with wide strides, nearly running. Halfway down the hall, he stopped and spoke briefly to a nurse, then turned and waved at Judy. Then he continued down the hall to where light poured out of an open room.

'You can sit here,' the nurse said pleasantly, offering a chair.

'Thank you.' It was hard-backed without arms, a chair for someone who had a moment to sit between duties. She unbuttoned her raincoat and let it fall around her. Down the hall a sense of something happening emanated from the room with the open door. The sounds were little more than whispers at this distance but they were the only sounds from either direction.

'Would you like a magazine, Mrs Goldblatt?'

It took her a moment to realize it was she who had been addressed, to raise her eyes and look at the nurse. 'Uh – yes – if you have one handy.'

Flustered at the appellation. Wondering if it was an assumption or if Marcel had said something in that brief stop at the desk. *My wife.*

The nurse opened a drawer and pulled out a worn copy of *Life* or *Look*. 'It's not very new,' she apologized.

'It doesn't matter. I haven't seen one for ages. Thank you.' She turned pages mindlessly. Cigarette ads. Cars. She glanced up and saw a tall, thin black man in some kind of white uniform run down the hall and enter the room Marcel was in. She watched the doorway for a minute but nothing else happened and she dropped her eyes to the magazine. As she turned the pages, she realized it was the issue on the assassination. There they were, the king and queen themselves, Jack and Jackie at the start of the trip, and there the famous strip of film that every American had seen a hundred times in the last six months. She hurried through the section, hoping there would be something lighter after it, but of course, there wasn't.

Leaving it open on her lap, she said, 'Do you like to work nights?'

'I don't mind. My husband works days and the children are still little so it works out best this way.'

'It must be hard.'

'It's the way things worked out.' The nurse looked down the hall. 'Excuse me,' she said, rising and hurrying away on soundless soles. Over the open door, a light had gone on.

For Judy the light seemed a signal of final distress. A feeling of nausea welled up within her, the ultimate threat to her equanimity. She kept her eyes on the open door down the hall as though she might pierce the wall and see within. A young man in a white coat stepped out of the room, looked at her, and went back in. It was not Marcel. She wondered if the woman inside, the woman dying, wanted to perform her last act under full lights before a large audience. She had asked for Marcel. Perhaps that was what she wanted, Marcel at the side of her bed with a single lamp, shaded, somewhere nearby. The company tonight was nobody's choice. Surely it was not Marcel's.

She was not sure how long she sat watching nothing. The magazine slid from her lap and when she put it on the desk, she saw the tall black man leave the room and go down the hall in the direction from which he had come. The nurse came next, sitting at her desk without a word and making a phone call in a quiet voice. A medical student left the room and then a doctor and following them was Marcel.

As she stood and walked to the centre of the hall, it struck her that he was at home here, that the reticence that had held him back at the apartment had evaporated as they got off the lift. This was his courtroom. Here he was neither patient nor visitor and he was without the apprehensions of either. He was not an outsider here, he was a member; he belonged. One day he would exchange the student's white coat for a more prestigious one but nothing else would change. This was his home.

He came rapidly, putting his arm around her as he reached her, and she fell in stride. 'You OK?' she asked in a hushed voice.

He shook his head.

Before they reached the lifts, he dropped his arm and broke away, pushing open a door on the right side of the hall. He left so suddenly that she kept walking several paces before she could signal herself to stop. Looking back she saw that the door he had gone through said MEN.

253

She felt frightened now, uncertain of her own ability to heal and comfort. She looked back down the hall. Something on wheels was being pulled out of the room with the open door. The long top of the cart was covered with sheets.

She turned back, pivoting so that she stood the way Marcel had left her. She heard the swinging door open and felt his arm around her and they resumed their march down the hall.

'Slowly,' she said softly.

His pace slowed and he said, 'OK.'

She pushed the Down button and the doors opened immediately. It had been waiting all this time for them. In a few minutes, they were in the car.

She thought unseemly prayers that they would find a parking space and the prayers were answered. Upstairs they undressed silently and got back into bed. His skin felt too cool and she rubbed his bare arm, trying to warm him. The passion that had seemed so limitless earlier in the day was gone as though it had never existed and to her surprise, he fell asleep almost immediately. It was she who lay awake, wary and watchful, until first light came from the living room. Then she too slept.

Six

———◆———

They awoke late, the sun streaming into the apartment. 'Let's go somewhere for breakfast,' Marcel said. 'You hungry?'

'Very.'

They walked diagonally across Washington Square Park and up University Place to the Cookery. There was a small table for two outside and they sat facing each other. He looked better this morning, clean-shaven, rested. They had not said much but they had walked closely and he had kissed the side of her face as they passed the pool in the park.

'Don't unpack your suitcase,' he said now, surprising her. 'Let's go uptown this afternoon. I'm tired of the Village. I don't want you living on West Third.'

'I don't mind, Marcel.'

'I mind.'

'No nostalgia?'

'None.'

'I always feel a longing for places I've left.'

'Because you left them too soon, or maybe soon enough. I outgrew this place a long time ago but I stayed because it was cheap and convenient and maybe because it bothered certain people that I was here and I enjoyed bothering them. I don't need that kind of enjoyment and it's not the place for you.'

'I really do love you,' she said.

'I thought you might.' His face looked very open, very endearing.

'Will you bring the kitchen table uptown?'

'It won't fit.'

'Yes it will. I'll find a place for it. And it's yours. You stripped it.'

The orange juice came and he drained his glass quickly. 'If it fits in the car, we'll take it.'

'OK.'

'Anything else I can do for you?' He looked very earnest, very obliging.

She shook her head. 'You've already done it.'

On Monday morning she mailed a report to Frenchy of what she had found in the farmhouse and how she had apportioned the items. A week later he called her.

'I've heard from Millie,' he said.

'Was I objective enough for her?'

'Overgenerous. She said giving Lillian two night tables and two lamps was far too much. She's decided to give the tables to Lillian and the lamps to her brother. That'll leave something for you. She said you forgot to take something for yourself.'

'Frenchy,' Judy said seriously, 'What did she want me to go out there for? Why couldn't she have made all these decisions herself the first time around?'

'I told you she was a little nutty. Maybe she didn't want to choose something for herself and be condemned as greedy. Anyway, she was very pleased with the arrangement, said Marcel was a joy to meet, and I think I'll have your cheque in the mail tomorrow.'

'She is nutty, isn't she?' Judy said, longing for confirmation.

'But a good soul,' Frenchy assured her.

It made her feel a little better about Millie's story. It made her able to set it aside.

A week later the dressing table with the large bevelled mirror was delivered to her apartment.

When Marcel's exams were over they spent a week at a cabin in Massachusetts. It was the first time they were together for consecutive days, consecutive meals, minute after minute and hour after hour. It was the first time they were both rested and unhurried, the first time they had all the time they wanted. She left happier than when they arrived. All that time had not been enough and all that closeness had not been stifling.

The drove back slowly, relishing the last of their time together. He stopped somewhere after lunch and they walked quietly in woods.

'I told the Rushes about you and me,' he said after a while.

'Oh?'

'Before we left. I didn't want them to hear it from anyone else.'

'How did they take it?'

'Predictably. No, not predictably. Regina's pleased. I think she takes full credit for making a match.'

'I'll give her three-quarters.'

'It's Morty that acted strangely. You know, for years I didn't make any effort to understand him and we didn't get along, we clashed all the time, but he tried and I know he felt a tremendous affection for me in spite of myself. Now, when I'd like to see things patched up, when I really try, I don't seem to get anywhere.'

'Is it me he disapproves of or our not being married?'

'I'm not sure.' He stopped walking. 'How could anyone disapprove of you?' he asked ingenuously and she laughed. 'It's something else, something I can't put my finger on. Maybe it's a family thing.'

'They never go to family weddings.'

'Regina's very close to her family.'

'I've never seen them once, in all the years I can remember.' She thought of Millie, the crazy cousin, and what she had said about Daddy and Regina.

'It doesn't matter.' He looked at his watch. 'We'd better get going or we'll hit the Sunday afternoon traffic.'

They walked lazily. He was such a pleasure to be with. They talked for hours and when they stopped talking, she was happy just having him nearby. If she had designed a man's body to suit her, it would have been his. Thinking about it, she kissed his cheek and he stopped and kissed her properly, holding her with the same undiminished desire she had sensed in him a week ago at the start of their holiday and a month ago when they had first lain on that bed in the old farmhouse.

'I've decided what kind of medicine I want to practise,' he said when they had resumed walking.

'So soon? You haven't even sampled all of it.'

'I think I've known all along. It isn't really a speciality because nobody seems to have made a career of it. I'd like to treat older people, elderly people. How does that sound to you?'

'I think you'd be very good at it. You have a nice way with people. They'll trust you. I just wonder why you made that choice.'

'It was a natural,' he said. 'I understand their anger.'

She had another week of holiday coming and he insisted that she take it without him because he could not get away. They went to court on her right-of-assembly case and won, bringing her congratulations from the partner who argued the case, and a raise on her first anniversary.

She waited till August to take her second week so that both her parents would be at their summer home in Pennsylvania. She had not seen them much since the end of May. Her mother, distressed at her living arrangements, would not invite both of them to dinner. Judy knew that this was the week she would have to straighten things out.

They talked after breakfast on her first full day, Daddy having gone off to look over the property, make repairs, enjoy one of the long solitary walks he took in summer. Edith Wolfe had been brought up the only child of wealthy parents – Grandpa French had made a fortune in the twenties and sold all the stock he owned early in 1929. Edith had lived a very proper life and she was ashamed of her daughter's behaviour. It was not an easy conversation and when it was over, Judy was not sure anything had been settled.

What had become more important was the realization of how much she missed Marcel. She chided herself for leaving on

Saturday when she could have spent the weekend with him. She found herself looking at her watch at frequent intervals, wishing it were time to call. When they finally spoke, it only made her miss him more.

She swam, she rode, she walked with her father and helped her mother with small tasks. A letter came from Marcel, written after their first telephone conversation. She had never seen his handwriting before, never imagined how he would put words together on paper. He put them together beautifully, legibly, emotionally, memorably.

In the middle of the week, she went down to swim before lunch and found her father drying off at the edge of the lake.

'Looks very calm,' she said.

'It is. And about as warm as it'll get this year.' He sat on one of the beach chairs they left permanently on the shore.

'Yes, I guess.'

'Your mother and I are very pleased you decided to spend this week with us. I don't suppose there'll be many more like this.'

She watched her foot making circles in the sand and said nothing. In a way that her mother could not, her father often touched something deeply sentimental in her.

'Your mum's not happy about the way you're living.'

'You're not either.' She remained standing but turned to face him.

'Perhaps for different reasons. You're a member of the bar. That happens to be very important to me. It's a membership, a status, that I think you should not take lightly.'

It surprised her sometimes that he could say such things and believe in what he was saying, as she was sure he did, when they both knew his own past. 'I'm not doing it to hurt anyone,' she said honestly. 'I know that I did once – at least partly. This is different.'

'Can you talk about that now?' her father asked.

'About Roy? Of course I can talk about it.' She sat, dropping the towel across her thighs. 'I could always talk about it.'

'You surprise me,' Jerold Wolfe said. 'You're so different from me and I always think we're very much alike.'

'I loved Roy very much,' she went on, not sure what he had meant, not sure that it was very important. 'And he loved me. Not at the beginning, maybe. At the beginning it was sort of a game. For both of us. But it changed. I could have married him but I chose not to.'

'One can't be sure about these things,' her father said.

But she was sure. In spite of what Annie had told her, she knew; but she was at a point in her life where knowing was enough or had lost its importance. She did not have to impress her father or anyone else that what she knew was true. Instead, she went on, knowing it was the only time she would ever talk to him about it, the only time he would ever ask.

'I left him because I wanted to be a certain kind of person, not one who destroyed other people's lives. I didn't want my own happiness founded on someone else's misery.'

'I'm glad you're that person.'

'I hope I am.' She shifted the towel, letting it fall down her legs to avoid sunburn. 'He's a very remarkable man,' she said. 'I probably learned more from him than from anyone else I've ever known, more even than from you.' She met his eyes openly and noticed, as though for the first time, that the hair along the sides of his face was greying, that on his chest also the hair had lost some of its colour. He had turned sixty-two earlier in the year but today it struck her that he was no longer young, that he was ageing, that one day he would be old, that she would not have him forever.

'Is something wrong?' he asked calmly and she knew that her face had betrayed her new knowledge and its accompanying fear.

She said, 'No,' softly and continued to look at him.

'Roy Kellems is a good lawyer,' her father said, 'and I respect that in him, admire it perhaps, but I'm sure you know that my respect and admiration have been quite limited since 1959.'

'Roy thinks a great deal of you. He never let an angry word from me go by without neutralizing it.' She spoke of him comfortably. He was a man many people thought they knew, but she knew him better than all of them, knew him and still respected and admired him without the limitations others, like her father, might set.

'I'd much prefer to talk about Marcel,' her father said.

'So would I.' The muscles sliding back to an easy norm, a flicker of something sexual where no one could see it but where she could feel and welcome it. 'I miss him.'

'Yes.' Her father looked more relaxed and the edge was gone from his voice. 'I've enjoyed knowing him these last four years. He's given me a great deal of satisfaction, a great deal of genuine pleasure.'

'I can't marry him,' Judy said, answering the question her father would not ask, feeling Marcel's absence sharply, thinking it had been easier talking about Roy because she did not miss Roy.

'You can do anything you want.' Like a message.

'Daddy – ' It was like dredging up the unmentionable. 'I cannot do to myself what I saw Diana go through. I cannot take the chance of having children. Don't you see – Roy was safe. The man I was seeing last fall was safe. They don't need children any more. Marcel does.'

'I haven't seen you marrying any of these "safe" men. I haven't seen you spending more than a few months with any of them. Does safe also mean impermanent? Is there a new definition I've failed to become aware of?'

'You know exactly what I mean. Don't bully me as if I were an obstreperous lawyer in your court.' She said it in a slightly teasing manner but she meant it. 'I care about him and I care about what becomes of him. His sister will never have children and if he marries me, the Goldblatt family will end right there.'

'I'm surprised sometimes,' Jerold Wolfe said, 'at how certain some people in their twenties are about what is right with a capital R.'

'How long should people in their twenties wait to find out?' she asked with some exasperation.

'Perhaps they shouldn't wait at all. Perhaps they should

admit, as the rest of us have, that they know very little about what is right.'

Sometimes she thought that of all the people she knew, her father understood things of the heart best. It was as if he knew how much she wanted Marcel at this minute, as if he understood those pangs that translated into sexual appetite, those feelings that could never be completely satisfied, only partly so as they whetted future appetites, making one always look forward with as much happiness as one had in looking back. 'I love him very much,' she said in a voice she could scarcely hear.

'You know, when I swim back across the lake late in the afternoon towards the end of August, the sun is very low and it's always in my eyes, painfully so at times. When I've nearly crossed the lake, I reach that little island with the big tree on it and because the sun is so low, one leaf at the top of the tree covers the sun and gives me welcome relief from the piercing glare. It's something I look forward to, that moment of peace at the end of that long swim, and I think sometimes, if a single leaf can cover the sun, what could my children do if they only tried.'

She looked at him while the tears that had welled up for Marcel spilled over now for her father and finally she said, 'I'll think about it.'

'That's all I ask,' her father said and, patting her back, he walked away.

In September, when her parents returned to the city, her mother called and invited them both for dinner.

262

Seven

It was cold and earlier than usual when Regina left the house. Downstairs the long car was waiting, the chauffeur leaving the driver's seat and reaching her door smoothly as she stepped out of the apartment house lobby with a bright 'Good morning' to the doorman. On the seat beside the driver a map lay open and after he had made the obligatory series of right turns to head in the direction they wanted, he drove north and west towards the George Washington Bridge. Today she was making her last trip to the family farm in New Jersey.

When Frenchy had called her about the property she owned, she had taken a moment to remember that she did, indeed, own property. Uncle Nate had put half the farm up for sale in 1947 to pay the gambling debts of his son, Arthur. Pained that a piece of that wonderful land should be sold for any reason, and further distressed that it must be sold for this one, she had bought it herself anonymously; only her cousin Jerold – and, of course, Morty – aware of the fact and the reason. Now there was a buyer who would pay a premium for both halves and Regina had told Frenchy that the profit of her share was to go to Millie, sweet Millie who had given her the coverlet from Grandmama's bed.

The sale had been marvellously lucrative and Millie had decided to holiday in Florida for the first time in her life, taking her sister, Adele, with her. Arthur lived somewhere in Florida, with or without his latest wife; it was hard sometimes to get such information from the sisters. That meant that none of the three would be there this frosty October morning.

The buyer was a developer – how, she wondered, could

anyone sell split-level houses with little green lawns thirty miles from Times Square? – and he was anxious to get a start on his building before the hard frost. This was the morning he was scheduled to bulldoze the houses still standing on the property and Regina was on her way to see them for the last time before they were reduced to memory.

She would be alone. She had asked Morty to come with her but he had declined. He had visited the farm only once since 1918 when his first wife, Aunt Maude, had died in childbirth, and that had been for Izzy's funeral, and he had refused to spend the night in the big house that Regina's grandfather had built, the house in which he had married Maude the year before she died. So she would be alone. Richard and Jeanne-Marie were in Japan or Vietnam and neither Henry not his sister Lillian would have the sentiment to see the farm again. That left only Jerold, and Regina had inquired carefully about his schedule. 'Leaves for court every morning at eight like clockwork,' Frenchy had said and she had felt relieved. She had not seen him for fifteen years. She would not see him again today.

The sun was behind them as they crossed the bridge, lighting the Hudson, the Palisades, the roller coaster in the amusement park high on top. Everything about the trip had changed. The route had changed and the conveyance had changed. Dirt roads had been paved, paved roads widened, widened roads divided, dual carriageways turned into super-highways. Fifteen years earlier the trolleys on Bloomfield Avenue had been laid to rest. When she asked Frank, the driver, he said Bloomfield Avenue was not on his map. They would take only main roads.

She tried to think of other things as they drove, of how much she wanted Morty to retire, of how pleased she was with Ernie's success in his marriage and his business, of how she looked forward to Thanksgiving when all the grandchildren would invade the apartment, of Adam who was twenty-one, Adam who was the reason of all reasons.

But all the thinking failed to drive away the old images,

Regina at seventeen with her hair newly cut and blowing in the wind as she sat on the trolley going up the hill to Caldwell, Jerold meeting her in the old Ford, Jerold taking her to a high hill, Jerold, always Jerold, and always too that house and those stairs and the bedroom with the tree outside the window. She knew the house was empty now, the old furniture distributed, sold, or given away, but the room was still there, just behind her closed lids, dreamy in the moonlight, bursting with a primitive urgency, that love which had been so right and so terribly wrong.

'I think this is it, Mrs Rush.'

She opened her eyes. They had approached from the wrong direction, traversed a highway that would one day cross the country. Nothing fitted in with the reality of her memory. To her right she could see the houses – how small they were this last October morning of their existence.

'Yes. Just turn in down that little drive. You can park near the other cars on the left. I'll walk around for a while.'

He pulled in next to a row of cars. A number of workmen were already on the site and a large yellow monster was moving towards Uncle Willy's square house where once she had sat in the kitchen and heard Aunt Eva tell her why she could not marry the man she loved. Funny that they were always yellow, the earth movers, bulldozers, house crushers. She got out of the car and walked to where she faced the buildings. Uncle Willy's house shuddered and collapsed into a pile of rubble and her body shuddered in sympathy, her eyes filling. If a house built with sturdy materials and undying love could be reduced to nothing so quickly, what could a life be worth?

The yellow monster moved on as she stood transfixed, a middle-aged woman in an expensive mink jacket who should perhaps have stayed at home, who should have known she could not watch dispassionately the destruction of the place where all her great passions had blossomed and been consummated. The ice house, the chicken coop, Millie's and Izzy's little house adjoining what had once been the most modern one of all, Uncle Nate's up near the road, the stand in front of it long gone, the stand where she had counted change for Millie and traded off hours to be with Jerold.

Gone, and the monster retreated, beeping in reverse, retrenched, assumed an offensive position and slowly made for Poppi's mansion. She was in terrible, wrenching tears now. She had done her best to keep it from happening, buying the property when Poppi died, not merely for Uncle Nate but, selfishly, for herself, because if the land was hers then the rest of it was hers too, alive and well in some hidden corner of a thankless universe.

The yellow machine nudged the house but the house stood firm, the tree, leafless, rising magnificently behind it. *On this spot I put first my shovel.* How could they all be gone? This was the Wolfe homestead. How had it come to this?

There was shouting and the machine, beeping, backed away to attack from a different angle. It charged again and the house shook, its empty windows gaping like the eyes of a sick animal. It won't fall, she thought. They're going to fail and I'm going to laugh. They'll keep the house, make it new again, and someone will live in it.

The machine disappeared behind the house and she heard the crash and the cheer from the men, saw the roof fall in, but the front, like some temporary Hollywood facade, stood bravely, daylight in the dust behind the upstairs windows, the empty doorway beckoning a parade of ghosts.

The yellow monster rounded the right end of the facade and a group of men in hard hats followed it, standing back to admire their unintended artistry. Then the great machine moved again, delicately this time, cautiously, and, barely touching the free-standing wall, pushed it so that it collapsed into its own cellar.

The dust settled slowly and the men moved away. They would have coffee now and rest after the arduousness of their early labour. She watched through the mist of her eyes and dust, the latter dissipating, the air clearing, revealing a pile of rubble with a thick, sturdy tree behind it, the shade tree

Grandmama had planted as a young, busty, beautiful woman, and beside it the figure of a man in a dark coat, looking in her direction.

He had come. She started towards him, making her way carefully on the hard, uneven surface. She kept her eyes on him across the space where a house had lived. They would never get that tree. Their architect would redesign to accommodate it. It would live into the next century as, surely, she would not. She skirted the remains of the house and he called, 'Careful,' and came to meet her. It was fifteen years.

'Hello, Jody.'

He kissed her, cold dry skin on warmer moist. 'Nothing quite like an old feeling, is there?' he said.

'Nothing in the world.'

'Let me look at you.' He took a step back, his hand still on her arm. 'You look wonderful. I'm glad my cousin Morty keeps you in furs and jewels. You wear them well.' He slid his arm across her furred back.

'I didn't expect you here today. I wouldn't have come if I'd known you were coming. How did you know they were doing it?'

'I have a son who still talks to me about unconfidential family matters.' He smiled. 'I didn't know you'd be here either. How's Morty?'

'He's fine. He'll be seventy-two next week.'

'And still working at that furious pace of his?'

'With a little moderation. Mostly because I've insisted. I asked him once, a few years ago when I very much wanted him to say yes, if he would give up the company.'

'But he didn't.'

'I shouldn't have asked. When a man loves two things almost equally, he can't give up either one of them and it isn't fair to ask it of him.'

'I expect you're right. I expect it's one of those great truths that you recognize only in looking back. Perhaps it's even true of women.'

'Perhaps it is,' she said, remembering.

He pulled his left cuff back and looked at the face of a gold wristwatch. 'Do you have time for a walk?'

'I think I have lots of time now.'

'Frenchy gave it to me,' he said, indicating the watch. 'When he passed the bar. To hurry me into the twentieth century. It's turned out to be quite convenient.'

She remembered that moment in Paris on the Avenue du Bois when he had pulled the old gold pocketwatch out for the first time and flicked it open. Paris was where she had met Morty, but in her deepest associations Paris had always meant Jerold. 'Are you aware of how much I love you?' she said.

'Aware?' They were walking unhurriedly toward the woods, passing just behind and below the ruins of the old Friedmann house. Any moment now Poppa would wave to her or Momma would call to have her run an errand. 'If you mean, do I sense it in you, yes. If you mean, do I feel it in myself, yes. If you mean, would I chuck it all and give it one last valiant try – yes.'

She reached into the silk-lined pocket of her mink jacket and pulled out the embroidered linen handkerchief that she had already used once this morning and patted her eyes.

'Will we talk about it now?' she asked.

'If you like.'

Fifteen years. A decision that changed lives, her life and Jerold's. Or perhaps a decision that kept them the same, left the families unsullied and merely rent two hearts. A decision made in great haste and considered in lengthy solitude. 'It was Adam mostly,' she said finally.

'I know.'

'He was only six.'

'It was never that I thought that you and I – '

'You don't have to tell me, Regina. I know.'

They had stopped walking and he turned to face her, to kiss her on the lips very softly as he had first kissed her when she was little more than a child, then to kiss her hard, with great emotion, their mouths hungry, as they had kissed when they were young, when they were twenty, when they were in Paris, when they were in New York, when they were in their forties, returning to each other. She knew his kisses as she knew his body, the first body she had ever seen, touched, loved, in the days when the slates were all clean, the lives ahead of them to live, when one word would have changed everything and she had not spoken it.

He let her go and she stood beside him, her head against his shoulder, his arms tightly around her, affording the protection and solace they had offered her since those long-ago times when he had been just a boy with a lot of promises, a lot of passion, a lot of love that would never fail.

They began walking again, his arm around her, holding her close, as though they were still those young people they had been, those cousins who should have married but instead did what was right and had never suffered for it – except when they saw each other.

'Adam's gone abroad for a year,' she said, speaking almost normally. 'Morty's softened his position a little and said he could have a year off before he starts to work. I think the younger ones benefit from our growing older.'

'They have in my family,' Jerold said, sounding not altogether content. 'I'm sure you know Judy's involved in a relationship that displeases me.'

'Don't be such a puritan, Jody. You would have lived with me if you could have.'

'That was different.'

'Was it?'

'Think of how much I loved you,' he said.

She swallowed. 'I do. Often and with great feeling.'

'I hope Judy feels that way. I can't think of anyone I'd rather see her spend her life with. It's the only mitigating factor, that her choice of companion is your protégé.'

'Mine? I should think you'd take at least half the credit for Marcel. Since that night you came in and picked up the pieces, I've rather thought we shared him. It's given me a good feeling. He couldn't be fonder of you if you'd fathered him.'

'Well.' He stopped and she could see in his face that he was moved. 'That's an unexpected pleasure, that we did it

269

together. He's certainly been the easiest of my children to raise.'

'That's because you were the right one to do it. He wasn't the easiest of mine.'

He said, 'Well,' again and she sensed that he was still considering what she had told him, that there was a child they shared, that they had done it in spite of history and genealogy. It gave a special meaning to this day, that she had been able to say it to him, to tell him something she had thought would remain forever unsaid. 'Have we missed the swimming hole?' he asked. They were nearly at the woods.

'To the left, I think.'

The paths were gone and the floor of the forest was crunchy with brown leaves.

'Where was it,' he asked suddenly, 'that I promised to meet you halfway?'

'Constantinople.'

'Yes, I thought it was. Edith asked me – some years ago – if we might include Turkey on a trip to Europe. Said she'd always wanted to see Istanbul, she called it. I told her – ' he laughed, 'that Istanbul was the last place on earth I wanted to visit. We went to Italy instead and travelled with Richard and Jeanne-Marie. A nice trip. You've never been there, have you?'

'No.' Something moved liquidly through the trees. 'There it is, Jody.'

The morning sun had not yet hit it and there was no sparkle but the rock was there, waiting to grow warm in the afternoon. Her throat had constricted. All those lost children, all that love. She took a step towards the pond, lifted a pebble and threw it in. The circles widened like families, becoming more distant, fading at the edges. Behind her, her cousin would be watching, thinking his own thoughts, of time gone, moments lost, a child shared. She had turned sixty in August and had not seen him in fifteen years and yet here he was, the thread that ran through her life, gold and shining and always there, the thread that wrapped that life up, all its pieces, in a neat, coherent package.

'It would be nice to see you from time to time,' he said from somewhere behind her. *If you mean, would I chuck it all and give it one last valiant try – yes.*

She turned so that she could face him but he was too far away to touch. 'Last time,' she said unsteadily, 'it took years, two at least, to begin to get back to something like normal. If it hadn't been for Adam, and later on, Marcel, I'm not sure I would have stuck with it. But I did. Morty's past seventy now and he needs some looking after. I couldn't see you, even over a cup of coffee, and go home with anything like equanimity.'

'I know. I shouldn't have asked.'

She went over to him and took his arm. 'If you hadn't, I would have gone home disappointed.'

They started walking back. 'We can't have you disappointed,' he said. 'Not on a day like this.' They were not far from Grandmama's shade tree now and a crew was working on removing the rubble of the farther buildings. 'Let me give you a lift home.'

'My car is here.'

'He won't mind going back alone. He may even enjoy it. Come. I'm sure even the most stringent moralists will allow a middle-aged Judge to drive his cousin home.'

They sat in the back of his limousine and held hands. The car had been parked at the far end of the workers' cars, where she would not have seen it from the road. Leaving, she watched out of the window. When the farm had disappeared, she leaned her head on his shoulder and closed her eyes. He found a station with old music and played it softly. Once or twice he lifted her hand and kissed it.

She opened her eyes and they were travelling south on Park Avenue. The driver turned left and pulled up before her building.

'Good-bye,' she said.

'Good-bye, dear.' He kissed her as the driver circled the car to open her door. 'Regina . . .'

She had slid away from him.

He reached into his coat pocket and pulled something out,

holding his hand in a fist. Resting it on the seat beside her, he opened his hand. Smiling up at her was the little Buddha.

She said, 'Oh,' and touched the worn stomach with a finger. He had given it to her that last morning fifteen years ago and she had put it back on the shelf a few hours later when Morty had come to take her home so that nothing in the house would be missing, nothing out of place. Edith could resume her position as wife and mistress of the house and never suspect that anyone else had entered the house in her absence.

'I told you once I was saving it for an important birthday,' he said. 'I think the one you just had was important enough.'

She took it in her hand and rubbed her thumb on the ivory. It looked rather worn, she thought, as though the last fifteen years had been something of a strain, as though it had been tossed around a bit, but hadn't they all? 'Thank you,' she said.

'You'll keep it this time, won't you?'

'Oh, yes.'

'I knew you would be there today. I wouldn't have gone otherwise.'

She squeezed his hand, left the car, and went upstairs to tell Morty she had seen her cousin Jerold for the first time in fifteen years.

Eight

It was a happiness without precedent. They loved each other. She got up early so that they could breakfast together and sometimes, when she was late getting home, he had put together a dinner. When she could, she got the car and drove to the hospital to pick him up at the end of the day. She met a handful of his friends that way and once caught a glimpse of Joy, Joy of the past. Judy was his present. He showed her off proudly, the way she showed him off.

She arranged her work so that she could do some of it at home in the evening when he was studying. That way there were more hours they could spend together.

Fern asked if it wasn't hard, with both of them occupied, to manage everything and Judy replied it was only half as hard as life had been when she was living alone. She wasn't *doing* things for him. They were helping each other. Fern said she sounded like a commercial for some new gadget.

In October she got an invitation from a woman lawyer a little older than she whom she had met at a conference on a case, asking her to an afternoon discussion meeting on Vietnam to be attended by women in the professions and the arts. Afternoon seemed rather a strange time – she did, after all, work – but she was concerned about Vietnam (Uncle Richard had written letters and articles about it) and she decided to go. She took some personal time off and went to the address on the invitation.

It was in an expensive building in the East Eighties, the residence of a doctor (male), and therein lay the clue. The group divided neatly into women in the professions and the arts and women *married* to people in the professions and the arts. She was somewhat stung at the discovery, wondering which of the two groups raised the status of the other, but the wives she spoke to turned out to be quite bright and concerned in their own right, not as spokesmen for their husbands. Some of them, in fact, had come in spite of their husbands' expressed disapproval.

She noted with some disappointment that the wives tended to be a better-looking lot and once during the afternoon, someone asked her what her husband did and when she said she wasn't married, the woman smiled and said, 'You're so pretty, I thought you must be married.'

A photojournalist who had just returned from Vietnam spoke for about twenty minutes, showing blow-ups of her pictures and drawing gasps from the audience. She spoke with passion and anger and the effect on the seated women was palpable.

Judy had told Fern about the meeting and Fern had said there was a *chance* she could give them some publicity, especially later if the group continued. When the main speaker had finished, the hostess of the afternoon made a few introductions -- the executive committee, this one and that one and Judy Wolfe -- 'Stand up, Judy. Let us get a look at you. Judy *may* be able to get us some publicity if we do our job well.'

She stood and smiled briefly. She was wearing a dark grey suit with a Chanel-type jacket. The professionals, she noted, wore less jewellery, mainly less that sparkled, and were dressed as though they had come from work, not from lunch at a midtown restaurant.

Then the food was served. A long table in the dining room had coffee and tea at either end and a hundred cakes and cookies along the sides. She waited till most of the crowd had been served and then took a cup of coffee and a small plate and walked along the table, looking at the pretty confections.

'Judy Wolfe,' a woman said as though making an announcement and Judy looked up into the face of a woman on the opposite side of the table. There was something distantly familiar about it but she could not place it in the repertoire of

274

faces of friends, parents' friends, business associates. She was a handsome woman, handsomely dressed, distinctly not one of the wives.

'I'm Annie Kellems,' the woman said, her eyes looking slightly playful.

'Mrs Kellems.' She was at a loss suddenly for anything else to say. She set the coffee cup down because her hand had lost its usual steadiness.

'You're a nice girl, Judy Wolfe,' Annie Kellems said, looking at her with large, direct eyes.

Judy put the plate down and the silver fork clattered thinly on the fine china. 'Not as nice as you, Mrs Kellems,' she said. Then she went into the bedroom, got her coat, and left the meeting.

There were weeks when he spent three nights at the hospital, and when he came home on the intervening ones, he was so tired he could do nothing but fall into bed for as many hours as he could sleep before getting up in the morning for his six-thirty rounds. But then there were weeks that were better, when they could spend time in the evening talking, making plans, putting everything aside and making love. She told herself it was better than being married because they retained the small sense of uncertainty that lovers had, the feeling of excitement, of urgency when they were together.

Letters came from his sister and he invited her to read them, as though offering a deeply personal side of himself to her. They were written in French, of course, and she always asked for a synopsis, after which they would talk about her a little, about his aunt Suzanne, about his increasing desire to return to France to find the family he had lived with during the war. It was something that had ignited that day at the farm, and she sensed that in some way she had been responsible, as had her father, as had, perhaps, Millie.

She wanted to go with him. She wanted to walk on the earth that had sustained him through the war, touch the hands of the people who had kept him safe. She wanted to see Suzanne, the widow, the sole survivor of her generation, whose influence was so strong that she could keep a woman of thirty-five from marrying the man she loved. And most of all, she wanted to meet Renée, his sister who was a lawyer and lacked the courage to fashion her own life.

She was happy. Early in November they were invited to dinner with the Rushes and although she was apprehensive, the dinner turned out to be a success. It was the first time she could remember meeting Morty. He was very tall and quite handsome, with grey hair and a delightful presence. It eased her concern to observe the Rushes. They were obviously very fond of each other. Their conversation was friendly and unforced. They were not two people biding their time in the same household. Before the evening was over, they had asked Marcel and Judy to spend Thanksgiving weekend at their Connecticut home. The Rushes were flying to Europe for the second half of November and the house would be empty.

She was touched by the gesture, by the thought that they considered Marcel one of their own. A few days later she found herself at the same office in the Empire State Building that she had visited the spring before on the day that Regina had suggested she look up Marcel. Her client was an elderly gentleman, a wealthy Jew who had come to this country just before the outbreak of war. He had some cousins – not very wealthy – who had emigrated to the States from Cuba after the downfall of Battista. One of them was having problems with immigration and her client asked if she would represent the cousin.

'I'd be happy to,' she said, pleased that he had come to accept her professionally.

'You understand I'm asking you to do this as a voluntary service,' he said.

'I understand and I'll be delighted to do it.'

'It'll be good practice. You'll learn something about the practical side of the law.'

She took the name and phone number of the Cuban cousin, said thank you once again, and left. It was a nice afternoon and

276

she wasn't expected back downtown. She felt good, very, very good, and because of that, she decided to drop in on Regina.

Regina opened the door to her office herself. 'Judy – come on in. How nice to see you.'

'Hi.' Judy kissed her cheek and dropped her briefcase near the door. 'I won't stay long. Just came to say thank you again. For Thanksgiving.'

'We're glad you can use the house. Take your coat off and sit down. It's getting raw out, isn't it?' Regina went back behind her desk and sat.

Judy pushed her gloves into her pockets and sat down in her coat, opening a button. Her face looked fresh and vibrant. 'Yes, but I've only walked a couple of blocks. It's really more bracing than raw.'

'It'll be more than bracing in Connecticut.'

'Marcel says it's one of his favourite places.'

'I think Marcel likes a quiet retreat once in a while.'

'Yes, and by the end of November he'll be ready – ' She broke off suddenly and her face changed. Her eyes were on something – something on the desk. Regina looked down fleetingly and saw the Buddha Jerold had given her only a few weeks ago. She had taken it to the design studio because Morty never came here, because she could keep it out in the open and enjoy it.

Judy inhaled in a gasp and looked up at Regina. 'You love my father, don't you?' she said in a low voice, as though, finally, she had matched the bits and pieces of rumour and fact that must have floated around her all her life.

Regina's hand was resting on the desk and she restrained the urge to snatch the evidence and whisk it away. 'Very much,' she said instead in a calm, steady voice that surprised her. 'And your uncle Richard too.'

'That's not what I mean,' Judy said with undisguised emotion.

'All the cousins,' Regina went on emphatically, trying to make a point she knew she believed in and wanted Judy to

277

believe in too. 'I was an only child and my cousins took the place of the brothers and sisters I never had.'

'*You know what I mean.* He *gave* that to you.' Judy's eyes were on the Buddha.

'It was a birthday present. I turned sixty in August. Sixty is a special birthday.'

'You still see him, don't you?' She had stood, the colour gone from her face.

'Judy, that's not so.' But she sounded less emphatic now, less than certain.

'It was you, wasn't it, that time when my mother packed us up and took us away?'

She knew even that. Why had he told her? Why did children have to be told things that were not meant for children to know? 'It wasn't me, Judy. Sit down, dear. Let's talk reasonably.'

'But you know about it. Does everyone in the world know about it?'

'Only one or two people and they will never say a word. I'm one of them. And I hold the key to the other.'

'It doesn't matter, it doesn't matter. It was because of you.'

'Judy, your father and I are cousins.'

'Lovers,' Judy corrected her. 'You're lovers. You've been lovers all your lives. Somebody told me and I thought she was a crazy old woman but she wasn't, was she? She was smarter than all the rest of them.'

Regina felt confused. Her eyes clouded as though she had missed something in the conversation. She shook her head slowly.

'Your cousin Millie.'

'Millie told you – ?'

'She said you would have to have been a fool not to know.'

Regina said, 'Millie,' again with plain amazement. Millie had known. 'Listen to me, Judy.'

'My mother is in the middle of all this.' Judy looked anguished. 'My mother is a good, kind, innocent person in the middle of all this.'

278

'Whatever happened between your father and me happened forty years ago, not today, not last week. I married a man that I loved and your father married a girl he was absolutely in love with.'

'What's the matter with you people?' Judy asked. 'Why did you make such a mess of things? Why didn't you just get married if you felt that way?'

'You know why we didn't marry,' Regina said and now she was in control again.

'Yes,' softly. 'I know.' She sat down again and closed her eyes. It was as though she had just found out there was really no freedom after all. The generations passed and nothing changed. A girl could do anything nowadays if she tried. She could get into law school, pass the bar, get hired by a good law firm, and still be trapped by the same genes that had trapped her father.

'Your dad and I are parents to six children,' Regina said. 'That's made a lot of things worthwhile.'

'Has it?'

Regina reached into a drawer, pulled out a tissue, and touched her eyes. It was the wrong thing to do, she knew. To make her denial credible she should remain unmoved. She should speak harshly. But she knew why Judy had not married Marcel and she wanted it finally to be over. She wanted an end. She wanted Judy to do what Regina herself had been unable to.

'It's different for you, Judy,' she said. 'The chances we couldn't take, you can take.'

But Judy had stopped listening. Her eyes were on the happy little Buddha. 'You can say what you like about forty years ago but there are things about my father that I know better than you do. He could have sent you flowers, he could have sent you jade or bronze or coral from his collection, but if he picked that – ' She stood and went to where she had left her briefcase. 'It didn't end forty years ago, did it? You don't have to answer,' she said quickly. 'We both know it didn't.' She looked at her watch. 'Give my regards to Morty. I've got to be getting home.'

They drove to Connecticut early on Thanksgiving morning and arrived well before noon. They dropped their luggage in the house and he took her to see the land. It was quite beautiful. Hidden in the woods there was a spring-fed lake that emptied into a creek far below by means of falls. The trees were bare but she could imagine them in the spring. She could imagine how beautiful it would be.

She had not told him about her encounter with Regina but she knew she would today. She needed him to tell her whom she was angry at. If her father had offered Regina the Buddha, why had Regina accepted it? They were married people with families. When you broke with someone, it was over. Judy knew that. She would not run to Roy Kellems or to anyone else she had known in the last four years. A relationship did not exist because of memories. It existed because two people worked to keep it alive.

'Want to sit?'

'OK.'

They were in a field near a low stone wall that had once perhaps been a property line. He sat against it and put his arm around her as she joined him. They were wearing identical white Irish sweaters that she had found in a special shop and bought as a special treat, and by coincidence, their trousers were both black, hers wool and his corduroy. In spite of the cold, she felt toasty.

'How's your Cuban?' he asked.

'Elusive.' This was the way they caught up with each other's lives, saving questions for quiet moments that did not come often enough, the way friends did, the way husbands and wives did. 'He's cancelled two appointments already. We have another for next week. I think immigration has set a date for a hearing and if he doesn't show up, it's going to make things tougher.'

'Has he told you what the problem is?'

'It's very hard to understand him, Marcel. His English is awful. I asked him to send me the papers he got but he never did.'

'Be patient with him. He's probably working at six jobs to keep his family going. Look, maybe next weekend we'll drive out to Brooklyn and you can talk to him at his apartment.'

It was like him, she thought, to make such an offer. The Cuban was like a patient. Besides, he was always more interested in her more practical cases, the ones in which an individual had a problem, rather than the ones in which a point of law was being argued, a principle, a test of some fundamental liberty. He talked about those cases with her, too, intelligently and thoughtfully, acknowledging that without the principle the individual had no redress, but his sentiment was with the Cuban, with his personal problem, with his history.

'I'll go myself,' she promised. 'You'll need the rest. You were exhausted last night.'

'But I slept. Like a log.'

'Tough day?'

'I don't remember. Ask me later. It'll come back. Did I eat dinner?'

'Yes.' She pushed him playfully with her shoulder. 'You ate dinner.'

'Then it couldn't have been that tough a day.'

'I love you.'

He murmured something agreeable and moved against her. 'It's seven months this week since you walked into my apartment.'

She turned her head and smiled at him. 'How can you possibly remember the date?'

'It was my birthday.'

'Oh, Marcel. And you never told me.'

'I had just come back from dinner at the Rushes. They gave me this.' Tightening his left arm around her, he reached across her with his right and pulled back the cuff of the sweater and the shirt underneath to bare the gold watch.

'I remember thinking it looked very new and shiny.'

'I think it's time we got married.'

'Marcel, I told you – '

281

'I know what you told me. I probably told you a lot of things too. Those are old things. Let's talk about new things today.'

'I can't have children,' she said, speaking of the oldest thing she knew.

'I'm not asking you to have children. I'm asking you to marry me.'

'It's the same thing.'

'It's not the same thing.'

'You should be thinking about marrying someone who can give you a family.' But she didn't want him to do anything of the sort. She wanted him for herself, forever.

'It's very important to me, that you be my wife.'

She looked at him again. He was very serious.

'There isn't a person in this country that's any more to me than a good friend. I don't want another good friend. I want someone who's more than that. You.'

'I've been thinking about your sister,' she said.

'No you haven't. Whenever you tell me you've been thinking about my sister I know you've been thinking about yourself. You've been brooding about something for weeks now.'

'It's true about my father and Regina, isn't it?'

He didn't answer for a moment. 'What difference does it make?' he said finally.

'Tell me whether you think it's true.'

'I think it could be.'

'He gave her something, a small piece from his collection. She keeps it at the design studio, I suppose so that her husband won't see it.'

'There's nothing wrong with giving small gifts.'

'Not that gift.'

'I lived in that house for years. Regina's not having an affair with anyone.'

'She didn't have to accept it.'

'She accepted it because he gave it to her.'

'I know.' She had wanted – unreasonably – for it to be Regina's fault. If she could absolve her father, if she could fix the blame elsewhere, it would be easier to bear.

282

'And it's all no more than a possibility.'

'She admitted it, Marcel. She talked about forty years ago. But he didn't give her the Buddha forty years ago. He gave it to her this year, for her birthday. She said – she said I knew why they hadn't married.'

'We aren't cousins, Judy.'

'You never saw Frenchy's first child.'

'Judy, I – just – want – you.' He said it deliberately, every word perfectly formed so that he could have been as American-born as she was. 'Nothing else. If the family doesn't survive, I don't care. I want to survive. I couldn't have said that to you when I met you that Christmas, but I can say it now. Children aren't part of anything I think about.'

'I need time,' she said, feeling him draw her closer.

'I'm not going anywhere.' He kissed her.

'I'm not either.'

He took her hand and pressed it against his penis, hard beneath the black corduroy of his trousers. She felt better, a question answered satisfactorily. If he wanted to survive, he would. Even if she left him, he would survive. But she didn't want to leave him. She wanted to believe that all he wanted was her.

'Let's go back.'

'You have an endless appetite for sex,' she said, not displeased. She kissed him.

'Not true. I have an endless appetite for you.'

'I like that better. So do I. For you.'

'Let's go back.'

He led her through fields, lawns and gardens to the kitchen door. She saw the kitchen in a kind of blur of colour and texture, blues, tiles perhaps hand-painted.

'We can have a fire,' he said, taking her to another room, quickly because there was a need, firmly because there was no doubt, but she had to make a brief detour because there was, as always, a concern. She could not chance a pregnancy.

The room was large and light and comfortable, soft furniture for lounging, a fireplace already laid, awaiting the match, a shaggy rug in reds and browns. He tossed two large pillows from the sofa onto the floor in front of the grate and put his arms around her. His cheeks were still cold but his mouth was warm and after a few moments, his hands. He was everything he had promised her in the spring. He was good to her. In every way he was good to her, from his concern about the elusive Cuban to satisfying her body's deepest needs. Today, she wanted to satisfy his. Today she wanted to take all the things he longed for and give them to him.

They dropped their white sweaters in a heap on the rug, then the shirts. She was wearing a lace bra in a cameo colour because he told her once he liked lace and it pleased her to please him. He said, 'Pretty,' and touched with his hands and then with his lips. It was so easy to please him, why couldn't she do it completely? All he wanted was to be with her, to have her as his wife. He didn't want children. He had told her that many times. Why couldn't she believe him, take him at face value as he took her? Why did she persist in second-guessing him? He was twenty-eight. Surely at that age he knew what he wanted.

Undressed, they lay on the rug, she beside him, bending over him to kiss, to caress, to arouse, to love in this best of all ways. She straddled him because she knew – she had learned – that this was what he liked best. There had been times when it was his passion that swept through her and ignited her own but today, now, she could feel herself leading, moving forward, down the narrowing channel. How well they suited each other, in all ways, and in this especially. She felt sweat spring to her skin, shoulders, back, and beneath her breasts, matching the glint on his. What a lovely man he was and so good to her, so good, so very good.

Exhausted, she lay on top of him, still gripping him with her knees, feeling the echoes of recent love. His arms were around her, holding her in place as the sweat evaporated, leaving her chilled.

'Cold?'

'A little.'

'I forgot to light a fire.'

'You lit a fire.'

He reached with one hand to the sofa and dragged down an afghan, hand-knit and in the same reds and browns as the rug, and shook it over her. She felt it fall lightly, feathery, the fringe caressing tenderly, as he did.

'Marcel.' She pulled the second pillow next to his and lay beside him. 'I want to do something for you.'

'What, sweetheart?'

'Anything. I want to get you something. Tell me what you want.'

'I don't want anything.'

'A glass of water,' she persisted. 'A drink. Let me make you a sandwich.' She moved to get up.

'Judy.' He held her arm to stop her. Then he said, 'Just water. With an ice cube.'

She got up and started for the door.

'Put something on.' he said.

She turned back. 'Why?'

'Please.'

She found the sweaters at the bottom of the pile and got into the larger one. It barely covered her buttocks. 'OK?'

He nodded and she threw a kiss and left. That element of puritanism surprised her but she found it endearing. In their bedroom she marched around nude and it did not bother him.

The tile floor of the kitchen was cool to her bare feet. She opened cabinets looking for a glass. The contents of the shelves were distinctly Regina as the contents of Edith Wolfe's shelves were distinctly hers. Here there were ceramic dishes and mugs painted with bright scenes. Regina and her father were so different. Their lives did not overlap except in family and Regina had little to do with family. She did not attend happy events, did not sit at the table with the cousins in her generation.

Judy closed the cabinet and moved on to another. For the first time. she thought she might understand the reason.

She found a glass, stemmed, that looked as though it might

285

be used for sherry and she filled it three-quarters with water
and then found the ice. Finally she located the trays and
selected a small silver one with a scalloped edge. In a drawer
there were linens and among them a place mat that fitted the
tray. It looked rather pretty, she thought, when she had it
arranged, like the trays that had served her through most of her
life, and still did when she visited her parents, but how happy
she was now, living her own way, how very happy.

She carried the tray into the room where Marcel waited. He
had lit the fire and it blazed brightly. He sat on the rug, his
back against the sofa, the two large pillows near him, and she
realized they were Regina's designs as the curtains were, as
perhaps the rug was.

She knelt carefully, setting the tray beside him.

'Why?' he said.

'Because I wanted to.' She felt unaccountably tearful, as
though she were about to leave him when, in fact, she was
about to stay. She sat on his other side, nearer the fire, and
rested her head on his shoulder. 'I just wanted to do something
for you,' she said.

He pulled the afghan to cover her legs, baring his own. In
the dark hair his genitals lay, soft and at rest. She ran her hand
over them lightly and left her arm across his lap. One did not
love this much very often.

He lifted the little sherry glass and drank half the water.
'Good water,' he said and she smiled against his shoulder,
which was now wet with tears. He put the glass down and
dipped two fingers in. 'Come here,' he said as though she were
elsewhere, and bathed her face around her eyes in the cold
water. 'Why can't it be simple?'

'I wish it were. I hate this feeling of being – impaired.'

'Don't say that, Judy. You've given me everything I ever
wanted – and a glass of water.'

'Let me have a taste.'

'I've put my fingers in it.'

'I don't care.'

He passed her the glass and she swallowed what was left,

286

licking the ice cube as it touched her lips. She leaned over him to replace the glass but it slipped from her fingers and as she said, 'Oh,' in dismay, it hit the edge of the silver tray and shattered.

'It's just a glass,' Marcel said. He lifted a few glistening shards and put them on the tray. 'Now all we need is the wedding ring.'

The ice cube was melting on the linen placemat, the wet stain slowly widening. 'I'll think about it,' she said.

Nine

———◇———

She did not see Regina again. It was Marcel's last year of medical school and he began applying for an internship. Davey took a short vacation without Marilyn and told Judy he needed to be alone once in a while. Judy and Marcel preferred to be together. She met his friends. He met hers. They talked about what to do with the apartment when the lease expired in the summer. She got the Cuban straightened out with immigration, at least for a while. He thanked her and sent one of his wife's cousins to her because his green card had been lifted. Her nephews grew bigger and more beautiful.

She did not think about the future. Her life had achieved a kind of perfection and she wanted to maintain it, just as it was, for as long as she could.

The fourth year of medical school was similar to the third. There were weeks when he came home every night and periods when he slept at the hospital three nights a week. She caught up with Fern and other friends on those nights and usually he managed to call her, at the apartment or at the office, just to say hello. He lost a patient and he mourned. He watched one heal and he was jubilant.

In March her firm began work on a new case with a juicy part for her. For days she dug into records, twice flying to Washington for the day. Late afternoons she met with the other lawyers working on the case, meetings that ended in the evening after suppers of sandwiches on the conference table.

The case coincided with the last of Marcel's clerkships requiring him to stay overnight at the hospital. On some of the nights he was home, she returned so late he was already asleep, exhausted from thirty-six hours of being awake. He would leave a note for her on the table along with the mail, something briefly informative, briefly affectionate. At the end he would tell her not to get up with him in the morning and sometimes, when his alarm went off (in the darkness) she would say, 'Hi,' and fall asleep for another hour, thinking how nice it would be to see him tonight, utterly forgetting that this was the night he would spend at the hospital. It was wearing and frustrating and ate even into alternate weekends.

But the case was exciting and none of the men seemed bothered by the late hours, even though some of them lived far enough away that they headed for Grand Central or Penn Station when the conference was over.

It was a Thursday and Marcel would be home. He had called at the office during the afternoon and left a message because she was out. She could not remember when they had last spoken face to face, or had a meal together, or kissed. She wanted desperately to get home early because tomorrow was Friday and, damn it, he was sleeping at the hospital again. But the conference dragged on and when she walked into the apartment, it was nine and there was a note from him on the table beside the opened letter from his sister that had arrived the day before.

'I'm beat,' his note read. 'But I'll see you Saturday and I *promise* we'll do something. Maybe just go to bed. (Together.) I love you. Marcel.'

She pulled her coat off and hung it up, stepped out of her shoes and walked in her stockinged feet. He would be asleep and she could be quieter without shoes. She went into the kitchen and opened the refrigerator. There was a portion of rice pudding and some lobster salad. He had stopped on the way home so that they would have something to eat. She closed the refrigerator. She had no appetite and she was disappointed. She looked at her watch. If she went to bed right now, she would be able to get up with him at five and cook them a good breakfast and *talk*.

Moving quietly, she undressed and showered. He was fast asleep, half on his stomach. She got into bed carefully and kissed his shoulder. He did not move. In a few minutes, she was asleep.

It was later but she did not know how much later. She had slept and now she was awake.

'Honey?' It was a cautious whisper. 'You awake?'

'Oh, Marcel, I missed you.' She felt his hand on her and as quickly as that, she wanted him. It was days since they had talked, nights – maybe a week – since they had made love. There were a hundred things she wanted to ask him – in the library this morning she had jotted down a list – but mostly, she wanted this. She reached out and touched his chest, his stomach, felt his penis, hard and big, as though they were already coming together instead of waking to each other's touch, and she discarded all physiological explanations that did not include sex, desire, love, you and me together, and moved toward him. She knew – it was not just a passing thought – that she ought to get up and take three minutes to insert the diaphragm but her period was due in a couple of days and it was safe, or safe enough.

He was as eager as she for the union, as willing to forgo the usual beginnings, the awakening having simply happened, the arousal having taken place in those first seconds, as though the week of separation, of missed phone calls, of affectionate notes, of accidental brushes in the night, had set the stage for the eventual coupling. It was quick, graceful, and fleetingly gratifying, *I'll make breakfast for you in the morning, darling*, and she slept very soundly afterward. When she awoke at five, she scarcely remembered it had happened although something in his manner at breakfast assured her it had.

When she was absolutely certain that she was pregnant, she found, to her surprise, that she was very calm, very well in control. Something had failed, the circle of rubber, the jelly in the tube, or – least likely – she herself. They had been together nearly a year and she had been at her firm nearly two. It was simply time to move on. The thought of abortion did not occur to her immediately but the thought of leaving did. As had happened once before in her life, she had overstayed her time. There was some money in savings, enough to get her somewhere – where, she did not know, just somewhere else.

There were a few things of which she was certain. She was a lawyer and she wanted to practise law. As much as she loved anything – except Marcel – she loved law. She could practise elsewhere. It was only necessary to study for another bar exam and take it. Nothing impossible there. The only thing that was impossible was leaving Marcel.

She knew she would have to time it carefully. Not in the middle of exams because he had to do well, but not afterwards, either, because it would be too late. She had to leave while all her choices were still open.

On a night when Marcel was at the hospital, she had dinner with Fern.

'You're looking disgustingly stylish,' she said over cocktails. 'Did you think you had cornered the market?'

'I knew I couldn't when you told me you had your own office. Every time I turn around, I elbow something. Yesterday it was three-quarters of a cup of coffee.'

Fern smiled indulgently. 'I got another raise. A *nice* raise. I'm now being asked what I think of series they're planning for the fall.'

'That's super.'

'And I've persuaded Jack and Vivien to visit New York in September. I've found a nice hotel that doesn't cost an arm and a leg and I'm paying for it.'

'Fern, that is really terrific.' She could see by the glow that Fern thought so too. 'Why don't you really give them a thrill and get married?'

Fern regarded her with a special glimmer that came only from Fern. She really looked great, sure of herself, handsome, well turned out. 'Whenever you give motherly advice to me, I have the feeling you're talking to yourself.'

'You and Marcel.'

'Maybe we're both right.'

'Maybe.'

'Something wrong?'

'Nothing at all,' Judy said easily. 'As I remember, I was suggesting that you get married and give Jack a thrill.'

'Dynamite lawyer,' Fern said. 'Never let them wander. You want to know the truth?'

Something in her almost said no. 'Sure I want to know the truth.'

'I have a happy, warm, periodic relationship that I don't want to give up.'

'Periodic. Fern, married men rarely come through.'

'Maybe this one's different.'

'Will you introduce him to Jack?'

'No.' Very firmly.

'I hope he's different.' She heard the note of sincerity in her voice, like a plea. Too many people threw away too much of their lives on hopeless cases and lived to regret it.

'He's a great man,' Fern said. 'And great men don't come around very often.'

'I know. I've known a couple.' Two. Exactly two.

'So what are you and your great man planning?'

'A trip west.' It had come up more easily than she had anticipated. 'You told me there were places along the way to camp out. I thought you might be able to let me in on the best ones.'

'What a nice idea.' Fern was plainly pleased. 'I'll put the map in the mail tomorrow with my favourite campsites circled. When are you leaving?'

'I'm not sure. A few weeks. I'll let you know before we go.'

'What a nice way to spend the summer,' Fern said. 'So what if you do elbow your coffee? Look at everything else you've got.'

'Yes. You're right. I'm really quite content.'

If she had an abortion, she would not have to go away. If she did it soon enough, she could arrange it for one of these days when he would not be home and if she needed rest, she could feign illness the following day. It was dangerous, of course, both physically and professionally. Her law firm did not know she shared an apartment with a man and the partners would surely not be pleased if she were involved in an abortion scandal. Not to mention the Bar Association.

But she knew several young women who had survived office abortions and a phone call would give her the necessary lead. It was something else that kept her from picking up the phone. It was the thing that she had never known for certain existed in her. The glob of tissue that she could not feel and probably would be unable to see was a child. If she went somewhere and had it, if it were whole and perfect . . .

But it was the other that kept her awake nights. If it weren't. Frenchy's child. It could happen to her as it had happened to him or to Davey. With each it had been the firstborn. She was older than either of her sisters-in-law had been and she had heard that such occurrences were more frequent with the increased age of the mother. In a few weeks she would be twenty-seven. Poor Rena had been scarcely twenty-one.

Anyway, there was time. Imperfect foetuses were often miscarried early in a pregnancy. A ride west in the old car might hasten it along. If she miscarried, she would know for certain. If she didn't, she could make a descision later. It was easier to put it off anyway. What would not be easy was leaving Marcel.

She went to a sporting goods store and asked what she would need for her trip. She paid for it in cash and said she would pick it up in a few weeks; she would let them know when. A sleeping bag. A tiny tent. Pills to purify water. Cooking utensils.

She missed her second period and realized that certain as she had thought she was, she had still hoped that some unfamiliar female complaint had been the cause of the problem. You're a realist, she told herself, recognizing the voice that had shouted at her in England six years ago. *You're pregnant. Do what has to be done*.

She gave Sheldon two weeks' notice. He was appalled, disbelieving. Take a leave, he said. You're a New Yorker. You'll hate California. We *want* you.

She said OK weakly and gave him a date. That was the moment she knew she was going to do it.

She called Fern and told her, thanking her for the map and all the useful notations. I'll send you postcards, she promised.

Everything taken care of except Marcel. She could not face him. He did not want children, or so he said, and now she was pregnant. If he *did* want children, he did not want the kind her family produced. It was a problem without a solution.

In the end, she decided to leave after he had gone off for the day. She would dress, drive to the sporting goods store and pick up the gear. Then she would cross the George Washington Bridge and be on her way.

Fern called her at work on one of her last days. 'You lied to me,' she said angrily.

'What do you mean?' Already she felt defeated. She had not even left and she had been found out.

'I just saw a schedule that says Marcel's class isn't graduating for over two weeks. How can you be leaving next week?'

'I –'

'You're leaving him.'

'Yes.'

'You *can't*, Judy.'

'It's a year. If I stay on, I'll never leave. He needs to marry someone who'll give him a family. I can't. You know that.'

'*Shit*!' The word must have resounded through the halls of the revered broadcasting company.

'Please.' Her voice wavered. 'This isn't easy for me.'

'You can't go *alone*.'

'You went alone, Fern. You said it was perfectly safe.'

'Stay in New York, Judy. Come to me for a while. Don't go far away by yourself.'

'Marcel's taken an internship here in New York. He doesn't have one out West. This is the best solution. If I stay, we'll see each other. He'll find me. It'll never be clean.'

'How many times in your life can you do this?' Fern asked in a low voice.

'I don't know. This is the last time. I promise. Just please keep it to yourself.'

'You listen to me. I want phone calls. Twice a week at least. If not, you better be prepared to have a state policeman drag you out of your sleeping bag one morning. Don't think I can't do it. We have affiliates all over the country and people who owe us, who owe me. Do you hear me?'

'Yes.'

'Twice a week.'

'Yes.'

'You need a goddamned spanking.'

Her hands were shaking when she hung up. She had planned so carefully and had already nearly been thwarted. But she trusted Fern. Fern would not betray her.

She began to feel queasy in the mornings and a taste had invaded her mouth, making even the thought of food disagreeable. Marcel had begun studying in earnest for his exams and over the weekend he took only a few hours off when they walked to Central Park, had some ice cream, and walked back.

'Nervous?' she asked.

'Exams always make me nervous.'

'But you do well.'

'I'll be OK.'

She got up with him on Monday morning. It was the first day in two years that she was unemployed. She scrambled eggs for him. She kissed him when she poured the coffee. She prayed she would keep breakfast down until he left.

'You look a little pale,' he said. 'You feeling all right?'

She nodded and offered her arm across the table. He gave her a smile and took her pulse as he had from time to time over the past year – that good year that was ending now, this very morning – half as a joke, half to dispute disputable diagnoses.

'Nice and slow,' he said. 'After exams, maybe we can get away for a weekend.'

'I'd like that.' She wondered how he could not know she

was on the verge of leaving. She reeked of departure. Her skin crawled with betrayal. If he did not leave soon, she would not be able to do it. She would weep and he would know.

He looked at his watch, brushed the napkin across his lips, and got up from the table.

'See you, sweetheart,' he said.

'Don't call me at the office. I won't be there most of the day.'

'Home on time?'

'Yes.'

He bent and kissed her and held her an extra second.

'Me too,' he said.

She watched him go, the lush dark hair, strong shoulders, nicely tapered rear. He turned quickly for a smile and a wave and the door closed. The sense of loss struck her like a wave and for a moment she thought she would be overpowered by grief, but the other asserted itself, sharply and uncompromisingly, and she hurried to the bathroom where she was politely sick.

The first day was the worst. She kept the radio on for company but the familiar stations began to fade somewhere in Pennsylvania and she had to hunt for others, disc jockeys with regional accents and the wrong kind of music. But they told her the time and that was what she wanted. He would be leaving the hospital now. He would be getting home. He would find her letter.

It has been the best year of my life . . .

She wondered how he would take it, which of the many possible feelings the letter and her departure would evoke, hurt, anger, pity, loss. There had been something in him last year, when they talked about Joy, that she had thought cavalier.

Do you sleep with her?

Sometimes.

But he was anything but cavalier with her. He needed her.

If I stay any longer, I might stay forever and whatever you say, that would be unfair to you.

296

Why had she written such rot? Why not just say, It's over, Marcel. I've decided to leave. Let him be angry. Anger could be productive in a way that loss could not.

In the last third of the day she drove into the sun. When the road headed directly west, it was almost blinding, something she had not thought of when making her plans. Why had she picked California anyway? Maybe because last time she had gone east. Maybe because California was a mystery, a place she had never visited, a place people raved about. The problem was, she didn't know anyone there and if she decided on an abortion, she did not know how to proceed.

But California was only the end of the line. She might find some enchanting place along the way and decide to remain, north in Montana or south in New Mexico. Fern's map went only to Kansas. After that she was on her own. She could pick and choose among the places to overnight. Something in that thought was pleasing, uplifting. She was on her own.

She drove until dark to reach the first place on Fern's map. She had started late and she wanted to feel that she was truly away before she stopped. The campsite was clean and attractive. She drove her car to the assigned spot and unloaded the gear. Everything was new, stiff, pristine, some things still in boxes and paper wrapping. Like a bride opening her trousseau on her wedding night, she unwrapped her utensils, the sleeping bag, the minuscule tent. Only she would never be a bride. She had left one man who wanted to marry her because it was wrong in one way and she had left another man who wanted to marry her because it was wrong in another way and she had as good as struck out. She had tried east and now she was trying west and there came a time when you had to say, enough. I am through. I cannot go on ruining people's lives, people whom I love, people like Marcel. The toll was too heavy, equally so on her. She had known when she was twenty-one that she could not marry and she knew now that she could not afford to love. She did not want Fern's kind of attachment, a man available at his wife's whim – what was wrong with her anyway? She knew marvellous people. Why should she settle for this?

That's right, Jude. Think about someone else's problems when your own are begging to be solved. What do you *want*?

Marcel. Nothing else ever. Get rid of this baby and see if he'll have you back. Marcel. Crawling into the tent. Marcel. Inching into the sleeping bag. She had never felt less in the mood for sex. What she wanted was the whole man. What she wanted was the life they had lived this winter, his life, and her life overlapping evenings and mornings and happy weekends. God, she missed him. Even during those times when they had kept their relationship alive with notes and promises, she had felt close to him. Now that was gone. In New York, which was hundreds of miles away, he was alone.

She drove west in the morning after her stomach settled. The states became real. After Pennsylvania there was really Ohio, after Ohio, Indiana. Accents changed. People smiled more readily, seemed more open, more willing to help. It was a nice country. There was life outside New York City.

On Wednesday evening she called Fern.

'Where are you?' Fern demanded. 'I'm worried sick about you.'

'In Illinois and why should you worry? Am I less competent a driver than you are?'

'It has nothing to do with competence. It has to do with choices. Judy, this is your home. Your job is here. Your family is here. *I'm* here for God's sake.'

'I need to think away from everyone.'

'You did that once before.'

'It was very rewarding.'

'You can't keep doing this.'

In the airlessness of the phone booth, she could not remember whether Fern had said it to her a hundred times before or whether she had said it herself. Or both. 'This is the last time.'

'Are you OK?'

'Fine. The map is wonderful. The people are marvellous. They're not like you but I think I could love them.'

'Why don't you stop off and see Jack and Vivien? I could call and let them – '

'I don't think so, Fern. There are things I have to sort out. I'll call you over the weekend.'

'Judy – '

'What?'

'Nothing. I have a lot to say and I don't want you to pay for it. Call me collect next time.'

She hung up and opened the door of the booth, inhaling the fresher air outside. Tomorrow she would cross into Missouri and then the East would really be behind her. She bought some postcards to send to her family and went into a small, homey-looking restaurant. She was only a half-hearted camper at best. She preferred being served in a restaurant. Most of all, she wanted to be home. With Marcel.

It was an easy trip to the campsite in Missouri the next day and she considered going farther. She could reach Kansas if she tried but she decided against it. If she arrived early enough, she would take a long walk. All this sitting made her feel uneasy. She wondered if there were horses around for hire. She hadn't ridden for a while and the thought of getting on a horse stirred an old longing. It did something else too. It made her think for the first time that if she had a daughter, she would buy her a horse.

The camping ground was the kind where you parked your car and carried your things to your campsite. Just for the exercise, she made it in two trips although she was sure she would be able to manage it in one when she left in the morning.

She had a good shower and sat with a book near her tent. This was her fourth day on the road and she was doing well. Last time she had left New York, she had needed help. She had gone to Regina. She would not be going to Regina again. She blamed Regina. The Buddha was Regina's fault. Edith Wolfe's unhappiness was Regina's fault. Everything that was imperfect in her family home was Regina's fault.

She could not blame her father. Men failed sometimes – it was as simple as that – and it was up to women to avert such failures. She had done it for Roy. Roy had gone back to Annie – *You're a nice girl, Judy Wolfe* – but perhaps only with the same inconstancy as he had shown before.

If Jerold Wolfe had given Regina Rush the Buddha, it was Regina's responsibility to turn it down. She was not sure why she felt this way. Perhaps she believed in a fundamental strength that women had and men only aspired to. Whatever it was, she knew she could not be friends with Regina now that she knew the truth.

She awoke on Friday morning with a sense of uncertainty mixed with a feeling of adventure. She had not yet made a decision on her course. This was the last location marked on Fern's map and she had to decide whether to continue west or to detour north or south.

But the decision would have to be made later. Getting up had become very unpleasant, a daily reminder that she had not yet acted, that something had to be done, that time was running out, that she did not have forever.

When she had washed and dressed she picked up the camping gear in both hands and started for the parking lot. It was a beautiful morning, clear and sweet-smelling. She told herself, as she had on Tuesday, Wednesday and Thursday mornings, that answers would come as she drove west, solutions would present themselves. But she would have to do something soon because if she didn't, she could end up like Diana, only worse. Diana had had Frenchy. Judy would be alone.

The familiar unpleasantness asserted itself and she detoured into the women's washrooms, feeling better when she emerged. She had lost a little weight but she had been eating less. Breakfast would come later, when she was on the road. She could not bear the smell or sight of food in the early morning.

She continued to the parking lot, an oval with a smattering of cars parked perpendicular to the edge at irregular intervals, a light, pre-season assortment. Hers was on the far side. She walked between the nearest two cars and then diagonally across the centre of the oval toward hers. It was right next to a pickup truck from Kentucky. As she reached the space between the pickup and the old VW, she saw him.

He was sitting on the ground with his back against the driver's door, wearing glasses, and reading from a textbook. She dropped her gear and he looked up, the picture of serenity.

'You have exams,' she said with a mixture of anger and despair.

'Next week. I'll be home in time.' He took his glasses off, folded them, and slid them in his shirt pocket.

'How did you find me?' Her voice was trembling.

'Fern called your father and your father called me. There are a lot of people back there who love you.'

'She had no right.'

'This isn't a question of rights.' He looked at her steadily. 'You pregnant?'

She nodded, her voice gone for the moment, her head dizzy. Nothing was a secret. Only in stories did pregnancy come as a surprise.

'How many periods have you missed?'

She held up two fingers in a V.

'Feeling OK?'

'No.' Barely audible.

'Try these.' He picked up a box of crackers from the ground beside him, nearer the front of the car where she could not see them, and held them out to her. 'Take them,' he said. 'They're for you. Why don't you sit down? I'm not going to touch you. I'm not taking you anywhere you don't want to go. You know me well enough by now. I just want to talk to you.'

'This is very painful for me,' she said. 'This is the conversation I wanted to avoid, although I suppose I owe it to you.'

He put the crackers in the space between them. 'Owe? We don't owe each other anything, Judy. I love you. That's the beginning and the end of it.'

She sat beside the pickup truck a few feet away from him and half a car's width between them. She reached over and took the box of crackers. It was unopened. He had brought it, knowing she was pregnant.

'Can I talk?' he asked.

'Go ahead.'

301

He closed the book and set it aside. He should be at the hospital now, making his morning rounds, instead of sitting on the ground in Missouri, talking. 'Just a couple of things,' he said. 'I called my sister.'

Caught by surprise, she felt a rush of elation. 'Did you really? What did she say?'

'She cried.' He met her eyes and then looked away. 'You were right about Renée. She needed someone to say, "Do it." I never thought I was the one. When the war ended, she was almost a mother to me.'

'Thank you,' Judy said.

He smiled a little. 'That's what Renée said. Anyway,' he took a breath, 'that was the first thing. The second thing is the baby. It's mine and I want it.'

She was chewing her second cracker, feeling her stomach begin to settle. 'You don't have to say things to be kind to me. We've talked about it enough over the last year. I know how you feel and you know how I feel.'

'I changed my mind. You were right about everything. I want offspring. I want my family to continue. I even think I want to give being a father a try. I learned a lot from you.'

'You can have it with someone else.'

'Sure. The way you can crawl into bed with someone else.'

'Don't say that.'

'That's what I came here for, to have my say. I want that child, Judy. That one.'

'This is my person and you have no right to tell me what to do with myself.'

'Don't talk to me about rights. That's a child, yours and mine. I want to give it a chance. Why didn't you have an abortion when you were in New York? You know who to call as well as I do.'

'I had to think.'

'Maybe you didn't want to.'

'Maybe I had to make up my mind.'

'Maybe you thought there was a chance it might turn out as perfect as we are.'

She did not answer. Time was running out, both here and for a rational decision. As perfect as we are. We were perfect, she thought, as perfect as two people could be.

'Your Cuban called,' he said matter-of-factly. 'The second Cuban.'

'I got him another lawyer.'

'He doesn't like the other lawyer. The other lawyer doesn't listen the way you did. The other lawyer doesn't have your patience.'

'We can't always have our first choices,' she said, speaking of herself and the Cuban at the same time. 'The other lawyer is very competent.'

'I asked Jerold to take care of it. He'll find someone else.'

'Is that all?' She no longer felt as though it were morning. Instead, it was evening, the end of a gruelling day. Everything she had thought was behind her was ahead of her again, the farewell, the parting, the whole mending process.

'No.' He shifted his weight slightly and turned so that he faced her. 'Is this what freedom means to you, leaving a job that you love and people that you love – people who love you – when things get tough? You know, I never spent three minutes of my life thinking about freedom until I met you. I never imagined that a person like my sister needed someone – a kid brother – to tell her that what she wanted to do was OK. I always did what I wanted – or thought I did. Only sometimes I used to wonder whether it was worth waking up tomorrow in the kind of world that allowed what happened to my family to happen. I can't tell you that you were the one that changed all that. There were a lot of people – Kellems, your father, Regina.' His voice trailed off as though there might have been others, as though he had gone back somewhere to dredge them up. 'I thought you had a real vision. I knew you were pregnant a few weeks ago and it hit me that I was happy, that you'd been right, that everything you'd said I really wanted, I really wanted. I thought you were just waiting to tell me.' His face was a face she would never forget, open, sincere. 'But if this is your idea of freedom, thanks, I'd rather stay a slave.'

'I was trying – ' It had become difficult to speak, harder to articulate. 'It wasn't just for me. I wanted it for you. I wanted you to be able to do whatever you wanted without feeling – ' she heard Fern using the word 'encumbered' all those years ago at Swarthmore ' – an obligation. I didn't want you giving anything up.' She used the back of her hand under one eye, then felt the tears on the other cheek.

'I haven't given anything up. You've taken it away. When I guessed you were pregnant, I was really pretty proud of you. I thought you'd done it finally, freed yourself from all the crap.'

'You still don't understand.'

'I know. Frenchy's baby. Jerold and Regina. Two good people who wanted nothing more out of life than to live it together. Is that what you want? You want to end up like them?'

I want you to act from love. . . . Her father's voice coming back through all those years, that day at Swarthmore after Davey's baby died, that crazy conversation that had made no sense to her. *The time will come and you'll remember we talked.* As though he had known then that this day would come, that she would be sitting on the gravelly ground in Missouri, trying to rethink the most important decision of her life. *I don't want you to weigh risks or to balance assets and liabilities or to try to corner the market on some useless commodity.* Her father in a dark coat and a hat, standing in the cold outside the dorm, having taken a detour on his way to Cincinnati in order to tell her meaningless things that she would never forget, telling her that once he had weighed pros and cons, that once he had done the right thing, that he did not want her making his mistakes. *The most important things we do in our lives have to do with love, and that's the way it should be.*

'Marcel.' She was crying freely now. *Make all your choices out of love.*

She whispered, 'No.' For the first time in a long time, she didn't care about anything.

She walked into the apartment as he turned the light on behind her.

'Get to bed,' he said gently.

She showered and got into bed, such a good bed, so comfortable after those nights in a sleeping bag on the hard ground. She could not quite remember what they had done with his rented car or what other arrangements they had made for the VW. She was home and she was almost ill with fatigue. Through the closed bedroom door she could hear him on the phone, talking now to her parents. He was tired too but not much of the French came through. They had trained him well these last two years. He drew now on stamina he had not known he possessed. He could think under strain, in the midst of fatigue, even after sitting up half the night in a parking lot in Missouri.

'She *is* home,' she heard him say in the muffled darkness and she knew he was talking to her mother. She could imagine her mother saying, 'She should come home for a few days, Marcel.'

She was home. It was a good feeling. She turned over, finding her most comfortable position. In the other room, Marcel said, 'Fern? Marcel Goldblatt.' And she slept.

She did not awaken when he got into bed but during the night she opened her eyes and moved and she felt him reach out and knew that tonight it was his turn to keep a vigil, that sleep would not come easily. In the morning she would tell him not to worry. She was home.

Ten

———◦———

It was not the easiest half year of her life but she kept busy and thought about it as little as possible, which turned out to be most of the time. Her mother, the eternal optimist, was delighted and her father, who was not given to jubilation, perhaps more so. They were especially pleased at the hastily arranged and sparsely attended marriage ceremony. Sheldon received her back with a kiss. To be fair to them, she finished her current work in November and took a leave.

It was an uneventful pregnancy but that did not ease the fear. They moved to a larger apartment in the same building, which strained the budget although Daddy excused Marcel's debt as a graduation gift from medical school, but she refused to furnish the extra bedroom, thinking that it would make an excellent office for two people who needed a place to do work at home. When the pains finally began, three days before her due date, she was alone, Marcel on one of the regular overnights of his internship. She waited until she was sure – until the day nurses were on duty and the message would not get lost – and made her phone calls, one to her doctor's answering service, which was returned in minutes, and several to the hospital to let Marcel know. Then she took her bag and got a taxi, congratulating herself on being a modern woman while wishing it had happened on a night he had been sleeping at home.

The fear that she had suppressed all those months possessed her during labour with accumulated fury.

'Maybe you should go away,' she said to him in a low voice as he sat at her bedside, excused for the day from his tasks. 'You must be tired.'

'I slept most of the night.'

'Maybe you should go away anyway.'

'I'm staying here. Don't say dumb things.'

The longest day of her life, the hardest, the most frightening. She would furnish the empty room after Christmas. She had already looked at desks and she would find an attractive sofa that converted into a double bed so that Renée and Claude could visit. The baby was quite still but the hearbeat was firm. Her doctor dropped in once in the morning and then after his office hours ended. She liked him. He was about fifty and very kind. Marcel had said he was the best. In January she would buy clothes and she would start riding again. They would get theatre tickets. They would resume their lives.

Marcel bathed her face and gave her boiled sweets to suck but when he asked her questions, she answered only by a movement of the head. She would not speak except to her doctor.

It was evening when they took her into the delivery room. There were so many people there she was grateful for Marcel because at least she could focus on someone she knew. The obstetrician was there, dressed for the occasion, an anaesthetist, a resident, women who must have been nurses, someone else. She had faced every other event in her life with such equanimity, even as she had done what she had not wanted to, that this fear gave her the sense of experiencing someone else's emotion. She lay on the table listening to two voices, her doctor's and her husband's, the first giving her instructions and the second reassuring her so softly that only she heard.

'There we go,' Marcel said with the first hint of excitement, moving from her side to get a better view. 'It's a girl, Judy,' and at almost the same moment, the voice of authority, 'It's a girl.'

Someone patted her arm, the anaesthetist. 'Nice going,' he said, as though it were a first for him too, as though he too had just discovered that it all happened exactly the way the gossip said.

'Looks very good, Mrs Goldblatt,' the doctor said with that absolute certainty that one always wanted from one's doctor and she let her breath out, only then aware she had been holding it since the first brief announcement. Like the voice at the end of the line, *Go ahead, New Haven*, and she thought, considering everything, it hadn't been so bad after all.

Daddy sent yellow roses and a card that said, 'I'm glad *someone* had the sense to have a daughter,' and Mother furnished the empty room as a gift to her first granddaughter. And when all the commotion was over and they were back at the apartment, Judy wrote a note to the office and said she thought she would really like to take a few months off rather than the six weeks she had originally requested. When she finished the letter, she wondered why she hadn't thought to ask for more time off to begin with. She was usually such a careful planner.

It was an unexpectedly hot day late in September. Simi (Simone after Marcel's mother) was happily at home with a nursemaid checked out by Edith Wolfe in her most thorough fashion. It had been refreshing to get back to work after Labour Day but on a day like this, Judy remembered with a touch of longing the easy days in July and August she had spent in Pennsylvania, some with and some without Marcel. Simi was a sweet, undemanding child who looked exactly like her father and had her mother's (Davey said) outgoing personality. She was weaned now and it had all been such a pleasure, it seemed a shame there would be no children to follow her.

Judy climbed the mountain of stairs to the entrance of 60 Centre Street, the beautiful Supreme Court Building, her briefcase in one hand and her suit jacket over her other arm where her bag hung from her shoulder. She was delivering some papers to one of the partners who was participating in a complicated civil case.

She could feel the sun as she mounted the steps, sweat forming on the arm that held the jacket, but it was good to be back. It was good to be part of it all again.

'Judith.'

A small flutter at the two syllables of her name and the voice that had spoken them. She turned to her right. He was standing a step below her, a short distance away. 'Hello, Roy.' She smiled because she was glad to see him and because he looked good, still lean, the hair still light, the glasses unchanged.

'You look wonderful.'

'Thank you.'

'I see you made it.' He glanced at the briefcase that she had set on the step below the one on which she stood, JW on fine black leather like the judge's. At the office, she was still Judy Wolfe.

'Three years ago. I'm – I'm really very happy.'

'I knew you would be. After all, it's the best.'

'I have a child, Roy, a little girl.' It was something she wanted to tell him, something she wanted him to know. 'She's nine months old now.'

'I'm very glad. You deserve to have a child. You deserve lots of good things.' So muted, so subdued. Seven years.

'How are Annie and the kids?'

'Very good,' he said with spirit, dropping his brown briefcase beside him. 'Got one in law school now. They're all achievers. I can't complain.'

'And Annie?'

'She's doing great things. Had a show of her paintings this summer, up in Provincetown. Did very well. Sold more of them than she thought she would.'

'I hope she didn't sell the portrait.'

'The portrait,' he said thoughtfully, as though he had to recall which painting she had referred to. 'She didn't even show it. She took it down a long time ago and put it away somewhere. Annie doesn't like it any more. Says it doesn't look like me.' Grey eyes that sometimes turned blue, thin lips that could look very hard except when there was a hint of a smile at the corners.

'You're teasing,' she said gently.

'Am I?'

Funny how young he made her feel, as though he were

someone from another generation the lower end of which had once, accidentally, overlapped her own, as their lives had. She smiled and looked down at his briefcase, her eyes passing over his left hand, ringless. 'You aren't wearing a wedding ring,' she said.

He lifted the hand briefly and looked at it. 'No. I took it off once, a long time ago, and afterward I decided not to put in on again. I don't like to go backward. Besides, its not being there is a kind of reminder.'

She didn't say anything, partly because she couldn't and partly because she didn't know what to say.

He picked up his briefcase. 'Well – ' He seemed rather at a loss for words himself. He looked at his watch. 'It's been good to see you, Judith.' He made a move to leave.

'Roy . . .'

He stopped where he was and fixed his eyes on her, suddenly very sober, a man who had never in his life lost his sobriety.

'I never said thank you.'

For a brief moment he seemed as overcome as she. Then the mouth softened and the eyes warmed. 'It was all my pleasure,' Roy Kellems said.

PART SIX

November 1967

One

━━━━◆◆◆━━━━

Calls that came in the night were never good news. Marcel answered when it rang in one of those hours between late Saturday and early Sunday. It was Marcel who could go from deep sleep to complete wakefulness in a matter of seconds. Now, in 1967, it was hard to remember a time when he had been unable to do it.

Judy listened to the conversation with eyes closed, hoping the usual hopes, that it wasn't her father, her mother, her brothers, their children. . . . Her own was safe in a crib, sleeping sweetly. She touched Marcel to reassure herself unnecessarily.

'Yes, what is it? . . . Oh, no . . . Where is he? . . . Good. Who's the cardiologist? . . . No, but I've heard the name . . . Yes. I'll call in the morning. You'd better get some rest . . . Yes . . . Right. Goodbye.'

'What is it?' She was awake now and scared.

'Morty,' he said, lying down again. 'Jesus.' A shudder ran through him. 'A heart attack. They were at a party. Regina drove him to the hospital.'

'Will he be all right?'

'We'll know in a few days. He just turned seventy-five.'

'I know.'

'I'll stop by and see Regina in the morning. She'll be a wreck. She's been asking him for years to retire and all he'd do is slow down a bit.'

'Who was that who called you?'

'Your father. The hospital called him to come and take Regina home.'

★ ★ ★

313

Afterward, Regina remembered so little about that night that she was not sure where they had been when he had started feeling ill, how she had managed to drive to the hospital, or how long she had sat in the waiting room. A nurse had coaxed her to go home, had offered at one point to go down and get her a taxi, but she had refused, weakly because she felt weak, but adamantly because she knew she could not leave him. Finally, someone had come whom she trusted and she had relented and gone home.

When she saw him the next day for the allotted three hundred seconds, she knew that he was more shocked at how she looked than she was at how he looked. And she knew – something in her signalled – that he felt pleased.

She had known women who stayed with their husbands because their husbands were a source of income, women who looked forward to the day they were left alone (with the cheque books and the portfolio), one woman, her cousin's wife, who had killed herself because she could no longer live with Henry and was not competent to live without him. Regina was none of those women. She had made a choice too, twenty years ago when her choices had been limited. She had come home and she had done her best. Money had not kept her, she was a full partner in the business, and the children were grown now – young Adam had turned twenty-five last month. What had kept her had been Morty. Now, the thought of losing him loomed as the greatest loss of her life.

He told her, in those first three hundred seconds, when he should have said nothing or very little, that he wanted her to go to the office, his office, sit at his desk, and preside over the company. She knew everything he did – he had seen to that over the years – and her presence in that office was now vital. She represented continuity.

She drove in that first morning in the chauffeured car as Morty had requested, feeling rusty, like an athlete retired so long he has forgotten the warm-up exercises, like a ballet dancer who can no longer find his position at the bar. She was four-fifths removed from the design studio, coming in no more

314

than once a week, having selected a capable replacement for herself. On the other four days she made the transition to the other life, the life she had thought, forty years earlier, that she would lead. She patronized the arts, crossing paths once or twice with Edith Wolfe; she lent her name and gave her time and money to civic and cultural projects that appealed to her; she read and studied. And finally, when she knew the time had come, she began to read all the letters from her cousin Richard Wolfe, slowly, carefully and painfully, starting with the first ones in the early 1920s, with the intention of editing and compiling them.

She did not complete the task. It was simply dropped, along with everything else that had brought her pleasure, in the aftermath of Morty's heart attack.

The secretary took her coat on Monday morning and asked the obvious question in a voice filled with genuine emotion.

'We think he'll be all right,' Regina said, having prepared the answer. 'Nothing will change here except that I'll take over for a while.' She looked at her watch. 'In twenty minutes, why don't you come in and we'll talk about today's schedule.'

The secretary opened the door to Morty's office for her and closed it softly behind her. The office was Morty's style, spare with sentimental touches. Designs by Regina Rush. On the wall, a few photographs and mementoes of the company and an Utrillo that was one of his favourites. The desk nearly clear except for a bevy of photographs that she had not looked at in years because when they spoke in this office, they sat together in the conference area, on the sofa, or on the comfortable chairs nearby.

She pulled the desk chair back and sat. The pictures were a shock. Ernie, Pat and their three children. Margot's wedding picture. Margot and Steve. Their children. Adam out of doors behind the house in Connecticut. All the rest were Regina. Regina in the late 1920s, in the wonderful coat with the fox collar that warmed the tips of her ears and nearly covered her nose as well. Regina in the thirties with a young Ernie. Regina with a child, Regina by herself. Looking at the photographs, one could believe that he had never loved any other woman besides her. There was a knock on the door and she realized that the twenty minutes had elapsed; the day had begun.

He lived, he improved, he was moved into a private room, and she began to relax although she knew that the great change had taken place. The company would not be the same again, nor would their lives. At the end of the week, she sat down in the evening and spoke to Adam.

Adam had been born in Morty's image. At twenty-five he was half an inch taller than his father and mirrored him physically in almost every way. The gait was the same. The faces were identical. The voice, although not quite so deep as his father's had the same quality and was often mistaken on the telephone. And after a year of wandering the earth after college and another year or so working on his own, he had shaved his beard and returned to Rush Industries as Ernie and Marcel had refused to.

'I thought he looked pretty good today,' Adam said, sitting in his father's chair in Regina's study. He had returned to the apartment from his own day after Morty's heart attack and his presence had been an unexpected pleasure for Regina.

'He does, yes.'

'You look like you could use a little sleep.'

'It's just hard getting back to a routine. I'm fine. Can I give you a drink, dear?'

'I don't think so.'

'You have some thinking to do, Adam.' She had decided to be direct. They knew each other well. Being nine years younger than Margot, he had spent many years as an only child and they had always been open with each other. 'Dad isn't coming back as head of Rush.'

He looked down, avoiding her eyes. They only say they want to know the truth, she thought, looking at the dark head. What they really want is hope. What they want is to know that nothing will change, ever.

'He's not that old, Mum. He doesn't act old or think old.'

'It isn't a matter of age,' she said, although it was very much

316

that, along with everything else. 'When Dad gets better, the doctor isn't going to let him do what he's been doing. And I'm not going to let him either.'

'That's not fair. He loves that company.'

'I know.' The mistress Morty never had, the exercise he never had time for, the education he never completed formally. 'I don't mean that he won't be available. I just mean he won't be *that* available. Adam, I'm sitting at Dad's desk because I'm his partner. There are several people who would like to sit there, people who would like the change a lot more than I want it. I'm not going to sit at that desk for the rest of my life, not even till I'm seventy-five. I'm a stopgap. I'm continuity. We've had many offers over the years to buy us out and we could probably sell within six months if we decided to.' She watched the look of disbelief creep up on Adam's face.

'You wouldn't,' he said.

'We wouldn't if we thought someone wanted it. But if it's just a job, we could sell and all of us could have plenty of income and do what we like, work at whatever we like, without all the responsibility, the trips, the hard work.' Her voice trailed off as she remembered it all, all the years, all the hard work.

'You know I want it,' Adam said.

'Think about it, dear. Think about Dad's life and how he's spent it. Think about it a lot. If you want it, we'll work together, all three of us. I think Dad wanted five more years to bring you along, but maybe we could do it in two or three. Just don't say yes too quickly.'

He sat another moment and then rose, still lanky, still not quite fully formed, but well on the way. 'Did you leave him once?' he asked, the question taking her by complete surprise. 'A long time ago? Because of Rush?'

'I? Leave Daddy?' She smiled as she said it, as though it were the most unreasonable thing she had ever been asked. 'Never, Adam. I never even thought of it.' Lying easily as her grandmother had lied to protect her daughter, to make sure Aunt Maude would be happily married, lying as Jerold should have when the question of his infidelity had come up in a conversation with his daughter, lying because the truth was worse and the truth was nobody's business but the participants'.

'I wasn't sure,' her son said.

'But you're sure now, Adam. Daddy hasn't been hard to live with. In many ways, I've been the tough one.'

He bent from his great height and kissed her cheek. 'I'll think,' he said.

On many Sundays Marcel took Simi out with Jerold. When Simi was very little, Judy had gone along, feeling the need to mother, but she sensed that the two men did not require her presence and once or twice she had almost felt an intruder. They were more than father-in-law and son-in-law. She teased sometimes that Marcel was the favourite son, although she knew that Daddy's relationship with her brothers was undiminished. It was a cold December Sunday, a few days prior to her parents' trip to a warm island, and she was squeezing Simi into a one-piece snowsuit, boots, mittens and finally hood, so that nothing showed but a round face with large eyes and a few soft curls of dark hair.

'Morty should be home in another week,' Marcel said, putting on his own warm gloves.

'Then he's doing well.'

'Looks like it. Maybe when he's back we'll run over to visit.' He said it casually but she knew it was meant for her to think about. She had not seen Regina since that day in her office three years ago, the day of the Buddha.

'Maybe,' she said.

'She'd like to see you, Judy.'

She was squatting on the hall floor, tying the cord that held the hood in place. She looked up at Marcel briefly and then kissed each of the puffy cheeks in front of her. Then she stood and rested her right hand on the hooded head, hardly aware it was there, just something you did when you had a child. 'I don't know, Marcel,' she said.

'Come on, Simi. Grandpa's waiting. *Tu veux parler français avec moi?*'

A shrill, 'No!' that could have been either French or English.

Marcel shrugged his shoulders in mock failure. 'See you,' he said, leaning over his daughter to kiss his wife.

She turned the double lock as they left and heard the little voice chirping down the hall to the lift. Everything that had happened to them was fortunate. In the spring Marcel would complete the residency that had been put together for him according to his wishes. He would set up the kind of practice he wanted. Judy had expanded the time she spent at the firm and the firm had turned out to be helpfully flexible. She was becoming an artful strategist whose opinions were solicited and respected. Even Frenchy had called her once on a case of his that was going to court and after he had outlined the facts and she had begun to talk, she had seen him smile – the way Daddy did sometimes – and later he had sent a cheque for a consultation fee.

And there was Simi. She bent to pick up a rag doll her mother had given Simi for her birthday. Two years old. It was hard now to remember life without her, life without Marcel, life without everything just the way it was now. Everything so good except Regina.

And then it struck her for the first time. It was silly, really. Daddy's affection for Marcel was genuine and it predated Simi, their marriage, even their falling in love. Funny that she had never seen it before. In a way, Marcel was a link to Regina.

Morty came home and he improved, but he was restless, frustrated at being weak and then frustrated at having so little to do. Regina and Adam conferred with him in his library and he made decisions as he always had, his mind sharp and quick, needing no notes, all the details in his head, like long ago when they were just beginning down on Worth Street. But the doctor refused to let him go back to the office, refused to let him chair meetings of his department heads, even if they came to the apartment.

319

'I've been kicked upstairs,' he said mournfully one evening when Regina had finished recounting her day at the office.

'Get well and let's do some travelling,' she said.

'You want to sell, Regina? Tell me the truth. Is it time for us to cash in?'

'I've thought about it,' she said. 'I've thought about it a great deal since November. I think I don't want to. I did once, but that was a long time ago. I'd like to give Adam a chance, if he wants to take it.'

'I thought you didn't want Adam to have it.'

'I never said that.'

'No, but I sensed it.' He was weighing words. 'You didn't want him to end up like me.'

It was February and cold out, too cold for him to take walks, too risky for him to chair meetings, too late for him to seize one good idea and turn it into a fortune. He had lost weight but he still had the old glint now and then; he sparkled in company. He was the same old Morty when the children visited. Everything that had ever been there was there now. It was only the physical capacity that had diminished.

'I wouldn't want him to turn out any other way,' she said.

Adam took on the travelling. She watched to see whether it tired him but instead, he appeared exhilarated. He was his father's son. After Morty returned from the hospital, she told Adam to go back to his apartment. A new normality settled upon them.

By April Morty was looking and feeling much better. He took walks and became stronger. He made a bargain with the doctor. If he improved through the summer, he would be allowed back to the office in September.

Only one or two part days a week, the doctor said. Only in an advisory capacity. As though Morty had ever stopped advising. As though one day had passed since the heart attack on which he had not expended some form of energy on behalf of Rush.

Regina had lunch brought in for her and Adam one rainy day

and she put the question to him. It was five months since Morty had been away.

'I thought I told you,' he said, raising his brows in a way that Morty did, as though it would clear his mind of the present confusion.

'You didn't tell me and I didn't ask. I wanted you to get a taste of all the things Dad has done by himself, the travelling especially.'

'I can handle it, Mum.'

'It's not whether you can handle it. It's a question of – ' She broke off, seeking a word.

'Love?' Adam supplied.

It was surely the right word but she had wanted to avoid it.

'The answer is no,' he said. 'I don't love Rush the way Dad does. I think I'm still fascinated with it. But each time the fascination wears off one small piece of the company, it's replaced with affection.'

'I see.' It was a more thoughtful answer than she had expected and in a way a little disappointing. Some remote corner of her being had hoped he would turn it down, hoped he would choose an income without the lifetime of hard work, without the strain of the physical and spiritual demands, hoped he would find something less gruelling to do with his life. It had been only a small hope.

Morty was not surprised. 'I knew he was hooked the first day he came to work for us,' he said, looking very satisfied. 'But I'm glad to hear it. I'm glad he told you. It means more when he says it to you. I think he tries to humour me.'

Regina smiled and touched his arm. 'We all try to humour you,' she said. 'It even seems to be working.'

'I'm feeling better, Regina. After the summer, I'll be able to work with Adam myself.'

At the beginning of June they drove to Connecticut, leaving behind the nurse who had plagued his days and the confinement of the apartment and the city. He exulted in the pleasure of the house, taking short walks before breakfast and longer ones in the afternoon. His colour improved and his spitits rose.

The second Sunday of their stay Regina awoke early when he did. He dressed quietly and started out of the room.

'I'll be right down,' she said sleepily and, as she had done more than a thousand times before in over forty years of marriage, she closed her eyes and awoke an hour later. She put on slippers and a robe, washed, and went downstairs. The breakfast table was set for two and the maid was sitting in the kitchen, reading the Sunday paper.

'Good morning,' Regina said. 'Where's my husband?'

'He went for his walk.'

Regina glanced at her watch. 'When?' she asked, faintly discomfited.

'Oh, maybe 'bout an hour ago.'

'An hour? And he hasn't come back?'

The black face looked suddenly frightened. 'No, ma'am. He just said he's goin' for a walk and he went out.'

Regina opened the kitchen door and went down the steps. 'Morty,' she called, looking left and right. 'Morty!' Faster, across the lawn, quickly toward the woods, following his usual route. 'Morty!' Holding her robe so she would not trip, panting because she had not run across a field in half a century. 'Morty!' With unimagined speed, flying over the grass. She entered the woods and slowed, still moving, still calling.

And then she saw him. 'Morty!' he was sitting at the base of a large tree, leaning against it, not moving. 'No,' she said in a half whisper. 'No, no, please no.' She reached him and knelt beside him. His head was forward as though he had fallen asleep sitting down and his cheek was cool. His glasses, folded in their case, were carefully placed in the breast pocket of his short-sleeved sports shirt.

Behind her she heard a sob and then a wail. 'Lilly-May,' she said without turning around, hearing the unsteadiness in her voice. There were people that had to be called, Ernie in New Jersey, Margot and Adam in New York, Marcel. She could not think. She could not choose which of them should hear it first, whose glorious Sunday should be the first to be ruined. 'I'd like you to call – There's a book with numbers.' The words were harder to say, the throat stiffening. 'Please call my cousin. Judge Wolfe. Ask him what I should do.' She was still kneeling, the debris of the woods starting to hurt her knees. 'I'll stay here with my husband.'

She heard the whimpering and footsteps recede and she moved herself into a sitting position. In the long wait that followed, she told him half a dozen things that she had never got around to saying, but which she was sure he knew anyway.

Two

———◦◦◦———

'How are you?' Marcel gave her a kiss and kept his hand on her arm.

'Not bad.' She looked drawn – it pained her to look in the mirror – but she no longer felt crushed. It was a month and although she had not yet begun to feel herself again, she had begun to want to. 'Let's sit in the living room.'

'That sounds kind of formal. Have you given up your study?'

'No. It's just that it's full of condolence letters and they're all very depressing. I'm taking some time each day to answer them and until it's done, I can't bear to go into the study for anything else. How are you, Marcel?'

'Fine.' He didn't look fine. He looked thin and tired.

'You're opening your office soon, aren't you?'

'Very soon. I've been doing a lot of running around but I think we're pretty much on our way now.'

'I hope you'll let me make you a little present for the new office.'

The suggestion seemed to deflate him. 'I don't think so,' he said. 'Not that I don't appreciate it. You've always been – you and Morty both – you've been more than generous.'

'We've been proud of you. You're the only doctor in the family.'

He smiled, looking as though the smile had surprised him. When it faded, he said, 'You know how much I appreciate everything you've both done for me. I wish Morty and I had been able to get along better.'

The son's burden. He had been brought up without a father and found himself now, at the age of thirty-two, with too many.

'You got along with him fine, Marcel. He would never have

324

forgiven himself if you had joined the company when there was something else you really wanted. He admired you for what you did. Morty only wanted one of his own to love his company the way he did. Jerold did the same with Frenchy a long time ago.'

'Sometimes I think that night you sent Jerold down to my place in the Village he should have given me a thrashing instead of a pep talk.'

'Jerold doesn't thrash people. That's why I sent him.'

'Sending him didn't make your life any easier, did it?' His dark eyes were very frank.

She was no longer sure what anyone knew, but she was fairly certain that Judy had not kept secret that last meeting nearly four years ago. 'Marcel, when someone dies, you find yourself reflecting, remembering turning points and wondering whether you turned in the right direction. Then you think about the future, where you're going, what your priorities are. I have only one. I want to see the family whole.'

'You're only one person, Regina. It's a varied family and there are strong wills.'

'I don't mind bending. Maybe you'll all see how flexible I am. Tell me,' she said quickly, changing the subject, 'how are your in-laws?'

'Jerold's fine. I've never seen him better. He turned sixty-six this year and I expect him to go on for a long time.'

'And Edith?' She watched him carefully.

'I'm not sure.'

'I wondered,' Regina said. 'When I saw her here, something made me uneasy.'

'It may be nothing.'

'But you don't think so.'

He took a long breath. 'Jerold's taken her to see someone.'

Regina nodded slightly and rose from the sofa. She walked to the mantel, tossing an affectionate glance at the Monet that hung above it, a gift from Morty when she was pregnant with Adam. Reminders. Everywhere one turned there were reminders. She took down the package and the envelope and came back to the sofa.

'This is for you,' she said, handing him the envelope. 'From all of us.'

He had stood when she had. Now he looked down at the proffered envelope as though it held bad news.

'And this is for Judy.' She put the small cube of a package on top of the envelope and waited for him to take both. The box was wooden and handcarved and had served some earlier purpose that she could not remember but it fitted its contents like a glove. The paper was a small print on tissue, tied with a narrow ribbon.

'I'll say thank you for both of us,' Marcel said. He put the envelope inside his jacket and the package in the outside pocket. Then, his arm around her, he kissed her cheek and they walked to the door.

'Let me know how Edith is,' she said.

'I will.'

'You know, I always wanted one of my children to study medicine. I never dreamed it would be you.'

'I could have told you that the day I got here. I wish I had.'

'It was much nicer coming as a surprise.' She rang for the lift. 'Give my love to Judy, dear.'

Fern was already at the table when Judy arrived, a few minutes later after an overlong meeting. She sat and caught her breath. 'Thanks for coming down to the netherworld.'

'Nonsense. I like an occasional reminder that New York continues to exist below Thirty-fourth Street. Sometimes I get the feeling that after Macy's it slides into the sea.'

'It probably does. Which accounts for most of the people I know down here thinking they're drowning.'

'But not you.'

'Well.' She unfolded the napkin and placed it on her lap. 'I am. But it's law that's keeping me afloat.' She opened her bag and pulled out a blue Tiffany box tied with white ribbon. 'Happy birthday. Now that you've dug holes in your ears, I thought you should have something to go through them.'

Fern looked at the box for a moment before accepting it. 'Thank you. I should have known it wasn't just a fun lunch.'

'It is a fun lunch. All our lunches are fun. Are they OK?' Fern had the box open and was sliding the earrings out of the blue pouch inside.

'Gorgeous. I can't wait to see them on.'

'Maybe if you show them off your sometime lover will cast out his wife and take you on.'

Fern smiled, looking rather wise and knowing for thirty-one. 'I don't think so, Judy.'

'He isn't – Fern, he's not using you, is he?'

'No. We have just the relationship that suits us both. You didn't feel used, did you?'

'That time? No. But the times were different.'

'They always are.'

'I saw him. I don't think I told you. Two summers ago, when Simi was very little.'

'Anything interesting?'

'Very interesting. I can't imagine running into Roy and not having it interesting. You met him. You must remember.'

'I remember.' She tucked the blue pouch into the blue box and closed it, slipping the box into her bag. 'I'm surprised that you never ask me about my guy.'

'Maybe I don't want to know. Maybe I think that you could have it all if you tried, the guy, the job, all the good feelings.'

'I can't.'

'God, Fern, if I had your nose, I think I would own the world.'

Fern looked pleased. 'You were the first person after Jack who told me I had a good nose.'

'Jack and I know noses.'

'How's your own family?'

It was the question she was least able to answer. 'My mother's not well.'

'I'm sorry.'

'She's been seeing a doctor since the summer and this is

November but no one'll tell me what's wrong. I'm sure Marcel knows but he says he isn't sure. They don't want to tell me because they all know I'll go to pieces when I find out. It's why I'm drowning.'

'I hope you'll keep me posted.'

She nodded and fiddled with food until she could speak again. 'On the brighter side, Marcel's got a beautiful office and real patients and one of these days, he's going to make a living from it.'

'That is bright. What about your wonderful uncle?'

'Oh, my uncle Richard's in the Far East, making trips into Vietnam with my aunt. One of her pictures made the *Times* last month. Page two. They covered the Democratic convention in Chicago and when they left for Vietnam, we all breathed a sigh of relief.' She smiled at the irony. 'Personally, I think they're crazy. Uncle Richard's almost sixty-five.'

'You don't understand anything about love, do you?'

'Oh, a few things I've picked up here and there.'

'They have kids?'

'One, my age. My cousin George. He's practising medicine on an Indian reservation in the Southwest.'

'That's different.'

'It may even be permanent. Word is he's got a Native American girlfriend. Hasn't sat very well with members of the family who don't think it's the right thing for a nice Jewish boy to do. Of course, George isn't Jewish. I don't think he's anything.'

'Nobody's anything any more. Your uncle's just led the way.'

'Maybe. He was everybody's ideal until we settled down to do what was expected of us. I wonder sometimes how Simi will turn out. I wonder if I would have the guts to send her off to visit Uncle Richard for a summer. Maybe I'll just keep her cloistered for a few decades.'

'*Judy!*'

Judy shrugged. 'Just for her own protection,' she said.

It became more than she had intended, more than she had imagined it could be. It became herself. She was Regina Rush of Rush Industries. The *Times* wrote a small article in the Sunday business section on the woman who had taken the reins, and one of the large soft drink companies made inquiries with an eye toward a merger. She turned the merger down flatly and Adam had the article framed as a gift.

It made her feel wonderful. It was over a year since Morty's heart attack and six months since his death. The books were good, the orders strong, new looms on order, production doing well. They were a company to contend with and she had done it herself. Morty had been right; she was a full partner.

And then one day in the spring of '69 it struck her that she was not doing it for Adam, not doing it because Morty had wanted it. She was doing it for herself. That was the day she called Adam into her office and told him that the time was coming when she would retire. That was the day that she got the date.

The call came from Edith Wolfe, Edith who had been so pretty and so happy and such a good wife to Jerold, but who was now doing battle against a disease that would not let her win. It was her sister-in-law. A helicopter had come in to evacuate the press but there had not been room on it for everyone. Richard, of course, had stayed behind so that Jeanne-Marie could be the first to safety. The helicopter had been shot down and no one aboard had survived. He was bringing her home. Regina listened to the grieved voice of her cousin's wife, her own grief beginning to take hold. The funeral would be at the little church downtown that Jeanne-Marie had been so fond of. What foolishness, Edith went on with unusual anger. Why couldn't they be like other people and take life easy in their sixties? What was it that kept them going?

Regina hung up. Two calls were waiting, one from Japan, and there was a sales meeting in half an hour that she was scheduled to attend. What kept them going? She wondered, fleetingly, whether Jeanne-Marie's film had come through the crash intact.

Marcel closed his office for the afternoon and they went downtown in the family car with Judy's parents. Davey had come down the night before and would ride with Frenchy and Diana.

Marcel had been stricken by the news. The few times he had met Jeanne-Marie they had spoken at length in French, liking each other greatly. Marcel was slightly older than their son and also a doctor. Jeanne-Marie was a warm, free, moving spirit. Marcel had never suffered his own parents' deaths and now he suffered them over and over as nonparents died. It was Judy who gave up being comforted in order to minister to her husband.

But of all of them, it was Mother who was most affected. Edith Wolfe wept into a handkerchief during the long trip to lower Manhattan. It was as though in mourning the death of her sister-in-law she had finally come to accept and mourn her own impending end.

The church was Italian Catholic in a neighbourhood that had retained the Old World and kept it new. Jeanne-Marie's passing blended the traditions of several cultures, including the one that rejected all the others. No visiting hours had been scheduled at the funeral home, much to the distress of the manager, who anticipated days of mourning before the burial. The funeral took place two days after Uncle Richard arrived in New York. He had arranged for a medley of French songs to be sung along with a few anti-war songs that had recently become popular.

The church was full of strangers. Here and there Judy spotted a famous face, television newscasters, sitting amid unfamiliar faces whom she took to be colleagues.

The family gathered near the front, to one side of the draped coffin. In the first row sat Uncle Richard, his son, George, and the beautiful black-haired girl who had only recently become a member of the family.

There were cousins everywhere. Crazy Millie sat between her sister and a man who was probably her brother, up from whatever sunny place he spent his worthless life. Regina sat beside Lillian, a contrast in faces, the one round and grief-stricken, the other thin and tight and condemnatory, her eyes on George's wife. Surely Lillian's idea of family would have to be stretched to accept this newest member.

But it was Judy's concept of family that changed during the funeral mass. There was not one Catholic among the relatives. When the time came to kneel, not one member of the family moved. These were the people related by blood and marriage to Jeanne-Marie Wolfe. It had never occurred to Judy to ask about family in France. She knew nothing about Jeanne-Marie's background. Uncle Richard had lived in Paris before the war and one day, the story went, he had come home with a wife. They had been married over thirty-five years.

She slipped her hand through Marcel's arm and held it. She herself had married a man with little family, a man from across an ocean, a man whose first language was different from hers. But they had a child now, as her cousin George would one day, enlarging the family, diversifying it, bringing in new spirits and talents and ideas and cultures as Jeanne-Marie had, Jeanne-Marie who had seemed more their own than some of the cousins who sat nearby.

She watched the priest go through the alien ritual, smelled incense, and wept for this member of the family who had sat beside her on a plane once during eight of the most difficult hours of her life. And suddenly she knew that she would like very much to have another child.

She waited until George had left for home and went down-town to visit her uncle, stopping along the way to pick up food, afraid that as a man alone he might starve.

'Judy,' he said, opening the door, 'aren't you sweet to come.'

She kissed him and handed him the bag.

'I'm a grubby old man today,' he said, carrying the bag to the kitchen. His face had a day's growth of beard and he was wearing what could only be described as a work shirt with a pair of old trousers that once must have fitted him better.

'It's such a nice house,' Judy said. 'Like a dolls house grown up.'

'We've lived in it since the war. On and off for about thirty years.'

They sat in the living room. 'I didn't know Jeanne-Marie was Catholic.'

'She wasn't.'

'But the funeral . . .'

'George wanted that. He's no more a Catholic than she was but he's kind of a traditionalist.'

'That's a nice way to be.'

'I suppose it's the way things go. I made the grand gesture, left home, country, convention, family, and my son returned to set down roots.'

'Not very conventional roots.'

'But roots all the same. He'll never leave that place. He's even learning their native language. Nice girl, he married. Did you get to meet her?'

'Just for a minute.'

'Very nice girl.' He looked thoughtful. He had lost weight. Perhaps that was why his clothes seemed to fit so badly.

'It was a beautiful church.'

'She liked that church. She used to take pictures sometimes of the priests hurrying to mass. Nice shadowy pictures. She took George there once, D-Day; he was six. She turned on the radio that morning and heard the invasion was on and she knew I'd be there with my trusty Waterman.' He tapped the place where a shirt pocket would be. 'Lost the damn thing in Vietnam. Filthy war. Had it thirty years. George never forgot that day. Said he'd never seen his mother pray before. Or after. She never told me about that. George did a long time afterwards. And Regina.'

'Regina?'

'She had them come over that evening, so they wouldn't be alone. I don't know what we'd have done over the years without Regina.' He looked around the living room. 'They never let us buy this house from them. We're permanent guests. Well, it's helped.'

332

'You were all so friendly when you were young.'

'We were a friendly family,' Uncle Richard acknowledged.

'But I've never seen her at a family affair.'

'Well – ' he hesitated, 'that was probably Morty's doing. He wasn't a family person the way Regina is. It's what Regina's always cared about, the family.' He was looking into the fireplace as if his thoughts were elsewhere.

'You know everything, don't you?' Judy said softly.

He looked up and gave her a half smile. 'Not nearly,' he said. 'But a lot more than most.'

'She wanted to marry my father, didn't she?'

A small sound – a chuckle – came from Richard Wolfe. 'Interesting the way stories get turned around,' he said, 'the way one's own hopes make them come out the right way – for you. I suppose that's part of the truth, that Regina wanted to marry my brother. It's a much bigger truth than that. Maybe all truths are bigger than the speakable part. Maybe one unspeakable part of that story is that it was Regina who saw to it that your father stayed with his family at a time when he might not have. But that's unspeakable, Judy. I'm sure you understand.'

'I didn't know, but I understand.'

'You know, I loved Rome.' He stood and walked to the front window. Shrubs grew halfway up the lower pane. The curtains were dusty. 'We could have stayed in Rome and she'd be alive. She'd had it with war. She'd had it after Spain. You weren't even around during Spain.' He turned away from the window. Seen down the length of the room, he looked even thinner, almost emaciated. 'It was only because of me that she went.'

'That's not true, Uncle Richard.' Judy stood, feeling his hurt and wanting to ease it regardless of the cost. 'We talked about it that time, when I came home for Grandpa Willy's funeral. She loved going with you. I think she looked forward to it. It was a different kind of war.' She had never consciously lied before to an adult, never lied so effusively, so convincingly. She half expected the earth to open up and and swallow her but she could not have done otherwise. Her uncle was alive and in pain and there was no need for the pain. If Jeanne-Marie had wanted to say no, she would have. She had been a strong personality, strong enough to change her husband's mind. It had been her choice not to.

'Well,' Uncle Richard said, 'I didn't know she'd ever said that.'

'She did. To me.'

He came and put an arm around her and patted her shoulder. 'Nice that my brother had a daughter. A nice daughter. I should offer you something to eat, shouldn't I?'

'No, there's something at home.'

'Then run along to your family. I'm not helpless. I appreciate the visit and the care package.'

'Take care of yourself.'

'Yes, I'll have to now, won't I?'

At the door she hugged him, touched his unshaven face and smiled.

'I'll take care of it,' he promised. 'Remember me uptown, Niece. It was good to see you. I think I've decided you're a nicer guy than I am.'

She wasn't quite sure what he meant but she wondered all the way home whether she had misjudged Regina very badly.

Three

On the last Friday in June of that year, 1969, Regina left her office at Rush Industries for the last time. She had kept the date a secret for as long as possible although she was aware that there was great speculation among the employees, both North and South. She had not changed the decor of the office, preferring to leave it as Morty had occupied it, a sign that she was merely an interim occupant. On the afternoon of the last day she took the photographs off the desk and packed them in her attaché case. Then she checked the drawers, removing only those things she considered personal possessions and leaving, with a smile, a half full box of Kleenex. Adam would get a kick out of opening that drawer on Monday.

The secretary stayed until almost the last minute, leaving finally when Regina said good-bye. The company would move very smoothly into new hands on Monday morning and the secretary was one of the people who would make that happen.

In the end it was Adam who was the more emotional of the two, coming to the office half an hour after closing, as they had planned, to escort her downstairs to the waiting limousine. Morty had said she should be driven to work and she had acceded. Adam was twenty-six and would take the subway most days. She liked that in Adam. He had been brought up with wealth and had developed a pleasant take-it-or-leave-it attitude towards it. He had his expensive tastes but they were visible only to those who knew him well.

'Got everything?' he asked, looking around the large office that he would one day decorate to suit himself, when he was able to let his father go a little more.

'I'm quite ready.'

They went to the door. He opened it and she passed through.

'Not looking back?' he asked.

'Not this time,' Regina said.

He did though, as if to see it for the last time as his father's office. He had called it. 'Dad's office' until very recently. When he came back on Monday morning, it would be his.

'Well, I guess we can go.'

'Want to stay awhile, Adam? I can go myself.'

'No. I think it ought to stay empty for a couple of days. Get used to the difference.'

She took his arm and they went downstairs to where the car was waiting and they drove to Park Avenue to have dinner together with the rest of the family, a celebration. She did not look back.

They visited Mother more and more often, sometimes just to sit and talk in the evening or on a weekend afternoon, and they came for dinner more often too. She still managed to get out but not as frequently as she wanted. Sometimes she was just content to stay home and rest. Sometimes she had no choice.

It was Thanksgiving and they sat around the dining room table like a small banquet, the whole family at one time. Mother was in good spirits and Davey was being especially entertaining.

In a lull in the conversation, Marcel said, 'I have some interesting news,' and the adults looked in his direction. 'I saw Regina yesterday. I think she has a beau – or at least an admirer.'

'How very nice,' Mother said with enthusiasm. 'Did she tell you?'

'We talked about it, yes.'

'She's a good-looking woman,' Davey said. 'And she sure as hell has plenty of money.'

'Davey!' Mother scolded.

'Oh, I don't think he's after her money,' Marcel said calmly. 'He's got enough of his own. Lives in England. His father and

Morty's father did business together in the twenties. Julian remembers Morty from his Paris days.'

It was a message, Judy thought. It was Regina's way of saying she was not a threat. It was a message for Judy.

'Have you met him, Marcel?' Mother asked, clearly interested.

'During the summer. I didn't know at the time what his relationship was to Regina. I thought he was just a visitor.'

'What is he like? Did he make a good impression on you? Is he as fine a person as Morty was?'

'Just as fine. Different, of course, but a warm personality. I'd even guess he's a bit younger than Regina.'

At that, Daddy laughed. 'Good for Regina. I think that should suit her very well. That's very good news, Marcel.'

'Maybe there'll be a family wedding,' Mother said optimistically.

'I don't think so,' Marcel said. 'I don't think Regina's going to marry again. I expect she may do something much less acceptable and rather more enjoyable one of these days.' He squeezed Judy's hand under the table and she reddened slightly.

Davey hooted.

'I'm sure Regina wouldn't,' Mother said.

'I hope she would.' Daddy was absolutely glowing. 'It's about time she did what she felt like doing without any limiting commitments.'

'Gee, Dad,' Davey said coyly, 'I wish we'd had this discussion a long time ago.'

Everyone laughed, including his wife, Marilyn, who looked a little startled.

'I thought we did, Davey. On more occasions than I'd like to remember.'

'Well,' Mother said, always the peacemaker, the mediator, the arbitrator, 'I'm very pleased for Regina.'

At home later, Judy went to a drawer and took out the package, still in its original wrapping, that Marcel had given

337

her over a year ago. She had never opened it but she knew that the Buddha was inside, knew it must be, knew it had been a peace offering from Regina. It had all become very awkward. She was sorry now that she knew as much as she knew, sorry that her knowledge had disrupted a life. She knew she should see Regina and talk to her, apologize for hurting her and even more for putting her in the position of having to disclose truths that were not Judy's business. She thought that one of these days, when the weather was nicer, after she had visited Mother she would walk over to Park Avenue and pay a call.

It was a bright Saturday in February. Marcel had morning office hours and they all ate a late lunch when he returned. Usually, Judy took Simi to see Mother but today, she decided to go alone. When they finished lunch, she put the small box in her bag, and made the short walk to the street with the family house.

'You just missed Davey,' Frenchy said, greeting her as she entered. 'He's gone back to Providence. They have a party tonight.'

'And you?'

'We have tickets for something. Forgive me if I don't remember what.'

'How is she?'

'In bed today. A little woozy.'

Judy shuddered. Rationally, she knew there would be no improvement, but its absence was always a disappointment.

Frenchy patted her shoulder. 'Easy. Go on up. I'm just leaving.'

Her mother, sitting against several pillows, looked extraordinary. She was as beautiful as Judy had ever seen her, her cheeks flushed as though she were happy or feverish and her eyes quite bright. Sometimes the medication did that to her. At least it did not put her to sleep. She was still there, all of her.

Judy sat and they talked. Mother missed Simi and Judy promised to bring her next week. Davey had been there and had taken lunch with them – 'You know Davey. All you need to do is offer him a free lunch' – Edith Wolfe smiled fondly.

338

Frenchy had just left. Frenchy was involved in a most interesting case, one of those new computer companies in competition with a much larger one and trouble all around. Very interesting, she said again, looking away.

'Daddy's hearing something quite unusual too,' Mother said after a moment. 'All these welfare rights cases that are coming up in the federal courts. Funny how one can have one opinion about a system and quite another about an individual who's part of it. I did something I've never done before. I told him what I thought.'

'You've never done that before?'

'Of course not. Not about a case.'

'Why not?'

'Surely it isn't my place, Judy. You don't expect Marcel to tell you how to think, do you?'

'Not how to think, no.'

'I wonder if he'll use it,' Edith Wolfe mused. 'My opinion.' She seemed the slightest bit disoriented. 'I wonder if – ' She broke off and closed her eyes for a moment. 'Do you remember Max Rosenberg, dear?' she asked suddenly.

The name jolted her. It was over twenty years. They never talked about it any more, she and her brothers. 'I remember,' she said cautiously.

'He really was something of a buffoon, wasn't he?' Edith Wolfe said mildly.

'I never cared for him.'

'But I did.'

The sentence hung between them. Judy could not respond. She watched her mother, whose eyes were somewhere else.

'I thought he was so fascinating, so brilliantly amusing, so *gallant*.' She laughed softly. 'He rather whirled me off my feet for a while. It wasn't very serious – or maybe it was – just some lunches now and then and a lot of silly talk that didn't amount to much, although I probably thought it did then. We even made plans. I wonder if I ever thought we would carry them through. That must have been 1947, after Daddy's grandfather died. Do you remember Poppi? You were very young then.'

'Yes.' Softly. 'He was very old.'

'Ninety-six or-seven when he died. Daddy's family has such longevity.' There was a touch of envy in her voice, a hint of sadness. 'It was one of those times when Daddy became – absorbed. You know how he can be, when he seems, sometimes, so far away?'

She nodded, starting to see it all, another piece falling into place, another shred she would have preferred not to know. In her bag a package with an ivory Buddha that she would not be able to deliver this afternoon.

'I suppose I wanted something just at that moment and there was Max, ready to give it. I never did anything, really, just withdrew. It was my way of saying, "I can't divide myself." Of course, that was why Daddy . . .' She stopped and looked very sober. 'All that trouble, he needed someone and I wasn't there for him. When I think of what I caused.'

'It wasn't you.' Judy took her mother's slim hand and held it between her two.

'Daddy was very good to me when it was over. Of course, he's ten times the man Max was. It was awful the way he treated Marian in the end. But it was a lovely time.' She closed her eyes.

'Would you like to sleep?'

Edith Wolfe moved down slightly under the cover. 'That would be nice,' she said.

Judy removed a pillow and watched her mother fall asleep. She leaned over to kiss the warm cheek and left the room. In the study at the front of the house, her father sat at his desk. She walked down the carpeted hall and stood at the door, looking in. On the walls were photographs Jeanne-Marie had taken of them when they were teenagers, three smiling, happy young people. Jeanne-Marie had loved family resemblances, parents and children and grandchildren. Perhaps Uncle Richard would put together a show one day in her memory.

'Hello, dear.' Daddy looked up from his desk. The black briefcase was open on the floor beside him and the desk was littered with papers covered with his handwriting. Nothing had changed in this room for thirty years.

Judy sat on a leather armchair. 'Mother told me about Mr Rosenberg.'

Her father's colour changed briefly, becoming pale before resuming its natural tone. 'I'm sorry she did that,' he said.

'You knew.'

'Yes.'

'And you kept it a secret.'

'Would you have done anything different?'

She felt her eyes filling. He had kept Mother's secret for twenty years to protect her, to preserve their marriage, perhaps because he loved her so much. 'No,' Judy said, not looking at him. She was a good advocate, a damned good one, but he was the better judge. 'Davey always knew.'

'Davey always seems to know everything.'

'I misjudged you,' she said.

'No. I think you judged me quite accurately.'

'I wish she hadn't told me. It was all gone. It wasn't part of my life any more.'

'Maybe you'll help me keep it our secret, Judy. There's no need for it to go beyond this room.'

She went to his desk and kissed him. Then she went downstairs and got her coat and bag. The maid appeared from nowhere and helped her on with her coat and held the door.

She walked west and kept going, Madison, Fifth, the park. She wanted comfort, but not from her father. He had given enough comfort to enough people and his wife was dying. Fern still lived west. On a Saturday afternoon there was a chance she would be home, taking care of Saturday chores for single women, cleaning, laundry, shopping, maybe a little heartbreak. She walked across Central Park as she had when she was young and had gone riding, when she was young and had a man beside her, when she was young and hated her father because he had kept his wife's secret at his own expense.

It was a different street and a different apartment. Fern had progressed in a decade. She lived nicely and owned good things. It was still a brownstone but there was a lot of brass and it was brightly polished. Judy pressed the button beside HALL

341

and waited. A moment later a young man, well dressed, opened the door from within and she slipped inside, still waiting for Fern's answering ring. Perhaps she was out. Perhaps today there would be no comfort as there had been once, long ago. That had been a Saturday too, when they had crossed the park.

She went up one flight and rang the doorbell.

'Coming,' Fern's voice sang out from the other end of the apartment. It was Saturday afternoon and she had been napping.

The door opened. 'Judy! Judy, hi.' Genuinely happy to see her, Fern in a long white terry robe stood aside as Judy entered. 'Sorry. You caught me – I know there's an expression. I have a guest.'

In *flagrante delicto*.

'I'm so sorry.' It came of being married, no, of being a parent, this thoughtlessness where single people were concerned. They conducted their lives differently, turned days around to suit them. With a three-year-old, one's life was rather circumscribed. She put her hand on the doorknob. 'I should have called. I was just completely thoughtless.'

'Don't go.' Fern sounded very sincere. 'You look cold. Come in and have some coffee with us.'

'I don't think – '

'Don't you want to know who my secret admirer is? After all this time?'

'You mean it's someone I know?' Her voice echoing her surprise. They didn't know any men in common. Or did they?

Fern led her through the apartment to the door of the bedroom. 'Come on out and see who's here,' she called.

Judy watched the closed door with an almost sickening apprehension. Someone she knew. The door opened and her eyes widened at the sight. A dark grey terrycloth bathrobe just like Fern's. A face she had known all her life, that sheepish grin that could belong to no other person.

'*Davey!*'

'Hiya, Jude. Sorry I missed you at the house. I had another appointment.'

'I – how long have you known each other?' Her head swimming.

'Since that first time you brought Fern home for Thanksgiving your first year at Swarthmore,' Davey said, looking lovingly at Fern, putting an arm around her.

'The first year.' Not just dizzy but nearly bursting. *The first year.* It had been at the beginning of their second year that . . . Davey's trip to Alaska that summer and his detour to visit the rabbinical college in Cincinnati. *Davey's detour.* She turned to look at Fern, whose face changed suddenly, the smile disappearing. Fern turned her head right and then left, a firm no.

'What a long time,' Judy said lamely, looking at Fern's fear and then moving her eyes to her brother's casual happiness.

'You remember,' he said easily. 'I was all hot about the rabbinate. It wouldn't've worked. Later on it was other things. But it's always been Fern.'

My brother who marries small round dark-haired women and lusts after this tall, fair, slender creature with the world's most beautiful nose.

'Look, I'll – talk to you both. Some other time though.' She turned back toward the door without saying good-bye.

Fern came with her. 'You're angry.'

'No. No, Fern. It's the last thing in the world I could be. It's just a little too much for one Saturday afternoon.'

On Central Park West she found a taxi to take her home.

'I couldn't let him know,' Fern said, putting her drink back on the little round paper coaster. They had met for a drink after work, just to talk. 'He was really set on this religious thing and I was the last person in the world he could marry. Besides, think of how it looked. Poor little girl from the boonies lassoes rich young man from the East Seventies.'

'Don't, Fern. Please.'

'I know you never thought of me that way, but your parents are only normal people with normal desires for their son. It wouldn't have surprised me if they had imagined I equated dollar signs with Davey. Only I didn't. I loved him.'

'How could you have cared what anyone thought?'

'That's me, Judy. It still is. They don't go away, the old fears. They just get packed a layer deeper.'

'But later, when the thing with Rena broke up, when he left rabbinical school, why not then?'

'He came back to me,' Fern said with a small smile of satisfaction. 'I thought when he married her it was over for good, but it wasn't. But at that point, he was talking about a life in academia and I had my sights on New York. You know me, girl with a dream.'

'Yes,' Judy said. 'I know you.'

'So I let him marry someone else.'

'Fern, if there's anything I can do.'

'Just don't tell him, please, about the baby.' Fern's eyes glistened with tears. She had wanted that baby. A dozen years later, it was still a loss.

'Of course I won't.'

'I did a good job, didn't I?' There was a note of pride. 'You really believed in my fictional guy from Kansas.'

'I believed. I believed everything. I believed Davey when he said he was staying in a hotel because he loved hotels.'

'He was with me.'

Judy smiled. 'He loved you better. Fern, you could make it work.'

'I couldn't. I would die being someone's wife in a small academic community. Wives don't have private offices, you know.'

Judy looked at the last remains of the sherry in her glass. She had begun to drink the very dry kind, Fino, when she could get it. It was pale and curled the tongue a little. It was how her head felt now, curled, tight, dry, withered. 'Well.' She saw the clock over the bar and knew the time had come. 'At least I don't have to worry about whether he'll treat you right.'

Davey showed up at noon on Saturday, an hour before Marcel would come home for lunch. He spent twenty minutes with Simi and then sat with his sister in the living room.

'I thought you'd guessed,' he said, reaching for an apple.

'Never.'

'All those times I came in for no reason at all.'

'Never,' she repeated. 'It just seemed nice to hear from you and I never questioned where you were or why or anything else.'

'You get a D for scepticism.'

'You get an A for originality. It was that summer you went to Alaska, wasn't it?'

'Fern tell you about that? Yeah, that was one great summer. I stopped off in Kansas for a couple of weeks and then went on to Cincinnati. By the time I'd been interviewed, I was a mess. Everything I wanted precluded everything else I wanted. So, like the brother you know so well, I let it ride for a while. Then I met Rena and I thought, maybe this is my chance to have it all. It's just that nothing worked.'

'Rena was a nice person, Davey.'

'How could I marry someone who wasn't a nice person?'

'So is Marilyn,' Judy said. 'It isn't kind, what you're doing to Marilyn.'

'Listen, Jude, if I wanted to be kind, I'd go into a monastery. I want what you want, but it didn't come as easily for me. I'm not complaining. I'm just saying I have to do it differently.'

'OK.'

'And this thing with Mum has messed me up.'

'I know.' During the week, Edith Wolfe had been in hospital for three days.

'I should have forgiven her.'

'You forgave her, Davey.'

'Yeah, but I waited too long. I should have forgiven her when I was a kid. I denied myself a mother when I needed one.'

'She was always there, Davey. She never accepted your denial. You know that. She's so pleased now that you come all the way down to see her.'

Davey said, 'Yeah,' and got up and went to the kitchen to

throw away his apple core, the well-trained husband who had been brought up with maids but who had accommodated, in small ways, to the level of an academic. 'I better get going,' he said, returning. 'They're expecting me for lunch.' He paused. 'I probably won't be there by the time you show.'

'That's OK.'

'I'll see you next week. We're all coming down for the weekend.'

'Good. Maybe we'll do something.'

They walked to the door and Davey gave her a hug. He opened the door and turned back with a slight frown. 'That's the first time you ever sounded as though you believed me. About old Maxwell Rosenberg.'

Judy smiled a small smile. 'I just realized some time ago that you were the messenger of truth.'

Davey gave her a bigger one. 'I like that,' he said.

Ten days later, beside the man she had loved all her life, Edith Wolfe died quietly.

It was the saddest funeral Regina had ever attended. She sat with her children and saw her cousins nearby, Lillian who had come in a fur coat, Millie who wept, Adele who sat stoically, Arthur who had flown from the South for the occasion. Only one cousin was missing. Henry, Lillian's brother, was absent, along with his rather new, quite young second wife.

'He has office hours,' Lillian had said curtly when asked. 'Doctors have a duty to their patients.'

It was a terrible funeral. There had been too many of them and this was the worst. She could not bear to look at Jerold or at his children.

They walked outside when it was over, a grey day with a chill that still smelled of snow, of winter, of endings. She saw Millie and hugged her and searched in her bag for a fresh handkerchief. Lillian approached and they kissed.

'Cold for March, isn't it?' Lillian said. She wore a black sealskin coat with a mink collar but she did not look warm.

Her face, which had always been thin, was now thin and lined. She was sixty-eight but she looked older; she looked worn.

'Very cold. I don't know how Jerold will manage. He'll be so alone.' Regina pressed her handkerchief to her eyes once again.

'Oh,' Lillian said off-handedly, 'with his looks and the money she's left him, he'll be married in a year.'

When she got home, Regina called England and told Julian she would arrive at the end of the week.

Four

———◦———

Judy was pleased that her father had chosen the Connaught. As a child, she had stayed there with her parents and brothers and now her own daughter would have a similar memory. It had been a glorious holiday. They had travelled. Together and separately, each of the adults indulging his own interests, reviving his own memories. Marcel had visited facilities that cared for the elderly; Daddy had been invited to lecture in the Netherlands and England; Judy had interviewed a man hoping for political asylum in the States. And Simi had had a wonderful time everywhere. They had all visited the Goldblatt clan in Paris and then Daddy had gone off alone while the three others made the pilgrimage to Marcel's wartime family.

Now they were in London for the last leg of their journey. Tomorrow Daddy would go to Cambridge where he would be the guest at a seminar, Marcel would go off to make his visits and accumulate data for a paper he was writing for a medical journal, and Judy would take Simi to see London, wonderful London of many memories. Best of all was the Connaught and Grosvenor Square, unchanged since her childhood. She could remember the day the five of them had arrived from the ship, Mother stepping out of the hired car, young and pretty and as happy to be in London as her daughter was today.

It was nearly eighteen months now and the first time they had persuaded Daddy to travel, eighteen months since she had last caught a glimpse of Regina at Mother's funeral.

It had been during the week of mourning they had observed after Mother's death that Judy had made up her mind that it must be done, that she must sit with Regina and talk, that she must apologize because she had not meant to hurt; she had

348

only echoed her own hurt. But the hurt was gone and anyway, it had been misplaced. She wanted peace.

A week after the funeral she had taken the box and walked over to Park Avenue.

'The Rush apartment,' she had said to the doorman, failing to read his look accurately until later. Up in the lift with the silent operator and then alone in the vestibule, pressing the bell.

It had been like a B movie, she had thought afterwards, the repentant cousin with her small wrapped box, the maid delivering the news.

'Mrs Rush has left for England, Mrs Goldblatt.'

'England.' As though the place were a jungle, as though the name were unknown.

'Three days ago. I can take a message for her.'

'England.' It was a place people went to work out their problems, to come to conclusions, to set their lives in order. 'Thank you,' she said. 'There's no message.'

Waiting alone for the lift, package and message undelivered. A B movie.

They were in London now and the package was in her suitcase. When Daddy came back from Cambridge, she would talk to him.

They sat in the sitting room of their suite taking afternoon tea. Marcel had taken Simi off to a museum. In three days in London, Simi had begun doing a respectable imitation of British English. Her French was flawless and had impressed her Parisian relatives, especially her Aunt Renée, who could see the resemblance to her own mother in the five-year-old face. A gifted child, Judy thought with enormous pleasure.

'One of my favourite cities,' Daddy said, setting the teacup in the saucer.

'Mine too. My mind stretches here.'

'And your legs, I think. You haven't been off them since we arrived.'

'I don't want to miss anything. I hope Simi remembers it as well as I.'

349

'She will. She's very much like you. A little more indulged, perhaps.'

'That's her grandfather's fault.'

He said, 'Mm,' and looked thoughtful. 'Small pleasures.'

She put her own cup down and patted her lips. 'Are you going to see Regina?'

He was clearly surprised, but only someone who knew him well could have detected it. 'So you know that too,' he said.

'For a long time. We had a conversation once and I was very unkind. I'm sorry for it.'

'Why don't you tell her?'

'I tried, but she had left for England.'

'And now you want me to do it for you.'

'I want you to know that whatever you do is OK with me.'

'My daughter giving me permission?' Jerold Wolfe asked mildly.

'Not permission. Just no objections.'

Her father smiled, his eyes on the tea tray. 'Judy,' he said, 'It may come as a surprise to you – perhaps even a disappointment – but I have never considered either your opinion or your feelings in my relationship with Regina.'

Unexpectedly, his admission elated her. For a while after Mother died, he had seemed so fragile. There was no fragility now in either his looks or his sentiments. 'I'm glad to hear it,' she said honestly.

She went to her bedroom and got the box out of her suitcase. Setting it on the coffee table, she said, 'If you see her, I'd appreciate your giving that to her. It belongs to her. I couldn't trust it to the post.'

'Why don't you sit down and finish your tea,' her father said, 'instead of running around quite so much.'

He was waiting for her when the train pulled in. Regina remembered a time nearly fifty years earlier when she had waited in another station for him to come home from college, secretly one day early, secretly so they could spend it together. Today the man's face handsomely overlaid the boy's profile.

Today was a sweeter day than the one nearly half a century ago. Today they were their own people.

'Hello, darling.' A kiss.

'Hello, Jody.'

'Did you leave a broken heart behind in the lowlands?'

'Probably.'

'You haven't married him, have you?'

'No.'

'Good.' He held a door for her and they went out into the street and got into a waiting taxi. 'I thought we'd have tea in our suite. The other three members of my energetic family are off for the afternoon.'

'Tea will be lovely.'

The call had come as she was dressing for an afternoon party in the next town, a garden party. It was the end of August and the gardens were all quite beautiful, lush and overgrown in that typical English way. I'm in London, he had said on the telephone. It's my last day. I'd like to see you. She had turned down Julian's offer of a car and taken the next train.

'I saw Suzanne,' Jerold said when the tea had arrived.

'Did she remember you?'

'Remembered me and, I thought, made some belated assumptions.'

Regina smiled. 'I fly to Paris about once a month to see her. We have a wonderful time together.'

'She's part of my family now,' Jerold said with an echo of the same wonderment she often felt herself at the way things had turned out.

'It's a good family.' She liked hearing his voice. More than any other, it had the power to comfort and reassure while evoking old passions, and perhaps some new ones. She would have preferred to listen for a while, to let it work its magic. 'I think it's more peaceful now,' she said, stirring herself. 'Your family.'

'Because you left?'

She nodded.

'You didn't have to leave.'

351

'I wanted peace, Jody. I wanted the important people to feel less threatened and I wanted the others to stop talking. Lillian said something once.'

'Lillian is a meddling woman who has never accepted the life that was given to her and never lifted a finger to change it. You owe her nothing. You owe nothing to anyone, Regina. Forget about peace. Peace is a boring state of affairs. Think instead about freedom. You're a free person. Do you know that?'

A floating feeling, as though bonds had dissolved at the sound of his voice. I am free. I owe nothing to anyone. 'I haven't thought about being free for fifty years.'

'I have. I've thought of very little else this month.'

Free. The debts all paid, the slate washed clean. Everyone taken care of except you and me. 'I want to take care of you,' she said, speaking freely.

Her cousin – whom she loved – rubbed the back of her hand with his own warm palm. 'I was about to make you a similar offer,' he said.

Sixty-seven and free. A dizzying sense of movement. A reward unexpected, not even hoped for. 'I wonder if we could do it all again.'

'Or try it for the first time.'

'Yes.' She smiled. Being free took some getting used to.

'By the way, Judy's left something for you.' He went to the desk and returned with a small package.

She recognized the paper. Judy had never opened it. A debt repaid and paid again. That sound when the cord is cut. She had heard it only once, when Adam was born, but it had stayed with her all her life, and she heard its echo now. The sound of freedom. The last bond. She offered him the box. 'I think it ought to go home with you, Jody.'

'Bring it along,' he said. 'When you come to stay.'

That night she told Julian she was leaving and the next day she packed her things and took a suite in a hotel in London to spend a few pleasant weeks by herself before going home.

Five

It was one of the good nights of the week. There were no evening office hours and Marcel had finished preparing for tomorrow's class in the new course he taught in geriatric care. It was a little after ten, Simi asleep, coffee and dessert plates still to be put in the dishwasher. Tomorrow, Judy would appear in court, but right now it was a nice, warm, comfortable night in November.

They were spread out on the sofa, his arm around her, newspapers scattered. They had been talking, catching up, making plans. There was a way now, still experimental, of testing to see if the foetus showed certain abnormalities. She had decided to take a chance. They had done so well with their first, she wanted to see what they could do with their second. Marcel was more than pleased. Their lives had taken shape and moved forward. Nothing was easy but everything was easier. In a couple of weeks, Regina was returning to New York and would join them all for Thanksgiving.

'I'm too tired to get up and go to bed,' Judy said.

He kissed the side of her forehead. 'I'll look in on my daughter and come back and help.'

He went to the back of the apartment and she heard a door open, heard his voice, low, saying a few words. Then he was back.

'Sleep Saturday,' he said, offering his hand.

'Simi has a birthday party. That cute little red-headed kid in her class.' She stood and the telephone rang.

'I'll go.' He glanced at his watch in an automatic way and answered in the kitchen.

She gathered the dishes from the coffee table and followed

him, running to rinse the dishes. When she turned the water off, she became aware of the conversation, of the tone of his voice, of the tension. It was not his answering service.

'You did exactly the right thing,' he said, speaking quickly but reassuringly. 'I'll be there in five minutes but I want you to call his regular doctor as soon as you hang up . . . Yes . . . That's right and I'll be right over.' He hung up with a bang and started for the door, stopping when he saw her at the sink, watching. 'It's Jerold. It sounds like a stroke, but I could be wrong.'

She said, 'No,' and backed away from him. '*No!*'

But he was sprinting to the front closet, throwing on a corduroy jacket because he had changed out of his day clothes when he came home.

'I'm going with you,' she called, making her feet move, following his path.

He turned and held her shoulders. 'You have a child sleeping in the bedroom,' he said firmly. 'You're staying here.'

'Marcel – ' She was almost in tears.

'You'll see him tomorrow.' Picking up the bag and opening the door in the same motion.

'Please,' she said. 'Please.'

'I'll call as soon as I can.' Already in the hall. Already on his way.

The door, well balanced, well oiled, and well adjusted, swung back and closed by itself and she walked listlessly to the living room to start her wait.

'He's OK.'

It was at least the third time he had said it, his arms around her just inside the door, his jacket still on, his face scratchy. Her tears had exploded as he came inside the apartment, and she could not make them stop. A little earlier, she had stepped into the study they shared and seen the black briefcase with the letters JW and after that, she had not been able to control the shaking, even though she had wrapped herself in a quilt.

'He's right-handed and it's affected his left side, which is fine. His speech is OK except for the left side of his face but that's probably temporary. He's alert and making sense.'

'How long – what about work?' She moved so she could see him, so that he could take his jacket off.

'We can't even make a prognosis for a few weeks, Judy. It's a long recovery.'

She moaned, realizing it only in the echo. She watched him hang up the jacket. His face was dark with beard. 'He can't retire, Marcel.' It was a plea. 'Maybe he can take a leave and go back later. I can't imagine him not going down to that court every morning.' She started for the bedroom, Marcel close behind. 'Regina won't let him retire,' she said with satisfaction.

'I'm not sure Regina will have much to say about it.' He unbuttoned his shirt and pulled it off. Then he sat on the edge of the bed, looking fatigued. 'Richard's going to call her in the morning. Your father said to tell her not to come. He said he's withdrawn the invitation.'

Six

————◆————

This time it was quite different; it was by appointment. As the lift stopped, the door to the apartment opened and Regina stepped out into the hall.

'You look wonderful, Judy,' she said, kissing her as though they had always been friends.

'Thank you. So do you. How was the flight?' They were inside now, the great apartment spreading before them, the paintings in the living room, the memorabilia of two long lives. She wondered if Regina would give it up now, sell it for some price unheard of in the thirties when they had first moved in.

'A little tiring but I read a good deal and slept a little. I like flying west. It stays light and there's the excitement of going home.' Regina held the door of her study open as Judy walked in. 'You may prefer one of the harder chairs, Judy. They're easier to get out of. You're one of those women who looks wonderful pregnant.'

'Thank you.'

'Marcel wrote how pleased you both were. It must be very satisfying to know that everything will be all right.' She poured coffee and offered a cup to Judy.

'It is. I couldn't have taken the chance otherwise.'

'I marvel at how things have changed.'

'I suppose it makes us less adventurous. Maybe the absence of all our new science made your generation more courageous. It certainly made you more adaptable. You gambled more readily.'

'Maybe we gambled less. The only member of the family who ever gambled often is my cousin Arthur and he's never come out a winner.'

'That's what Daddy says.'

As though something very profound had been said, a silence settled over them.

'How is he?' Regina asked finally.

'He's really fine.' Judy said, hearing herself use the same voice that she always used when describing her father's health, a tone of strong reassurance. 'If he had broken an arm or a leg, he'd be himself again now. It's just that he wasn't able to go back to court and it's depressed him.'

'But he'll be there tomorrow?'

'I guarantee it.' Judy smiled. It had not been easy but she had done it, not only because she wanted her father to go, but because she wanted to do something for Regina, something right. So much in life was beyond one's control – Fern and Davey, the lost babies – it was rewarding to act as a catalyst in an event that should have, perhaps, happened long ago. 'He's going alone in his own car so that he can leave whenever he wants,' she admitted. 'By the way, Uncle Richard is flying in tonight.'

'Then they'll all be there.'

'I think so.'

'You've been very good to me, Judy.'

'I'm sorry for all those years.'

'Those years are gone. We can forget them.'

'We'd like you to ride with us tomorrow. There're just the three of us and it's a big car.'

'I accept.'

'It's Simi's first wedding and she's very excited. You should see her dress. It's all smocking and lace.'

'Those are always the prettiest ones.'

Judy put her cup down and looked at her watch. The arrangements had been made and now it was past eight and she had had a long day. She stood, feeling the small ache in her back that signalled the need for rest. Still, she did not want to go. 'It's a wonderful apartment,' she said, seeing it for the first time as Regina's home, not as a place that reminded her of somewhere else, of the Rosenbergs'.

'We raised four children here.'

'Four? Oh yes, of course. It was four, wasn't it?' She passed through the doorway and stopped at the stairs. How many Christmases ago had that been when the slim, dark-haired, angry boy had come down and stopped just there, stopped to look at her? 'How can you say you're not a gambler, Regina? When I think of all the chances you took.' That boy on those stairs, leaving a good life in England and coming home to see Daddy.

'Maybe when it all turns out right, you just think of it as good judgement.'

'I hope it all turns out right tomorrow, not just for my father. I want it to turn out right for you too.'

'Thank you, Judy. I think it will.'

Judy went on to the door. She did not share Regina's optimism although she wanted to believe in it. She had worked hard to get him to agree to attend this wedding but she had no sense that he would do any more than be present. A long time had passed since his high spirits of the preceding fall.

'Did the test tell you whether it would be a boy or a girl?'

The question brought her back. 'It did,' she said, 'and we're very pleased. But we've decided to keep it a secret.'

'A very good decision,' Regina said approvingly as they reached the door. 'Secrets are best kept by the people they concern. I'm glad you came, Judy. I look forward to tomorrow.'

'It's Regina!' Millie, birdlike, peered through thick lenses as Regina approached the table. 'What a nice dress, Regina. I didn't know you were coming.'

'I told you she was,' Lillian said drily. 'I see you're wearing blue again. You always wore blue to weddings.'

'It's my favourite colour.' Regina bent and kissed Lillian. 'I'm so sorry,' she said. 'I don't know what to say.'

Lillian reached into her petit point bag, a memento of a trip to Vienna, pulled out a lacy handkerchief, and pressed it to her eyes. 'They shouldn't have had the wedding,' she sniffed.

'I don't think they stop weddings for an uncle,' Millie said with childlike innocence, 'do they, Adele?'

'Hardly.'

'I'm not talking about uncles,' Lillian said with fury. 'I'm talking about *my brother*.'

'Don't snap,' Adele said. 'You're a snappish woman. It's why no one sits next to you.'

Lillian's eyes circled the table with its four places filled and four still vacant. 'No one's sitting next to anyone,' she said with an air of triumph.

'Regina, dear.'

She turned to see Richard beside her, his face tanned as only the Southwest could tan a face. Raising her chin, she kissed him warmly while Adele, plump in a shapeless, dark dress, mumbled something.

'I'm told he'll be here,' Richard said so that no one else could hear, but across the table Adele eyed them with an old suspicion.

'I have Judy's solemn word.'

'My cousin who is still a dreamer,' he said with a smile and moved around the table to greet Millie, then Adele, and lastly Lillian, pausing to convey condolences, and sitting, finally, between her and Adele, the first man at the table. Lillian smiled gloatingly.

'Have any of you seen my brother?' he asked.

'You don't mean Jerold's coming, do you?' Millie asked in surprise. 'I heard he was quite feeble since his stroke.'

Richard looked severely distressed. 'Jerold is not feeble. He's been fully recovered for months.'

'Well, he can sit between my sister and me,' Adele offered. 'If he needs help, we'll be there.'

Richard sighed, turned to Lillian and spoke in a low voice.

'Lillian thought Mr What's-His-Name might be sitting in the extra seat,' Millie said in her high-pitched voice, turning toward Regina.

'Mr What's-His-Hame wasn't invited.' Regina smiled at her cousin.

'You see, Lillian? Mr What's-His-Name isn't sitting in Henry's place after all.' Millie turned to watch a group of children parade by the table. 'Oh, aren't they adorable! Aren't they the cutest things? Which one is your great-granddaughter, Lillian?'

'The one with the halo,' Lillian retorted.

'Well, Millie, good to see you.' Arthur waddled toward the table. 'Adele – how are my sisters?' He kissed them both and paused for air. 'Richard, it's been a while, hasn't it? And Regina! Well, this is a treat. All the way in from Paris, are you?'

'London,' Millie corrected. 'Regina's just back from her gentleman friend in England.'

'London, Paris, what's the difference? It's good to have a family wedding although I can't think how I'm related to the groom.'

'To the bride, Brother,' Adele said gently. 'The bride is Lillian's daughter's – '

'Well, it's all the same. It's a wedding. Lillian!' Arthur crooked his head so he could see around the flowers. 'Oh, Lillian, what a blow. Our poor Henry.' Arthur began to cough and Millie stood and held his arm, patting his back until the attack subsided.

'Well,' he said, a trifle subdued, 'I think I'll take my place between my two lovely sisters.'

'No, dear, you can't do that,' Milly said shrilly. 'We're saving that seat for Jerold, in case he needs help. You sit between Regina and me, that's a good brother.'

Nodding and pursing his lips understandingly, Arthur did as he was told. Quite suddenly, there was a sound of weeping.

'I knew I'd be the one left out,' Lillian sobbed. 'You've never treated me well, none of you, leaving me with my dead brother's chair empty next to me. You take pleasure in seeing me miserable.'

Richard put a hand on her back and Regina slid one place to her left. 'It's all right, dear,' she said softly. 'I'll keep you company.'

'Ah, my brother,' Richard said and everyone at the table turned to look.

He looked remarkably well, Regina thought, but thinner than the last time she had seen him, that August afternoon in London last summer. He was flanked by Judy, looking almost a duplicate of her beautiful mother, and a boy who, Regina realized, was Frenchy's son. Judy was talking to Jerold as they walked and young Michael was trying to hold his grandfather's arm and being shrugged off rather forcefully. Judy looked at Regina and smiled. The sisters seated him in the appointed place and Regina could no longer see him because of the flowers. They sat exactly opposite each other.

Regina turned to Arthur, who sat on the other side of the ghost of Cousin Henry. 'I can't remember the last time I saw you,' she said. 'I think you were between wives.'

'Very likely,' Arthur said in his hoarse voice. 'Lost my last one, you know.'

'I didn't know. I'm sorry.'

'A year the last of this month and I haven't been the same since. Passed away in her sleep. Wonderful woman. Best of the lot and I should know. Had three of them. Like to find one more to take me through what's left of this life.'

The music began; waiters filled wine glasses; there was a collective sound of spoons clinking on china.

'I suppose there's one blessing in being old,' Lillian said. 'They put us far from the music – if you can call it music nowadays. Mmh!' She made a sound of distaste and extricated a half-eaten strawberry from her mouth. 'Why do they pick them if they aren't ripe?'

Adele leaned toward Richard. 'Shall I help Jerold with his fruit?' she asked.

'Adele,' Richard said with obvious anger, 'if you have a question for Jerold, ask him. And the answer to that one is *no*.'

It was the first time Regina had ever seen him lose his temper and the intensity of his anger delighted her. Jerold's faculties had not been impaired. He had walked without help. He had resented those who thought he needed it.

The soup came and went. Regina saw Adam's head float above all the others on the dance floor and she smiled at him. In the fall he would marry the tall, beautiful girl who moved so gracefully with him. One day there would be more grandchildren. Ernie's oldest daughter was talking about marriage. In a few years there would be a great-grandchild. It was lovely to have them all but she was a free woman; she enjoyed them when they were there and then she pursued her own life, her own interests, the passions that still moved her. Beside her the ghost of Cousin Henry stared at his uneaten fruit.

'Aren't they just precious?' Millie said. 'Over there, the children's table.'

Regina turned to look. They were precious, tiny and frilly and all smiles, turned out for their first wedding.

'What was our first wedding?' Adele asked.

'Mine, I suppose,' Lillian said as though she wished otherwise.

'Oh, no, Lillian,' Millie corrected her. 'It was years before yours. It was Aunt Maude's. Remember?'

The mood at the table suddenly changed.

'That's right,' Richard said. 'I was the ring bearer. It was – let me see – we'd just gone into the war. It must have been 1917.'

'Fifty-five years,' Lillian said with amazement. 'Wait just a moment and I'll tell you the date. Grandmama had it all arranged that Uncle Mortimer would be a married man when he registered for the draft and that was Tuesday the fifth of June. They were married on Sunday the third. The third! Today is Saturday the third. It's their anniversary, fifty-five years ago today!'

Millie began to laugh her high-pitched laugh. 'Fifty-five years and we're still at the children's table.'

'So we are,' her brother seconded. 'Still at the children's table.'

'I remember how Lillian begged to sit with the grown-ups,' Adele said. 'We were just babies, she said. Not good enough for a young lady like her.'

'I caught the bouquet.' Lillian sounded as though she would like the chance to give it back.

'And wasn't Aunt Maude beautiful,' Adele said reverently. 'Wasn't she the most beautiful woman this family has ever produced. That white silk dress billowing all over and all those beautiful ladies and Poppi's Pierce-Arrow . . .'

'And Uncle Mortimer,' Millie crooned. 'I never saw a man in my whole life as handsome as he was. He was the man I wanted to marry.'

'He was the man we all wanted to marry,' Lillian said.

There was a sudden silence and the three women turned collectively toward Regina. She smiled and looked at the flowers. She had lived the life they had all desired, married the man of all their dreams and like their grandfather before them, in their old age they had forgotten who the man was.

'He was quite wonderful,' she said in a clear voice, asserting her right as his wife and partner.

'Well, that was some wedding,' Richard said evenly, restoring calm. 'Henry wouldn't eat and Arthur ate too much.'

Lillian hooted. 'Didn't he though.'

'Poor Henry,' Millie said in a subdued voice. 'He had a hard life, Lillian.'

Lillian reached for her handkerchief again. 'I don't know how I'll get along without him,' she sniffed. 'I don't know what I'll do now that he's gone. My brother's supported me since the day he opened his office. I don't know how I'll manage now.'

Regina stiffened and looked at Lillian and Lillian, meeting her eyes, quickly covered her mouth with slender fingers. The disclosure had stunned Regina and clearly horrified Lillian, who was mumbling disclaimers. Morty had been right, after all. Lillian had been well taken care of. Regina's cheques had gone for the fur coat, the trips, the petit point bag. Nearly forty years of cheques.

Harold appeared behind Millie and Millie left the table to dance with him, a man past forty with the face his father would have had if he had lived long enough. Richard whispered to Lillian and they left the table together.

Arthur cleared his throat and laid a fat cigar on an ashtray. 'Well,' he said, clearly embarrrassed, 'here I am left with the two most beautiful girls in the family and I can't think which of them I'd rather dance with.'

'Dance with Adele,' Regina said. 'I'll stay and keep Jerold company.'

Arthur hoisted himself out of his chair and accompanied his sister to the dance floor. Watching them go, Regina left her seat and took the one next to Jerold. In front of him, a plate full of food had not been touched.

'Hello, Jody,' she said softly.

He shook his head and said nothing.

'I waited for your letters.'

The lined handsome face seemed unrelentingly sorrowful. 'Regina.' He still had not looked at her. 'I don't write letters any more.'

'You mean you don't write them to me.'

'That's right. That is exactly right.'

'I want you to dance with me.'

He looked at her finally with an air of frustration. Then he pushed his chair back and stood, turning so that she was on his right, and took her arm.

'Does the left arm give you trouble?' she asked.

'Some.'

'My fingers bother me once in a while,' she said lightly. 'In my sleep sometimes and in cold weather. I wear mittens in the winter, the way the children do.'

They began to dance at the edge of the floor. The music was slow and some of the younger people had sat down at the completion of one of those mad group affairs that had become popular in her absence.

'Go back to England,' Jerold said.

'I've left England. I packed all my bags.'

'You had a good life there.' He spoke carefully, fluently, flawlessly. 'I'm an old man, Regina.'

'No.'

The music stopped and he guided her to the corner of the large room where a door led to the lobby.

'Anything can happen to me now.'

'It's happened already and you've survived it. I want us to be the first to go to China. I want to visit Istanbul and see the Blue Mosque. I want what we promised each other.'

Jerold shook his head slowly.

'We live such a long time in our family. There are so many good years ahead.'

'Regina –'

'I told you once – it was before I went to Paris – I said I wanted to take care of you, Jody.' Once on a high hill with the wind blowing and the future descending on her like a shroud, like a cloud that would cover the sun forever. 'That's what I've come home for, to keep my promise.' *My cousin who is still a dreamer.*

She saw his eyes fill and he reached into a pocket and pulled out a handkerchief, turning away from her to use it.

'Have a good trip, Regina,' he said and started back across the empty dance floor to the table.

She watched him in the blur that was her unaided vision, an old man returning to a table of old men and women.

'Hi, Grandma,' a young voice said beside her.

'Hello, Lisa. How nice you look tonight.'

'Thanks. See you later.'

'Yes, dear.'

He had reached the table. She could see them quite clearly now, Lillian complaining to Uncle Jack that she was too old to sit at the children's table, little round Arthur with a collection of empty wine glasses in front of him, reaching across the table for yet another, Millie and Adele in the dresses Aunt Bertha had sewn for them for the wonderful occasion, the marriage of Aunt Maude, Henry pouting over the food on his plate, Richard trying to be gallant, and Jerold, the handsomest of the lot at fifteen, offering the world to little Regina in her pale blue silk dress. There was a fanfare and Grandmama pirouetted across the living room – I am so happy – into Uncle Willy's arms. I am so happy. I am so happy.

It was all a blur. Regina opened the door and walked across the lobby to the checkroom, claiming the little cape of sable that she had bought for herself one day this past winter on a quick trip to Denmark.

She slipped it over her shoulders and walked out in the dark, a free woman walking freely. They would miss her inside. The meal had not ended and there were festivities ahead. Perhaps, she thought, they might even gossip. She felt very much as she had the day she had put fifty cents in her pocket and gone to have her hair cut for the first time. Free.

At the curb was a silver-grey limousine. The door opened as she reached it and the man in uniform got out and said, 'Good evening, ma'am.'

'This is Judge Wolfe's car, isn't it?'

'Yes, ma'am.'

'I'm to wait for him here.'

He opened the back door and she slid across the seat to the far side. The door closed with an expensive thud and she sat in the cool, air-conditioned darkness, thinking. It had been a pretty wedding. Lillian and her daughter were not on the best of terms but Lillian had come to her grand-daughter's wedding just the same, as they all would, to all the weddings, all except Regina.

It was half an hour later when she heard the voices, Judy admonishing her father to be careful of something, Davey laughing, Marcel, an exchange of good nights. The driver left the car and said something to Jerold.

'In the car?' she heard Jerold respond, the sound of his voice blurred, as her natural vision was, through the insulated walls of the heavy automobile.

The rear door opened and the light sprang on, hurting her eyes. She shielded them with her hand as someone took the seat beside her. The door closed and the light disappeared.

'You're a damned stubborn woman, Regina,' her cousin said.

'And what a long time it's taken,' she said with satisfaction. 'I've made up my mind about something.' A week ago she could not have imagined saying this. Now it seemed like the easiest thing in the world. 'This was my last wedding. I spent

366

twenty-five years wishing I could go to a family wedding and now that I've come, I'm disappointed. They've all changed.'

'Changed? They haven't changed in sixty years.'

'Then what's happened?'

'What's happened is they haven't changed. What's happened is they're exactly the same as they were sixty years ago. You send her cheques, don't you? Lillian.'

'Yes.'

'Ungrateful woman.'

'What about you and me, Jody? Have we changed? Has the statute of limitations run out on our promises?'

'Regina – ' He took her icy left hand in his good warm right one. He leaned forward and said. 'Will you turn that damned cooling system off?'

The faint whirring receded almost immediately.

'You should see a doctor about your fingers,' he said gently.

'I might do that. I forget most of the time. It's such a small thing.'

'Nothing is small if it causes you pain. What am I going to do with you, Regina?'

'I suppose you'll think of something.'

He leaned forward again and said, 'What are you waiting for?'

'Are you going home, Judge?' the voice came back.

'Of course I'm going home. Where else would I go at this time of night?'

'Yes, sir.'

The car pulled out of line and Jerold leaned back and stretched his legs. 'You could wear those little white gloves, he said.

'They don't wear them any more.'

'Don't they?'

'And they don't ride the El or sail the seven seas. They fly. But they still climb the Great Wall of China.'

'Well.' He took her hand again and rubbed it on his cheek. 'I suppose there's still time for me to learn something.'

Fontana Paperbacks: Fiction

Fontana is a leading paperback publisher of both non-fiction, popular and academic, and fiction. Below are some recent fiction titles.

- ☐ SEEDS OF YESTERDAY Virginia Andrews £2.50
- ☐ SONG OF RHANNA Christine Marion Fraser £2.50
- ☐ JEDDER'S LAND Maureen O'Donoghue £1.95
- ☐ THE WARLORD Malcolm Bosse £2.95
- ☐ TREASON'S HARBOUR Patrick O'Brian £2.50
- ☐ FUTURES Freda Bright £1.95
- ☐ THE DEMON LOVER Victoria Holt £2.50
- ☐ FIREPRINT Geoffrey Jenkins £2.50
- ☐ DEATH AND THE DANCING FOOTMAN Ngaio Marsh £1.75
- ☐ THE 'CAINE' MUTINY Herman Wouk £2.50
- ☐ LIVERPOOL DAISY Helen Forrester £1.95
- ☐ OUT OF A DREAM Diana Anthony £1.75
- ☐ SHARPE'S ENEMY Bernard Cornwell £1.95

You can buy Fontana paperbacks at your local bookshop or newsagent. Or you can order them from Fontana Paperbacks, Cash Sales Department, Box 29, Douglas, Isle of Man. Please send a cheque, postal or money order (not currency) worth the purchase price plus 15p per book for postage (maximum postage required is £3).

NAME (Block letters) _____

ADDRESS _____

_____

_____